Praise for the novels of Jan Siegel

The Witch Queen

"Siegel spins a wonderful world where magic and modern mundanity rub shoulders. It's a place where an evil demon rules an office tower in the heart of the financial district and all old houses have ghosts and goblins if only you've the eyes to see them."
—*St. John's Telegram* (Newfoundland)

"A new twist on an old tale of passion rekindled and love betrayed . . . Siegel creates complex, believable characters caught in a web of treachery and intrigue."
—*Library Journal*

"Confident, thoughtful prose, intelligent plotting, and likable characters distinguish this trilogy from the common lot. Arthurian mythology blends seamlessly with other traditions, creating a rich web of allusions."
—*VOYA*

"Siegel does some distinctive, startling things. . . . She writes in a quiet but uncommonly witty style that can soar into eloquence or mute into dread as needed. . . . She uses myth and legend in daringly eclectic ways."
—*Publishers Weekly*

Please turn the page for more reviews. . . .

The Dragon Charmer

"Engrossing . . . Jan Siegel's writing is lively, erudite, and often poetic."
—*Starburst*

"Magical . . . The narrative has an eerie, chilling quality, enhanced by the descriptions of horrible creatures heard but not seen."
—*Romantic Times*

"Delightful . . . It's refreshing and a welcome change to find someone producing skillful, entertaining contemporary fantasies."
—*Science Fiction Chronicle*

"Jan Siegel came onto the scene with considerable panache in *Prospero's Children*. Now *The Dragon Charmer* continues the tale [and] her inventive powers shine."
—*Locus*

"Highly imaginative and darkly charming."
—*Publishers Weekly*

Prospero's Children

Also by Jan Siegel

PROSPERO'S CHILDREN
THE DRAGON QUEEN

JAN SIEGEL

THE WITCH QUEEN

BALLANTINE BOOKS • NEW YORK

The Witch Queen is a work of fiction. Names, places, and incidents either are products of the author's imagination or are used fictitiously.

A Del Rey® Book
Published by The Random House Publishing Group

www.delreydigital.com

ISBN 0-345-44259-8

Manufactured in the United States of America

First Hardcover Edition: August 2002
First Mass Market Edition: October 2003

OPM   10   9   8   7   6   5   4   3   2   1

PRAYER

Ah, once I lived my life in every breath,
I gave my first love to a unicorn
and rode the shadows on the edge of death
and pierced my heart with his enchanted horn.
I saw the mountains soar ice-white, cloud-tall,
and moonfoam on an endless waterfall,
and felt the petals of my flesh unfold,
and mountains, waterfalls, and heartbeats rolled
down long blue valleys to a distant sea.
Oh Lord, even the pain was dear to me,
if Lord there be.

And now my life is filled with little things,
little moments crowding little days,
my thought has shackles where it once had wings
and narrow vistas overstretch my gaze,
and daily work, and daily growing care
trundle me down the road to God-knows-where
if God is there.
I fear the hour when the world turns gray
and in the hollow midnight try to pray;
mountains and waterfalls have flowed away
leaving me nothing much to say,
nothing but questions, till my thoughts run dry—
I ask and ask, but never hear reply:
Is there a dream to set my spirit free?

In all the dead void of eternity
is there a God—and Love—and Phantasy—
or only me?
Is there Another, Lord, or can there be
no God but me?

THE WITCH QUEEN

Prologue

Enter First Witch

The name of the island was Æeea, which, however you attempt to pronounce it, sounds like a scream. It was a gold-green jigsaw fragment of land set far away from any other shore, laced with foam and compassed with the blue-shaded contours of the sea. Near at hand, the gold dulled to yellow: slivers of yellow sand along the coastline, dust-yellow roads, yellow earth and rock showing through the olive groves on the steep climb to the sky. The central crag was tall enough to hook the clouds; in ancient times the natives believed such clouds concealed the more questionable activities of their gods. Nowadays, the former fishermen and peasant farmers catered to the discerning tourist, telling stories of smugglers and shipwrecks, of nymphs and heroes, and of the famous enchantress who had once lived there in exile, snaring foolish travelers in the silken webs of her hair. Æeea was overlooked by the main vacation companies: only the specialists sent their customers to a location with little nightlife and no plate smashing in the quiet tavernas. Most of the more sumptuous villas were owned by wealthy mainlanders who wanted a bolt-hole far from the madding crowd of more commercial destinations.

The villa above Hekati Beach was one of these. More modern than most, it had seaward walls of tinted glass, black marble pillars, cubist furniture standing tiptoe on blood-colored Persian carpets. There was a courtyard, completely enclosed, where orchids jostled for breathing space in the jungle air and

the cold silver notes of falling water made the only music. At
its heart the latest incumbent had planted a budding tree grown
from a cutting—a thrusting, eager sapling, whiplash-slender,
already putting forth leaves shaped like those of an oak but
larger and veined with a sap that was red. The house was re-
putedly the property of a shipping magnate, a billionaire so
reclusive that no one knew his name or had ever seen his face,
but he would loan or rent it to friends, colleagues, strangers,
unsocial lessees who wanted to bathe on a private beach far
from the prying eyes of native peasant or vulgar tourist. The
latest tenant had been there since the spring, cared for by an
ancient crone who seemed to the local tradespeople to be
willfully deaf and all but dumb, selecting her purchases with
grunts and hearing neither greeting nor question. Her back
was hunched, and between many wrinkles the slits of her eyes
appeared to have no whites, only the beady black gleam of
iris and pupil. The few who had glimpsed the mistress declared she was as young as her servant was old, and as beautiful as the hag was ugly, yet she too was aloof even by the
standards of the house. They said she did not lie in the sun,
fearing perhaps to blemish the pallor of her perfect skin, but
swam in the waters of the cove by moonlight, naked but for
the dark veil of her hair. In the neighboring village the men
speculated, talking in whispers over the last metaxa of a goddess beyond compare, and the women said she must be disfigured or diseased. She had a pet even stranger than her
servant, a huge sphinx cat hairless as a baby, its skin piebald,
grayish-white marked with bruise-black patches. It had been
seen hunting on the mountain slopes above her garden; someone claimed to have watched it kill a snake.

Behind the glass walls of her house, the woman heard the
villagers' stories, though her servant never spoke, and smiled
to herself, a sweet, secret smile that showed no teeth. She still
bathed by night, secure in the power of the moon, and by day
she stayed in a darkened room, lighting a cold fire on the cold

marble hearth, and gazing, gazing into the smoke. Sometimes she sat in the courtyard, where little sun found its way through the vine-trellised canopy. No cicadas strummed here, though the slopes beyond throbbed with their gypsy sawing; no bee buzzed, or not for long. The hungry orchids snapped up all insect life in their spotted mouths. There was no sound but the water. The woman would sit among the carnivorous plants, dressed in a thin red garment spotted like an orchid, with the black ripples of her hair falling around her shoulders. Watching the tree. The cat came to her there and rubbed its bald flank against her limbs, purring. "Will it fruit, Nehemet?" she would murmur. "It grows, but will it fruit? And if it does, what fruit will it bear?" And she would touch the leaves with her pale fingertips—leaves that trembled at that contact, not after but before, as though in anticipation.

For Panioti, son of the woman who owned the village general store and gift shop, there came a night when the last metaxa was a drink too much. He was handsome as only a child of the sun can be, high of cheekbone and brown of skin, with the gloss of youth on him like velvet down and the idle assurance of absolute beauty. In the summer, he minded the shop for his mother and made love to all the prettiest visitors; in the off-season, he went to college in Athens, took life seriously, studied to be an engineer. "I do not believe in the loveliness of this unknown siren," he maintained over the second to last drink, "or she would not hide herself. A beautiful woman puts on her smallest bikini and shows off her body on the beach. Has anyone seen her?" But none of those present had. "There you are. I won't take her charms on trust; like any rumor, they will have grown in the telling. I want proof. I want to see her with my own eyes, swimming naked in the moonlight. *Then* I will believe her a goddess."

"Why don't you?" said one of his companions. "Hide in the olive grove down by the rocks. See for yourself."

"He would never dare," said another. "Bet you five thousand drachma."

By the last drink, the bet was on.

The cove was inaccessible save by the path down from the house, so the following evening Panioti swam around the headland, coming ashore on the rocks in order to leave no footprints, and concealed himself among the olive trees at the base of the slope. He carried in a waterproof case a camera, the kind that would take pictures in the dark without need of a flash, and a bottle of beer. He sat under the leaves in the fading sunset, leopard spotted with shadow, drinking the beer slowly, slowly, to make it last. The dark had come down before the bottle was empty, and he thrust it upright into the sandy soil. He waited, impatient with the crawling hours, held to his vigil only by the thought of his friends' scorn if he were to return too soon. At long last his wristwatch showed the hands drawing toward midnight. *Now* she will come, he thought, or I shall leave. But I do not think she will come.

He first saw her as a white movement on the path, her form apparently wreathed in a glittering mist, her dark hair fading into darkness. She seemed to glide over the uneven ground with a motion that was smooth and altogether silent; he almost fancied her feet did not touch the earth. The hair prickled on his neck. For a moment he could have believed her a pagan spirit, a creature of another kind whose flesh and substance were not of this world. Then as she descended to the beach he realized the mist effect was a loose, transparent garment that she unfastened and shed on the sand; her body glowed in the moonlight, slender and shapely as an alabaster nymph, a cold, perfect thing. She raised her arms to the sky as if in greeting to some forgotten deity, then she walked out into the water. The sea was calm and all but waveless: it took her with barely a ripple. He saw her head for a while as a black nodule silhouetted against the sea glimmer, then it dipped and vanished. Belatedly, he remembered the camera, extracting it from its case, waiting for her to reemerge. He half wondered if she would show in a photograph or if, like some supernatural being, she would leave no imprint on celluloid. He moved forward, lying along the rocks, poised and ready; but the swimmer did not return. She was gone so long his breath shortened in fear and he put the camera aside, braced to plunge in in a search he knew would be hopeless.

She reappeared quite suddenly, within yards of the rocks where he lay. He thought her eyes were wide open, staring through the night with the same dilated gaze with which she must have pierced the darkness undersea. She began to swim toward the shore—toward *him*—with a sleek, invisible stroke. Then abruptly she rose from the water; the sea streamed from her limbs; her black hair clung wetly to breasts, shoulders, back. For the first time, he saw her face, dim in the moonglow but not dim enough—he looked into eyes deep as the abyss and bright with a luster that was not of the moon; he saw the lips parted as if in hunger . . . He tried to move, to flee, forgetful of the camera, of the bet, of his manly pride; but his legs were rooted. The whisper of her voice seemed to reach into his soul.

"Do I look fair to you, peasant?" She swept back her hair, thrusting her breasts toward him, pale hemispheres surmounted by nipples that jutted like thorns. "Look your fill. Tell me, did you feel bold coming here? Did you feel daring—sneaking among the rocks to gawp, and ogle, and boast to your friends? What will you say to them when you return—*if* you return? That you have seen Venus Infernalis, Aphrodite risen from a watery grave, reborn from the spume of the sea god's ecstasy? What will you say?"

Closer she came and closer; his spirit recoiled, but his muscles were locked and his body shuddered.

"Nothing," he managed. "I will say nothing. I swear."

"I know you will say nothing." She was gentle now, touching a cold finger to his face. "Do you know the fate of those who spy on the goddess? One was struck blind, another transformed into a stag and torn to pieces by his own dogs. But you have no dog, and the blind can still see with the eyes of the mind. So I will blank your mind and put your soul in your eyes. You came here to see me, to behold the mystery of my beauty. I will give you your heart's desire. Your eyes will be enchanted, lidless and sleepless, fixed on me forever. Does that sound good to you?" Her hands slid across his cheeks, cupped around his sockets. His skin shrank from the contact.

"Please," he mumbled, and "No . . ." but her mouth smiled and her fingers probed unheeding.

In a velvet sky the moon pulled a wisp of cloud over her face, hiding her gaze from what followed.

The next morning a rumor circulated through the village that the woman and her servant had left in the small hours, taking the hairless cat and uprooting plants from the courtyard. The taxi driver who had driven them to the airport confirmed it, though his tip had been so generous he had gotten drunk for a week and was consequently confused. For some reason, the house was not occupied again. The owner left it untenanted and uncared for; the bloodred carpets faded, and only the orchids thrived.

They found Panioti two days later, borne on the sea currents some way from Hekati. He had not drowned and there was no visible injury on his body, save where his eyeballs had been plucked out. But that was not a story they told the tourists.

Part One

Succor

I ⌒⌒⌒⌒

It was New Year's Eve 2000. Under the eaves of the Wroke-wood, the ancient house of Wrokeby normally brooded in silence, a haphazard sprawl of huddled rooms, writhen stair-cases, arthritic beams, and creaking floors, its thick walls at-tacked from without by monstrous creepers and gnawed from within by mice, beetles, and dry rot. English Heritage had no mandate here: shadows prowled the empty corridors, drafts fingered the drapes, water demons gurgled in the plumbing. The Fitzherberts who originally built the house had, through the vicissitudes of history, subsequently knocked it down, razed it, burnt it, and built it up again, constructing the priest's hole, burrowing the secret passages, and locking unwanted wives and lunatic relatives in the more inaccessible attics un-til the family expired of inbreeding and ownership passed to a private trust. Now it was leased to members of the nouveau riche, who enjoyed decrying its many inconveniences and complained formally only when the domestic staff fell through the moldering floorboards and threatened to sue. The latest tenant was one Kaspar Walgrim, an investment banker with a self-made reputation for cast-iron judgment and stainless steel integrity. He liked to mention the house in passing to colleagues and clients, but he rarely got around to visiting it. Until tonight. Tonight, Wrokeby was having a ball.

Lights had invaded the unoccupied rooms and furtive cor-ridors: clusters of candles, fairy stars set in flower trumpets, globes that spun and flashed. The shadows were confused, shredded into tissue-thin layers and dancing a tarantella across floor and walls; the glancing illumination showed costumes historical and fantastical, fantastical-historical, and merely erotic wandering the unhallowed halls. Music blared and thumped from various sources: Abba in the ballroom, Queen in the gallery, grunge in the stables. The Norman church tower that was the oldest part of the building had been hung with red lanterns, and stray guests sat on the twisting stair smoking, snorting, and pill popping, until some of them could actually see the headless ghost of William Fitzherbert watching them in horror from under his own arm. Spiders that had lurked undisturbed for generations scuttled into hiding. In the kitchen, a poltergeist worked among the drinks, adding unexpected ingredients, but no one noticed.

Suddenly, all over the house—all over the country—the music stopped. Midnight struck. Those who were still conscious laughed and wept and kissed and hugged with more than their customary exuberance: it was, after all, the second millennium, and mere survival was something worth celebrating. The unsteady throng caroled "Auld Lang Syne," a ballad written expressly to be sung by inebriates. Some revelers removed masks, others removed clothing (not necessarily their own). One hapless youth threw up over the balustrade of the gallery in the misguided belief that he was vomiting into the moat. There was no moat. In the dining hall, a beauty with long black hair and in a trailing gown of tattered chiffon refused to unmask, telling her light-hearted molester: "I am Morgause, queen of air and darkness. Who are you to look upon the unknown enchantment of my face?"

"More—gauze?" hazarded her admirer, touching the chiffon.

"Sister of Morgan Le Fay," said a celebrated literary critic, thinly disguised under the scaly features and curling horns of a low-grade demon. "Mother—according to some—of the traitor Mordred. I think the lady has been reading T. H. White."

"Who was he?" asked a tall blonde in a leather corselette, sporting short spiked hair and long spiked heels. Behind a mask of scarlet feathers her eyes gleamed black. She did not listen to the answer; instead, her lips moved on words that the demon critic could not quite hear.

After a brief tussle, Morgause lost her visor and a couple of hairpieces, revealing a flushed Dana Walgrim, daughter of their host. She lunged at her molester, stumbled over her dress, and crashed to the floor; they heard the thud of her head hitting the parquet. There was a moment when the conversation stopped dead. Then people rushed forward and said the things people usually do under the circumstances: "Lift her head—No, don't move her—She's not badly hurt—There's no blood— Give her air—Get some water—Give her *brandy*—She'll come around." She did not come around. Someone went to look for her brother; someone else called an ambulance. "No point," said Lucas Walgrim, arriving on the scene with the slightly blank expression of a person who has gone from very drunk to very sober in a matter of seconds. "We'll take her ourselves. My car's in the drive."

"You'll lose your license," said a nervous pirate.

"I'll be careful."

He scooped Dana into his arms; helpful hands supported her head and hitched up the long folds of her dress. As they went out the literary critic opined, turning back to the spike-haired blonde, "Drugs. And they only let her out of rehab three months ago."

But the blonde had vanished.

In a small room some distance from the action, Kaspar Walgrim was oblivious to his daughter's misfortune. One or two people had gone to search for him, thinking that news of the accident might be of interest, although father and child were barely on speaking terms. But they could not find him.

The room where Walgrim sat was reached through the back of a wardrobe in the main bedchamber, the yielding panels revealing not a secret country of snow and magic, but an office equipped by a previous owner with an obsolete computer on the desk and books jacketed thickly with dust. Beside the computer lay a pristine sheet of paper headed *Tenancy Agreement*. Words wrote themselves in strangely spiky italics across the page. Kaspar Walgrim was not watching. His flannel-gray eyes had misted over like a windshield in cold weather. He was handsome in a chilly, bankeresque fashion, with an adamantine jaw and a mouth like the slit in a money box, but his present rigidity of expression was unnatural, the stony blankness of a zombie. The angled desk lamp illumined his face from below, underwriting browbone and cheekbone and cupping his eyes in pouches of light. At his hand stood a glass filled with a red liquid that was not wine. Behind him, a solitary voice dripped words into his ears as smoothly as honey from a spoon. A hand with supple fingers and nails like silver claws crept along his shoulder. "I like this place," said the voice. "It will suit me. You will be happy to rent it to me . . . for nothing. For gratitude. For succor. *Per siéquor. Escri né luthor.* You will be happy . . ."

"I will be happy."

"It is well. You will remember how I healed your spirit, in gratitude, as in a dream, a vision. You will remember sensation, pleasure, peace." The hand slid down across his chest; the man gave a deep groan that might have been ecstasy. "Do you remember?"

"I remember."

"Finish your drink."

Kaspar Walgrim drank. The liquid in his glass held the light as if it were trapped there.

The spiked blond hair was screwed into a ball on the desk. The knife-blade heels prowled to and fro, stabbing the floorboards. The bird mask seemed to blend with the face of its wearer, transforming her into some exotic raptor, unhuman and predatory.

When he was told, Kaspar Walgrim signed the paper.

The year was barely an hour old when a cab pulled up outside a house in Pimlico. This was smart Pimlico, the part that likes to pretend it is tonier than it is. The house was cream-colored Georgian in a square of the same, which surrounded a garden that fenced off would-be trespassers with genteel railings. Two young women got out of the taxi, fumbling for their respective wallets. One found hers and paid the fare; the other scattered the contents of her handbag on the pavement and bent down to retrieve them, snatching at a stray tampon. The girl who paid was slender and not very tall, perhaps five foot five: the streetlamp glowed on the auburn lowlights in her short designer haircut. Her coat hung open to reveal a minimalist figure, gray chiffoned and silver frosted for the occasion. Her features might have been described as elfin if it had not been for a glossy coating of makeup and an immaculate veneer of self-assurance. She looked exquisitely groomed, successful, competent—she had booked the taxi, one of the few available, three months in advance and had negotiated both fare and tip at the time. Her name was Fern Capel.

She was a witch.

Her companion gave up on the tampon, which had rolled into the gutter, collected her other belongings, and straightened up. She had a lot of heavy dark hair that had started the evening piled on her head but was now beginning to escape from bondage, a wayward wrap, and a dress patterned in sequined flowers that was slightly the wrong shape for the body inside. Her face was in a state of nature save for a little blusher and some lipstick, most of which had been smudged off. For all that she had an elusive attraction that her friend lacked, an air of warmth and vulnerability. The deep-set eyes were soft

behind concealing lashes and the faintly tragic mouth suggested a temperament too often prone to both sympathy and
empathy. In fact, Gaynor Mobberley was not long out of her
latest disastrous relationship, this time with a neurotic flautist
who had trashed her flat when she attempted to end the affair.
She had been staying with Fern ever since.

They went indoors and up the stairs to the second-floor
apartment. "It was a good party," Gaynor hazarded, extricat-
ing the few remaining pins and an overburdened butterfly clip
from her hair.

"No, it wasn't," said Fern. "It was dire. The food was quiche
and the champagne was blanc de blanc. We only went for the
view of the fireworks. Like all the other guests. What were you
discussing so intimately with our host?"

"He and Vanessa are having problems," said Gaynor unhappily. "He wants to buy me lunch and tell me all about it."

"You attract men with hang-ups like a blocked drain attracts flies," Fern said brutally. "So what did you say?"

Gaynor fluffed. "I couldn't think of an excuse to get out
of it."

"You don't need an excuse. Just say no. Like the antidrug
campaign." Fern pressed the button on her answering machine, which was flashing to indicate a message.

A male voice invaded the room on a wave of background
noise. "Hi, sis. Just ringing to wish you a Happy New Year. I
think we're in Ulan Bator, but I'm not quite sure: the fermented mare's milk tends to cloud my geography. Anyway,
we're in a yurt somewhere and a wizened rustic is strumming
his souzouki . . ."

"Bouzouki," murmured Fern. "Which is Greek, not Mon-
golian. Idiot." What music they could hear was pure disco,
Eastern Eurostyle.

"*Shine jiliin bayar hurgeye,* as they say over here," her
brother concluded. "Be seeing you." *Bleep.*

"*Shin jillian* what?" echoed Gaynor.

"God knows," said Fern. "He's probably showing off. Still," she added rather too pointedly, "he hasn't any hang-ups."

"I know," said Gaynor, reminded uncomfortably of her abortive non-affair with Fern's younger brother. "That's what scared me. It gave me nothing to hold on to. Anyhow, he's obviously airbrushed me from his memory. You said you told him I was staying here, but . . . well, he didn't even mention my name."

"He doesn't have to," Fern responded. "He wouldn't normally bother to phone just to wish me Happy New Year. I suspect he called for your benefit, not mine."

"We never even slept together," Gaynor said. "Just one kiss . . ."

"Exactly," said Fern. "You're the one that got away. A career angler like Will could never get over that. You couldn't have done better if you'd tried." Gaynor flushed. "I'm sorry," Fern resumed. "I know you weren't trying. Look . . . there's a bottle of Veuve Clicquot in the fridge. Let's have our own celebration."

They discarded coats and wraps, kicked off their shoes. Fern deposited her jewelry on a low table, took a couple of glasses from a cabinet, and fetched the champagne. After a cautious interval, the cork gave a satisfactory pop. "Happy New Year." Fern curled up in a big armchair, tucking her legs under her.

Gaynor, on the sofa, sat knees together, feet apart. "Happy New Century. It's got to be better than the old one."

"It doesn't start quite yet," her friend pointed out. "Two thousand and one is the first year of the century. This is the in-between year, the millennium year. The year everything can change."

"Will it?" asked Gaynor. "Can you *see*?"

"I'm a witch, not a seeress. Everything can change any year. Any *day*. Dates aren't magical—I think. All the same . . ." Her expression altered, hardening to alertness. She set down her glass. "There's something here. Now. Something . . . that doesn't belong." Her skin prickled with an unearthly static. The striation of green in her eyes seemed to intensify until they shone with a feline brilliance between the shadow-painted lids. Her gaze was fixed on the shelving at the far end of the room, where a vase rocked slightly on its base for no visible reason. Without looking, she reached for the switch on the table lamp. There was a click, and the room was in semidarkness. In the corner beside the vase there seemed to be a nucleus of shadow deeper than those around it. The light had concealed it, but in the gloom it had substance and the suggestion of a shape. A very small shape, hunch-shouldered and shrinking from the witch's stare. The glow of the street-lamps filtering through the curtains tinted the dark with a faint orange glimmer, and as Gaynor's vision adjusted, it appeared to her that the shape was trembling, though that might have been the uncertainty of its materialization. It began to fade, but Fern moved her hand with a Command hardly louder than a whisper, soft strange words that seemed to travel through the air like a zephyr of power. *"Vissari! Inbar fiassé . . ."* The shadow condensed, petrifying into solidity. Fern pressed the light switch.

And there it was, a being perhaps three feet high assembled at random from a collection of mismatched body parts. Over-long arms enwrapped it, the stumpy legs were crooked, mottled fragments of clothing hung like rags of skin from its sides. Slanting eyes, indigo-black from edge to edge, peered between sheltering fingers. A narrow crest of hair bristled on the top of its head and its ears were tufted like those of a lynx. It was a monster in miniature, an aberration, ludicrously out of place in the civilized interior.

Neither girl looked particularly shocked to see it.

"A goblin," said Fern, "but not resident. And I didn't ask anyone to advertise."

"How could it come in uninvited?" asked Gaynor. "I thought that was against the Ultimate Laws."

"Some creatures are too simple or too small for such laws. Like cockroaches, they go everywhere. Still . . . this is a witch's flat. Even a cockroach should be more careful." She addressed the intruder directly. "Who are you, and what are you doing here?"

The goblin mumbled inaudibly.

"Louder," said Fern. *"Intona!"*

"Not a *house-goblin*," the creature said with evident contempt. "I'm a burglar."

"What have you stolen?" asked Fern.

"Nothing," the goblin admitted. "Yet."

"You know who I am?"

Mumble.

"Good," said Fern. "So you came here to steal something specific, from me. I expect you thought I would be out much later on Millennium New Year's Eve. Who sent you?"

Warty lids flickered briefly over the watchful eyes. "No one."

"Was it Az—Was it the Old Spirit?" said Gaynor.

"He wouldn't use an ordinary goblin," said Fern. "He thinks they're beneath him." She lifted her hand, pointing at the intruder with forked fingers, murmuring words too soft to be heard. A tiny gleam of light played about her fingertips, like the sparkle in a champagne glass. *"Who sent you?"*

The goblin held its breath, flinched, squeezed its eyes tight shut, and then opened them very wide. "The queen!" it squeaked. "I steal for the queen! Not for gods or demons! I'm a *royal* burglar, I am! I—"

"Mabb," said Fern, relaxing slowly. "I see. I suppose she . . . Of course, I know what she wants. Tell her it isn't here, and it's not mine anyway. It's held in trust, tell her, a sacred trust. It's not a thing to be stolen or bartered. Say I know she will understand this, because she is a true queen who appreciates the value of honor."

"Who's Mabb?" asked Gaynor *sotto voce*.

"The queen of the goblins," whispered Fern. "Not much fairy in her, so I hear."

"*Does* she appreciate the value of honor?"

"I doubt it, but I'm told she responds to flattery. We'll see." She raised her voice again. "What's your name?"

The goblin pondered the question, evidently considering whether it was safe to answer. "Some call me Skuldunder," he conceded eventually.

"Well, Skuldunder," said Fern, "since you're here, and it's a special occasion, will you have some champagne?"

"Is it good?" The goblin scrambled down from the shelf and approached warily, radiating suspicion.

"Have you never stolen any?"

There was a shrug, as if Skuldunder was reluctant to admit to any shortfall in his criminal activities.

Fern took another glass from the cupboard and half filled it. "Try it," she said.

The goblin sniffed, sipped, grimaced.

"We will drink to your queen," Fern announced. "Queen Mabb!"

They drank solemnly. When Fern judged their visitor was sufficiently at ease she left him with Gaynor and went to her room, returning presently with a small quilted bag unzipped to show the contents. "These are gifts for your queen," she told Skuldunder, "as a gesture of friendship and respect. I have heard she is a great beauty—" Fern uttered the unaccustomed lie without a wince "—so I have chosen presents to adorn her loveliness. These colored powders can be daubed onto her eyelids; the gold liquid in this bottle, when applied to her fingernails, will set hard; in this tube is a special stick for tinting her lips. There is also a hand mirror and a brooch." She indicated a piece of costume jewelry in the shape of a butterfly, set with blue and green brilliants. "Tell her I honor her, but the Sleer Bronaw, the Spear of Grief, is something I and my people hold in trust. It is not mine to give up."

Skuldunder nodded with an air of doubtful comprehension, accepting the quilted bag gingerly, as if it were a thing of great price. Then he drained his glass, choked, bowed clumsily to the two women, and made an awkward exit through a window that Fern had hastily opened. "I don't think it will dematerialize," she said, referring to his burden. "I hope you can manage . . ." But the goblin had already disappeared into the shadows of the street.

"What was that all about?" Gaynor demanded as Fern closed the window.

"The Sleer Bronaw is the spear Bradachin brought with him from Scotland when he first came to Dale House," Fern explained. "It's still there, as far as I know. I believe it has some mythic significance; Ragginbone thinks so, at any rate." Bradachin, the house-goblin who inhabited her family's Yorkshire home, had migrated from a Scottish castle after the new owners converted it into a hotel. Ragginbone was an old friend, a tramp who might once have been a wizard and now led a footloose existence in search of troubles he could not prevent, accompanied by a faithful dog with the mien of a she-wolf. "It's unusual for something like that to be left in the care of a goblin, but Bradachin knows what he's doing. I think. You saw him use it once, remember?"

"I remember." There was a short silence. Then Gaynor said: "Why would Mabb want it?"

"I'm not sure. Ragginbone told me someone had offered her a trade, but that was a long time ago. I suppose she must have latched on to the idea again; he says her mind leaps to and fro like a grasshopper on speed—or words to that effect. Anyhow, none of the werefolk are focused in Time the way humans are."

"It was an interesting start to the New Year," Gaynor volunteered. "A goblin burglar." She gave a sudden little shiver of reaction, still unused to encounters with such beings.

"Maybe," said Fern. "Maybe—it was a portent."

When the bottle was empty, they went to bed, each to her own thoughts.

Gaynor lay awake a long time as two-year-old memories surfaced, memories of magic and danger—and of Will. Somehow, even in her darkest recollections, it was the image of Will that predominated. There were bats—she hated bats— flying out of a TV set, swarming around her, tangling in her hair, hooking on to her pajamas. And Will rushing to her rescue, holding her in his arms . . . She was waiting behind a locked door for the entrance of her jailer, clutching a heavy china bowl with which she hoped to stun him, only it was Will—Will!—who came, Will who had escaped and come back to find her. Will was beside her in the car when the engine wouldn't start, and she switched on the light to see the morlochs crawling over the chassis, pressing their hungry mouths against the windshield. Will whom she had kissed only once, and left, because he had too much charm and no hang-ups, and he could never want someone like her for more than a brief encounter, a short fling ending in long regret. "He's your brother," she had said to Fern, as if that settled the matter, the implications unspoken. He's your brother—if he breaks my heart it will damage our friendship, perhaps for good. But her heart, if not broken, was already bruised and tender, throbbing painfully at the mention of Will's name, at the sound of his voice on a machine. Ulan Bator . . . what was he doing in Ulan Bator? She had been so busy trying to suppress her reaction, she had not even thought to ask. She knew he had turned from painting to photography and abandoned his thesis in midstream, ultimately taking up the video camera and joining with a kindred spirit to form their own production company. Whether they had any actual commissions or not was a moot point, but Fern had told her they were working on a series of films exploring little-known cultures, presumably in little-known parts of the world. Such as Ulan Bator, wherever that might be. (Mongolia?) And what the hell was a yurt? It sounded like a particularly vicious form of yogurt, probably made from the fermented mare's milk to which Will had alluded.

Gaynor drifted eventually into a dream of bats and goblins, where she and Will were trapped in a car sinking slowly into a bog of blackberry-flavored yurt, but a morloch pulled Will out through the window, and she was left to drown on her own. Fortunately, by the next morning, she had forgotten all about it.

Fern stayed awake even longer, speculating about Mabb, and the goblin burglar, and the spear whose story she had never heard, the ill-omened Spear of Grief. She remembered it as something very old, rust spotted, the blade edge pitted as if Time had bitten into it with visible teeth. It had no aura of potency or enchantment, no spell runes engraved on shaft or head. It was just a hunk of metal, long neglected, with no more power than a garden rake. Yet she had seen it kill, and swiftly. She wondered whose tears had rusted the ancient blade, earning the weapon its name. And inevitably, like Gaynor, she slipped from speculation into recollection, losing control of her thought and letting it stray where it would. She roamed once more through the rootscape of the Eternal Tree, in a world of interlacing tubers, secret mosses, skulking fungi, until she found a single black fruit on a low bough, ripening into a head that opened ice-blue eyes at her and said: "You." She remembered the smell of fire, and the dragon rising, and the one voice to which both she and the dragon had listened. The voice of the dragon charmer. But the head was burned and the voice stilled, for ever and ever. And her thought shrank, reaching farther back and farther, seeking the pain that was older and deeper, spear-deep in her spirit, though the wound, if not healed, was all but forgotten. Now she probed even there, needing the pain, the loss, the guilt, fearing to find herself heart-whole again for all time. And so at last she came to a beach at sunset and saw Rafarl Dévornine rising like a god from the golden waves.

But she had been so young then, only sixteen, in an age ten thousand years gone. And now I am different, she thought. In Atlantis, they thought I was a star fallen from the heavens. But now I am a witch—not a pagan witch from a dream of the past but a witch of today, a twenty-first-century witch. My skills may be ancient but my spirit is as modern as a microchip. As modern as a hamburger. Would I love him, if I met him now? When Someday comes, when in the dance of eternity our paths recross, will I even *know* him, or he me? And the tears started, not from the return of pain but from its loss. The lack of pain hurt more, and there was an ache inside her that was not her heart. Gaynor suffers, Fern thought, her Gift for friendship showing her what the other sought to hide. But at least Gaynor suffers because she loves. I have lost all the love I ever had, and it will not come again, because you love like that just once, and then it's gone for good. I must be a fickle creature, to love so deeply and forget so fast.

And her tears dried, because she saw them as an indulgence, playing at grief, and she lay in the dark empty of all feeling, hollow and cold, until at last she slept.

It was one of those dreams where you don't know you're dreaming. She moved through it as if she were an onlooker behind her own eyes, with no control over her actions, traversing the city with the desperate certainty of someone who was utterly resolved on a dreadful errand. It was a winter evening, and the glare of the metropolis faded the stars. Many-windowed cliffs rose above her, glittering with lights; modern sculptures settled their steel coils on marble plinths; three-cornered courtyards flaunted fountains, polished plaques, automatic doors. Recent rain had left sprawling puddles at the roadside that reflected headlights and streetlamps in glancing flashes. In places the city looked familiar, but at other times it seemed to change its nature, showing glimpses of an underlying world, alien and sinister. Sudden alleyways opened between buildings, thick with shadows that were darker and older than the nightfall. Flights of steps zigzagged down into nether regions far below the Underground, where crowds of what might be people heaved like boiling soup. Faces passed by, picked out briefly in the lamplight, with unhuman features and tufted ears. It came to Fern that she was looking for something, something she did not want to find, driven by a compulsion that she could not control. She had always believed in the freedom to choose—between right and wrong, good and evil, character and anti-character, the choices that shape the soul. But she knew now that she had already chosen, made a choice that could not be unmade, and her feet were set on a deadly path.

Presently she came to the turning that she sought, a pedestrian walk that passed under an arch in a façade of opaque windows. When she emerged at the other end of the tunnel she was in an open square. It was large—far too large for the buildings that enclosed it on the outside, as if she had passed through a dimensional kink into some alternative space. Stones paving stretched away on either hand; distant groups moved to and fro, busy as ants in their unknown affairs. In front of her, broad steps spread out like low waves on an endless beach, and above them rose the tower. She had been expecting it, she knew—she had been seeking it—but nonetheless the sight gave her a sick jolt in her stomach, a horror of what she was about to do, her fearful necessary errand. The tower was taller than the surrounding buildings, taller than the whole city, a cubist edifice of blind glass and black steel climbing to an impossible height, terminating in a single spire that seemed to pierce the pallor of the clouds. Reflected lights gleamed like drowning stars in its crystal walls, but she could see nothing of what lay within. It was of the city and yet not of it, an architectural fungus: the urban maze nourished it as a hapless tree nourishes a parasitic growth that will ultimately devour its host. For this was the tower at the heart of all evil, the Dark Tower of legend and fairy tale, rebuilt in the modern world on foundations as old as pain. Fern looked up, and up, until her neck cricked, then dragged her gaze away and slowly mounted the steps to the main entrance.

Guards stood on either side, scarlet coated and braided across the shoulders. They might have been ordinary commissionaires were it not for the masks of dark metal covering their faces. Iron lids blinked once in the eye slits as Fern passed between them. The double doors opened by invisible means and she entered a vast lobby agleam with black marble. A dim figure slid from behind the reception desk. A voice without tone or gender said: "He is waiting for you. Follow me." She followed.

Behind the reception area there was a cylindrical shaft rising out of a deep well that appeared to be surrounded by subterranean levels and ascending beyond the eye's reach. Each story was connected to the shaft by a narrow bridge unprotected by rail or balustrade, open to the drop beneath. Transparent elevators traveled up and down, ovoid bubbles suspended around a central stem. Fern flinched inwardly from the bridge, but her legs carried her across uncaring. The elevator door closed behind them and they began to climb, gently for the first few seconds and then with accelerating speed, until the passing stories blurred and her stomach plunged and her brain seemed to be squashed against her skull. When they stopped her guide stepped out, unaffected, unassisting. An automaton. For a moment she clutched the door frame, pinching her nose and exhaling forcefully to pop her ears. She didn't look down. She didn't speculate how far it was to the bottom. Her legs were unsteady now and the bridge appeared much narrower, a slender gangplank over an abyss. Her guide had halted on the other side. She thought: It looks like a test, but it isn't. It's a lure, a taunt. A challenge.

But she could not turn back.

She crossed over, keeping her gaze ahead. They moved on. Now they were on an escalator that crawled around the tower against the outer wall. At the top, another door slid back, admitting them to an office.

The office. The seat of darkness. Neither a sorcerer's cell nor an unholy fane but an office suited to the most senior of executives. Spacious. Luxurious. Floor-to-ceiling windows, liquid sweeps of curtain, a carpet soft and deep as fur. In the middle of the room, a desk of polished ebony, and on it a file covered in red, an old-fashioned quill pen, and a dagger that might have been mistaken for a letter opener but wasn't. There was a name stamped on the file but she did not read it: she knew it was hers. Her guide had retreated; if there were other people in the room she did not see them. Only *him.* Beyond the huge windows there were no city lights: just the slow-moving stars and the double-pronged horn of the moon, very big and close now, floating between two tiers of cloud. A scarlet-shaded lamp cast a rusty glow across the desktop.

He sat outside the light. Neither moonbeam nor starfire reached his unseen features. She thought he wore a suit, but it did not matter. All she could see was the hint of a glimmer in narrowed eyes.

Perhaps he smiled.

"I knew you would come to me," he said, "in the end."

If she spoke—if she acknowledged him—she could not hear. The only voice she heard was his: a voice that was old, and cold, and infinitely familiar.

"You resisted longer than I expected," he went on. "That is good. The strength of your resistance is the measure of my victory. But now the fight is over. Your Gift will be mine, uniting us, power with power, binding you to me. Serve me well, and I will set you among the highest in this world. Betray me, and retribution will come swiftly, but its duration will be long and slow. Do you understand?"

But she was in the grip of other fears. She felt the anxiety within her, sharp as a blade.

"The one you care for will be restored," he said. "But it must be through me. Only through me. None other has the power."

Though she heard no sound, she seemed to be pleading with him, torn between a loathing of such a bargain and the urgency of her need.

"Can you doubt me?" he demanded, and the savagery of eons was in his voice. "Do you know who I am? Have you forgotten?" He got to his feet, circling the desk in one smooth motion, seizing her arm. Struggle was futile: she was impelled toward the glass wall. His grasp was like a manacle; her muscles turned to water at his touch. She sensed him behind her as a crowding darkness, too solid for shadow, a faceless potency. "Look down," he ordered. She saw a thin carpet of cloud, moon silvered, and then it parted, and far below there were lights—the lights not of one city but of many, distant and dim as the Milky Way, a glistening scatterdust spreading away without boundary or horizon, until it was lost in infinity. "Behold! There are all the nations of the world, all the men of wealth and influence, all the greed, ambition, desperation, all the evil deeds and good intentions—and in the end, it all comes to me. Everything comes to me. This tower is built on their dreams and paid for with their blood. Where they sow, I reap, and so it will always be, until the Pit that can never be filled overflows at the last." His tone softened, becoming a whisper that insinuated itself into the very pith of her thought. "Without me, you will be nothing, mere flotsam swept away on the current of Time. With me—ah, with me, all this will be at your feet."

She felt the sense of defeat lying heavy on her spirit. The

vision was taken away; the clouds closed. She was led back to the desk. The red file was open now to reveal some sort of legal document with curling black calligraphy on cream-colored paper. She did not read it. She knew what it said.

"Hold out your arm."

The knife nicked her vein, a tiny V-shaped cut from which the blood ran in a long scarlet trickle.

"You will keep the scar forever," he said. "It is my mark. *Now sign.*"

She dipped the quill in her own blood. The nib made a thin scratching noise as she began to write.

Behind her eyes, behind her mind, the other Fern—the Fern who was dreaming—screamed her horror and defiance in the prison of her own head. *No! No . . .*

She woke up.

The sweat was pouring off her, as if a moment earlier she had been raging with fever, but now she was cold. Unlike Gaynor, for Fern there was no merciful oblivion. The dream was real and terrible—a witch's dream, a seeing-beyond-the-world, a chink into the future. *Azmordis.* Her mouth shaped the name, though no sound came out, and the darkness swallowed it. Azmordis, the Oldest Spirit, her ancient enemy who lusted for her power, the Gift of her kind, and schemed for her destruction. Azmordis who was both god and demon, feeding off men's worship—and their fears. But she had stood alone against him, and defeated him, and held to the truth she knew.

Until now.

She got up, shivering, and went into the kitchen, and made herself cocoa with a generous measure of whiskey, and prepared a hot water bottle. It seemed a long way till daylight.

II ~~~~~

At Wrokeby, the house-goblin was no longer playing polter-geist. He lurked in corners and crannies, in the folds of curtains, in the spaces under shadows. The newcomer did not appear to notice him, but he sensed that sooner or later she would sweep through every nook and niche, scouring the house of unwanted inmates. He watched her when he dared, peering out of knotholes and plaster cracks. He was a strange, wizened creature, stick thin and undersized even for a goblin, with skin the color of aging newspaper and a long pointed face like a hairless rat. His name when he had last heard it was Dibbuck, though he had forgotten why. The piebald cat that prowled the corridors could either see him or scent him, and she hunted him like the rodent he resembled, but so far he had been too quick for her. He had known the terrain for centuries; the cat was an invader on unfamiliar ground. But the presence of Nehemet made him more nervous and furtive than ever. Still he crept and spied, half in fascination, half in terror, knowing in the murky recesses of his brain that the house in his care was being misused, its heritage defiled and its atmosphere contaminated for some purpose he could not guess.

The smaller sitting room now had black velvet curtains and no chairs, with signs and sigils painted on the bare floor where once there had been Persian rugs. A pale fire burned sometimes on a hearth long unused, but the goblin would avoid the room, fearing the cold hiss of its unseen flames and the flickering glow that probed under the door. Instead he ventured to the cellar, hiding in shadows as old as the house itself. The wine racks had been removed and shelves installed, stacked with bottles of unknown liquids and glass jars whose contents he did not want to examine too closely. One bottle stood on a table by itself, with a circle drawn around it and cabbalistic words written in red along the perimeter. It had a crystal stopper sealed in wax, as if the contents were of great value, yet it appeared empty: he could see the wall through it. But there came an evening when he saw it had clouded over, filled with what looked like mist, and in the mist was a shape that writhed against the sides, struggling to escape. He skittered out of the room, and did not return for many days.

On the upper floors he found those Fitzherberts who had stayed this side of Death, their shrunken spirits rooted in age-old patterns of behavior, clinging to passions and hatreds whose causes were long forgotten. They dwelt in the past, seeing little of the real world, animate memories endowed with just a glimmer of thought, an atom of being. Yet even they felt an unfamiliar chill spreading through every artery of the house. "What is this?" asked Sir William, in the church tower. "Who is she, to come here and disturb us—we who have been here so long? This is all that we have."

"I do not know," said the goblin, "but when she passes, I feel a draft blowing straight from eternity."

The ghost faded from view, fearful or ineffectual, and the goblin skulked the passageways, alone with his dread. At last he went back to the cellar, drawn, as are all werefolk, by the imminence of strong magic, mesmerized and repelled.

She wore a green dress that appeared to have no seams, adhering to her body like a living growth, whispering when she moved. There were threads of dull red in the material like the veins in a leaf. Her shadow leaped from wall to wall as she lit the candles, and her hair lifted although the air was stifling and still. The cat followed her, its skin puckered into goose-flesh, arching its back against her legs. There was a smell in the cellar that did not belong there, a smell of roots and earth and uncurling fronds: the goblin was an indoor creature and it took him a while to identify it, although his elongated nose quivered with more-than-human sensitivity. He avoided looking at the woman directly, lest she feel his gaze. Instead he watched her sidelong, catching the flicker of white fingers as she touched flasks and pots, checking their contents, unscrewing the occasional lid, sniffing, replacing. And all the while she talked to her feline companion in a ripple of soft words. These herbs are running low . . . the slumbertop toadstools are too dry . . . these worm eggs will hatch if the air reaches them . . . At the end of one shelf he saw a jar he had not noticed before, containing what looked like a pair of eyeballs floating in some clear fluid. He could see the brown circle of iris and the black pupil, and broken fragments of blood vessel trailing around them. He knew they could not be alive, but they hung against the glass, fixed on *her*, moving when she moved . . .

He drew back, covering his face, afraid even to brush her thought with his crooked stare. When he looked again, she was standing by a long table. It was entirely taken up by an irregular object some six feet in length, bundled in cloth. Very carefully she uncovered it, crooning as if to a child, and Dibbuck smelled the odor more strongly—the smell of a hungry forest, where the trees claw at one another in their fight to reach the sun. Her back was turned toward him, screening much of the object from his view, but he could make out a few slender branches, a torn taproot, leaves that trembled at her caress. She moistened it with drops from various bottles, murmuring a singsong chant that might have been part spell, part lullaby. It had no tune, but its tunelessness invaded the goblin's head, making him dizzy. When she had finished she covered the sapling again, taking care not to tear even the corner of a leaf.

He thought muzzily: It is evil. It should be destroyed. But his small store of courage and resource was almost exhausted.

"The workmen come tomorrow," she told the cat. "They will repair the conservatory, making it proof against weather and watching eyes. Then my Tree may grow in safety once more." The cat mewed, a thin, angry sound. The woman threw back her head as if harkening to some distant cry, and the candle flames streamed sideways, and a wind blew from another place, tasting of dankness and dew, and leaf shadows scurried across the floor. Then she laughed, and all was quiet.

The goblin waited some time after she had quit the cellar before he dared to follow.

He knew now that he must leave Wrokeby—leave or be destroyed—yet still he hung on. This was his place, his care, the purpose of his meager existence: a house-goblin stayed with the house until it crumbled. The era of technology and change had driven some from their old haunts, but such uprootings were rare, and few of goblinkind could survive the subsequent humiliation and exile. Only the strongest were able to move on, and Dibbuck was not strong. Yet deep in his scrawny body there was a fiber of toughness, a vestigial resolve. He did not think of seeking help: he knew of no help to seek. But he did not quite give up. Despite his fear of Nehemet, he stole down his native galleries in the woman's swath, and eavesdropped on her communings with her pet, and listened to the muttering of schemes and spells he did not understand. Once, when she was absent for the day, he even sneaked into her bedroom, peering under the bed for discarded dreams, fingering the creams and lotions on the dressing table. Their packaging was glossy and up-to-date, but he could read a little and they seemed to have magical properties, erasing wrinkles and endowing the user with the radiance of permanent youth. He avoided the mirror lest it catch and hold his reflection, but, glancing up, he saw her face there, moon pale and glowing with an unearthly glamour. "It works," she said. "On me, everything works. I was old, ages old, but now I am young forever." He knew she spoke not to him but to herself, and the mirror was replaying the memory, responding to his curiosity. Panic overcame him, and he fled.

On the tower stair he found the head of Sir William. He tried to seize the hair, but it had less substance than a cobweb. "Go now," said Dibbuck. "They say there is a Gate for mortals through which you can leave this place. Find it, before it is too late."

"I rejected the Gate," said the head haughtily. "I was not done with this world."

"Be done with it now," said the goblin. "Her power grows."

"I was the power here," said Sir William, "long ago . . ."

Despairing, Dibbuck left him, running through the house and uttering his warning unheeded to the ghosts too venerable to be visible anymore, the drafts that had once been passing feet, the water sprites who gurgled through the antique plumbing, the imp who liked to extinguish the fire in the oven. A house as old as Wrokeby has many tenants, phantom memories buried in the very stones. In the kitchen he saw the woman's only servant, a hagling with the eyes of the werekind. She lunged at him with a rolling pin, moving with great swiftness for all her apparent age and rheumatics, but he dodged the blow and faded into the wall, though he had to wait an hour and more before he could slip past her up the stairs. He made his way to the conservatory, a Victorian addition that had been severely damaged fifty years earlier in a storm. Now three builders were there, working with unusual speed and very few cups of tea. The one in charge was a gypsy with a gray-streaked ponytail and a narrow, wary face. "We finish quickly and she'll pay us well," he told the others. "But don't skimp on anything. She'll know."

"She's a looker, isn't she?" said the youngest, a youth barely seventeen. "That figure, and that hair, and all."

"Don't even think of it," said the gypsy. "She can see you thinking." He stared at the spot where the goblin stood, so that for a moment Dibbuck thought he was observed, though the man made no sign. But later, when they were gone, the goblin found a biscuit left there, something no one had done for him through years beyond count. He ate it slowly, savoring the chocolate coating, feeling braver for the gift, the small gesture of friendship and respect, revitalized by the impact of sugar on his system. Perhaps it was that which gave him the impetus to investigate the attics.

He did not like the top of the house. His sense of time was vague, and he recalled only too clearly a wayward daughter of the family who had been locked up there behind iron bars and padlocked doors, supposedly for the benefit of her soul. Amy Fitzherbert had had the misfortune to suffer from manic depression and what was probably Tourette's syndrome in an age when a depression was a hole in the ground and sin had yet to evolve into syndrome. She had been fed through the bars like an animal, and like an animal she had reacted, ranting and screaming and bruising herself against the walls. Dibbuck had been too terrified to go near her. In death, her spirit had moved on, but the atmosphere there was still dark and disturbed from the Furies who had plagued her.

That evening he climbed the topmost stair and crept through the main attics, his ears strained for the slightest of sounds. There were no ghosts here, only a few spiders, a dead beetle, a scattering of mouse droppings by the wainscoting. But it seemed to Dibbuck that this was the quiet of waiting, a quiet that harkened to his listening, that saw his unseen presence. And in the dust there were footprints, well-defined and recent: the prints of a woman's shoes. But the chocolate was strong in him and he went on until he reached the door to Amy's prison, and saw the striped shadow of the bars beyond, and heard what might have been a moan from within. Amy had moaned in her sleep, tormented by many-headed dreams, and he thought she was back there, the woman had raised her spirit for some dreadful purpose; but still he took a step forward, the last step before the spell barrier hit him. The force of it flung him several yards, punching him into the physical world and tumbling him over and over. He picked himself up, twitching with shock. The half-open door was vibrating in the backlash of the spell, and behind it the shadow bars stretched across the floor, but another darkness loomed against them, growing nearer and larger, blotting them out. It had no recognizable shape, but it seemed to be huge and shaggy, and he thought it was thrusting itself against the bars like a caged beast. The plea that reached him was little more than a snarl, the voice of some creature close to the edge of madness.

Let me out . . .

Letmeout letmeout letmeout letmeout . . .

For the third time in recent weeks Dibbuck ran, fleeing a domain that had once been his.

Lucas Walgrim sat at his sister's bedside in a private nursing home in Queen Square. Their father visited dutifully once a week, going into prearranged huddles with various doctors, signing checks whenever required. Dana was wired up to the latest technology, surrounded by bouquets she could not see, examined, analyzed, pampered. The nursing home sent grateful thanks for a generous donation. Nothing happened. Dana's pulse remained steady but slow, so slow, and her face was waxen, as if she were already dead. Lucas would sit beside her through the lengthening afternoons, a neglected laptop on the cabinet by the bed, watching for a quiver of movement, a twinge, a change, waiting until he almost forgot what he was waiting for. She did not toss or turn; her breast barely heaved beneath the lace of her nightgown. They combed her thick dark hair twice a day, spreading it over the pillow: there was

never a strand out of place. In oblivion her mouth lost its customary pout and slackened into an illusion of repose, but he
saw no peace in her face, only absence. He tried talking to her,
calling her, certain he could reach her wherever she had gone;
but no answer came. As children they had been close, thrown
in each other's company by a workaholic father and an alco-
holic mother. Eight years the elder, Lucas had alternately bul-
lied and protected his little sister, fighting all her battles,
allowing no one else to tease or taunt her. As an adult, he had
been her final recourse when boyfriends abandoned her and
girlfriends let her down. But in the last few years he had been
busy at the City desk where his father had installed him, and
she had turned to hard drugs and heavy drinking for the moral
support that she lacked. He told himself that guilt was futile,
and she had made her own decisions, but it did not lessen the
pain. She was his sister whom he had always loved, the little
rabbit he had mocked for her shyness and her fears, and she
had gone, and he could not find her.

At his office in the City colleagues eyed his vacant chair
and said he was losing his grip. The malicious claimed he had
succeeded only by paternal favors, and he did not have a grip
to lose. His latest girlfriend, finding him inattentive, dated another man. In the nursing home the staff watched him covertly,
the women (and some of the men) with a slightly wistful degree of commiseration. Purists maintained that he was far
from handsome, his bones too bony, his cheeks too sharply
sunken, the brows too straight and somber above his shadowed eyes. But the ensemble of his face, with its bristling black
hair and taut, tight mouth, exuded force if not vitality, compulsion if not charisma. Those who were not attracted still
found themselves intrigued, noting his air of controlled tension, his apparent lack of humor or charm. In Queen Square
they thought the better of him for his meaningless vigil, and
offered him tea that he invariably refused, and ignored the occasional cigarette that he would smoke by the open window.

He was not a habitual smoker, but it was something to do, a way of expressing frustration. The bouquets came via florists and had little scent, but their perfume filled his imagination, sweet as decay, and only the acrid tang of tobacco would eradicate it.

He came there late one night after a party—a party with much shrieking and squirting of champagne and dropping of trousers. He had drunk as much of the champagne as found its way into his glass, but it did not cheer him: champagne cheers only those who are feeling cheerful already, which is why it is normally drunk solely on special occasions or by the very rich. At the nursing home he sat in his usual chair, staring at his sister with a kind of gray patience, all thought suspended, while his life unraveled around him. There were goals that had been important to him: career success, a high earning potential, independence, self-respect. And the respect of his father. He had told himself often that this last need was an emotional cliché, a well-worn plotline that did not apply to him, but sometimes it had been easy to lapse into the pattern—easier than suspecting that the dark hunger that ate his soul came from no one but himself. And now all the strands of his existence were breaking away, leaving nothing but internal emptiness. The excess of alcohol gave him the illusion that his perceptions were sharpened rather than clouded and he saw Dana's face in great detail: her pallor appeared yellowish against the white of the pillow, her lips bloodless. He did not touch her, avoiding the contact with flesh that felt cold and dead. Somewhere in the paralysis of his brain he thought: I need help.

He thought aloud.

The unfamiliar words touched a chord deeper than memory. Without realizing it, he drifted into a daydream. He was in a city—not a modern city but a city of long ago, with pillars and colonnades and statues of men and beasts, and the dome of a temple rising above it all flashing fire at the sun. He heard

the creak of wooden wheels on paving, saw the slaves shovel-
ing horse dung with the marks of the lash on their backs.
There was a girl standing beside him, a girl whose black hair
fell straight to her waist and whose eyes were the pure tur-
quoise of sea shallows. "—help," she was saying. "You must
help me—" but her face changed, dissolving slowly, the contours re-forming to a different design, and he was in the dark,
and a red glimmer of torchlight showed him close-cropped
hair and features that seemed to be etched in steel. The first
face had been beautiful, but this one was somehow familiar;
he saw it with a pang of recognition as sharp as toothache.
There was a name on his lips—a name he knew well—but it
was snatched away, and he was jerked abruptly, not knowing
where he was, reaching for the name as if it were the key to
his soul.

One of the male nurses was leaning over him, clasping his
shoulder with a scrubbed pink hand. "You called out," he explained. "I was outside. I think you said: 'I need help.'"

"Yes," said Lucas. "I did. I do."

The young man smiled a smile that was reassuring—a little too reassuring, and knowing, and not quite human.

"Help will be found," he told Lucas.

A damp spring ripened slowly into the disappointment of
summer. Wizened countrymen read the signs—"The birds be
nesting high this year," "The hawthorn be blooming early," "I
seed a ladybird with eight spots"—and claimed it would be
hot. It wasn't. In London Gaynor moved back into her refur-
bished flat and stoically withstood the advances of her host of
New Year's Eve in his quest for extramarital sympathy. Will
Capel returned from Outer Mongolia and invited his sister to
dinner, escorting her to the threshold of the Caprice before
recollecting that all he could afford was McDonald's. Fern
drank a brandy too many, picked up the tab, and went home to
dream the dream again, waking to horror and a sudden rush

of nausea. In Queen Square, Dana Walgrim did not stir. Lucas devoted more time to the pursuit of venture capitalism, doing adventurous things with other people's capital, but rivals said he had lost his focus, and the specter that haunted him was not that of greed. And at Wrokeby the hovering sun ran its fingers over the façade of the house and poked a pallid ray through an upper window, withdrawing it in haste as the swish of a curtain threatened to sever it from its source.

It was late May, and the clouds darkened the long evening into a premature dusk. The sunset was in retreat beyond the Wrokewood, its last light snarled in the treetops on Farsee Hill. Three trees stood there, all dead, struck by lightning during the same storm that had shattered the conservatory at the house, and although there was fresh growth around each bole, the three crowns were bare, leafless spars jutting skyward like stretching arms. Folklorists pointed out that Farsee Hill was a contraction of pharisee, or fairy, and liked to suggest some connection with an occult curse, the breaking of a taboo, the crossing of a forbidden boundary, though no one had yet come up with a plot for the undiscovered story. That evening, the clouds seemed to be building up not for a storm but for Night, the ancient Night that was before electricity and lamps and candles, before Man stole the secret of fire from the gods. The dark crept down over wood and hill, smothering the last of the sun. In the smaller sitting room, another light leaped into being, an ice-blue flame that crackled and danced over coals that glittered like crystal. On the floor, the circle took fire in a hissing trail that swept around the perimeter at thought-speed. The witch stood outside it, close to the hearth. Her dress was white, sewn with sequins or mirror chips that flung back the wereglow in tiny darts of light. But her hair was shadow-black, and her eyes held more Night than all the dark beyond the curtains.

Dibbuck crouched in the passage, watching the flicker beneath the door. He heard her voice chanting, sometimes harsh, sometimes soft and sweet as the whisper of a June breeze. He could feel the slow buildup of the magic in the room beyond, the pull of power carefully dammed. The tongue of light from under the door licked across the floorboards, roving from side to side as though seeking him out. He cowered against the wall, shivering, afraid to stay, unable to run. He did not fear the dark, but the Night that loomed over him now seemed bottomless as the Pit; he could not imagine reaching another dawn. Within the room the chant swelled: the woman's voice was full of echoes, as if the thin entities of air and shadow had added their hunger to hers. There was a *whoosh*, as of rushing flame, and the door flew open.

The wereglow sliced down the passage like a blade, missing the goblin by inches. It cut a path through the darkness, a band of white radiance brighter than full moonlight, stretching down the stair and beyond, piercing the very heart of the house. And then Dibbuck heard the summons, though it was in a language he did not understand, felt it reaching out, along the path, tugging at him, drawing him in. He pulled his large ears forward, flattening them against his skull with clutching hands, shutting out all sound. But still he could sense the compulsion dragging at his feet, and he dug his many toes into crevices in the wood and wrenched a splinter from the wainscoting, driving it through his own instep, pinning himself to the floor with a mumbled word that might have been flimsy goblin magic or a snatch of godless prayer. He had closed his eyes, but when his ears were covered he reopened them. And he knew that if he endured another thousand years, he would never forget what he saw.

There was a mist pouring past him along the beam of light—a mist of dim shapes, formless as amoebas, empty faces with half-forgotten features, filmy hands wavering like starfish, floating shreds of clothing and hair. Even though his ears were blocked he seemed to hear a buzzing in his head, as if far-off cries of desperation and despair had been reduced to little more than the chittering of insects. He wanted to listen, but he dared not lest he respond to the summons and lose himself in that incorporeal tide. He saw the topless torso of Sir William grasping his own head by its wispy locks: the eyes met his for an instant in a fierce, helpless stare. He glimpsed the tonsure of a priest slain in the Civil War; a coachman's curling whip and flapping greatcoat; the swollen belly of a housemaid impregnated by her master. And among them the fluid gleam of water sprites and the small shadowy beings who had lived for centuries under brick or stone, now no longer able to remember what they were or who they had once been. Even the imp from the oven was there, trailing in the rear, clutching in vain at the door frame until he was wrenched into the vortex of the spell.

When the stream of phantoms had finally passed, Dibbuck plucked out the splinter and limped forward, still blocking his ears, until he could just see into the room. The pain in his foot went unregarded as he watched what followed, too petrified even to shiver. Within the circle, the ghosts were drawn into a whirling, shuddering tornado, a pillar that climbed from floor to ceiling, bending this way and that as the spirits within struggled to escape. Distorted features spun around the outside— writhing lips, stretching eyes. The witch stood on the periphery with her arms outspread, as if she held the very substance of the air in her hands. The spell soared to a crescendo; the tornado spun into a blur. Then the chant stopped on a single word, imperative as fate: *"Uvalé!"* And again: *"Uvalé néancharne!"* Blue lightning ripped upward, searing through the pillar. There was a crack that shook the room, and inside the circle the floor opened.

The swirl of ghosts was sucked down as if by an enormous vacuum, vanishing into the hole with horrifying speed. The goblin caught one final glimpse of Sir William, losing hold of his head for the first time since his death, his mouth a gape of absolute terror. Then he was gone. What lay below Dibbuck could not see, save that it was altogether dark. The last phantom drained away; the circle was empty. At a word from the witch, the crack closed. On the far side of the room he registered the presence of Nehemet, sitting bolt upright like an Egyptian statue; the light of the spellfire shone balefully in her slanted eyes. Slowly, one step at a time, he inched backward. Then he began to run.

"We missed one," said the woman. "One spying, prying little rat. I do not tolerate spies. Find him."

The cat sprang.

But Dibbuck had grown adept at running and dodging of late, and he was fast. The injury to his foot was insubstantial as his flesh; it hurt but hardly hindered him. He fled with a curious hobbling gait down the twisting stairs and along the maze of corridors, through doors both open and shut, over shadow and under shadow. Nehemet might have been swifter, but her solidity hampered her, and at the main door she had to stop, mewing savagely and scratching at the panels. Outside, Dibbuck was still running. He did not hesitate or look back. Through the Wrokewood he ran and up Farsee Hill, and in the shelter of three trees he halted to rest, hoping that in this place his wild cousins of long ago might have some power to keep him from pursuit.

The conservatory was completed; the gypsy and his co-workers had been paid and dismissed. "You have not found him," Morgus said to the sphinx cat. "Well. It is not important. He was only a goblin, a creature of cobwebs and corners, less trouble than a dormouse. We have greater matters at hand." It was now four days since the exorcism, and the house grew very still when she passed: the curtains did not breathe, the stairs did not creak. Somewhere deep in its ancient mortar, in the marrow of its walls, the house felt lonely for its age-long occupants, lonely and uncomprehending. It sensed the invasion of alien lights, the laying down of new shadows, the

incursion of elementals lured by the force of dark magic. It
missed the familiar ghosts, as a stray dog given a well-meaning
bath misses its native fleas. Inside, the atmosphere changed,
becoming bleak and watchful, though no one was watching
anymore.

The prisoner in the attic felt it, if only because there was
nothing else to feel. Morgus rarely visited him anymore, even
to gloat, so he would talk to himself, and the house, and a
moth that was slight enough to slip past the spells, until he
grew impatient with it and crushed it in one vicious sweep of
his hand. He had the strength to wrench the iron bars from
their sockets and snap the chains that bound him as if they
were made of rust, but magic reinforced both chain and bar,
and though he tugged until his muscles tore, it was futile.
"What is she doing?" he would ask the house, and when it
made no answer he could sense the new silence and stillness
permeating from below. He lay long hours with his ear to the
floor, listening. He knew when the ghosts were gone, and
he heard the padding of Nehemet's paws as she hunted, and
the softest rumor of Morgus's voice grated like a saw on his
thought. Sometimes he would howl like a beast—like the
beast he was—but nobody came, and the sound bounced off
the walls of his prison and returned to him, finding no way
out. Sometimes he wept, hot red tears of frustration and rage
that steamed when they touched the ground. And then he would
curse Morgus, and the attic prison, and the whole world, until
he was hoarse with cursing, and in the silence that followed
his lips would shape the name of his friend—his one friend in
all the history of time—and he would call for help in a moth-
like whisper, and crush his mouth against the floor in the anguish of the unheard.

In the reconstructed conservatory, Morgus was planting the
Tree. It was midnight, under the pale stare of an incurious
moon. The triangular panes of the roof cast radiating lines of
shadow around the stone pot in which Morgus placed the

sapling. Here was a different kind of magic, a magic of vitality and growth: the air shimmered faintly about the bole, and the leaves rippled, and the sap ascended eagerly through slender trunk and thrusting twig with a throb like the beat of blood. Morgus crooned her eerie lullabies and fed it from assorted vials, and the cat sat by, motionless as Bastet save for the twitch of her tail. "We are on the soil of Britain, *my* island, my kingdom," said the witch. "Here, you can grow tall and strong. Fill my flagons with your sap, and bring forth fruit for me— fruit that will swell and ripen—whatever that fruit may be." She gathered up the discarded wrappings and left the conservatory, Nehemet at her heels. Behind them, unseen, the heavy base of the urn began very slowly to split, millimeter by millimeter, as the severed taproot forced its way through stone and tile, flooring and foundation, down into the earth beneath.

"I wish you'd stop giving me advice," Will Capel complained. He and his sister were returning from Great-Aunt Edie's funeral in the West Country, an event that many of her relatives felt was long overdue. She had ended her days in a retirement home near Torquay, but this had not prevented her from descending on hapless family members for Christmas, Easter, weddings, anniversaries, and christenings, not to mention the funerals of those less hardy than herself. Since Aunt Edie had been ninety-one when she died, Fern felt excessive grief was not called for. While she drove, she found she was remembering her own aborted wedding—and Aunt Edie's hovering presence there, usually clutching a small cup of sherry.

"What did you say?"

"I *said*, I wish you would stop giving me advice."

"I didn't," Fern said serenely. "I never give advice."

"It's the *way* you never give advice," said Will. "I can feel the advice you're not giving me radiating out from your brain in telepathic pulses. And there's your expression."

"I haven't got an expression."

"Yes, you have. It's your favorite cool, you-can't-guess-what-I'm-thinking expression. If we were playing poker, I'd know you had a particularly sneaky royal flush. As it is, I'd be prepared to bet you're thinking about Aunt Edie's last trip to Yorkshire and your wedding-that-wasn't, and that means you're about to criticize my love life."

"Your love life," said Fern, "is entirely your own affair. Or several affairs, as the case may be."

"You see?" said Will. "Love life. Criticism."

Fern sucked her lip in an attempt to suppress a smile. "I hate to disappoint."

Will gave a grin that stiffened gradually into something more artificial. "How is Gaynor?"

"You've been a long time asking," Fern said lightly. Her eyes were on the road; Will found that her profile was no longer something he could read. "She got over the flautist very quickly, which may indicate that there was not much to get over. A recent news bulletin told me she was still resisting the advances of Hugh, the slightly estranged husband of Vanessa. However, sources close to Miss Mobberley inform me that she may not be able to hold out. When men cry on her shoulder, she has a tendency to go soggy inside."

"Has she tried waterproof clothing?" said Will, a little too sharply. "Anyway, I didn't want a résumé of her sexual activities. I just wanted to know how—she—is."

"Last weekend," said Fern scrupulously, "she was perfectly well."

There was complete silence for almost a mile. Since Fern had decided recently she did not want music on while she drove, believing it was a serious distraction, the quiet was as noticeable as a blackout in a shopping mall.

Eventually Will said, changing the subject without apology: "I may be going to India later this year." Fern made an interrogative noise. "Looks like Roger and I might have got our first real commission. Someone at BBC 2 likes the Himalayan idea. You know: tales of the hidden kingdoms. Power politics in Buddhism, the true origins of Shangri-la, that kind of stuff. I told you about it in the Caprice."

"If it comes off," said Fern, "*you* can take *me* to the Caprice."

"I *did* take you to the Caprice!"

"Next time," his sister said darkly, "you pay for it as well."

It was late by the time they reached London, and Will accepted an invitation to share take-out in Fern's flat. They bought an assortment of Thai nibbles and a bottle of chardonnay and took them back to Pimlico. Once inside, Fern switched on lamps, drew the curtains, lit a scented candle. "There's something about funerals," she said. "The smell always stays with you. That damp, rusty sort of smell you get when people take out the black coat they haven't worn for years and then stand around for too long in the rain."

"It didn't rain," Will pointed out, uncorking the wine.

"The air was wet," Fern insisted.

It was after they had sat down and were opening up the cartons that she went suddenly still and quiet. "What is it?" Will asked, watching her face change.

Fern said nothing for a few seconds. When she spoke again, it was a half-tone louder. "Show yourself. This is my brother: his presence need not trouble you. He is accustomed to the ways of your folk." And, after a pause: "I don't wish to Command you. That would be discourteous, and I should deeply regret any further discourtesy. You know I want friendly relations with the queen."

The queen? Will mouthed, his eyebrows shooting upward.

Fern ignored him. Her gaze had focused on a place at the foot of the curtains where the drapes were bunched together in many folds beside the looping leaves of a potted plant. Presently, Will saw some of the shadows detach themselves and move forward, taking shape in the light . . . a diminutive, ungainly shape, hunch shouldered and bowlegged, with long simian arms. Fern noticed his patchwork clothing looked newer than last time and he had acquired a species of malformed hat, squashed low over his brow, with the words "By Appoyntmnt" embroidered on it in crooked stitches. His tufted ears were thrust through slits in the brim; his sloe eyes gazed slyly from underneath.

"Skuldunder," Fern acknowledged.

"Who invited you in?" Will demanded.

"It isn't necessary," Fern sighed. "He's a burglar. We've met before. He usually burgles on behalf of Mabb, queen of the goblins. So are you here on private business, or does this visit have an official sanction?"

"The queen sent me," the goblin prated, briefly inflating his hollow chest. "She says, she is graciously pleased to accept your gifts and . . . and your friendship. It is a great honor."

"For whom?" Will murmured, fascinated. Fern stood unobtrusively on his foot.

"A great honor," the goblin repeated. "She knows you are a powerful witch, but she believes you mean no harm to her and her people. And me," he added, throwing Fern an apprehensive glance and clutching his hat brim for support.

"Of course not," said Fern. "I would prefer not to harm anyone." Will, noting the language of diplomacy, thought the statement held an element of warning, but Skuldunder appeared tentatively relieved. "Have a glass of wine," she continued. "Is there something I can do for the queen?"

"It is she who has sent me to help you," the goblin declared. "She says she will overlook the matter of the bodkin—"

"Bodkin?" Fern frowned. "Oh—the spear."

The goblin took a wary mouthful of chardonnay. "There is Trouble," he announced, giving the word an audible capital T. "We have heard of another witch, one perhaps more powerful than yourself. We think she is new to this country. She is performing great magics, sorcery of a kind beyond our ken. The queen felt you should know of this."

"The queen is wise," Fern said, adding, in an aside to Will: "It may be nothing. Some street witch playing games with fireworks, or an old woman who looked at Mabb sideways and gave her a spot on her nose. All the same . . ." She turned back to the goblin. "Does she have a name, this witch?"

"We do not know it," said Skuldunder.

"An address?"

"She has taken over a mansion north of this city. Already she has done great evil there. It was the property of a human family who died out years ago, and few mortals came to trouble it, leaving it to the ghosts and lesser creatures of the otherworld. But she made a terrible spell to purge it, and now they are all gone, and the only beings who dwell there are those who have come in her train."

"An exorcism," said Fern.

"Ethnic cleansing," said Will.

"Exorcism is not necessarily terrible," Fern elaborated. "It shows lost spirits how to pass the Gate: that is all."

But Skuldunder was shaking his head and kneading his hat brim with nervous fingers. "No—no—it wasn't like that. We think she—she *opened the abyss*. They were all sucked through—all of them. Into *nothingness* . . ." He was trembling visibly. "Only the house-goblin escaped. He is very old, and not as brave and cunning as those of us who live wild, but he did well. He fled from the house and hid in a place where the old magic lingers. Her minions could not find him there. We don't know how long he was in hiding; he could not tell us. Some of the queen's folk came across him when they were hunting toads. He must have wandered a fair way from his hiding place by then."

"The name of the house?" asked Fern.

Skuldunder frowned. "It was a name of rooks," he said. "Rooks and oak trees. Roake House . . . something like that."

"And all we know about this witch is what the house-goblin has told you?"

"Yes . . . But he is very frightened. He did not want to leave the house, and now he is lost and confused, even among his own people. Truly, he has seen dreadful things."

"House-goblins frighten easily," said Fern. "Most of them, anyway. Tell the queen . . . tell the queen I would like to question him myself. This matter of another witch could be important; our information must be carefully sifted. Since this is such a serious issue, perhaps the queen would honor me with her presence here. Then we could consider the problem together."

"Here?" said Skuldunder. "The queen?"

"She would be my most royal guest," said Fern—implying, Will thought, that lesser royalty came to her flat on a regular basis.

"I will ask her," Skuldunder said doubtfully. He retreated toward the window, fading into a pattern of shadows.

"Well?" Will inquired.

"It's probably nothing," Fern conceded. "A storm in an acorn cup. I'm just curious to meet Mabb. Ragginbone is too aloof. Even a witch needs friends."

"Especially a witch," said her brother.

"She reminds me of another case I had," said the new doctor. The medical team who briefed Kaspar Walgrim normally varied little, but every so often they would call for a second opinion, and a third, and a fourth, and another check would wing its way toward the clinic's bank balance. The doctors accepted advice to prove they were not rigid or hidebound; Walgrim needed both the input of wisdom and the output of checks to prove he was doing something. The regularity of his attendance had fallen with the passage of time; now he came only once a fortnight, or once a month.

"What is the point?" he said to his son. "She doesn't know

we're here." But Lucas was still there, night after night, though his days were filled with a feverish intensity of work that he hoped might divert his mind if not his heart. He was on hand when the new doctor dropped in—not a fifth opinion so much as an interested party, an expert in coma cases to whom Dana was a novelty specimen. At the remark, which was addressed to the colleague accompanying him, something in Lucas's brain switched to *alert*.

"It was when I was up in Yorkshire," the doctor continued. "Another girl—a bit older than this one, but not much. I don't know if that's significant. She had a history of what looked like psychosomatic symptoms, and the case itself had several bizarre features . . . However, there's nothing like that here. It just seems to have started in the same way: a night out, too much to drink, and then total blackout. Slowed heart rate—" he lifted an eyelid "—eyes turned up. No known allergies?"

"None," said the other.

"No physical injury?"

"A minor contusion on the head. Nothing serious. Her skull is normal. Erm . . . this is her brother."

"Lucas Walgrim," he introduced himself, extending a hand. "What happened to the girl in Yorkshire?"

"She revived. Very suddenly. After about a week." For no obvious reason, the doctor looked uncomfortable. "She discharged herself the same day."

"The *same* day?" His fellow medic was startled.

The new doctor shrugged. "It was an odd business. One moment, barely alive; the next, sitting up, throwing her weight around, getting out of bed. I believe the first thing she did was to dump her fiancé. Most people would have given themselves a couple of days to think it over, but not her. She was . . . difficult."

I like her already, thought Lucas. I want Dana up and about, being *difficult* with doctors.

He said: "I'd like to talk to that girl."

"You know that's not possible. Patient confidentiality."

"You've already breached that confidentiality," Lucas pointed out, utilizing a manner that had been honed to an edge in backrooms and boardrooms. "You've discussed various aspects of her case with someone outside your profession. I want to talk to her. Arrange it."

"Out of the question."

His colleague interceded with a smoothness doubtless oiled by the size and regularity of the Walgrim checks. "Perhaps we can deal with this another way. If my associate were to contact the patient in question and explain the position, giving her your name and number, I'm sure—under the circumstances—she would be willing to get in touch with you. Although I'm afraid she won't be of much help. The patient rarely understands the illness: that's why they come—"

"Thank you," Lucas cut in. "I'd be grateful if you would do that. I'll expect to hear something shortly."

The new doctor looked unconvinced, but was hustled from the room. Lucas turned back to his sister, but his attention was no longer focused on her. Something in his posture had changed: his body was rigid, taut as wire, the anticipation strong in him, filling all his thoughts. He could not sleep but his mind slipped; he was in a time outside Time, and the figure in the bed, though still white and immobile, was not that of Dana. Other images crowded in on him, flickering through his brain so fast he could not pin them down: a mass of leaves shuddering in an unnatural wind—what looked like a disembodied head—more leaves—gray fields—water falling into a basin of stone—horns—fire—and then the figure again, but now her breathing had quickened, and her eyelids lifted, and he saw she was the second girl in his dream of weeks before, a girl sharp and bright as steel, with a glint of true green in her eyes. And then the world jolted back into place, and there in the bed was Dana, and his heart hammered as if he had been running.

"What is happening to me?" he whispered, and inside his head a voice that was almost—but not quite—a part of his thought answered him. *It is the Gift. Don't fear it. Don't fight it. It will guide you.*

The Gift. In Atlantis long ago the aura of the Lodestone had infected mortal men, endowing the earthly with unearthly powers. The Lodestone was broken and Atlantis sank beneath the waves, but the mutant gene had already spread throughout the world, and it was passed on, dominant, often dormant, warping all who abused it. They were called the Gifted, Prospero's Children, the Crooked Ones, the Accursed. Lucas did not understand what had altered him, but he felt its influence growing, opening his vision on new dimensions, twisting his thought. But this was the way to restore his sister, the way to redemption. There was no other road.

It was one in the morning before he left the nursing home, walking toward his Knightsbridge flat as if indifferent to the distance and the hour, until a taxi driver accosted him and insisted on taking him home.

Fern was in her office about a week later when the call came in. She worked for a PR company in Wardour Street with a short list of stressed-out employees and a long list of lucrative and temperamental clients. She had recently risen to a directorship, partly because of her diplomatic skills with the aforementioned clientele. When she picked up the phone she was in a meeting to discuss the launch of *Woof!*, a new glossy magazine on celebrity pets, and it was a few minutes before she absorbed what the call was about. "Sorry? Say that again? You want me to . . . No, I don't think we should have Coquette; she goes to absolutely everything these days, it'll be news if we can keep her out . . . His sister? And who's he? . . . Sushi's always reliable, provided we get the best . . . Sorry?" By the end of a confused conversation, she found she had written down a name and number with only the haziest idea of why.

It was several days before she got around to using them.

"Hello? I'd like to speak to Lucas Walgrim. Fern Capel . . ."

Presently a male voice said rather brusquely: "Miss Capel? I'm afraid I—"

"I understood you wanted me to call you," Fern said with frigid courtesy. "A clinic in Yorkshire where I spent a brief stay a couple of years ago got in touch with me. I was a coma patient there. They said you had a sister in a similar condition . . ."

"Yes." Even through the telephone, Fern detected the slowing of pace, the shift in focus. "I'm so glad you called. I may be clutching at straws, but Dana collapsed under circumstances that I'm told parallel yours—"

"Really? Who told you?"

"A doctor was indiscreet. He didn't name you, but I pressed him to put you in contact with me. I hope you don't object?"

"N-no." Fern wasn't sure. "It's just—I don't think there's anything I can do for you. I lost consciousness, I was out for about a week, then I recovered. It didn't teach me anything about diagnosis."

"There's nothing to diagnose. She just lies there, hardly breathing. Her heartbeat's slowed to hibernation rate. She's been like that for months. Since New Year's Eve." A pause. "I wanted to talk to someone who's been there, who *knows*. Perhaps I could buy you lunch?"

His determination was a tangible thing, reaching out, compelling her.

"I'm awfully busy right now . . ."

"What about a drink?"

Fern hesitated, then gave in. "All right. But I really don't see how I can help you."

"Tomorrow? After work?"

They agreed on a place and time, and Fern hung up, preparing to put the matter out of her mind. But it nagged at her, though she did not know why, and she lay awake far into the night, picturing the unknown girl lying as she had lain, death white, death still, wired up to the mechanics of life support, heart monitor, drip, catheter, for month after month after month . . .

III ∽∽∽∽

The hardest thing was being back inside Time. I had spent so long in a dimension where no time passed, where the illusory seasons revolved endlessly in the same circle, never progressing, never changing, where day and darkness were mere variations in the light. I had spent so long—but "long" was a word that did not apply there, for in the realm of the Tree there is no duration. A millennium or a millionth of a second, it is all one. The Tree has grown and grown until it can grow no further, and it is held in stasis, bearing its seedless fruit, bending the space around it as a black hole bends the stuff of the universe. (I know about these things, you see. I have watched them in the spellfire, the witches and wizards of science poking at the stars.) I glutted myself on the power of the Tree and was reborn from the power of the river, after *she* burned me in the pale fire of sorcery. And then I could not go back. I called the birds to me: the blue-banded magpies, the heavy-beaked ravens, the woodpeckers and tree creepers. I sent them across the worlds to the cave beneath the roots where I and my coven sister had dwelt, to bring me my herbs and powders, my potions and crystals. I bound tiny water-skins about the necks of the woodpeckers, and taught them to tap the bark until it bled sap, and return to me when the vessel was full. The sap of the Tree has a potency I alone have ever learned: from it I can make a draft that will drain individual thought, leaving the intoxicated mind to think whatever I de-

54

sire. Last, I summoned the great owl, wisest of birds, and told him to find for me the single branch hidden in the cave, wrapped in silk, the branch I had plucked long before with many rituals, and to bear it carefully back. I planted it in my island retreat, fearing it might not root, but the magic was strong in it, and it grew.

I chose the island because of my coven sister Sysselore, who lived there once. In those days she was Syrcé the enchantress, young and beautiful, and lost sailors came to her with their lean brown bodies, and she turned them into pigs, and grew thin on a diet of lean pork. I hoped the island would be a place of transition, where I could reaccustom myself to the living world. The sudden racing of Time made me sick, so there were moments when I could not stand, and I would lie down on a bed that seemed to tilt and rock like a speeding carriage on an uneven road. Even when the nausea passed, there was the terror of it, of being trapped in the rush of Now, snatching in vain at seconds, minutes, hours that are gone before you can take hold of them. I could not believe I used to live like this: only the iron of my need and the steel of my will kept me from flight. But as Time moved on, so I became habituated to it.

There were more people on the island than in ancient days; humans have bred like locusts, and the earth is overrun. Many have strange customs: they lie in the sun and go brown like peasants, and the women show their bodies to all men instead of a chosen few. I do not lie in the sun; white skin is the acme of beauty, and I am beautiful again. The fire purged me, the river healed me, and I emerged from the waters of Death as Venus reborn, a Venus of the night, star pale and shadow dark. I turn from the sun now, preferring the softer light of the moon, the moon who has always been a friend to witchkind. In the moonlight I am a goddess, and a man came to spy on me, like the ill-fated heroes of legend and folktale, and I plucked the eyes from his head and the spirit from his body, that he might spy on me forever. But when I look in the mirror I see the old Morgus there still, the power-bloated mountain of flesh not eroded but compressed, constricted into a form of slenderness and beauty. The lissome figure is somehow subtly gross, and the loveliness of my face is like a shifting veil over the face beneath. That realization fills me with a joy that is not of this earth, for I know that the dark within is strong in me, and beauty alone is a shallow, insipid thing without the power beneath the skin. And sometimes, in that same reflection, I seem to see the Eternal Tree, winding its twig-tendrils and root-tendrils in my hair, and blending its night with the shadows in my eyes. That is the sweetest of all, for with the Tree, I am immortal, both human and unhuman, and I can challenge even Azmordis for the throne of the world.

I left the island after the incident with the man. There would be curiosity and questions, and though I could deal with both I did not wish to be troubled. And so I came home at last, to Britain, which was called Logrèz, the land where I was born and where I will one day rule alone. Let Azmordis flee to the barbarian countries across the western sea! This was my place, and it will be mine again, until the stars fall. I hid in the cave in Prydwen where Merlin is said to have slept more than fifteen hundred years ago; but he is not there now. But I have had enough of caves. The entrance was concealed with enchantments older than mine, and in the gloom of that safety I lit the spellfire and sought a house to suit both queen and witch.

I had conjured a creature to be my servant, part hag, part kobold; I bought her labor for a bag of storms. When seven times seven years are done, and she is free of me, she will open it and raze the village where she was scorned and stoned at some remote time in a forgotten past. She rarely talks, which pleases me; I know these things about her because I have seen the pictures in her mind. But she is sharp of ear and eye, adequate at housework, and skilled in the kitchen, and the loyalty that I have purchased is mine absolutely. Her meaningless vengeance binds her to me more surely than any spell. And I have Nehemet, Nehemet the goblin cat, who was not conjured but came to me, there on the island, as if she had been waiting. Who she is, or what she is, I do not know. Her name came with her, spoken clearly into my thought, though she has never spoken again. Goblin cats are rare; according to one legend they were the pets of the king of the Underworld, losing their fur because they did not need it in the heat from the pits of Hel. But Nehemet is no mere animal: there is an old intelligence in her gaze, and her poise is that of a feline deity who steps haughtily from a new-opened tomb. She is my familiar, in every way. Somewhen in the passing centuries we have met before.

I am glad they are both female. I prefer to surround myself with females, whatever their kind. Men are to be manipulated or enslaved; they are necessary for procreation, but that is all. I loved a man once, if love is the word: that desire that can never be sated, that madness where even suffering is dear to the heart. I lay with him and he took me to the place where sweetness is pain and pain is bliss, and in the cold gray morning he looked on me and turned away and left me alone for always. So I took my love and buried it deep in my spirit, so deep that I have never found where it lies. He was my half brother, and he became the High King, but the son I bore him was his downfall, though it gained me nothing. Enough of him. I remember Morgun, my blood-sister, my twin. As children we played together, exchanging kisses, touching each other's nipples until they swelled like spring buds. But in the end she turned to the love of men, submitting to the rule of lords and masters, and betrayed me, and herself, and died in bitterness. I saw her head, hanging on the Eternal Tree, vowing even then to be my doom. Now there is only one man in my house—if man you can call him—and he is in chains.

I brought my possessions and my entourage to Wrokeby

after New Year's Eve. I have a use for both the house and its owner: Kaspar Walgrim is a monarch in a world I do not know, the world of Money. And Money, like magic, is the key to power. With magic you can bemaze the minds of men, but with Money you can buy their souls. Walgrim is one of the rulers in the realm of Money: they call it the City, Londinium of old, Caer Lunn. The High King never kept his seat there, but the head of Bran the Blessed was once entombed beneath its white tower, gazing outward over the land, shielding it from enemies. But my half brother dug the head up, saying it was a pagan thing, and he could hold his kingdom alone; only the kingdom was lost and the god of greed sits on the throne where a hundred kings have sat before, playing the games of power and spending their people's gold. I need Money, and Walgrim has my magic in his blood. He will harvest the City's gold for me.

Wrokeby is an old house by the standards of today, though its first stones were laid long after I quit the world. But there are bones underneath, green and rotten now, which were flesh when I was born: I can feel them there, reaching up to me through the dark earth. I cannot destroy them without uprooting the house itself, but I have cleaned out the ghosts that cluttered every empty room, even the imp that made mischief in the kitchen. Grodda, my servant, complained it was always extinguishing the flame in the stove. I opened the abyss and they were sucked through; I heard their thin wailing, felt their helpless terror. It is long and long since I have tasted such terror, even from flimsy, lifeless beings such as these: I drank it like wine. My half brother laid down the knightly precepts: help the oppressed, outface fear, do nothing dishonorable. The laws of Succor, Valor, Honor. But they were for warriors and heroes, not for women and witches. We were to be loved and left, abused and disempowered. And so I made precepts of my own, turning his on their heads: oppress the helpless, wield fear, honor nothing. *Succor. Valor. Honor.* I have never forgotten those three words. It was good to feel fear again, the fear of lesser, weaker creatures. It makes me strong, stronger than I have felt in time outside Time. There was little fear to feed on beneath the Eternal Tree.

Only the house-goblin escaped, though Nehemet hunted for him. Goblin cats were so called not merely because of their appearance, but because goblins were once their prey. She is a skilled huntress, but he fled the house, and she did not find him. But it does not matter. Away from the house he will pine, and despair will shrivel him like an autumn leaf. He must be gone by now.

I moved my prisoner here, from the borders of the Underworld where I had caught and bound him. The house on the island was not suitable, but here there is an attic room already equipped with locks and bolts and bars. I secured him with many chains, and I locked the locks, and bolted the bolts, and walled him in with spells stronger than bars. He did not speak, not then, but sometimes I hear him snarling, two stories above me, chewing on his own fury. Soon the nightmares will begin, and he will howl like a beast in the darkness, and then I will visit him, and watch him grovel, and whine for mercy, and call me "Mother." I have not yet decided on his punishment, only that it will be slow, sweet and slow, and before I am done he will be offering me the soul he does not have—the soul he longs for and dreams of—for a moment of surcease.

I like to feel them around me: my collection. Not the corpse cuttings and cold relics that warriors prize, but living trophies. My prisoner, the girl who mocked me, the eyes of the spy. And one day, *she* will be there. *She* who failed me, and cheated me, and made my own blood rise up against me. For she is in this world, this Time. Somewhere she lives and breathes, wakes and sleeps, unsuspecting, believing me dead. I named her Morcadis, my coven sister, my disciple, and my weapon. I would have made her as Morgun, my long-dead twin—Morgun as she should have been—sharing her body, owning her soul. But she escaped from the domain of the Tree, and when Sysselore and I followed she turned on us with the crystal fire, and we burned. Sysselore was gone in an instant, but I had my mantle of flesh—flesh and power—and I crawled to the icy river, and plunged in, and was remade. And now I have returned to the world alone, to reclaim my kingdom—my island of Britain—to challenge Azmordis himself for the dominion of Men.

But first I will find *her*, and pluck out her heart while she yet lives, and fry it, and she may watch me eat.

Fern found the note on her doormat before she went to work. The paper was pale brown and shredded around the edges; from the print on the back it might have been the flyleaf of an old book. The writing was in greenish-blue ink, with many splotches, the words ill-formed and badly spelled. "The queane wil come and see you to nite at midnite. She sends you greting." There was no signature, but Fern suspected that this was because Skuldunder, if he was the scribe, could not manage to spell his own name. She folded the note carefully, put it in her jacket pocket, and went to the office. She had half promised to keep Will informed of any developments, but a busy day left her little leisure for personal calls and anyway, she did not want to have to disclose where she was going earlier in the evening. There was no real reason for her reluctance, or none she could identify, but the thought of the forthcoming meeting with Lucas Walgrim filled her with both impatience and unease. Impatience because she was sure it was a waste of time—her time and his—unease because it would touch on matters that were too near the bone, too close to the heart, to be discussed with a stranger. But she could not let him down. Good manners ensnared her.

"How will you recognize me?" she had asked. "Carnation boutonniere? Rolled-up copy of *Hello!*?"

"I'll know you," he had said, with a quiet certainty that was unnerving.

Not for the first time in her life, she wished she wasn't quite so well brought up.

They met in a City bar not long after six. Fern arrived in time to get a small table to herself, setting her coat over the spare chair before the bulk of the rush-hour drinkers flooded in. She checked each new arrival, particularly the men on their own, trying to match a face to the voice on the telephone. At one point, a young man stood in the entrance for a couple of minutes, peering around the room, and she thought with a sense of resignation: This is it; but it wasn't. He had the pink-faced, slightly smug good looks that youth so often assumes when it has too much money, but there was no sign of the single-mindedness or the underlying tension she had detected in the brief telephone conversation. He moved across the room, waylaying a blonde who had been screened by a pillar, and Fern switched off her expression of polite welcome and stirred the froth into her cappuccino.

When he finally arrived, only five minutes late although it seemed like much longer, he caught her off guard. She was expecting someone who would pause, gaze about him, vacillate; but he came toward her without hesitation or doubt, sat in the empty chair with no invitation. "Miss Capel. Hello. I'm Lucas Walgrim."

Her initial reaction was that this was not a face she would trust. Attractive in the wrong way, with that taut-boned, clenched-in look, like a person who is accustomed to suppressing all emotion. A suggestion of something unsafe, an element of ruthlessness carefully concealed. No sense of humor. Under the black straight line of his brows his eyes were a startling light gray, nearly silver. She had never liked pale eyes. A lack of pigment, she had been told in her school years. Lack of color, lack of warmth, lack of soul.

She said: "How did you recognize me?"

"I've seen you before." She was the girl in his dream of the city, though older, the girl he had seen waking from oblivion. But there was no sign of the intense, arresting creature he remembered. She was just a classic London type, more woman than girl, discreetly power-suited, elegantly pretty, well-mannered, aloof, so inscrutable that she appeared almost bland.

She asked: "Where?" and he didn't know how to answer. He could not tell this cool sophisticate that he had seen her in his dreams. Instead, he was conveniently distracted by a waitress and ordered coffee and whiskey for himself and, at Fern's request, a gin and tonic for her. Then he adopted boardroom tactics, changing the subject before she had time to repeat her question.

"It was good of you to come. You said you were busy, so I won't keep you. If I could just tell you about my sister—"

"And then what?" Fern knew he had deliberately evaded her earlier question and was beginning to feel uneasy in a totally different way.

"I don't know. I was hoping it might strike a chord of some kind. I'm going on instinct here. I don't have anything else to go on."

"I honestly don't think I'll be much help. What you need is some kind of support group . . ."

"*No.* What I need is someone who's *been there*—wherever Dana's gone. Can't you just try to talk to me?"

"All right." Fern felt cornered. "What exactly happened to your sister?"

"We had a New Year's Eve bash at my father's place in the country. I wasn't in the room at the time, but I'm told Dana fell and hit her head. Not very hard. The doctors said she shouldn't even have had a concussion. When she passed out—well, I thought it was drink or drugs. She's had a problem with both. I took her to the hospital, but they said she hadn't taken anything and her alcohol level was high but not excessive. She just didn't come around. They couldn't understand it. They waffled about 'abnormal reactions,' that sort of crap, but it was obvious they were stumped. She hasn't even twitched an eyelid since then. Her pulse is so slow she's barely alive. I heard it was like that with you."

"A little," Fern acknowledged. "I was *very* drunk, I blacked out, I stayed out. Then, a week or so later, I came around. That's really all I can tell you."

His eyes looked lighter, she noticed, because of the shadows beneath. "No, it isn't," he said. "I *know* it isn't. Tell me where you went when you were unconscious."

He noted with interest that her expression became, if possible, a shade blander. "Answer my question," she said.

"Which question?" he queried unnecessarily.

"The one you dodged."

He paused, thinking it over. "You might not believe me: that's why I didn't answer. I saw you in a dream. Twice. Nothing sentimental, don't get that idea. The second time you were in a hospital bed, regaining consciousness. I only saw you for an instant, but the picture was very sharp. Too sharp for dreaming. You looked . . . intensely alive. More than now."

He realized too late that he had been offensive, but her manner merely cooled a little further. She inquired noncommittally: "Do you often have such dreams? Dreams that stay with you?"

"Occasionally. Did you dream when you were in a coma?"

"No." Their drinks arrived, covering a momentary stalemate. When the waitress had retreated, Fern pursued: "You said you dreamed about me twice. What happened in the first one?"

"It didn't make sense. There was a city—an ancient city— a bit like Ephesus in Turkey, only not in ruins—and a girl asking me for help. Then it changed suddenly, the way dreams do, and we were in the dark somewhere, and the girl turned into you. She looked much younger—fourteen, fifteen—but it was definitely you. The strange thing . . ."

"Yes?"

"I recognized you. I mean, the person I was *in the dream* recognized you. Whoever you were." When she did not respond, he added: "Do you follow me?"

"Yes." Both expression and tone seemed to have passed beyond circumspection into a realm of absolute detachment. She sounded so remote, so blank, he knew that his words had meant something to her. Her drink was untouched, her hand frozen in the act of lifting her glass.

When he saw that she wasn't going to elucidate he said: "Your turn."

"My . . . turn?"

"You were going to tell me what happened when you were comatose. If you didn't dream . . . ?"

"I couldn't," she said slowly. "I wasn't there. I was— outside my body, outside the world." She concluded with a furtive smile: "You might not believe me, of course."

"Where were you?"

"Under a tree."

"Where? In a wood? A field? What kind of tree?"

He knew the questions were meaningless, but she answered them. "The only kind of tree—the first tree. The Tree all other trees are trying to be, and failing. No wood, no field. Just Tree. Under the Tree, there was a cave, with three witches. It's always three, isn't it? The magic number. I was the third."

"Are you a witch?" he asked, unsmiling. She looked very unmagical, with her sleek short hair and svelte besuited figure. But it troubled him that she did not either affirm or deny it. She glanced down at her hand—her left hand—as if it did not belong to her, and remembered her gin and tonic, and sipped it, slowly, as though she were performing an exercise in self-restraint. He had developed similar methods in business, learning to curb his occasional impetuosity, to suppress any inner weakness or self-doubt, to control every nuance of his manner. But she does it naturally, he thought. Without trying.

"What happened next?" he persisted. "You woke up?"

She gave a small shake of the head. "I had to find the way back. It was difficult. Dangerous. I had a guide . . . At this party, when your sister passed out, do you remember anything unusual? Or peculiar?" He saw the alteration in her attitude, a new alertness in her looks, and experienced a pang that might have been hope, and might have been fear.

"There were people taking coke, taking E, taking the latest thing in feel-good designer drugs. They were drinking thirty-year-old Scotch and forty-year-old brandy and absinthe and champagne. Some were discussing literature and French cuisine, religion and sex. Others were talking to the furniture. Many were incapable of talking at all. Nearly everyone was in fancy dress. How unusual do you want?"

If he was witty, Fern did not laugh. (No sense of humor, he thought.) "Did anyone see . . . a bird, an animal, a phantom? Something unexpected or uncanny?"

"At least six people saw a headless ghost in the old tower—one or two had a conversation with it—but I understand that's par for the course. Several of the guests wore animal costumes. I noticed a woman with a bird mask, rather beautiful and predatory, but—no, not that I know of. Nothing *real*."

"What is real," sighed Fern. It wasn't a question.

There was a silence that he felt he should not break. She was looking at him in a way people rarely look at each other in a civilized society, as if she were assessing him, without either animosity or liking, fishing for clues to his character, trying to peer into his very soul. She made no attempt to disguise that look, and he thought it changed her, bringing her closer to his memory of the girl in the dreams. He found himself responding in kind, scanning her face as if it were the estimated output from some new investment project, or a painting he admired that rumor told him might be a fake.

Eventually she said: "You really believe your sister's condition isn't . . . mere oblivion, don't you? You think she's somewhere else?"

"Mm."

"And I expect," she went on, "you sometimes know things without knowing *how*. You're very good at second-guessing the market, or whatever it is you do in the City. Your colleagues think it's sinister; they may suspect you have access to inside information."

"I don't make many mistakes," he conceded.

"You have a Gift," she said lightly—so lightly that he knew the phrase meant more than it said, and he heard the importance of the final word.

"So I've been told."

"By whom?" Her tone had sharpened.

"There was a nurse at the clinic late one night. He was from an agency, filling in for someone who was off sick; he hasn't been back since. He told me that there are people with certain powers . . . that I might be one of them."

He has power, she thought. I can sense it coming off him like static. He has power, and he uses it, but he doesn't know how. He's like I was before I *learned* witchcraft: he's playing by feel. Only it's far more dangerous, because he's desperate, living on the edge. If his control should snap . . .

She asked: "Does your sister have this Gift?"

"I don't think so. Her only real talent is for making a mess of her life." After a minute, he went on: "I didn't do enough for her."

It was a bald statement of fact, not an apology, but for the first time Fern came close to liking him. "You're doing something now," she said. "*We're* doing something. At least, we're going to try."

She looked into his eyes: smile met smile. There had been

few smiles throughout the meeting and these were understated, hers close-lipped, his tight-lipped, curiously similar. Something passed between them in that moment, something slight and intangible, connecting them.

Fern said: "There's a lot here I don't understand. Most of it, to be frank. It could be that your sister's spirit was taken because of you, or even instead of you, but I've no idea by whom." The one who stole my spirit is dead, she thought, but there's a new witch at large in the world, according to the goblins. I must learn more from Mabb. "I have to make some inquiries."

"Whom do you ask," he said skeptically, "about something like this? A medium?"

"A medium is just a middleman," Fern said. "Or middlewoman. I don't need one. I'd like to visit your sister, if I may. I don't suppose it will tell me anything, but I want to see her."

"I'll arrange it." Suddenly, he gave her a full smile, gentling the tautness of his face. She noticed that there was a single broken tooth in his lower jaw, a relic perhaps of some childhood accident. He obviously hadn't cared enough to have it capped, and that tiny act of indifference made her warm to him another degree or two.

He said: "I knew you'd help." He didn't thank her.

"I'll do what I can," Fern responded. She didn't promise.

Fern went home by tube, so absorbed in her own thoughts that she almost missed her stop. When she got back to the flat she made preparations diligently, her mind elsewhere. She set out bottles, glasses, candles. Knowing she had left it too late, she tried to call Will, but on his home number she got a machine and his mobile phone was switched off. But she did get through to Gaynor.

"What are you doing tonight?"

"I've already done it," Gaynor said. "I went to a dreary film at an arts cinema with Hugh, I think because he hoped it would impress me, and then he told me that Vanessa doesn't understand him, and then I declined to have sex with him again—I mean, I declined again, not that I had sex with him before—and now he says *I* don't understand him either, but—"

"Why should you want to?" said Fern. "Forget about Hugh; this is important. Can you come around? I'm expecting a visit from royalty and I think I'd like someone else here. It saves explaining afterward."

There was a short pause. "Did you say *royalty*?"

"Not that kind. Mabb, the goblin queen. Skuldunder dropped in the other night and I asked him to arrange it. I wasn't going to tell you about it—"

"Why not?"

"I didn't want you involved," Fern temporized. "After last time . . ."

"Look, I was scared last time, and I'll probably be scared again, especially if there are bats. I scare easily. But it doesn't matter. I'm your best friend. We're supposed to be a team."

"*Are* we?"

"Yes, of course. You, me, and . . . and Will."

"Some team," said Fern. "Two members don't even speak to each other. The Lone Pine Five had better look out."

"Do you want me to come around or not?" Gaynor interjected.

"Yes, I do. Something's happening, and I need to talk it over. You're nearer than Ragginbone—"

"Thanks a lot."

"—and you don't wear a smelly coat. Come around now?"

Gaynor came. Fern had already made coffee, and they sat down amid a scattering of candles while she described her meeting with Lucas Walgrim and the information she had received from Skuldunder.

"You think there's a connection?" Gaynor asked.

"Maybe. In magic, there are no coincidences. It's very difficult for someone to separate another human soul from its body. I've been doing some reading in the last couple of years—Ragginbone gave me a load of stuff—and even the spells for it are obscure. It takes a *lot* of power. The Old Spirit can do it, but he's not human, and he has to have the consent of his victim. He seems to be able to bend the rules sometimes; after all, I didn't actually consent the night I was taken, but I *had* called him, and I was unconscious, and vulnerable. But when Morgus sent the owl for me I should have been able to return to myself instead of being wrenched into another dimension. She took you once, too, remember? Only you were the wrong person so she sent you back again. Apparently, she used to collect souls. She would seal them in djinn bottles or inanimate objects—"

"Gin bottles?" Gaynor queried.

"D-J-I-N-N. The point is, she was very powerful. There is no record of Zohrâne managing spirit-body separation, though the evidence suggests Merlin could, and maybe Medea. It's impossible to be sure when there's so little contemporary documentation. Mostly people wrote centuries afterward about what magicians did, basing it on legend and hearsay."

"I didn't know there was *anything* contemporary to Merlin or Medea," Gaynor said. Her job was the study and restoration of old books and manuscripts—the older the better—and a glimmer of professional enthusiasm had come into her eye.

Her friend reverted firmly to the original subject. "As far as I can tell, it takes a special kind of concentration to split someone from their physical body. I couldn't begin to do it, though I can separate *myself*—that's quite simple; many people do it in dreams with no spell involved. You only need to be a little Gifted. The majority of people have *some* magic in them, even if they never use it. But Morgus's power was exceptional. It looks as if Dana Walgrim's spirit was stolen, like mine—only Morgus is dead. So we're looking for someone with the same kind of power, which is not a nice thought. And

Skuldunder has already come to me with a story of a new witch who may be both powerful and evil . . ."

"Are you sure Morgus is dead?"

"Of course I am. I saw her burn." Fern's expression assumed a certain fixity, concealing unknown emotion. "I killed her."

Gaynor knew she was trespassing in private territory. "She deserved it," she offered, aware it was no consolation.

" 'Many who die deserve life. Can you give it to them?' " Fern retorted, quoting Tolkien, and there were sharp edges in her voice. She leaned forward too quickly, reaching for the coffeepot, knocking a candle from its holder and crying out in pain as the flame seared her left hand.

"Put it under the tap," said Gaynor, fielding the candle with rather more caution.

"It doesn't hurt much."

"Yes, but you know it will. Why *have* you got all these candles? The place looks like a fire hazard."

"Atmosphere," said Fern on her way to the kitchen. "Atmosphere is very important to werefolk. And Mabb *is* royalty, of a sort. I thought I should make an effort."

"You said she would come at midnight," said Gaynor, glancing at the clock. "She's late,"

"Of course she is," Fern responded from the next room, over the sound of the tap running. "Punctuality may be the politeness of kings, but she's a queen. Ragginbone told me about her. Outside her own kind, her prestige is limited, so she exercises caprice whenever she can. She's behaving like any Hollywood superstar, keeping the audience waiting."

Gaynor was staring fixedly at the curtains over the central window. The unstable candle flames made the shadows move; creases that should have been motionless seemed to twitch into life. She tried to picture a shape or shapes there, developing slowly. She was sure she could see something—the crook of an elbow, the point of an ear—when the smell reached her.

It was a smell both animal and vegetable, a rank, hot, stoaty smell mingled with the green stink of an overripe bog. It invaded her nostrils from somewhere just to the left of her chair, making her gorge rise. She gasped: "Fern—!" even as she looked around.

The goblin was standing barely a yard away. Her appearance was almost as vivid as her odor, the large head swiveling curiously on a worm-supple neck, the stick-thin limbs dressed in some garment made from dying flowers and spidersilk, with a rag of fawn skin over one shoulder. Wings plucked from a swallowtail butterfly fluttered in vain behind her. Another butterfly, in blue and green brilliants, secured the fawn skin; her nails were painted gold; the lids of her slanting eyes were zebra striped in cream and bronze. A crown of leaves, set with the wing cases of beetles, adorned hair as short and colorless as mouse fur, and by way of a scepter she held a peeled switch as tall as herself, topped with a bunch of feathers and the skull of a small bird. Gaynor found herself thinking irresistibly that the queen resembled a nightmare version of a flower fairy who has recently raided a children's makeup counter. She made a desperate attempt to rearrange her expression into something polite.

"You must be the witch," said the goblin, lifting her chin in order to look down her nose. "I honor you with my presence."

"Thank you, but . . . I'm not a witch," Gaynor stammered. "I'm just her friend."

"Councillor," said Fern, resuming her place on the sofa. "We are indeed honored." Her tone was courteous but not fulsome. She's a natural diplomat, Gaynor thought. It must be the years in PR. "May I offer your highness some refreshment?"

The queen gave a brief nod and Fern mixed her a concoction of vodka, sugar, and strawberry coulis, which seemed to meet with royal approval. Gaynor, remembering Skuldunder's reaction to the wine, wondered secretly if she had any previous experience of alcohol. Having accepted the drink,

Mabb seated herself in a chair opposite, leaning her switch against it. Her eyes, black from edge to edge, gleamed in the candlelight like jet beads.

"It is well that you have come," Fern went on. "This new witch, if she is indeed powerful, could be a threat to both werefolk and Men. In time of danger it is necessary that those of us with wisdom and knowledge should take counsel together."

"What wisdom does *she* have?" Mabb demanded, flashing a glare at Gaynor. "I have not talked to a witch in many a hundred year. I do not talk to ordinary mortals at all."

"She is not ordinary," said Fern. "She may be young, but she is learned in the ancient histories, and wiser than I. She stood at my side in a time of great peril, and did not flinch."

Yes, I did, I flinched frequently, Gaynor said, but only to herself.

Mabb evidently decided she would condescend to approve the extra councillor. "Loyalty to one another is a human thing," she said. "I am told it is important to you. Goblins are loyal only to me."

"We may have different customs," said Fern, "but we can still be allies. I am gratified to see your highness wears my gifts."

"They please me," said the queen, scanning her gilded nails. "More gifts would be acceptable, and would confirm our alliance."

"Of course," said Fern. "When our meeting is concluded, I have other gifts for you. But first, I need to know more of this witch."

Mabb made a strange gesture, like a parody of one Fern had learned to use in summoning. "Skuldunder!"

The burglar materialized hesitantly.

"Bring the exile," ordered the queen.

Skuldunder duly vanished, reappearing presently with another goblin in tow. He looked as brown and wrinkled as a dried apple, and there was the stamp of past terror on his face, but now he seemed in the grip of a lassitude that exceeded even fear. "He was a house-goblin," the queen explained with a flicker of contempt, "but he was forced to flee his house. He withers from loss and shame." She turned to her subjects. "This witch is my friend, our ally. She is not like the rest of witchkind. You must tell her about the sorceress who drove you from your house. I command you!"

The old goblin shivered a little and blinked, but said nothing.

"What is his name?" asked Fern.

"Dibbuck," said Skuldunder.

"Dibbuck." Fern dropped to the floor, bringing herself on a level with his vacant gaze. "I need your help. I have to learn all I can about this woman, in case I have to dispose of her. I know it's hard for you to talk about it, especially to someone like me, but please try. It may be vital." And, after a pause: "Is she young or old?"

"Young," said Dibbuck at last. His voice was not soft but faint, as if it had already begun to fade. "Young-looking. Old inside."

"Could you describe her?"

But this Dibbuck did not seem able to do. Goblins, Fern realized, see humans differently, not feature for feature but more as we see animals. "Green dress," he volunteered, and then: "White dress." For some reason he shuddered. "Much hair."

This was hardly unique, Fern reflected. Most witches favored long hair. Perhaps that was why she kept her own so short.

She groped for the right questions to ask. "Do you know when she came to the house?"

Dibbuck was largely oblivious to dates. "The party," he said. "Big party." A faraway echo of remembered mischief brightened his face. "I added things to the drinks. Salt. Red pepper. There were many people in many clothes. Long clothes, short clothes. Masks."

"Fancy dress?" Fern said quickly.

Dibbuck looked bewildered.

"Never mind. So the witch was there?"

"Didn't see her. Too many people. But she was there after." He added: "The hag came later, and the cat, and the gypsy."

Fern tried to elicit further details, with limited success. The hag appeared to be some kind of servant, the gypsy maybe a temporary worker. "Tell me about the cat."

"It was a goblin cat," interrupted the queen. "A sallowfang. He was afraid of it."

"What's a goblin cat?"

"They were the cats of the king of the Underworld," Mabb explained, with the complacency of a child who has access to privileged information. "They have no fur, and their skin is black or white, sometimes striped or piebald. They are bigger than normal cats, and very cunning." She concluded, with a narrowing of the eyes: "They used to hunt goblins."

"A sphinx cat," suggested Gaynor. "I've never seen one, but I know they're hairless."

"These sound as if they're magical, or part magical," said Fern. "Could be a relative."

"This one chased him," said Mabb, indicating Dibbuck. "He was lucky to escape. A sallowfang can smell a spider in a rainstorm."

"What about the household ghosts?" said Fern. "Skuldunder said something about an exorcism."

"She made the circle," Dibbuck said, "in the spellchamber. I saw them all streaming in—they couldn't resist—Sir William—the kitchen imp—little memories like insects, buzzing. I pinned myself to the floor with a splinter, so I couldn't go. They were trapped in the circle, spinning around and around. Then she . . ." His voice ran down like a clockwork toy into silence.

"She opened the abyss," Mabb finished for him. "I thought my servant told you."

"You mean—Limbo?" hazarded Gaynor.

"Limbo is a place of sleep and dreams," Mabb responded impatiently. "It is a part of *this* world. The abyss is between worlds. It is—emptiness. They say those who are cast into it may be swallowed up forever. When mortals die they pass the Gate. *We* go to Limbo, until this world is remade. But no one may return from the abyss until *all* worlds are changed. I thought even humans would know that."

"We have our own lore," said Fern. "It must take a great deal of power to open a gap between worlds . . ."

"And for what?" Mabb sounded savage with indignation. "A few ragged phantoms—an imp or two—a handful of degenerates. So much power—for so *little*. She is mad, this witch. Mad and dangerous. She might do *anything*."

For all her eccentric appearance and freakish temperament, thought Fern, the goblin queen showed a vein of common sense. "Can you recall her name?" she asked Dibbuck, but he shook his head. "The name of the house, then?"

"Wrokeby." His face twisted in sudden pain.

"Is there anything else I should know?"

Dibbuck looked confused. "The prisoner," he said eventually. "In the attic."

"What kind of prisoner? Was it a girl?"

"No . . . Couldn't see. Something—huge, hideous . . . A monster."

Not Dana Walgrim, Fern concluded. "What else?"

Dibbuck mumbled inaudibly, gazing into corners, seeking inspiration or merely a germ of hope. "She had a tree," he said. "In the cellar."

"A tree in the *cellar*?" Fern was baffled. "How could a tree grow in the dark?"

"Seeds grow in the dark," said Mabb. "Plant magic is very old; maybe the witchkind do not use it now. You take a seed, a fortune seed or a love seed, and as it germinates so your fortune waxes or your lover's affection increases. They used to be popular: mortals are always obsessed with wealth or love. If the seed does not sprout, then you have no fortune, no love."

"Not a seed," said Dibbuck. "It was a tree, a young tree. It was uprooted, but it was alive. I smelled the forest; I saw the leaves move. She wrapped it in silk, and fed it, and sang to it."

"Does this ritual mean anything to you?" Fern asked Mabb, inadvertently forgetting to give her her royal title.

But Mabb, too, had forgotten her dignity. Possibly the vodka had affected her. "I have never heard of such a thing," she said. "A woman who wraps a tree in swaddling clothes and lullabies it to sleep sounds to me more foolish than magical. Perhaps, if she is besotted with these fancies, she may not be dangerous after all. When I wanted to play at motherhood, I would steal a babe from a rabbit's burrow, or a woodman's cradle, not pluck a bunch of dead twigs. Of course," she added with an eye on Fern, "that was long ago. I have outgrown such folly. Besides, human babies scream all the time. It becomes tiresome."

"So I'm told," said Fern. "I need to think about all this. Your highness, may I have some means of calling on you and your servants again, should it be necessary? This witch may indeed be mad or foolish, but I fear otherwise. I must make a spell of farsight, and then I may know what further questions to ask your subject."

"I will have the royal burglar pass by here othernights," Mabb decreed magnanimously. "If you wish to speak with him, pin a mistletoe sprig to your door."

"It's out of season," Fern pointed out.

"Well." Mabb shrugged. "Any leaves will do." She waited a minute, beginning to tap her foot. "You mentioned gifts . . ."

Fern went into her bedroom for a hasty trawl through her makeup drawer and jewel box.

* * *

"*Can* you make a spell of farsight?" Gaynor asked when they were alone.

"I could light the spellfire," Fern said, "if I had any crystals. That might tell me something. Do you want a G and T?"

"Actually," said Gaynor, "just tea would be good. I'll make it."

"No, it's all right." Fern headed for the kitchen.

"Are you—are you going to tell Will about this?"

"Probably." There was a pause filled with the noise of gurgling water, and the click of a switch on the kettle. "Why?"

Gaynor stiffened her sinews, screwing her courage, such as it was, to the sticking point. "I just think you should. Because he's your brother. Because three heads are better than two. Because we're a team."

"Are we?"

"You said so."

"I think that was your idea." Fern came to the kitchen doorway, propping herself against the frame. "Last time you both nearly got killed. That's not going to happen again. I can protect myself, but I can't always protect you, so you *must*—you must *promise*—do exactly what I say, and stay out of trouble. I don't like the sound of this witch. I didn't fully understand what Skuldunder meant when he said she opened the abyss, but I do now. You must promise me—"

"No," said Gaynor baldly. "I mean, I could say it, but it wouldn't be true, and anyway, you haven't the *right*. I may not be Gifted like you, but that doesn't mean you can control me or exclude me. Or Will. I got involved last time because you were in denial, and now I'm involved for good. You can't change that." She spoke in a hurry, determined to get the words out before Fern could interrupt or she lost her nerve.

After a minute the set look that was becoming habitual to Fern relaxed. "Sorry," she said unexpectedly. "I've been a control freak from childhood. Years of managing Dad. Just . . .

be careful this time. No rushing off into the dragon's den. Please."

"No fear," said Gaynor with an uncertain smile.

Fern returned to the kettle, reemerging presently with two mugs of tea, both overfull. As she set them down the contents of the left one splashed over the rim. "Damn," she said. "Not again." She sucked at the injury, then lowered her hand, extending it until it was directly under the lamplight. "Gaynor . . ." The scald mark faded even as she watched, leaving her skin unblemished. There was no other burn to be seen.

"What did you do?" Gaynor demanded. "Is it more magic?"

"Maybe," said Fern, "but not mine." There was a long moment while recollection and doubt turned over in her mind. "This happened before . . . when I set fire to Morgus. My hand was burned. Kal made me dip it in the river . . ."

"The river healed you, didn't it?" Gaynor said. "It was the Styx. Remember Achilles. Supposing . . . you're invulnerable? I mean, your hand . . . Have you hurt it at all since then?"

"I don't know. A scratch or two. I wasn't paying attention."

"You might not have noticed," Gaynor said.

"There's only one way to find out," said Fern. She thrust her hand into the nearest candle flame. Gaynor saw her face whiten and her lips clench and cried out in protest. Fern withdrew it, trembling: her palm was red and already puckering into blisters. But as they watched the blisters sank, the angry ridges smoothed, the red dimmed to pink and vanished altogether. They stared at each other, incredulous and amazed. Then Fern got up and fetched a fruit knife from the kitchen. "It works for burns," she said. "Let's try something different." She jabbed the blade into her finger. The cut opened, filling with blood—and closed, flesh binding with flesh, leaving no scar.

"Please don't try breaking any bones," Gaynor begged. "I've never been into self-abuse, even if it's someone else."

"I don't think I could," said Fern. "It may heal straight after, but I feel pain first."

They were still discussing the implications of their discovery when a glance at the clock showed a startled Gaynor that it was past three. "Stay over," Fern suggested. "You left your washcloth behind anyway, and I think the Body Shop night cream must be yours."

Gaynor was already in bed when Fern appeared in the doorway, silhouetted against the light beyond. Gaynor could not see her face clearly, but she was somehow aware that it had changed. "If the river healed my hand," Fern said, "supposing—supposing it healed Morgus?"

"She was dead," Gaynor insisted. "You said she was dead."

"She was alive when she crawled to the river and threw herself in. I never saw the body. I should have thought of it before. She knew the power of the river: that's why she did it. And if it worked—if it healed her—then she must be invulnerable now, mustn't she? *Completely* invulnerable. Invincible."

"We don't *know*," said Gaynor unhappily.

"No, we don't," Fern agreed. "It's late, we're tired, this may be only a brainstorm. In the morning everything will look different . . ."

"I hope so," Gaynor said.

In the morning it was a gray, ordinary sort of day, the kind of day on which it is difficult to believe in witches and dark sorcery and impossible to believe in summer. But Fern had seen many such days and she was not to be deceived, even in the heart of London: she could sense the evil moving under the skin of the city. She left Gaynor with assurances that she would tell her everything and went to work, trying to focus on the forthcoming magazine launch, and failing. Lucas rang just before lunch, saying could she come to the clinic that evening. The assumption that her time was his annoyed her, but instinct told her she was being petty so she agreed.

"She's in love," opined a colleague, watching her through a glass partition. "She has all the symptoms: abstraction, absent-mindedness, personal calls from unknown men . . ."

"She doesn't have a glow of happiness," said a PA.

"Happiness? What's that got to do with love? You poor innocent girl . . ."

Fern, oblivious to the speculation she aroused, retouched her makeup before leaving the office and took a taxi to the Queen Square clinic. Lucas was waiting for her in reception. She registered privately that he was definitely attractive, or might be if he smiled. He did not smile. He said hello, thanked her for coming, and suggested: "Call me Luc," when she greeted him formally. L-U-C, he explained, like the French. Poseur, she decided. They went up in an elevator, passed an office where a male nurse nodded a greeting, and walked the length of a corridor to a private room with an impeccable display of flowers and the customary array of life support systems. There was a view over the square, a white glimpse of sky atop the buildings. The obligatory water jug was untouched, the bed linen drawn up smoothly under the sleeper's arms. Fern found herself thinking: This is how my family felt, when it was me. This is what they saw. She had seen herself in dream or vision, when her spirit was far away, and it seemed to her this girl's face was the same, pale and empty, a wax mask framed in the dark shadows of her hair. She was sure now, if she had ever doubted, that Dana Walgrim's soul had been stolen, torn from its fleshly home and sent who knew where. But there was one difference that struck her disagreeably. Fern knew she had been watched over, protected—by onetime wizard and present tramp Ragginbone, by her father, her brother, her friend; by the local vicar and his wife. Her vacant body had been constantly guarded and cared for. Yet Dana seemed to have only her brother and the nurses. The flowers had been professionally arranged. There was nothing personal in the room, nothing disordered. No one had sat on the bed or moved the chairs all day. "Where are the rest of your family?" Fern asked. "Surely there should be people here—relatives, friends?"

"She didn't have any real friends," Luc said, not noticing the insidious past tense. "My father comes now and then. His helplessness distresses him."

"Yes," said Fern ambiguously. "It is distressing."

"Her best friend went to Australia about a year ago."

"Call her," said Fern. "Fly her over here. You can afford it." A statement, not a question. "It's important for her to know that she's loved, that people want her back."

"Do you think she can *see*—?"

"Maybe." She remembered the Atlantean veil that Gaynor had knotted round her shoulders, a scarf of protection. Dana could have no such thing, but there were other possibilities. "Does she still have a special toy from when she was a child—a favorite teddy or something?"

"I never thought of that." Luc frowned. "Stupid of me. There was a teddy bear that used to belong to my grandmother; it was called William—never Bill, always William, I don't know why. One of its ears fell off and the au pair sewed it on again the wrong way around. I suspect it's an antique, probably worth a fortune in today's market. Dana might still have it. I'll go over to her flat later."

"Good."

"It won't help to find it, though, will it? Are you just giving me something to do? Keep him occupied, keep him from panicking, make him feel *useful*." The light eyes held hers.

"I told you," Fern said, "it will help her to know she's loved. She has to *want* to come back, or she may not be able to."

"I've tried to be here for her." His tone was level, but the words sounded faintly defensive.

"And before?" Fern inquired, almost without thinking.

He did not answer. He was holding his sister's hand, looking down into her face. "Have you any idea where she's gone?"

"I have an idea," Fern admitted. "I just don't know if it's the right one. I saw someone last night who told me something that might be relevant."

"Research, or coincidence?"

"Not research, but . . . there are no coincidences, only patterns. Fragments, so they say, of the greater pattern. It depends on what you believe."

"No pattern," Luc said bleakly. "Just chaos." And then: "What did you learn?"

"I'm not sure yet. I need you to answer a couple of questions."

"Okay."

"What's the name of your father's country house where your sister fainted?"

"Wrokeby," he said. "With a W." He saw the slight alteration in her expression. "Was that what you wanted—needed—to hear?"

"I'm afraid so."

"Afraid?"

"Never mind. It ties in, but there's still too much I don't understand. At that party, were there many people you didn't know?"

"About half of them, I should think. Anyway, I told you, everyone was in fancy dress. Costumes, wigs, bizarre makeup, masks. I couldn't always recognize the ones I *did* know."

"The person I want would be a woman—"

"That really cuts down the list of suspects."

Fern ignored his sarcasm. "Perhaps dressed as a witch."

"There must have been several witches. No pointy hats: the glamorous kind. Come to think of it, Dana went as a witch of sorts. Yards of ragged chiffon and hair extensions. Medieval meets New Age. Not Morgan Le Fay, but some name like that. She'd been reading T. H. White."

He saw Fern stiffen; for a moment, her face was as pale as the girl in the bed.

"Morgus?"

"I think so."

Fern went to the window; her fingers gripped the sill. In the cloud-cast sky, a chink of blue opened up, like an illusion of hope. She thought: Morgus is out there. She's out there and she's invulnerable. And if she isn't looking for me, then I have to look for her. At Wrokeby—Wrokeby with a W. Her stomach knotted in fear; her heartbeat quickened. I'm not ready. I can't face her, not again, not yet, not now. If she cannot be killed . . . She struggled to conquer physical weakness and mental block. It seemed to her a long time before she turned around, managing at least the semblance of calm.

"I must go away," she said. "This weekend. I have to go to Yorkshire. There's someone I need to consult." Like a doctor, she thought, a specialist—in witchcraft. "I'll call you when I get back."

"You'd better have all my numbers." He gave her a business card with office and cell phone, wrote his home number on the back. "Should I really fly her friend over from Oz? She may not want to come: she's pregnant."

"Leave it for now."

She's scared, he thought. Behind that immaculate face, she's really scared . . .

He said: "So what can I do—apart from the teddy bear?"

"Think of her," said Fern. "You have the Gift. Look for her in your dreams. You can find all sorts of things in dreams."

"I know," he said.

The dream came to him when he was barely asleep, plunging him from a state of half-waking into a world of turbulent darkness, with no interim of quiet slumber, no gradual descent through the many layers of the subconscious. This was not the sleep-spun region of fairy nightmares and haphazard imaginings: this was a different reality, violent and harsh. He stood on wooden planks that heaved and tilted, clinging to a great wheel. Water streamed across the boards and black rain drove in his face and lashed at his body. His clothes were clammy rags, his long hair—he had worn long hair, in his teens—whipped around his neck, almost cutting his skin. He was on the deck of a ship—no, a boat, some kind of fishing vessel, less than forty feet long, with a single mast and sail splitting under the impact of a savage wind. Giant waves reared up like cliffs on either hand, spume capped; thunder boomed; greenish lightning darted from the tumult of the clouds. There were other people on the boat with him, half a dozen or so, hauling on the rigging, clutching the base of the mast, but he could not call out to them, he was isolated in a vortex of chaos. His teeth chattered from terror and cold.

As long as he could remember, he had been afraid of the sea. In childhood, his worst nightmares had been of a huge tsunami, a great wall of blue-green water rolling over the land to engulf him. He climbed the nearest hills, but they were never high enough, and he would waken, sweat sodden and shaking, convinced he was drowning. His father made him learn to swim at five, believing that would cure him, but the enforced proximity of water taught him only to hide his fear, not to conquer it. The dreams faded as he grew older, but not the phobia. He once spent three days on a friend's yacht, a trip undertaken in a spirit of icy determination, and the whole time he was pale and silent, unable to eat. His friend thought he was seasick; but he was never seasick. After his mother's death in a car crash when he was nineteen he woke gasping from a dream that he was actually drowned, lying on the seabed while tiny creatures picked at his flesh and his bones poked through and a mermaid with eyes like bits of glass came to stare at him. And now here he was, pitchforked somehow onto a tiny boat in the heart of a hurricane. He did not know how he came there, or why; he knew only fear. He thought: This is madness, folly and madness, we must use the engines, radio for help; but there were no engines, no radio.

He heard the hissing crack. Lightning struck the mast, and it broke. The sail was in shreds. Someone screamed, perhaps a man overboard, a dreadful long ululation that sounded hardly human anymore; but he could do nothing. He hung on to the helm because that was all there was. And at last it came to him that he was in charge, he was the captain, he had led the others into this, the madness and the folly were all his. The realization dragged him down like a great stone, down through the breaking timbers of the boat into the black water. And there was the mermaid with her strange flat eyes, her living hair crackling with storm static, her arms reaching for him.

Afterward, he did not want to remember the dying. It was more vivid than dream, more real than memory. The sea closing over him, and him trying to breathe, but his breath was sea, and there was sea in his lungs, in his ears, in his head, and the terrible infinite struggle, and the slow uprush of darkness that took everything away . . .

He woke between clinging sheets, and the throb in his ears became the hum of the city, and a glance at the clock told him only minutes had passed since he'd gone to bed. He sat up, gulping air, and lay down again slowly, eyes wide as if he were afraid to close them.

You can find all sorts of things in dreams . . .

But that night he slept little, and did not dream again.

IV ᕙᕒᕒᕒᕒᕗ

Fern left work early on Friday and drove to Yorkshire. It was still daylight when she came over the moors: great cloud bastions were building up in the sky; giant shadows traveled ponderously across the landscape. At one point she pulled over, getting out of the car to catch an advancing band of sunlight. The moor stretched away on each hand, green with summer, heather tufted, humming with insect life. She took off her jacket, unbuttoned her shirt at the neck, and let the wind ruffle her sleek hair. To the casual observer—had there been one—she was a city girl shedding the trappings of an urban lifestyle in preparation for a country weekend. But Fern knew she was crossing a boundary, both familiar and imaginary, from the superficial realities of her routine existence to a world where reality was unstable and everything was dark and different. Yet now the very boundaries had changed: the dark otherworld had come even to London and lurked around corners, and under paving stones, and in the blackness beyond the streetlamps. So she stood in the sun and bared her throat to the wind as a gesture of acknowledgment and acceptance. I am Fernanda Morcadis, she told the clouds and the plateau and the indifferent bees. I am of the witchkind, Prospero's Children. It is everything else which is unreal.

The dog came bounding over the grasses as she got back into the car. It might have been a German shepherd, except that the brindling of its fur included brown and gray rather than tan and its face was more pointed and wilder, and there was a speed in its movement and a light in its yellow eyes that no domestic animal could match. It came over to Fern and waited, panting slightly, tongue lolling between wicked teeth, while she caressed its rain-damp ruff. "Lougarry," she said. "Tell your master to come to the house. I need his help."

Go carefully, said the thought in her head. *These are troubled times.*

Then the creature turned and sped away. The sun disappeared, and in the gloom beneath a vast cloud the moor changed, becoming cold and unfriendly. Fern shut the door and teased the engine into life. As she drove off a sudden squall struck, almost blinding her: the wipers struggled ineffectually to clear the windshield. The rain passed, but the murk still lingered, turning the world to gray. Yarrowdale lay ahead, a narrow valley winding down from the North York Moors to the windswept beaches of the North Sea.

As she swung onto the road that led down to the village she had her lights on, but the oncoming car showed none. It appeared as if from nowhere, on her side of the road, heading straight toward her. She swerved onto the verge, her heart in her mouth, and it shot past without slowing. Fern braked to a stop and leaned forward, breathing deep and slow to calm herself. Her headlights had shone directly into the approaching vehicle, and she was sure that what she had seen was no freak of fancy. For one instant of panic she had faced the driver of the other car, and she had glimpsed not a human visage but a grinning death's-head grasping the wheel with hands of bone.

She waited a few minutes before restarting the engine. Then she drove gently down the valley, turning off at Dale House. Lights in the windows indicated that Mrs. Wicklow, their local housekeeper and theoretically long past retirement, had come to welcome her. She parked the car and went indoors.

The big kitchen at the back was warm from the stove and smelled of cooking. Mrs. Wicklow had been widowed the previous year and with the departure of Will, who had been loosely affiliated with York University before he abandoned his M.A., she had suffered a dearth of recipients for her generous cuisine. Fern's father, Robin, paid Mrs. Wicklow regardless of what she did, but she claimed she was too young to accept a pension and took whatever opportunities there were to justify her wages. To Fern, she was family. They embraced, and Mrs. Wicklow produced gin and tonics for both of them. Her Christian name was reputed to be Dorothy, but no one ever used it; for all their intimacy Fern still called her "Mrs. Wicklow" without thinking.

"There's trouble," the housekeeper said sapiently. "I can see it in your face."

"I had a close shave in the car," Fern said. "Some idiot driving like a maniac on the wrong side of the road."

"That'll be one of the vicar's boys," Mrs. Wicklow deduced. "Expelled from school halfway through term and he's pinched his dad's car twice that I know of. That poor Maggie's out of her mind with t' worry of it. Vicar's children are always the worst: it's like t' devil goes after them special. But that wasn't what I meant. I was thinking of t' other kind of trouble. T' kind we had before. The old man's been around since New Year's Eve: that's always a sign. Him and t' dog. Mr. Watchman or Skin'n'Bones or whatever he calls himself. You'd better have him around to a decent supper tomorrow. Don't know how he keeps body and soul together."

"Habit," Fern murmured.

She went to her room early, after Mrs. Wicklow had gone home. She pulled out a box from under the bed—a box that had once belonged to Alison Redmond, who had come to stay one bright morning fourteen years ago and had died in a flood where no water should have been. And because of her, Fern thought, I am who I am. I might never have known I had the Gift, if it wasn't for Alimond.

Inside the box, there were a pair of dragonskin gloves, a videocassette that Fern had only played once, a handwritten book, the writing changing gradually from an antique script into a modern scrawl, and a number of miniature phials whose labels she had never deciphered. In a compartment she had missed previously she found a leather bag of dull bluish crystals and a small receptacle containing a silver-gray powder. Fern put on the gloves: they seemed to meld with her hands, and the mottled patterns shifted and changed without help from the light. "It is time," she said to herself, and the realization made her shiver. The mad driver, whoever he might be, was just part of the picture, an emissary of Azmordis, a wild card, a manic phantom who had picked up her description from somewhere. In the otherworld, she was wanted. She knew that now. She removed the gloves again and went to bed, lying awake in the dark.

The house-goblin considered coming in to talk, but he knew Fern had a human concept of privacy, so he went downstairs to the kitchen and drank the whiskey she had remembered to leave out for him.

Ragginbone came to the house the following evening. He was old, old and tough, like an oak tree that has weathered many winters; his clothes were shabby, gray-brown and gray-green, blending with the moorland. The greatcoat that he had worn through all seasons had been abandoned in favor of a misshapen jacket of antiquated cut hanging almost to his knees. Atop his head he wore a wide-brimmed hat that would have been pointed at the crown if it had not been permanently dented. But the eyes beneath his hat brim were gold-green and bright as spring, and the rare smile that rearranged his wrinkles was as warm as ever. To the villagers he was Mr.

Watchman, Ragginbone the tramp, but to Fern he was Cara-
candal Brokenwand, ex-wizard, Watcher of history, a man of
many names and many travels, of short words and tall tales,
her mentor, insofar as she had one, her friend since she was
sixteen. And the wolf-dog with him was Lougarry, with the
soul of a woman in the body of a beast, and a silent voice that
could be heard only in the minds of a few.

They sat long over their dinner after Mrs. Wicklow had
gone, while Lougarry lay in her accustomed place by the
stove. Fern related everything that had happened and the conclusions she had drawn, and Ragginbone's smile grew even
rarer, and the lines deepened on his brow. "Mabb is a chancy
ally," he said at one point. "Goblins are by their very nature
untrustworthy, and the female of the species is invariably
more extreme than the male. More vicious, more capricious,
shallower of heart, sharper of whim. Be wary."

"Sexist," said Fern.

"I was born in a sexist age. Experience has not taught me
to think differently. To generalize: men are rash and cow-
ardly, women are prudent and brave, men are strong in the
arm, women are strong in the heart, men are stupid and cunning, women subtle and devious. Men are self-centered, soft-
centered creatures, armored in loud words and harsh deeds.
Women are gentle and fragile, selfless beyond sense, and
steel to the core."

"Is that how you see me?"

His face creased. "You are a woman of your time. Beside
you, steel is pliable. Your spirit was cut from diamond."

"Is that a compliment?"

"Neither compliment nor insult, merely an opinion." He
reached for the wine bottle, topped off both glasses. "Go on
with your story."

The light was failing now, and the shadow of the hill leaned
over the house. Fern switched on a single lamp and lit the
only candles she could find, fixing them in a serviceable iron

candelabra that dated from an era before electricity. Night crept slowly into the room, filling up the cracks between cupboards and under the fridge and tallboy. The wine bottle was empty, and Fern poured whiskey into three tumblers. "There's always whiskey in this house," she remarked. "The vodka runs out, and the gin, but never the Scotch. I suspect Bradachin of doctoring Mrs. Wicklow's regular shopping list."

"There's nae harm in it," said a thickly accented voice. "Nae harm and muckle guid. Usquebaugh warms the belly and strengthens the heart, and we'll hae need o' strong hearts in the days to come, I'm thinking."

The house-goblin appeared from nowhere in particular and climbed on a chair, accepting the glass that Fern pushed toward him. He was a reddish, hairy creature, tall for his kind, limping from a malformed limb or old wound but spider-swift in his movements. He had come from a castle in Scotland that had been converted into a luxury hotel, dealing with the trauma of his exile by bringing the spirit of the McCrackens with him. He played the bagpipes in the small hours, and filled the dour Yorkshire house with the echoes of great halls, and high towers, and dreams of the wind off the loch. Both Fern and Ragginbone knew him to be courageous beyond the custom of his folk, stubborn, resourceful, and loyal. He had spent all his history with a family of fierce fighters, passionate feuders, and hopeless plotters, and some of their skills and their prejudices had rubbed off on him, setting him apart from his own people. Mabb had banished him from her court, when she troubled to remember it, for excessive fealty to Man, but Bradachin was still attached to his queen.

"So ye've had speech with the maidy," he commented. "For all her kittle follies, she's nae fool. What o' this witch, then? Can ye be siccar she's the one ye met afore?"

"I'll have to see her," said Fern. "Morgus is—unmistakable."

"She may look different," Ragginbone said thoughtfully. "She was severely burnt: her flesh melted. You always said you thought much of her bloating was stored power rather than fat. She may have been working on a regeneration spell during all her sojourn beneath the Tree, burying it in her own body, waiting for the appropriate trigger. The fire might have killed, but the river healed and the spell was set in motion. The excess power would be used up, the rest absorbed into her new body. I would expect her to resemble the woman she was in her former life, not the grotesque hag you knew. Anyway, witches are vain. She would never return to the world without doing something to restore her looks."

"You're saying she may be young again," said Fern. "Young and beautiful—and invincible. I killed her once . . . must I do it again? And how do you kill someone who cannot be hurt?"

"There'll be a way," said Ragginbone. "There is always a way. Trust in stories. The Achilles' heel, the Cyclops's eye, the brazen stopper that releases the giant's blood . . . But Bradachin is right: we must be sure. It is time to be a witch indeed, Fernanda. You must draw the circle."

"I know," Fern acknowledged. "That's why I came here." She looked down at her hands, which were child-sized, the nails tinted like bits of shell. Inadequate hands for all that she needed to grasp. "I found crystals and fire powder in the box. Alimond used the front room, Will's old studio—"

"No. There are bad memories there. Magic wakes magic. Let them sleep. I think . . . I shall come with you to London. There is one I know who will help. He won't like it, but he *will* help."

"Mayhap I maun be coming, too," said Bradachin with an air of reluctance that deceived no one.

It was left to Fern to dissuade him. "You are a house-goblin," she said. "Your duty is here, with the house. Anyway, there has to be someone to keep an eye on the place. As Ragginbone said, too much has happened here in the past, and . . . trouble wakens trouble. As I turned into Yarrowdale, a car nearly hit me. It was coming straight at me—I had to swerve onto the verge to avoid it—and whatever was driving it wasn't human. Morgus is not our only problem: the Old Spirit has more reason than ever to hate us. *He's* always preferred to seek me out here, away from civilization. If there are any developments, I can get a message to you." Wisely, she gave him no time to argue. "You can use the telephone?"

"Ay, but—"

"Good. When magic fails, there is always technology." She turned to include the former wizard, pushing the discussion past the danger point. "What do you make of this business with the tree?"

"It is . . . disturbing," Ragginbone admitted. "I am wondering if she has brought a cutting from the Eternal Tree out of its native dimension into the real world. I do not know what would happen if one did. It might wither instantly, unable to bear the pressure of Time and life. Or—"

"The Eternal Tree exists in stasis," Fern said. "It has enormous power—a kind of treeish hunger—I felt that—but it *couldn't* grow any more, it couldn't reach out any farther. It was trapped in timelessness, in a cycle that went nowhere. When I bore the—the fruit here I was told it would rot far more quickly: that is the nature of fruit. And it was seedless. But maybe if you brought something living into this world— something with the potential for growth . . ."

"It would grow," Ragginbone said somberly. "As a theory, it is all too viable. Bring here a twig, a leaf, a toadstool, a blade of grass. The pulse of the Tree is in it, and the restraints of its usual environment are removed. On reflection, perhaps that is what caused the great birds who roost there—the owls, the raptors, the eagle, and the roc—to far outgrow their everyday cousins. They fly between worlds, and the Tree's hunger is in their blood. It is not a comfortable thought. But Morgus must plant her sapling: it will need earth and water, sunlight and shade. It cannot take root in the air or flourish in a silken shroud."

"And have ye asked yoursel," Bradachin interjected, "if sic a tree grew in *this* world, what kind o' apples wid it be bearing?"

"That," said Ragginbone dryly, "was the question I was trying to avoid."

That night Fern slept little, troubled by a confusion of dreams. She saw the Dark Tower where Azmordis ruled in the city, and the same tower on a barren plain—it was stone now, and ruinous, but she knew it was the same—and eager tendrils came groping through the fractured walls, twining themselves around and around it until the tower was a great tree, and a million leaves unfurled, choking the sky. And *there* was a single fruit, swelling, ripening, till it became a living head, with features that at first she did not recognize. (The heads of the dead grow like apples on the Eternal Tree, until they are plucked, or fall and rot, and the wild hog devours them. All who have done evil must hang a season there . . .) And then the eyelids split, and the lips parted, and she knew herself.

"What are you doing here?" she demanded.

"Penance," said the head. "For all that I did, and all that I did not do. For the friend I failed, and the love I forgot, and the blood on my burned hand, and the blood on the hand that was whole."

"The blood I shed with my burned hand has risen up against me," Fern said. "My other hand is clean."

"Not for long," said the head.

"What friend have I failed? Tell me!"

"Search your heart."

"I did not forget my love!"

"Search your head."

The scene changed, and she was back in Atlantis, the golden city in the Forbidden Past—Atlantis before the Fall. When she was sixteen she had been there, and loved and lost, and won and failed, and drowned in the great storm and crawled up on a beach of stars somewhere beyond the end of space. And she had known ever since that nothing would fill her like Atlantis: no sight, no scent, no place, no love. But it was long, long ago, many thousand lifetimes to all but her, and when the dream showed her her love—her Raf—climbing out of the fountain, shaking the water drops from his hair, his face was a blur, and all she remembered was the sudden brightness of his smile, and the tooth missing in his lower jaw. She cried out: "My heart does not forget!" but he did not hear her, and when she turned there was the head again, smiling her own smile, and it rotted and shriveled before her eyes, and the wild pig came raging through the undergrowth . . .

She woke to absolute stillness, so that even her pulse seemed to have stopped. She got up and went to the window, but there was nothing outside save the night. Not an owl hooted. She stood there for some while, feeling herself menaced, knowing her enemy was neither near nor far, and watchful, and wore many faces.

The Tree grows faster now, in the soil of Logrèz. Once, I could encircle the trunk with my fingers, but it thickens daily, quivering at the contact of my clasping hand. I have watched the leaves reaching for the evening sunlight, and seen how the sap glows like bright blood when the dimming light reaches back. Whoever built the original conservatory was a fool, situating it so that it faces north, occluded by the nearby wood; but it suits my purposes. I did not dare plant the Tree outdoors: it could gorge itself on too much light and air, and grow beyond containment. After so long outside Time, in a dimension where the light was spun from its own thought and the air was its stale breath, I know the risks of exposing it to the stimulus of reality. It will not flower, or if it does, flower and leaf are too much alike for the observer to differentiate, but it *will* fruit, it must fruit. I have given it all my love, and it must give me issue—whatever that issue may be.

I sent the nightmares to the prisoner three nights ago. Nehemet sat watching while I heated the cauldron, adding two drops of the precious sap to a recipe as old as evil. She was so still she might have been a ceramic statue, clumsily painted so the clay tone showed through the thin coating of black and white. Her skin looked smooth and matte, wrinkling around the joints, like human skin. Her ugliness fascinates me. Perhaps because it is hairless her face has a kind of bony intensity that you normally see only in the primates: something close to expression, which is rare in any beast. But I am not yet sure what Nehemet's expression may mean.

I poured my thoughts into the cauldron, and saw the mixture heave and sink, taking their shape, dissolving, re-forming, until at last they streamed upward in a column of black fume, passing through ceiling and floor, through brick barrier and spell barrier, seeking their victim. He did not cry out, not then. He is strong in a crude, primitive way, even as the Stone men were strong—strong to withstand weather and disease, hardy hunters, brutal lovers. And he is intelligent; if he were not, there would be no satisfaction in tormenting him. When I went to him tonight I could hear him moaning from the stairwell, but as soon as he saw me he was silent. The nightmares clung to him, crawling over him, close as a miasma, insubstantial as smoke. They probed with shadow fingers through flesh and bone, twisting the eyeballs in his sockets, the visions in his head. Red tears ran down his face, streaking the moonscape of pitted skin and jagged skull. I drew nearer, watching, riveted, as he writhed and wept. And then he jackknifed, for an instant—a second—shaking off his incubi, lunging for me with one huge fist. His strength was such that the spell barrier throbbed and sang at the blow, but it held, throwing him backward, and even as he fell the nightmares were on him again.

"Shall I call them off?" I asked him when I had studied him awhile. "Would you plead with me—would you *beg* me—to call them off?"

He made no answer, save for the stifled grunts of suffering.

"There is a small task you can do for me," I said. "Agree, and I will give you a respite—for a little time. For the duration of your task, at least." He knew I would not let him go. But he must have hope, or he will not endure. I will give him neither the labor of life nor the freedom of death, but I will *offer* both, and let him grasp at them in vain, and see his bitterness when he is left always empty.

I have many uses for him, and he shall serve my purposes, even while I feed off his pain.

"Will you accept my task?" I murmured, in a voice softer than the rasp of his breathing. "For an atom of quiet, a moment of deliverance? You have no other chance. *She* will not remember you. You were a pawn in her plans, a mere dupe, to be discarded when you had done your part. I alone have never abandoned you—and I never will. My child . . . my blood . . . Do not gnaw yourself in anger: I will have vengeance for us both. Her soft small face will not look so fair when I am done with it. Do not fear . . ."

In the end, he agreed. But it was a gradual end, long and slow in the coming, and I tasted every drop of his anguish, sweet as wine on the tongue. At last I ordered the nightmares to withdraw, sending them back to the empty cauldron that waited in the basement below. Later, I would melt them down, remake them in some other form. He was slumped against the wall, dumb now, mine to command. The sweat lay on him like slime and his own dirt befouled the floor.

"You are a mere beast," I said, "but a beast with brain—or brain enough for my needs. There is something I want—from the Eternal Tree."

I saw the flicker in his eyes as he glimpsed a chance of escape. But it died swiftly: he knew I would not be that careless.

"You will be released," I told him, smiling, mocking. "You will go freely from here, and freely return. If not . . . well, I shall put a spell on you, so the nightmares will find you, wherever you hide, and then they will never let you go. No hole will be small enough to conceal you, no shadow dark enough. Do you understand?"

He did not nod or speak, but his silence was assent.

"Then go to the Tree. You know the way. You explored all the paths of the ancient Underworld long ago, creeping like a thief through the caverns of legend. You have no soul to lose; you may sneak where others would not venture. On the Tree the heads are ripening. The one I want should be there now. She may not look as you remember—in the early season the heads are mostly still young, though they age fast—but you will know her, she will tell you her name. Bring me my coven sister Sysselore, who was Syrcé the enchantress . . . We were together so long, I would not be without her. Even in death I want her to see my triumph, and envy me."

"She will rot in days," he said harshly. "Maybe in hours."

"Fool! Do you doubt me still? I can brew a potion that will keep an apple as crisp as the instant it was picked—for months, even years. I will pickle the head in hell-broth, and it will stay sweet and firm for as long as I require. But carry her back quickly: those who die old are swiftest to degenerate."

"And then?" he asked, unable to exclude the faintest note of desperation—half hope, half fear—from his voice.

I smiled at him—for is he not my son?—savoring his illusions, toying with his trapped mind, his pliant emotions. "Then we shall see."

Later, when I opened the barrier, I marked him with the sigil Agares, the symbol of Finding. The acid burned deep into his skin, but though he hissed and sweated, he could not move until the brand was fixed. To remove it, he would have to flay his own brow to the bone.

"Return promptly," I whispered, "lest I become impatient." Then I let him go.

Tomorrow, there will be other matters. I must begin the

search for *her*. When the moon is at the full, I will prepare the circle.

"We should wait for the full moon," said Ragginbone. "The circle is more powerful at that time."

"We can't wait," Fern said tensely. "Morgus won't be content with collecting souls. Her Gift is formidable, and the strength of the Eternal Tree is in her. I must know what she's doing."

"Remember, she won't yet have realized that you know she's alive. You are young and inexperienced: by using the circle, you may betray yourself. I don't want to damage your confidence—"

"I haven't any," Fern interrupted, unsmiling. She was driving as they talked, and she did not take her eyes off the road.

"All I'm saying is that everyone makes mistakes. The more powerful the individual, the greater their capacity for error. Morgus has already shown her hand by what she did to this girl: her ego gives her away. So we have a slight advantage, a sliver of time. Full moon is in a few days. Don't slip up through impatience."

"I want to get on with it," Fern said baldly, "because I am afraid."

"Fear is healthy, but you should not let it guide you. In the conflict to come, the main responsibility may rest with you—though we cannot be sure of that—but you have friends and allies, known and unknown, and you must have faith in them. Even in Atlantis, among strangers, you found help. There is always help, if your intentions are good. Or so I like to believe. Don't try to take the whole burden on yourself."

"Last time, Will and Gaynor were in danger," Fern reminded him. "I couldn't bear it if they were hurt, or—or killed."

"The choice is not yours," Ragginbone retorted seriously.

There was a pause while the banks of the motorway rolled

past, a bridge arced over them, a lorry roared by in the middle lane, going too fast.

"When I killed Morgus," Fern said suddenly, "I mean, when I thought I did—it was unreal. I was pure spirit, detached from my body, trapped in the otherworld. A world where myths come true. I cut a head from the Tree and brought it back here. It was only when I saw the head in the context of reality that I felt horror. Under the Tree—in the caverns of Hel—everything was like a dream. My feelings were vivid, often intense, but not quite . . . normal. Since then, there have been moments when I have told myself: *I killed.* I killed a fellow human being—even if she was a psychotic witch queen with her mind stuck in the Dark Ages and her ambition fixed on an improbable future. It was only bearable because of the unreality factor: I never actually had to come to terms with it. I don't know if I can do it again. Here. In the real world. *I don't know if I can kill her.*"

"You may not have to," said Ragginbone, and there was gentleness in his gaze, though she did not see it. "Don't waste time agonizing. Right now, you should worry more about whether *she* will kill *you*."

"That makes me feel better," said Fern.

More motorway streamed beneath them; huge blue or green signs warned of approaching exits, distance from London, the next gas station or eatery. From time to time long rows of cones sprang up with apparently no other function than to congest the traffic flow. Reality, Ragginbone reflected, was every bit as strange as the surreal dimensions that clung around the edge.

Several miles later Fern resumed: "Where do you think I should do it?"

"Do what?" asked Ragginbone, emerging from temporary abstraction.

"The circle."

"Ah . . ."

"I thought of my flat, but there's a fitted carpet and anyway, even if you pushed back all the furniture there wouldn't be a lot of space. How big does the circle have to be?"

"Big enough," said Ragginbone unhelpfully. "If it's too small you will constrict the magic and it could burst the boundary or even explode. Besides, you need to maintain a safe distance between you and whomever—or whatever— you summon. The perimeter of the circle is your security. Too small, and the spell is overconcentrated. Too large, and it becomes stretched, so you cannot sustain it. That may have been why the circle Alimond made in your old barn all those years ago broke so easily. It was too big for her power."

"We should have done it at Dale House," said Fern. "I can't think of anywhere else large enough. We may have to rent a studio or something."

"Possibly," said Ragginbone. "However . . . there's a place I know that would be suitable. If I can persuade the owner."

Fern considered this. "Who *is* the owner?" she inquired suspiciously.

"He is Gifted—after a fashion. A street wizard, a potion peddler . . . There were many like him once. They drew horoscopes, and sold love philters, and checked the auguries for one side or both before history's forgotten skirmishes. Those with real power lived until they grew weary and then passed the Gate. Some had their throats cut in dark alleyways by whoever lost the latest skirmish, or choked on their own potions, or were tortured for secrets they did not possess. Religious organizations accounted for a good few. But this one . . . well, I think you could say he got stuck. Stuck in the past, more than four hundred years ago, but existing in the present. Out of sight, out of date, out of touch. He shut himself away from the world in his hermit's cave, and he never leaves. Or so he claims. Food is delivered and therefore presumably paid for, though heaven knows how. The building was reconstructed above him about a century ago, but he has spells enough to hide himself from the hapless and the curious. He says he has no contact with either witchkind or werefolk, but I'm not sure if I believe that. It may be wishful thinking on his part."

"He sees you," Fern pointed out. "Evidently."

"Reluctantly," Ragginbone amended. "He can be useful. He did me a favor when you were last in trouble. And I would not like him to be used by the wrong people."

"You mean," Fern translated, "you used him, but you don't want him doing any favors for anyone else."

Ragginbone smiled his appreciation, but did not answer.

"So where is this hermitage of his?" Fern demanded. "A desolate moor—a Welsh mountainside—a gloomy forest—if there is any gloomy forest left in this country, which I doubt."

"It's in the jungle," said Ragginbone.

"The *jungle*?"

"The urban jungle. Lost in the crowd—the easiest place to lose yourself in the modern world. He has one basement in an underground warren, one door among a million doors. In the country, people peer and question; in the city, who cares? Who notices?"

Fern said: "You mean he's in *London*?"

"Soho," said Ragginbone.

In Soho, anything can happen. There are strange secret bars that only open at three in the morning, clubs that switch their decor and their names every couple of months, people who change their identities, their faces, their sex. Buildings interconnect, with rooftop escape routes and hidden passageways. Subterranean kitchens steam and bubble. Sex shops and strip shows are available alongside the smartest restaurants, the coolest dives. In what was currently the most fashionable nightclub in town, Luc Walgrim was dancing. Most Englishmen dance badly: they are too inhibited, too protective of their machismo; they think dancing is for women and gays. But Luc was an exception. His style was deliberately restrained, his slow, snaky movements met the rhythm of the music at every other beat, his expression was that of someone whose mind was far away. His partner, intrigued, writhed closer, and then, when that expression did not alter, writhed away again. Luc did not notice. He felt alienated, out of place, not merely because it was Saturday night and he was sober—he had been drinking steadily but without apparent effect, and had achieved that state of black, illusory sobriety in which too many people think they are capable of driving a car. The wall on one side was all mirror, and for a moment, catching the reflection of the gyrating crowd, he thought he saw a carnival of dancers with animal heads, not masks but real animals, with red tongues and whiteless eyes . . . He looked for his own face, and it was gray and vulpine, fang toothed and point eared. He turned away and moved back toward the bar, trying to talk to friends, mouth to ear, against the clamor of the music, but all he could hear of their answers was braying, cackling, screeching. He ordered a cocktail from a barman who looked suddenly like a donkey, thinking rather too late that he had been unwise to stick with the absinthe.

Without conscious effort he found himself picturing Fern Capel appearing on the far side of the room, walking toward him. It was impossible to imagine her with the head of a beast; even on such short acquaintance, he sensed that she was always only herself. Yet he had very little idea who that self really was. He visualized her moving among the frenetic dancers with still, quiet purpose; the strobe lighting did not touch her; her face was isolated in its own pallor. Her lips parted and he knew she spoke, though he could not hear what she said. Then the image dissolved into the melee of the nightclub, and there were the animals again, making their animal noises, jerking their human limbs in a clumsy fandango. He called out, or thought he did—*Help me*—and there was a whisper in his head, louder than the surrounding cacophony: "Come with me." It took all the self-discipline he could muster not to run from the club.

Outside, he went where his feet took him. Past the statue of Eros, along Piccadilly, across Hyde Park Corner and on to Knightsbridge. The traffic was scarcer now, the beggars were asleep. Cabs curb-crawled suggestively at his heels, but he waved them away. In a doorway, he saw someone huddled in a blanket, moaning, but when he bent over hesitantly, she stared at him with glazed eyes and said she was fine. She may be dead by morning, he thought, and I can do nothing. Or she may be alive, and looking for another fix of whatever she is fixed on, and I can still do nothing. My sister's body lies in a hospital ward, and I have done nothing. He had found her teddy bear that day and laid it beside her, telling the nurses not to remove it. They indulged him. His father had not been to see Dana for nearly three weeks. Anger, frustration, guilt, despair had all gone cold inside him, and now the absinthe filled his mind with phantoms.

He was approaching his father's Knightsbridge home. It loomed over him in all its pale elegance, teetering above porch and pillar, slices of yellow light showing between half-drawn curtains. He was dimly aware that it was very late, surely too late for Kaspar, who rarely kept such hours. The front door opened inward and Luc retreated, moving from shadow to shadow, sheltering behind a gatepost. A woman came out wrapped in a full-length velvet evening cloak, black or some very dark color; his father followed. At least, he assumed it was his father, but he could not be sure, because the man had the head of a dog—a lean hound's head with dumb, obedient eyes. The woman's face was invisible, hidden in the lee of her hood. A car that must have been parked farther along the road drew up beside them, silent as smoke; the man opened the car door. The woman turned to say goodnight, and Luc saw under the hood.

He had been expecting some kind of cat, domestic or wild, a chocolate-tipped Siamese or a mottled ocelot. But the face beneath the hood belonged to neither animal nor human. The eyes were enormous, staring, deep as midnight; the skin shriveled against the skull. There was no nose, only two holes like pits set just above the mouth. The shrunken lips drew back from a ragged array of teeth. Even in his bemused condition Luc reeled, knocking his temple against the post, stifling an oath before it could escape. The woman got into the car. His father closed the door and stood watching while it drove away; then he went back inside the house. Luc slid to the ground and rested his brow on his hands, fighting in vain for some kind of clarity.

Fern telephoned his flat as soon as she returned to London. "Hello," said the machine. "This is Luc. Leave a message, and I may get back to you." It did not sound promising. She considered trying his mobile, but guessed he was at the hospital and it would be better not to disturb him. Instead, while Ragginbone went off on affairs of his own, she decided to marshal her troops. One particular meeting was long overdue.

"Oh," Gaynor said rather lamely. "I didn't expect to see you."

"Nor I you," said Will.

"I knew, if I told you, you'd create difficulties." Fern addressed the two of them impartially. "I've had enough of this idiocy. Sit down. I got you to come here because I need you—both of you. Ragginbone says I should accept help, and you—" she looked at Gaynor "—said you were already a part of this, and you—" she turned to Will "—well, you always have been. According to Gaynor, you're my team, so behave like one. You have to work together. Talking to each other would be a start."

"I never stopped talking to Gaynor," Will said, with only a

trace element of frigidity. "I simply haven't had the opportunity to do so—for quite some time."

"I'm in the book," Gaynor said before she could stop herself.

"I didn't know I was supposed to telephone you," Will responded evenly. "Somehow, that wasn't quite the message that came across."

"I didn't mean—"

"You ran off in such a hurry, you forgot to leave me your number."

"You could have gotten it from Fern! No—I mean, that wasn't what I . . . Look, if you'd wanted to talk to me, you would have called. You always do what you want; I know that. So when you didn't call, or—or anything, I assumed you didn't . . . want to."

"You seem to have worked out my motives very easily," Will said, masking uncertainty with sarcasm.

Gaynor fidgeted with her hair, a lifelong nervous habit, but did not attempt to reply.

"Time's up," Fern said, glancing pointedly at her watch. "If that was apology and reconciliation, I didn't think much of it, but it will have to do. We have serious matters to discuss. All the evidence indicates Morgus is back—"

"Back?" Will repeated. "But she's *dead*. Are we talking some kind of ghost, or a *tannasgeal*—or has someone been fruit picking on the Eternal Tree?"

"You're behind," said Fern. "Take your mind off your personal problems, and I'll fill you in."

In the end, she brought them both up to date, concluding with a brief account of her discussions with Ragginbone. In asking questions and debating possibilities, Will and Gaynor forgot their mutual embarrassment and inevitably began to talk to each other as well as Fern.

"What I don't understand," Will said finally, "is where Azmordis—sorry, the Old Spirit—fits into all this. And don't say he's out of it this time, because I won't believe you. He's never out of the game for long. He's like God or the devil: where Man goes, he goes."

"He's played both god and devil down the ages," Fern said. "And we were credulous: we fell for it. We worshiped him and feared him. He's grown strong on that. All the same . . ."

"He wants you on his side," Will persisted, "and you've turned him down twice. Could he be sending you this recurring dream to try to mesmerize you somehow? Third time—"

"Third time lucky?" Fern finished for him. "Perhaps. But I'm not a child now; he would find it very hard to get inside my head. My Gift is more developed: it guards me. Besides, if the dream is meant to mesmerize, it isn't working. It just fills me with horror. Worse each time . . . Let's leave it for the moment. Right now, Morgus is the problem."

"She can't be as dangerous as the Old Spirit," said Gaynor. "Can she?"

"In some ways she's more dangerous. He's been in the real world since the beginning; he knows how it works. He's become a part of what Ragginbone calls the greater pattern, an evil part maybe, but still only a part. His goals of corruption and despair are woven into the fate of the world, an underlying theme to our goals of happiness and decency and universal sharing. Morgus is different. She's lived too long outside. Her attitudes are those of the Dark Age. If she's heard of nuclear weapons, you can bet she thinks radioactive fallout is a kind of diabolical magic, something you could stop with a spell of Command. I suspect—I fear—that to her modern society is a toy shop full of entertaining new gadgets. Heaven knows what she may do with them."

"What you are saying," Will summarized, "is that the Old Spirit knows how to play cricket, but cheats, whereas Morgus thinks it's croquet."

"And plays by witches' rules," Gaynor added.

"Witches' rules," Fern echoed. "One of these days I must find out what they are."

* * *

She spoke to Luc the next day. He sounded distracted and told her at least three times he had found the teddy.

"Good," said Fern, giving up. "Hang on to it."

"Did you find out anything in York?"

"Not York, Yorkshire. I didn't go there to find out anything. I went to consult someone, and I consulted. Finding out comes next. Excuse me, but . . . are you quite all right?"

"Not really," he admitted. "A two-day hangover. The headache doesn't want to go."

"What *were* you drinking?"

"Absinthe."

"Absinthe makes the heart grow fonder," Fern quipped. "Sorry, that must be as old as the hills. It's poisonous, isn't it? I should have warned you, be very careful with alcohol at the moment. It lays your mind wide open. Anything could get in."

"I know," said Luc. "I think it did. I kept seeing people with animal heads. I looked in the mirror and even I had one. You were the only person who was normal."

"I wasn't there," Fern said, disconcerted.

"No, but . . . I imagined you."

"What sort of head did you have?"

"Something gray and foxy," he said. "Look, I'm not sure if it's important, what happened next, but maybe I ought to tell you. It wasn't a dream, but it felt like one, and you said I should focus on my dreams. Afterward, I went around to my father's house. I was walking home from this club and it's more or less on the way to my place. There was a voice in my head, and I walked and walked, and then I was there. He came out with a woman. He didn't see me; I just watched. He had the head of a dog, maybe a wolfhound, all lean and silvery, but his eyes were stupid. The woman had a cloak and hood. She got in a car and was driven away."

"What kind of animal was she?" Fern asked.

"Not an animal. I saw her for only a second. She looked—

hideous. A skull face with staring eyes, and no nose, and jagged teeth . . . This sounds insane, doesn't it? I was probably hallucinating."

"Probably," said Fern. "Could you ask your father who she was?"

"I rang him this morning. Said I was passing in a taxi the other night, and I'd seen him with someone. She's a Mrs. Mordaunt, Melissa Mordaunt. Apparently she's renting Wrokeby from him. His voice was strange when he spoke of her. He said something about *gratitude* . . ."

"He's lending her the house out of gratitude?" Fern hazarded. "But for what?"

"He never feels gratitude," Luc said flatly.

"I think," said Fern, "you'd better tell me more about your father."

Ragginbone called around that evening. "My friend in Soho has agreed," he said. "We can use his basement."

"When?" asked Fern.

"Friday," said Ragginbone. "The night of the full moon."

It is full moon tomorrow. I will make the circle, and call up the spirits, even the oldest and strongest, and put them to the question. I will summon Azmordis himself, if need be, but I *will* find her. I will find her in the end.

 Part Two

Valor

V ❧❧❧

In the city, you cannot see the night sky. Traffic pollution thickens the air, and the reflected glare of a million street-lamps fades out the stars. The constellations are numberless and stretch into infinity, yet a tiny cluster of man-made lights can dim their far flung fires out of existence. And the moon is paled, and hides its concave profile behind the hunched shoulders of buildings and the jagged crests of walls, and in the blur of unclean fogs. For the city is the unreal place, where nature and magic are diminished, set at a distance, and Man reigns supreme in the jungle of his own creation, controlling, manipulating, lost, and alone. Only the full moon is big enough, and bright enough, to impinge on the cityscape. And in the summer when the moon is hugest, the concrete towers cannot hide it, and it rolls into view around every corner. The glow is stronger than the electric lamps, and the creatures of the city gaze up into its golden face and remember who they really are.

On that Friday night the sky was clear and the moon seemed larger than ever, its brow lined and pitted with mountain ranges, its cheeks smooth with oceans of dust. It peered over the rooftops into the alleyway called Selena Place, and touched briefly on a shop window hooded with a shabby canopy, where a few stuffed birds showed their molting plumage in a glass case against a background of unswept cobwebs and unlit shadows. Soho was busy, but the alley was relatively quiet;

people came and went soft-footed from both the social club
and the unsocial, mumbling names not necessarily their own
into discreet intercoms. A ginger cat that was diligently exca-
vating a garbage can twitched at the moon's touch on its fur
and glanced up quickly with a glitter of eyes. It returned to
foraging, ignoring a passerby, looking up again only when a
group of four turned the corner. In front strode an old man
whose broad-brimmed hat and flapping jacket made him resemble the traditional concept of Fagin; a much younger man
and two women came on his heels. The cat surveyed them for
a moment and then shot up a vertical wall and through a broken pane. No one paid any attention. Beside the hooded window, the door of a shop that never opened trembled under the
impact of multiple knocks.

"Maybe he's gone," said Fern, after a pause.

"Never." Ragginbone lowered his mouth to the keyhole
and began to mutter words they could not hear, words that
crept through the crack and into the darkness beyond. The
door began to shiver of its own accord; chains rattled inside.
They caught the sound of scurrying feet and scraping bolts;
the door jerked open to the limit of a safety chain; part of a
face appeared in the gap. A pale subterranean face with a single boot-button eye. A smell of unwashed clothing wafted
toward them.

"Moonspittle," said Ragginbone. "Let us in."

"Too many. Two too many." Or possibly *too too many*. The
fluting whisper was thin with fear, shrill with obstinacy. "Go
away."

"We will never go away," Ragginbone said. "There is
power here. Feel it. You can shut it out but you cannot make us
leave. We will wait for as long as it takes."

"No . . ."

"*They* will see us waiting. They will want to know why.
They will want to know who is here, making us wait so long."

They? Fern mouthed.

"His bogeymen," Ragginbone explained, sotto voce. "Whoever they are. Probably everybody."

The safety chain was released; the door opened wider. A hand plucked Ragginbone inside. The others followed.

They found themselves groping in almost complete blackness. "Mind the furniture," said the voice of their host, receding ahead of them. With great presence of mind Fern grabbed the skirts of Ragginbone's jacket, simultaneously reaching behind her for Gaynor's hand. Will bumped into what might have been a small table, but it sidled away from him. Ragginbone said: "This way," and presently a dim light appeared at what must have been the far end of the room. They crammed into a narrow passage and descended a twisty stair where all but Fern had to duck under the roof beam, and then they were in the basement.

Minimal lighting revealed the shop owner, his small round body bundled in peeling layers of cardigan, his spindle legs inadequately trousered, exposing knobbed anklebones above his threadbare slippers. Tufts of hair stood out around his scalp like cloud wisps around a barren hilltop. He carried with him an odor of closed cupboards, stale woolens, things long forgotten left at the back of unopened drawers. His skin was bleached like that of some cave-dwelling creature who had never seen daylight, let alone sun. "You are not," he began, and then paused, losing the sentence, then finding it again. "Welcome here."

"We're sorry to intrude," Fern said scrupulously. "We need your help."

"You are . . . the witch?"

"I hope so." The flicker of a smile did not conceal her apprehension.

"Too young," he said. "Too green."

"She has the Gift," said Ragginbone. "I was very little older when I first drew the circle. And I think the power is stronger in her . . ."

Moonspittle looked unconvinced. "These others," he said. "You never mentioned any others."

"My brother, Will," said Fern, "and my friend Gaynor. We work together."

"The Gifted always stand alone."

"That explains a lot," Will murmured. "Isolation leads to arrogance, alienation from reality . . . No wonder so many of them go insane."

Ragginbone shot him a curiously bright look. "Enough talk," he said. "We have things to do."

The basement was unexpectedly large, book walled and low ceilinged, as if the weight of the buildings above had crushed the available space into breadth rather than height, and shelves and volumes were packed together like a many-layered sandwich. At one end was a conspiratorial huddle of chairs and occasional tables; at the other, a wooden bench was cluttered with chipped glass retorts, convoluted tubes, odd-shaped jars, and even a Bunsen burner. The inadequate lighting was further obscured by huge lampshades whose trailing fringes resembled jungle undergrowth. Fern found a fireplace hiding behind a screen and asked for a brush to sweep it out. "We do not need the fire," said Moonspittle, and he might have paled if he had not been so pale already; but Fern insisted. No brush was forthcoming, so she settled for an old rag that must have been used as a duster for several centuries. The others shifted furniture, rolled back odds and ends of carpet. The shadow of past magics was clear on the bare floor: the circle burned into the boards, and around it the dim tracery of ancient runes. While they prepared the room the ginger cat appeared from somewhere, getting under their feet, rubbing its moth-eaten flank against their ankles. "Mogwit," said Moonspittle, and picked the cat up, crooning over it. Fern helped herself to fire crystals and silver-gray spell-powder from his store, not wanting to draw on her own limited supplies, but he made no protest. Ragginbone applied a match to various gray-yellow lumps of wax; the electric lamps were extinguished, and in the candlelight the basement seemed to change. Too many sorceries had been performed there, and the fallout had eaten into the walls like dry rot, animating at a whisper. The darkness thickened; the furniture receded, shuffling away from the circle. Fern hissed: *"Fiumé!"* and the crystals in the grate spat blue flame. New shadows sprang up, leaping toward a ceiling that appeared suddenly higher, lost in gloom.

She found she was shaking with a mixture of fear and excitement, but excitement was the stronger. Now that it had finally begun—now that she was putting her Gift to the test, exercising her power for the first time in the deepest magics— she felt the touch of intoxication, the heady surge of an inner force that seemed to have no limits, no restraints. She moved around the circle, sifting the powder along the rim, chanting softly the words she had been taught. The rumor of the city was silenced; there was no sound but the quiet cadences of her voice murmuring the syllables of power in the tongue of Atlantis, the language of the Stone. When she had completed the circuit the powder ignited at her fingertip, kindling to a glimmer that curved away from her around the perimeter. Within, the space expanded until the straining boundary encased both depth and distance. Gaynor drew close to Will; involuntarily, he put his arm around her. Moonspittle shrank into a chair, clasping the restless cat to his chest. Ragginbone leaned forward; under lowered brows his eyes glinted like diamonds in a mine.

"She has gone too far," Moonspittle said with a quaver. "Feel it! Too far—"

"What does he mean?" Will asked.

"The circle is a channel," said Ragginbone. "She has opened it up a long way . . ."

Fern did not hear them. The magic filled her, absorbing every sense. She was both possessor and possessed. At the hub of the circle a figure took shape, molded in smoke: a woman veiled in red. Her substance appeared unstable, as if several forms were combined within a single outline, and she held in many hands a white marble marked with colored rings, which was the most solid thing about her. She lifted the veil, and bones shone beneath her changing faces, and her eye sockets were empty. She spoke through blurred lips in a distant chorus.

"Who are you to summon the sisterhood of seeresses? We do not recognize you."

"I am Morcadis," said Fern. "Surely a seeress would know me."

The marble was set in a hollow socket and glowed into life, fixing her with its terrible stare. "One of us has sought for you, but found you not. In the future, we will remember you."

"I thought seeresses could *see* the future."

"Only our sister Skætha could do that, but the burden was too great, and now she sleeps, never to reawaken."

"Then tell me the present. I need to know about Morgus, who anointed herself queen of witches. I thought she died in the fire, but that wasn't so, was it?"

"She shriveled into a maggot, and the maggot grew to a fetus, and the fetus became a woman who was born again from the River of the Dead."

"Did she return to the Tree?" Fern asked, knowing the answer.

"The spells that hid it from us have worn thin," the sisterhood said slowly. "The Cave of Roots is unoccupied, and only the birds fly between the worlds. Yet a thief prowls there even now, one that you knew."

"Who?" Fern said quickly.

"He is horned like a ram and clawed like a lion, and he was named for a king's sword, but the name was altered and degraded, becoming a byword for a beast."

"Kal," said Fern. She had not thought of him in a long while. "What is he doing there, now Morgus has gone?"

"He steals a fruit from the Tree."

"Who is it?"

"It is barely ripe; we cannot see. Release us: we have told you all that we can."

"Not yet." Fern made a swift gesture, tightening her grip on the perimeter. "I believe—I am sure—Morgus is at a place called Wrokeby, a country house somewhere. Can you see *her*?"

"We will not make the attempt," the sisterhood responded. "She has always concealed herself in black enchantments that may injure our gaze. We have only one Eye; we do not wish to have it blinded."

Fern glanced at Ragginbone, who gave a slight nod.

"Are there more questions," the woman asked, "or may we go?"

"One more," said Fern. "Did the River make Morgus invulnerable?"

"No blade can wound her, no poison choke her. But she is still mortal, and all mortals are vulnerable. Everything that lives must die."

"That is no answer," Fern said.

"It is all that we know."

"Thank you," Fern sighed, loosing her hold on the magic. The sisterhood removed the Eye and faded into vacancy.

"None other has ever . . . thanked us. We will remember you . . ."

In the dimness beyond the circle, Gaynor found she was pinching Will's arm. She heard Moonspittle mutter: "The Gifted do not need such courtesies." The cat writhed in his grip, spitting back at the fire.

Ragginbone said to Fern: "Don't overreach yourself." But Fern was already pacing the perimeter again, repeating the liturgy of summoning. This time, the vapor at the center condensed swiftly, darkening and solidifying into the figure of a man almost seven feet tall with the antlers of a stag. A doeskin covered little of a body where the muscles swelled like giant pods and vein stems entwined forearm and calf. His coloring was dark, not African dark or Asian dark, but a dark of the spirit, deeper than a deep tan, green tinted from the shadows of forest and jungle. The matted pelt on his head and chest was bronze-black; the eyes were set aslant under sweeping brows that met unnaturally low. His nostrils flared at the unwholesome smells of the stale basement and the traffic-ridden city beyond.

"Cerne," Fern said. "I give you greeting."

"Greeting, witch. Why do you call on me? I have no love for your kind."

"You once did," said Fern, "if love is the term. That is why I summoned you."

"Love was not the term," Cerne responded. "Love was the sentence. She hungered, and I fed her. She was more beautiful than you, taller, and her hair was midnight-black, and her skin was like cream. I bathed in her skin, and slept in her hair, and filled her with my lifeless seed, and she took it, and performed an abomination. I have no more love for witches."

"She plucked a spirit from the dark," said Fern, "and sealed it in her womb, and gave a life, if not a soul, to your son."

"He is not my son. The immortals bear no children: we have no need. Like the mountains we grow, enduring age-long, and like them we are ground into dust. Our life is the world's life. We may sleep, or sink into Limbo, but we cannot pass the Gate. My—son—is a blasphemy against the Ultimate Law."

"It wasn't his fault," Fern protested, provoked to unplanned indignation. "He had no will in the matter. He was born, and he suffers. You should care."

There was a pause, then Cerne threw back his head and

laughed. And laughed. The red cavern of his mouth was open wide, and she saw old bloodstains on his teeth, and the steam of his breath in his nostril pits. "Harken to the witch! I am the lord of the wilderness, the hunter in the night, a killer of both the weak and the strong. Men have worshiped me, and set aside for me the best cut of the roast, and sacrificed their own kin on my altars. And I should *care*? A sorceress stole my spawn and magicked it into existence—*and I should care*? What folly is this? Did you call me here to plead for the brute beast that is Morgus's brat? Would you defy the Ultimate Powers?"

"If they were wrong," Fern said doggedly. "Everyone has a right to love, or at least compassion, no matter how they were made. But that isn't why I called you. I have Morgus to deal with. I thought you would know her—her weaknesses."

"You are so close to the droppings of her womb—ask *her*."

"We are forever enemies. I burned her with fire crystals by the River of Death, but she crawled into the water, and was restored, and now no weapon can touch her. Yet I must kill her."

"*You* kill *her*?" She felt the smolder of his gaze probing her body. "The aura of magic is bright around you, but you are still small, and slender as a peeled wand. There is no strength in you for such a contest."

"I have strengths you cannot see," Fern said, hoping it was true. "I have to stop her. There is no one else who can."

"Then I wish you good fortune," said Cerne, with something that might have been a smile or snarl. "When I learned what she had done, I would have spitted her with these—" he indicated his antlers "—but she slipped from me, and shielded herself with spells, and after the beast squirmed free of her loins I knew I needed no other vengeance. Nonetheless, may the dark powers guide your hand. She has enjoyed life too long."

"I doubt if she enjoys it," said Fern.

He could tell her no more. She thanked him, as she had the

sisterhood, and released the spell. She was beginning to feel drained, and there were still other spirits to summon, and questions to ask, and she seemed to have received no answers, only more questions. Ragginbone poured her something from one of the glass retorts—something that looked ancient and mellow and tasted like cooking brandy.

Then she resumed the spell.

The full moon shone straight through the window into my spellchamber. The climate seems to have grown warmer since the old days: I opened the casement, giving the light a clear path, and the air that followed it was mild, smelling of the wood beyond. Then I drew the curtains over the other windows, lit the blue fire. I wanted to open the circle a long way, to reach far and deep, and the spellfire empowers me. Flimsy spirits, primitive and crude, had begun to cluster among the roof beams and under the tiles, sucked in by the vacuum of the ghostless house; I could see some of them seeping through the ceiling like a shadowy stain. They are mere elementals, individually ineffectual, but in swarms they have the insidious strength of massed bacteria. My dark magics attract the most basic type, the sort who are drawn to acts of power and pride. They both feed them and feed off them, surrounding the circle with their miasma. Nehemet saw them, too; I noticed her gazing upward, with the spell glimmer in her eyes.

I moved around the periphery, chanting the ancient words. In the center, moonlight met firelight, silver mingling with blue. There was a mistiness at that point that grew slowly denser; too slowly. Vague shapes interlocked, failing to materialize. I saw the veil of the seeress, and phantom fingers clasping the Eye, but they were too many, a whole sisterhood in a single entity. Their voices sounded somehow remote, as if echoing from within the Wrokewood, or floating down a moonbeam. "We are weary. Do not call us now. We will not speak again."

"Then go," I said. "All save one. I summon Léopana Pthaia. Let her come before me!"

The multiple figure dwindled into a solitary shape squat and rounded like the idols of the Mother, with the claws of an animal dangling between her bare breasts and a scarlet cloth over her sable features. The Black Seeress. She removed the cloth, showing the nose spread wide across her face, and the unsmiling curve of protuberant lips. Her bones were not visible, for she is the most powerful of the remaining seeresses, and the closest to mortal flesh, and it is not for her complexion that she is called the Black. She fixed the Eye in her left socket, and the ring of the iris darkened against its sudden glow.

"I am the Pthaia," she said. "What do you want of me?"

"I did not summon the sisterhood. Why did you not come alone?"

"We were bound together. There is too much magic in the night. Question me, and be done."

"There is one that I must find. She was named Fernanda, but I rechristened her Morcadis, in honor of her Gift. I would have made her my coven sister and mixed my blood with hers, but she betrayed me and fled, seeking my death. But I live, and have returned to the world, and will take back my kingdom! Yet first I must have my revenge. Where is she?"

"Neither too far, nor too near. Look for her, and you waste your sight."

"Why is that?" I demanded. Léopana was not usually so cryptic.

"*She* will find *you*. Have patience, and she will come. She is only a circle away."

"What do you mean? Speak more plainly!"

"I have spoken. You are clever, Morgus, and you rank high among the Gifted, and you think yourself beautiful. The River of Death has sealed your flesh against all weapons that bite, so you are as untouchable as a god. Yet I say to you, beware!

You are too proud, daughter of the north, too greedy, too vengeful; but there are those who are prouder and hungrier, and whose enmity runs deeper. Do not measure yourself against the greater foe, or overlook the lesser."

I felt her anger, and I knew her words sprang from that source, and were not a warning but a curse. The Eye smoldered but could not pierce. "I did not summon you for advice," I said. "Damn me with visions, or be silent. Have you nothing more to tell me?"

"Everything that lives . . . must die . . ." Her voice grew faint, and she plucked out the Eye, pulling the veil over her face and vanishing without dismissal. My grip on the magic seemed to be erratic, though I did not know why, and I poured my will back into the circle, drawing taut the perimeter, reaching out beyond the boundaries of the night. An old, old crone appeared briefly at the heart of the spell, half bald and dressed in corpse clothes, mumbling to herself. I knew her, of course: Hexaté, who had made herself a goddess among witches, and drunk the blood of a thousand sacrifices, and grown fat on human flesh; but she was nothing now. A senile hag who gibbered and cackled, sinking toward a sleep from which she might never awaken. For the immortals, senility can last a long time, and the sleep must be profound indeed that can carry them into Limbo. I banished her without questions, though she remembered my name, and I called on another of the old ones, the first spirits who have remained to consort with Men. He was manifest as a slight figure scarcely four feet high, his anatomy undeveloped, his face infantine and pure, save for the eyes. I say *he* as a matter of convenience and custom, but in fact the sex of the Child is not known, and his androgynous features may look sometimes more feminine, sometimes closer to those of a boy. He wore a tunic of white samite and a wreath of leaves on moon-gilded curls.

"Eriost," I greeted him, "who is also called Vallorn, Idunor,

Sifril the Ever Young, by your names I bind you. Answer my questions."

"You have left too many out," said the Child. "I am also Teagan the Beautiful, and Maharac the Corrupter, and Varli the Slayer. Question me as you wish, but you cannot compel my answer."

"I do not need to," I said. "The question is direct but the answer is obscure, and I think you will not know it."

"Ask," said Eriost.

"Even the Black Seeress answered me only with riddles and curses. You are too ignorant—"

"Ask!"

"I seek one Fernanda Morcadis, a witch of untried Gift and stolen skills. Yet it seems that her inexpert nets are too subtle for the gaze of the wise and farseeing."

A frown puckered the creaseless forehead; the knowing eyes glowed like marsh gas. "I feel no subtlety," he said. "There is something else, something—" And then he was gone. There was no warning: he disappeared like a light suddenly extinguished, leaving the circle empty. I stared, caught my breath—released it in a torrent of Atlantean. The suspense seemed to endure a long time, but in reality it was only moments. Then he was back, and the glow dimmed in his eyes.

"She has no subtlety," he repeated, and anger disfigured his innocence. "But she has power—though it may be less than yours—and the courage to use it. She will come to you—she will come soon—and when she does, you must kill her. Don't hesitate, don't try to trap her. *Kill.* Or you will not see another sun."

"You overestimate her," I said. "My Gift is greater, my will stronger. No weapon can harm me, not even the guns of the modern world. When I have her, I will snap her like green wood."

"Green wood bends," said Eriost. "You called me: heed my

words. She has a treasure you have never had. Mortals value it highly."

"What is that?"

"Friends."

I cursed him away, scorning his fears. What need have I for friends, when I can collect souls and imprison them in flagon and jar, when I can whistle the birds from the Eternal Tree and enslave both beast and man to my slightest whim? Friends are a weakness: they drain your emotions, hurt you, betray. I have Nehemet for a companion, and with the head of Sysselore I shall have whatever conversation I require. I wish Morcadis joy in her friendships. They will destroy her.

Nehemet wormed herself between my legs as if in affection, but I need none. Even ordinary cats are not by nature affectionate: they offer caresses and purring to gain the saucer of cream, the plate of fish. And Nehemet is a goblin cat, whose kind love only the hunt. Her gestures are a matter of style, a feline affectation.

She retreated, adopting her usual pose of statuesque immobility, while I invoked some of the lesser spirits who attend the practices of sorcery. If Morcadis had been using her Gift, they should have sensed it. They are akin to the elementals but far stronger, beings who rarely act but merely *are*. Their coming can bring temperature changes, freaks of weather, moods of oppression and foreboding, sounds and smells from the environment where they first flourished. Some are composites, spirit clusters of a hundred or more united in cloud form. Others make themselves visible with human features, or the masks and limbs of beasts.

They came and went at the hub of the circle in an unholy procession: Boros brought the howling of icy winds, Mallebolg the ogre was mantled in his own gloom, Cthorn appeared as a monstrous blob frilled with lip, Oedaphor bulged with a thousand unmatching eyes. Yet those eyes had seen too

little, and the others wailed, or groaned, or slobbered their ignorance.

"I seek a witch with friends," I told them. "That is rare
enough. Who are her friends? I *must know*."

But no one could answer me.

There was a girl, I remembered. The wrong girl. My emissary had taken her by accident, finding her in the same house
with Morcadis, and I had sent her back without learning her
name. She wore her hair very long for these days, and her
eyes were dark and frightened, like those of a nervous animal
paralyzed by the gaze of a predator. I could not call her, but I
searched deep in my memory to find her face, re-creating it
diligently in the nucleus of the spell, summoning her with her
own image. It takes great strength to perform such a feat, and
I felt myself growing faint from the strain of it, striving to
flow along the current of the magic, to reach the source of that
face and draw it to me. There was an instant when *something*
connected, and the power of the circle redoubled, and lightning stabbed upward from the perimeter, and the invading
moonbeams turned red.

And then she was there.

"Concentrate," said Ragginbone. "You *must* remain in control, or the results could be fatal."

"I can't reach him," Fern said, and her intensity was almost
savage. "I know he's there—I can *feel* him—but I can't reach
him."

"He's dangerous—unpredictable—half-monster. He may
resist your call. Expending your energies for such as he is
folly."

"I swore to be his friend," Fern said. "It's too long since I
spoke with him."

"You choose your friends ill," Ragginbone muttered, but
his mouth was wry.

"I know." She took a slow breath, repeated the summons.

"Kaliban, sword child, man-beast, conceived in sorcery from an empty seed, I, Morcadis, call you. Son of the demon, son of the witch, come to me! By your soul I conjure you! *Venya! Fiassé!*"

A darkness solidified at the circle's heart, growing horns. Red eyes gleamed in the werelight. A voice that was little more than a growl said: "I have no soul."

"Yet you came." Fern was panting from the force she had exerted.

"Your call reached a long way, little witch. Even beyond the world. I wondered . . . what evil have I done to merit so insistent a summons?" He grew more defined as he spoke, and the firegleam lit his face, showing the mark burned deep into his brow.

"What is *that*?" Fern demanded, and the direction of her gaze made no gesture necessary. "Who—"

But he withdrew back into darkness, shrinking inward upon himself, vanishing as swiftly as a genie into a bottle. "Kal!" Fern cried. "Come back! Kal!"—calling him not as a witch calls a spirit but as a mortal to a long-lost companion.

He did not come. In the circle, there was a blur of glitter and light, and another figure materialized abruptly. A small figure, leaf crowned and dressed in white, with the soft perfect features of a child. Fern had seen it once before, watching another invocation from behind a chair. "—wrong," it said. Its voice was sexless and pure. "What form of witchery is this? Who called me here?"

"You were not called," Fern said coldly. "Begone!"

She began the motion of dismissal—and stopped short, arrested by his next words.

"I seek a witch named Morcadis."

"Why?"

"You are she?"

"Why?"

"Your enemy has found you—"

"Good." Fern raised her hand. "Tell Morgus, since you have become her page boy, that *I* have found *her*. *Envarré!*"

The Child disappeared instantly. Ragginbone took Fern's arm, but anger had strengthened her, and she did not need support. "Bravado," he said. "It sounded well, even if it wasn't."

Moonspittle was muttering apprehensively, presumably to his cat. "Who—or what—was *that*?" asked Will.

"A spirit," said Ragginbone. "One of the oldest, despite its appearance."

"Evil?"

"Neither evil nor good, but, like so many of the old ones, it inclines the more to evil, or at least to mischief. Its preferred apparition is in accordance with its mind-set. It has no known gender, but can assume the semblance of either." He turned back to Fern. "You should not have admitted it."

"I didn't," said Fern. "It was just *there*."

"You must have relaxed your grip."

"No. I would have sensed that."

"The circle is too open," Moonspittle averred. "Anything can get in. Look now!"

Fern had not attempted a further summons, but in the midst of the spellground a gray dimness was gathering, coiling in upon itself, changing shape. Fern launched into another incantation, securing the boundary, but whatever was trying to manifest itself came from within, and did not need to violate the perimeter. There was a noise of wind, and the room grew bitterly cold. The liquid froze in the retorts, forcing out stoppers, causing one to burst with a sound like a gunshot; fluid leaking from another dripped into an icicle from the edge of the bench. Frost crackled along the spines of books. Gaynor's teeth chattered; Fern felt her fingers growing numb. In the circle, a blizzard swirled, and at its heart there were eyes as hard as winter. "Boros," Ragginbone said, through cold-stiffened lips. Fern croaked a dismissal, and the blizzard seemed to sag, losing momentum, and the eyes blinked and were gone, and warmth seeped back into the basement. The spellfire leaped in the grate, but it gave out little heat, though its core could have melted metal. In the background, Moonspittle could be heard complaining in a routine manner about the damage.

"He's right," Ragginbone said. "You appear to be attracting undesirable elementals. This is becoming dangerous. Close the circle."

Fern gave a quick shake of her head. "I am not done yet."

Nor was the spell. The last of the snowflakes were sucked into a blackness that bulged and grew, straining this way and that as if something with too many body parts was smothered in the gloom and struggling to escape. It did not want to be dismissed, grunting and bellowing with several voices. "Mallebolg the ogre," Ragginbone said helpfully. "He has three heads and a number of different personalities, none of them pleasant. God knows where he came from."

It took Fern some minutes to dispose of him, and even then the blackness did not disperse, merely turning paler and brown around the edges, settling into a featureless mass that simply sat there, pulsating very slightly like an animated blancmange. Gradually, some of it extruded into a species of double frill, fat and fleshy, which spread until it encircled over half the blancmange. Then it spoke.

"I am Cthorn," it said. "I have come. Feed me."

Fern uttered the familiar words of dismissal, but she was growing weary again and desperate, and they seemed to hold less force. A section of the lips extrapolated, shaping themselves into a tube—there was a sucking noise, a gulp—and her spell was swallowed up. The blancmange grew a little, ominously.

It said: *"More."*

For a second or two, Fern felt the upsurge of panic.

"Try fire," Will suggested.

This time, when Fern hurled her order, there was raw authority in her tone. The tube of lip shot outward, and Fern threw in the final *"Fiumé!"* even as it devoured the spell. Flame seared through the soft mouth parts; the lips crumpled and turned black; the whole blancmange began to shudder. Then it imploded, engulfed in its own substance, eviscerating the very core of the magic. Gaps appeared in the circle as the spellpowder was whipped into the vortex. Fern picked up the wrong jar, swore, swapped it, tried to fill in the chinks. The magic was flowing back now, leaking out into the room. The bookshelves heaved in a solid, moving wave. The ceiling arched upward until the distended plaster began to split and fragments floated down like leaves. The floor shifted uneasily beneath their feet. The cat had turned into a ball of madness: both Ragginbone and Moonspittle struggled to restrain him, flayed by whirling claws. Will threw his arms around Gaynor just as she reached to brush the plaster from her hair, inadvertently knocking him in the eye. Both of them gasped out breathless apologies. Something with too many eyes materialized in several parts of the room at once, staring out from chair back and book-spine, from grimy lithograph and splintered bell jar. Fern had abandoned the spellpowder and was fighting to regain control, ignoring a growing sense of helplessness.

"Orcalé nef-heleix . . . Vardé nessantor . . . Ai Morcadis thinéfissé . . . vardé!"

The eyes winked out. The perimeter was still broken, but the magic seemed to be contained, held within a boundary of pure will. The spellfire flared, blue flames licking around the pelmet, and in its livid glare Fern's face, too, looked blue, pinched with effort. "End it!" cried Ragginbone, but she rushed on, babbling the new summons in a frenzy of haste, before her strength failed altogether. "Dana!" she called, into the night, into the void. "Prisoner or wanderer, come to me!"

And for a few moments she was there—not the well-tended body in the hospital bed but as she must have looked at the party, with a swirl of hair not her own and the chiffon

tatters of her costume. Under the makeup her eyes were
frightened; her hands seemed to push at an invisible wall. At
first she did not appear to see her summoner, but then her
gaze focused on Fern, and she grew still, and the tip of her
nose flattened as if pressed against a glass. Her lips moved
soundlessly, but they could all read the words. *Help me . . .*

She vanished without dismissal into a surge of darkness.
The epicenter of the circle grew storm-black. An image developed in the murk: a girl's face, transparent as a hologram,
shining faintly. Fern murmured, bemused: *"Gaynor?"* Ragginbone's shout of warning came too late. Gaynor had slipped
from Will's grasp, stepped through a break in the perimeter.
There was a second when her features melded with those in
the circle, then she, too, vanished.

What happened next was something Fern would never remember very clearly: Will's panic, Ragginbone's harsh admonition, Moonspittle's squeak of protest. She was unable to
think anymore and ceased to try; instinct took over. "You'll
have to maintain the circle," she found herself saying, probably to Moonspittle. "Seal the boundary. Don't let anything
through. If you can hold the spell, I'll be back." She didn't
wait for objection or restraint. Her will was firm, her mind
empty. She had no plan of action, no doubt, and in that instant, no fear.

She stepped into the circle, spoke one word. *"Envardo!"* *I
follow.*

She followed.

At first, Gaynor thought she hadn't moved. She couldn't
recall entering the circle, only being there. There was a brief
uprush of light, a sensation of falling—and then the spinning
tunnel of radiance slowed, subsided, and she was left standing
as before, except that now the perimeter was unbroken. She
looked up, and saw the full moon streaming through an open
window, its light blending with the werelight so that she had

to narrow her eyes against the brightness. The only window in the basement had been small and high up, screened with cloth or brown paper. She began to be frightened—not very frightened, not yet, but frightened enough. She stared around her, trying to see beyond the circle, but all she could make out was a soaring darkness of vast black drapes depending from some vault far above. Then she saw the woman. A tall woman in a pale dress that glittered when she moved. Her hair hung down her back in a thick clotted mass; her bare arms were as white as the dress. The fire glow limned her figure with blue. Long afterward, Gaynor said: "Her face was beautiful, but it was like something in a surrealist painting. If you looked at it from a different angle, you knew it would be utterly horrible."

The woman asked: "What is your name?" Her voice was soft and sweet as the smell of decay.

Gaynor did not want to reply, but she knew she must. "Gaynor."

"That sounds like a modern contraction. The name I knew was Gwennifer. How interesting. So *you* are Gwennifer."

"I don't understand."

"Playing the idiot, is that it? It makes no difference. I used you before; I shall use you again. You were always invaluable to my plans. I gather you have befriended Morcadis now. Your folly—or hers. Where is she?"

"I think—outside the circle . . ."

"That's no answer. Tell me the truth: the magic binds you. Where is she?"

The pressure of her insistence was almost suffocating Gaynor; she struggled to breathe. Half choking, she could manage no other response. "Outside . . . the circle . . ."

And then Morgus realized what had happened. Two circles, two spells, drawn together in a single magical bond . . . *"Uvalé!"* she screamed, and a gap appeared along the rim where the flame flicker went out. She raised her hand. "Come to me!"

Gaynor felt herself impelled toward the break in the circle. She knew that to leave the spellground would be disastrous, but she could not seem to resist. Outside the perimeter, the dark shrank to normal proportions, becoming sweeping curtains against a paneled wall. A cat waited there, stone still, its hairless body blotched black and white. She thought the expression on its wizened face was one of total malevolence. Unable to stop herself, she set foot out of the magic, into the room.

The sudden cry behind her snapped the compulsion like overstrained elastic. "*Xiss!* Stop! I command you!" A hand seized her wrist, wrenching her back into the circle with such violence that she stumbled and fell. She tried to rise, clutching her rescuer. Outside the perimeter, Morgus was swaying from side to side like a cobra about to strike. Her eyes slitted; her mouth widened into a smile without laughter, all hunger and teeth. In front of her, the goblin cat began to prowl to and fro along the edge of the break, as though searching for that weakening in the barrier that would allow ingress.

"Morcadis," said the witch, very quietly, and "Fernanda Morcadis," louder now and clear as a chime.

"You were looking for me," said Fern. "I have come." She was breathless from the abrupt translocation, thrown off balance by Gaynor's desperate grip.

"I like your friend," Morgus went on, her manner lightening deceptively. "I knew her of old: she was always venial in sin, soft-hearted and soft-headed. A liability to all who stood by her. I shall enjoy questioning her again."

"She is young," said Fern, puzzled. "You have met before only briefly, in a dream."

"Youth!" Morgus said scornfully. "An illusion. Do I not look young to you? Everything is reborn, recycled, remade, even the spirit. She is Gwennifer the adulteress, though she has grown very plain. She cannot change."

"The world of Time has made you mad," said Fern. "You

are seeing old enemies in new faces. I thought *I* was the one you feared."

"Feared?" Morgus's tone was like silk. "Oh, no, my most diligent pupil. You betrayed me and tried to kill me, but all you achieved was to initiate my regenesis. I used to think I could not return without you, and indeed you have brought me back. You have made me invulnerable, unkillable. I have the power of the Gift and the power of the Tree and the power of the River. What have you got with which to challenge me? Nothing. I will take your little Gwennifer and sew up her lips with her own hair, and stitch back her eyelids, and she will have to watch the fate I will prepare for you, and it will be long and slow, and before I am done—"

"I will beg for death," Fern interrupted. "I know. They always say that." She was afraid now, and angry at her own fear, and every bit of emotion showed beneath the bravado. The circle closed at a word, rekindling to a glittering thread, but it made a flimsy barricade against the might of the witch queen. Fern knew she had only seconds to take them back—back to the cellar in Soho—and she tried to gather her remaining power, her Gift, but instinct was failing her and she had little idea what to do, or how. Morgus made a convoluted gesture and uttered a strange hoarse sound deep in her throat, a cry from an age before speech, and the boards at their feet began to split in many places, and green stems came through, thick and serpent strong, twining their ankles, holding them fast. Gaynor stifled a scream. In moments more tendrils had looped her body, pinning her arms to her sides; Fern snatched hers free just in time.

"I have you!" Morgus gloated. *"I have you!"*

She lifted both hands—

—and *something* shot out of the air in front of Fern and hit Morgus full in the chest. The force of its trajectory blew a hole in the perimeter that could not be mended; the witch queen reeled at the impact, borne backward, losing her grip.

Fern felt the snake lock slacken about her legs and kicked the
stems away, stamping them into the floor. Gaynor followed
her example. Morgus beat off her attacker and stood there
gasping, her dress ripped and red stained, her half-exposed
breasts swollen into tumuli from the arousal of power. Claw
slashes were closing slowly in her white skin, leaving residual blood trails that crisped into hardness against nipple and
ribs. The invader had dropped to the floor and crouched there,
yowling. Its ginger fur was discolored in the blue light and
much of it stood on end, bristling with magical static. It yowled
in the unmistakable language of cat fight and garbage raid.

Mogwit.

"Grab him!" Fern cried. "I have to concentrate."

Gaynor lunged just as Nehemet pounced. There was a moment of confused struggle: she felt her arm torn and never
knew which animal was responsible. Then she was back in
what remained of the circle, clutching a raging bundle of ginger fur. Nehemet threatened, her mouth stretched in a hiss;
but she did not attempt to spring after them. Morgus began a
charm or curse that was never finished. Fern felt her body
grow rigid with the buildup of power: she forced mind and
will, Gift and spell to converge in one instance, one word.
Gaynor felt her wrist seized, heard the Command—and the
circle spun into a hoop of flame, blurring, thickening. Light
swallowed them . . .

. . . and they were back in Soho.

It was Moonspittle who had secured the perimeter, controlled if not actually coerced by Ragginbone. Will, handed
the cat with a curt order to hold tight, had underestimated
Mogwit's strength: more than a hundred years as a wizard's
familiar had not only extended life but enhanced muscle
tone, though the cat's intelligence seemed to have lapsed into
second kittenhood. Once the circle was empty Fern and Moonspittle closed the spell on a shriek of rage that came from no-

where in the room. The fires sank, the electric lights were switched on, and the basement reverted to its own brand of normality. They presented the owner with his promised reward, a new ball for his pet and a collection of pornographic postcards from the Edwardian era, which Ragginbone had found in a secondhand bookshop. "That cat almost certainly saved our lives," Fern said. "I'll come back tomorrow and bring him some salmon."

"Smoked," said Moonspittle. "He likes it smoked."

"Nothing but the best," Fern assured him.

They took a taxi back to her flat. Ragginbone reserved his strictures for their return; Will didn't. They were recuperating in Fern's living room over wine and coffee before the tide of recrimination finally began to subside.

"Well," said Ragginbone judicially, "and how did Morgus look to you?"

"She's lost weight," said Fern. "I'm afraid—it's been transmuted into power in some way. She spent centuries in hibernation, feeding off the Tree, and now she's stronger. She said she has the power of the Gift, and the power of the Tree, and the power of the River . . . and I could *feel* it around me, against me. It was too much. I couldn't fight it."

"But you did," said Gaynor.

"We were lucky," Fern said somberly. "Just lucky. You can't rely on that."

"Still," Ragginbone remarked, "it's something to know the luck is with you. And Morgus *has* a weakness: that much is clear. The sisterhood told us: All that lives must die. It remains only to find a way."

"At least we know where she is," said Will.

"Does she know where we are?" asked Fern.

"We must hope not," said Ragginbone. "I doubt if the elementals had enough time to absorb their location. Meanwhile, we have various avenues to investigate. It might be worth having another word with Mabb: she's capricious and undependable, but the goblins seem to be deeply involved in this affair and she may have further information. Her folk have quick ears; they hear many rumors. Then there's this man Morgus has enspelled . . ."

"The superbanker," said Will. "Very rich, very powerful. That's always suspect. You don't get to be rich and powerful by being a warm, caring person."

"Precisely. Also his son, Lucas."

"Luc," said Fern. "I told you, he's Gifted. I'm sure of it. I'll be in touch with him." She felt a flicker of pleasure at the idea, a reaction she was determined not to reveal, but the feeling faded on another resolve, equally secret, less a determination than a compulsion. There was someone else she had to find, a friendship neglected, a debt unpaid. Kal. And if anyone knew Morgus's weak spot, it would be him.

She went to bed later that night thinking not of Luc, but of a half monster, double horned and lion clawed, who had once been her guide in the dark.

VI ✦✦✦✦

On Saturday morning, the light crept belatedly into the shop that never opened. Dawn had done little to illuminate the interior, but as the sun ascended a few adventurous rays found their way into the alley, past bleared glass and barred grille, sending two or three thin slivers of brilliance needling into the gloom. Ragginbone was lying on a couch at the back, well past sleep, thinking the long slow thoughts that came from a long slow life. The couch was hard and too short for his height, but the centuries had toughened him against all discomforts and he was conscious of only one physical lack, the warmth of Lougarry's body pressed against his side. He had left her in Yorkshire—her kind were ill-at-ease in the city—and he missed her silent companionship, her constancy, her soft unspoken whisper in his mind. Presently, he was distracted by the invasion of a newspaper inserted forcibly through the creaking mail slot. He rose to retrieve it, surprised that Moonspittle should have any such contact with modern life; but it was not one of the national dailies, only a local newsheet distributed free to anyone with an accessible door. Ragginbone sat down to peruse it, but instead found himself watching the darts of stray sunshine that traveled across the floor, until cloud or building cut them off for good. Their tiny glimmer revealed glimpses of mounded bric-a-brac dating back hundreds of years, shapeless hunks of abandoned furniture, many-pronged objects that might be

139

candelabra or the antlers of decayed hunting trophies. Everything was dim with age and dust, save for the occasional chink where a glint of residual color peeped through. Ragginbone wondered idly what secrets might be buried there, under the cobwebs and the dirt. When the sun had moved on, his gaze returned to the paper. It was difficult to read in the poor light—he switched on a nearby table lamp, but there was no bulb in it—however, his sight had sharpened with the development of his Gift, and though his powers were mainly gone now, that was one of many side effects that had remained. He was poring over an article about rescue archaeology on a site in King's Cross when Fern arrived.

Ragginbone admitted her; she had not yet mastered the knock that would summon Moonspittle. "I've brought the smoked salmon," she said.

Mogwit appeared from the nether regions, drawn by some mysterious feline instinct, and pressed himself against her legs, meowing persistently. His attentions continued even on the stair, where she almost fell over him. In the basement, Moonspittle accepted the salmon without thanks and presented it to the cat on a cracked saucer, whereupon Mogwit proceeded to toy with it like a disappointed gourmet.

"Maybe it isn't fresh enough," Moonspittle suggested.

"It isn't supposed to be fresh," said Fern. "It's smoked."

They left the cat to his mind games and Moonspittle prepared an evil-smelling beverage that he insisted was tea. Ragginbone drank it because he had drunk worse things in the sixteenth century; Fern drank out of politeness. "I've been wondering," she said tentatively, "I've got only a limited supply of fire crystals and spellpowder. Where do I go to restock?"

"All the same stuff," Moonspittle responded. "Spellpowder is made from crystals. Ground down, mixed with . . . something. Only one supplier. If he isn't dead. Haven't seen him for a while."

"You haven't seen most people for a while," Ragginbone pointed out. "How long?"

"Saw him—oh, in 1850. Remember very well. He had a calendar. He liked to keep track of time." Moonspittle's tone implied this was a rare eccentricity.

"What's his name?" said Fern.

"Neb Goathless." It was Ragginbone who answered. "He's a dwarf—one of the true dwarves, not just a short human. There were many in the old days, but they were fond of war, and now they are all but extinct. He controls the processing and sale of the crystals, but the number of his customers must have fallen to almost nothing through the twentieth century. The witchkind have become so few. I can't think of anyone who has been in contact with him recently. He may indeed be dead."

"Where do the crystals come from?" Fern inquired. "Are they man-made, or—?"

"They come from the mines," Ragginbone explained. "The mines of Gol. It's a place in the otherworld, deeper than Hades: there used to be many entrances from the real world, in caverns and subterranean tunnels, but they have been sealed off. There is only one way in now, and it's guarded by afreets. I went there once—just once. Visitors are not allowed in the mines: they are dark and perilous."

"I'd imagine they are," sighed Fern. "I suppose I shall have to go and see this Neb Goathless one day. Do you know the way?"

"Maybe," said Ragginbone; and: "He used to deliver," volunteered Moonspittle. "To special customers. He knew I didn't go out."

"Anyway," Ragginbone concluded, "you have enough supplies for now. It would be hazardous to attempt further magic at the moment; elementals like Cthorn and Oedaphor are still around, and they would almost certainly be drawn to it. Now we need more mundane research." As he spoke, his thought strayed to the newspaper stuffed in his jacket pocket. Perhaps that was why he missed the unnatural blankness of Fern's assent.

"Of course," she said. "I'd better get going. Thanks for the—the tea."

As she left the room, she noticed Mogwit had polished off the salmon and was now curled in a chair, looking, with his patchy fur and smug expression, the picture of feline raffishness. He ignored his benefactress completely.

That evening, she drew the curtains in her flat well before dark. She had canceled a visit to the cinema with friends, pleading PMS, and although she hovered on the verge of calling Gaynor, even lifting the receiver and starting to dial, after a moment she replaced it in the cradle, aborting the call before it was made. She was learning the value of backup in a dangerous situation, though it went against her instincts; that night she had many reasons for wanting to act alone. With Ragginbone's warning in mind she spent a long time in preparation, screening the room with spells of concealment and protection, a web of magics that would allow only the most insubstantial elementals to pass. She blocked the chimney and placed a handful of fire crystals in the grate, igniting them at a word. A few drops from one of the phials damped down the bluish flames, producing instead a thick pale smoke that coiled out into the room, thinning to a mist that blurred vision and stung the eyes. She spoke the incantation she had learned in the Cave of Roots beneath the Eternal Tree, in the days when she was Morgus's apprentice, her spirit stolen from her body and held captive at the witch's whim. The smoke drew together, condensing into a swirl opaque as porridge, which spun around an epicenter and darkened to the color of storms. The picture developed slowly, dark on dark. A glimmer of light grew between writhing pillars: a cave, with stalagmites springing to support the roof, and the red gleam of torches, and the creak of a huge wheel revolving ponderously in the background. Dimly she made out the human figure spread-eagled against the spokes, a giant of a man all muscle and bone, the ribs straining at his torso, the knotted sinews in his arms almost bursting the skin. Here and there she could see the spikes that held him in place thrusting through his flesh, and the dark blood that drizzled down his limbs. The wheel turned; his mouth opened in a scream that she could not hear; sometimes sound was late in coming to the spell. The picture focused on his face, upside down: the throbbing bulge of his throat, the ridged lines of jaw and cheekbone, the white half-moons of his eyes, upturned in his head. Fern wanted to look away but she could not. Sound arrived as a shriek, earsplitting, agonized, abruptly cut off. Everything went black.

Other images followed, some faintly familiar, some strange, many of them horrible. A path winding through gray meadows in a light that was neither day nor dusk, and the back view of a man striding steadily, purposefully, and far behind him a frail ghost whose robe trailed like a shroud. A river of molten lava, rippled with fire; spirits danced in the vapors above it, and something that was not a bird plunged screeching from a ledge, skimming the heat on featherless wings. Then a cauldron full of a red viscous liquid swimming with pale noodles that might have been entrails; an eye popped to the surface, and a severed hand, only to sink from view again. The cauldron was made of black metal, but presently it began to glow dull red, and the contents bubbled into steam, and shapes poured out, rising like smoke or scrambling over the rim—human shapes patched together from broken limbs and shattered skulls. One came toward Fern as if rushing out of the picture: its nose was crushed and a sword swipe had split both lip and jaw, but its eyes shone with an unholy glow. She murmured a soft word, and it vanished abruptly, the image clouding into darkness. There was a long drawn-out pause;

then the scene lightened gradually into a green glimmer filtering between many leaves. They resembled oak leaves, but
larger, and they rustled gently as if filled with muted whispering. The spell-scene pulled back, showing a fat yellow fruit
ripening slowly out of sight of the sun. The process appeared
to accelerate: irregular lumps swelled on either side, ears unfurled like petals, eyeballs bulged against sealed lids. Hair
came last, sprouting from the crown and flowing down to
great length. A tiny white spider began crawling up one dark-
gold strand. The sallow rind warmed to pink; the eyes opened.
She's beautiful, thought Fern, and: *I know her.* But the woman
she had known was old and withered, all greed and furtive
malice; this was a witch from an enchanted island, radiant
with youth. Yet the look in her eyes was the same.

Sysselore, Fern said to herself. *This is the head of Sysselore.*

A dark hand intruded, wielding a notched hunting knife. It
cut the stem, and the head was gone.

The picture changed. In a corridor full of shadows Fern
glimpsed a retreating figure moving with swift pace and lilt-
ing hips. Her white dress glittered in the dim light. Then there
was a hill with three trees blackened from a lightning strike;
then bare moorland and a wolf running that might have been
Lougarry. These images passed very quickly; dark returned.
She was back in the caves. But this time the Underworld was
empty, save for the faint twittering of the ghosts and the water
notes of the spring of Lethe, sweet enough to erase all pain,
and memory, and love. As Fern watched a shadow crossed the
picture; she caught sight of a curling horn, an eye that gleamed
red under a lowering brow, the massive hunch of a shoulder.
At its flank hung a pouch whose function Fern recognized:
hair spilled from the top, and a white spiderlet scuttled to
safety within. Fern recalled seeing such spiders during her
sojourn beneath the Tree: they grew into arachnoid monsters
the size of dinner plates. The spell-scene followed the creature through cavern and tunnel: it seemed to be part man, part

beast, clothed in skins or its own fur, moving silently on taloned paws. "Kal!" Fern hissed, knowing he would not hear. He must be running errands for Morgus, though not willingly, she was sure. Perhaps that was why he would not stay, when she had called him to the circle. Ragginbone had told her the rune on his forehead looked like the rune of Finding; he might have feared to betray her whereabouts to his mother.

The scene shifted again, melting into a grayness of rain. Wipers swept across a windshield. Then—as on the road to Yarrowdale—she saw a vehicle rushing toward her, something huge, maybe a lorry, and headlights blinking in her eyes, and behind the oncoming wheel a brief vision of a death's-head, its mouth fixed in a lipless grin. She felt rather than heard someone scream, and knew it was herself—

She found she had doubled over as if at a blow, shaking. She straightened cautiously, half afraid to look, but the smoke scene had moved on. Now the rain was black, streaked with lamplight and neon, and beyond it reared the glittering façades of banks and brokerage houses. She felt herself drawn into the picture, swept along crowded pavement, through snarling traffic. She tried to resist, knowing her destination, but the magic had taken over. The Dark Tower soared ahead of her. She was sucked up the endless shaft, whirled away on the escalator. And there was the office, the desk, the suit beyond, though as ever the spell avoided his gaze. But the red file was missing. Instead, she found she had produced her own file and set it in front of him. The knife slashed a shadowy arm, and something dripped from it that might have passed for blood. "Sign," said a voice she thought was hers. He picked up the quill—

The magic shrank inward, distorting the image into cubist fragments; then suddenly it imploded, and there was only smoke. She was in her own living room, sitting cross-legged before the fireplace, and the crystals were spilling out of the grate, and torn vapors hung on the air. She unblocked the chimney and let them go. Only when the last wisp of fume had departed did she unbind the protection spells and open the window to admit the midnight breeze.

Before she went to bed, she plucked an ivy twig from the square's garden and taped it to the front door.

On the Sunday, Will and Gaynor met for lunch at a riverside pub in Hammersmith. They paid on ordering, causing a brief tussle over the bill that Will won. He was nervous, and consequently annoyed with himself, and brushed aside her offer to pay with unusual curtness. Two years before, at the end of a period of danger and growing intimacy, she had walked out on him without saying good-bye—a brand of rejection that was rare in Will's experience—and the wound to his ego still smarted. If there was more than ego involved, he suppressed the notion. Although he was chronically broke and his production company had yet to produce anything, he had never gone short of girlfriends: generally long-legged, high-minded beauties who made it a point of honor to pay their way. Gaynor's legs were not particularly long and her face was not particularly beautiful, lending itself more to sweetness, sadness, and sympathy than any expression of assurance and poise, but she had her own independence.

"Are you sure?" she said.

Grunt.

"I'd really much rather—"

"No."

"It's just that Fern says you're not awfully well off at . . . the moment . . ."

"Fern says? The voice of the oracle? I didn't know financial omniscience was part of her Gift. I'm doing fine. Take this."

He thrust a glass of lager toward her. Gaynor accepted it meekly, embarrassed by her own lack of tact. They found seats on an outdoor terrace overlooking the Thames; the gray river took the duller gray of the sky and sheened it with silver.

A breeze off the water freshened the stuffy city air. There was a short silence, then they both crashed into conversation at once.

"It's been too long since we—"

"I'm sorry I—"

They stopped, abandoning both sentences unfinished. Will pulled himself together first. "Why don't we start with the weather? That's a nice, safe subject that should keep us both away from any areas of potential awkwardness."

"It hasn't been a great summer so far," Gaynor complied.

"Very English," Will agreed. "Cloudy skies, occasional showers, lots of isobars."

"I always expect to see those wavy lines passing overhead," Gaynor offered.

"You may yet," said Will. "As we both know, anything can happen, and when we're around, it usually does. I'd only just got over the events of 'ninety-eight when Fate hit me with more last Friday. The gate-crashers were particularly nasty."

"The thing with the lips . . ." Gaynor shivered. "Did Fern actually kill it?" She knew enough about magic to be aware that otherworldly beings could rarely be depended on to die promptly.

" 'Fraid not. Ragginbone says it's an elemental, so it can sprout up again anytime. Apparently, it's attracted to acts of sorcery—but I can't imagine Fern's in a hurry to try any more of that. She was pretty horrified when you just stepped into the circle and disappeared." He added, rather more softly: "We all were."

Gaynor thought it prudent to ignore the softness. "You don't think she'd try something alone?"

Will opened his mouth to refute the suggestion and then shut it again, recollecting past experiences. "I hope not," he said shortly. "She's not stupid. She must know she isn't ready to confront Morgus."

"She knows." Gaynor's words were bleak with memory.

The arrival of their food created a welcome intermission.

"Did Morgus say anything to you?" Will asked, dispensing cutlery.

"Oh, yes. It was very strange: she talked as if she knew me, not my face but my name. She said I looked different—plainer. Maybe she thought I was a reincarnation or something. She called me Gwennifer."

"Guinevere," said Will. "That's where Gaynor comes from. You must know that."

"I never really thought about it. It always seemed too glamorous a name for me." Suddenly she laughed. "You don't suppose she really thought I was a reincarnation of the original Guinevere—Arthur's queen—the ultimate femme fatale? Me? That would be utterly ridiculous."

"Not from where I'm sitting," said Will. His smile narrowed his eyes to bright slits, blue against a freckle-topped tan. His hair was blond from what little sun the season had provided. She thought she saw new lines on his forehead, evidence of maturity, or so she hoped, and a sudden warmth rushed through her that was both wonderful and terrifying, heating her cheeks to a glow. The garlic mushrooms on her plate became mysteriously uneatable.

"I never saw you blush before," Will continued presently. "You should do it more often. It suits you."

"I don't get many opportunities," said Gaynor.

"That's not what I hear. According to Fern, some man is always dumping his troubles on you."

"Yes," Gaynor replied before she could stop herself, "but that doesn't make me blush." Panicked that she might incriminate herself further, she rushed on. "We were talking about Morgus. Fern can't deal with her till we find her weakness, whatever that is—"

"If she has one."

"The seeresses sort of implied it, didn't they? Everything that lives must die."

"That isn't prophecy, that's common sense," Will retorted. "*I* might have said it."

"Really?" murmured Gaynor, with a furtive grin.

There was a brief check in Will's manner; this time, his eyes narrowed without the smile. "The real issue," he declaimed in an edged voice, "is what *we* can do. Fern has the Gift, but we have gifts of our own. I can't immediately remember yours, but *I* have common sense. And there are more ways than magic of finding things out."

"You mean ancient manuscripts," Gaynor said. "I could look up some stuff about Morgus. She must get a few mentions."

"Ancient manuscripts, modern manuscripts. Questions. People. I told Ragginbone we'd investigate the superbanker."

Gaynor forgot to balk at the "we." "I know nothing about banking," she said. "Nor do you. I don't even know any bankers."

"Yes, you do. Everybody knows a banker nowadays. It's one of those embarrassing facts of life. A couple of generations ago everybody knew a bishop; now it's bankers. I can think of at least two old school friends who are in high finance. One of them's in prison, but it's the same thing."

"I don't know any," Gaynor maintained. "I—oh, shit."

Will cast her a questioning look.

"Actually, I do," Gaynor confessed. "It had slipped my mind. Wishful nonthinking. Hugh."

"Hugh who?" Will uttered owl-like. Hadn't Fern mentioned someone called Hugh?

"Hugh Fairbairn. He's married to a friend of Fern's—an acquaintance really—called Vanessa, only he says she doesn't appreciate him. He likes me. I've had to refuse to—to appreciate him twice already."

"Good." Will picked up a fry that had long gone cold and took an absentminded bite. "We can dispense with his help. I'll get hold of Adam. He's already declined to invest in my production company, so he owes me."

"I'm afraid I don't understand."

"He failed in his allegiance to our old school tie," Will explained.

"You never wear a tie."

Will abandoned the fry and shoved his largely untouched plate to one side. Gaynor's garlic mushrooms were beginning to look soggy. "Why don't you just drink up and I'll get another round?" Will suggested.

The conversation deteriorated rapidly when Gaynor wanted to pay for it.

In the small hours of the morning a mist had oozed out of the ground and hung in pale ribbons along the verges of the Wrokewood, screening the façade of the house. The walls showed only their stony roots rising out of grass and gravel. Above the mist, pointed roofs and gnarly chimneys floated as if detached from their moorings. The stump of the old tower was completely hidden. Such mists normally kept to the open fields, but rain had dampened the earth and the mild air drew the moisture upward into fogs that were thicker and more extensive than usual. A benighted local, on the road after a drunken party, saw the disembodied gables outlined against the predawn gloom and hurried away, sobered and shivering. The house had never had a bad reputation, but with the arrival of the latest tenant there had been some mutterings. Builders and deliverymen had talked of a changed atmosphere. The evacuation of the ghosts had produced strange ripples, which touched sensitive minds. The nervous reveler, quickening his pace on the three-mile walk to his home village, did not see the mist curdling in the wake of a passing figure, or the clawed feet padding beneath the veil, across the grass to the house. There was no knock or chime, but the front door opened and someone went inside. A little of the mist went with him and hung around the entrance hall, making the air clammy.

"You have it?" said Morgus.

For answer, he passed her the pouch at his side. It was heavy, and long tresses of hair spilled over the top. Morgus seized a handful of the hair and lifted the contents clear of the bag. "My coven sister," she said. "My Sysselore. It is *good* to see you again."

"I will rot swiftly in this world," snapped the head. "Why bring me here? What have we to say to each other that we have not said before, many times?"

"I have missed your sweet discourse," said Morgus. "Fear not: you will rot only at my pleasure. I have potions that will preserve you in this form for as long as I wish. Of course, I may let you age a little first. Your cheek is smoother than it was, but I might prefer to see the Sysselore I knew and loved."

"You look younger, too," said the head. "Maggot magic, no doubt. It doesn't suit you."

"Naughty," Morgus chided, pinching the cheek so that sap spread like a bruise under the rind. "You seem to have forgotten your courtesies. Am I not still your queen?"

She turned to Kaliban, who had shrunk back into the shadows. "You have done well, though it took you too long. Enough of freedom. Get you to your attic, and for a while I may let you sleep in peace, if it pleases me."

"Take this brand off my brow."

"The brand is there for good. With it, I can find you, wherever you may skulk. Now go, or I will set the nightmares on you!"

He made a half move toward the door, visibly torn, and her smile widened. Seeing it, he wheeled and began to climb the stair. She followed him, carrying the head, ready to reseal the spells that bound him. The bag lay where she had tossed it, discarded. The cat Nehemet came, and probed it with a curious paw, and sniffed at it, and let it be. When the cat had gone a white spiderling emerged and scuttled across the floor. On the Tree it had been scarcely bigger than an aphid, but now it had grown to thumbnail size. The vitality of this new dimension surged through its tiny body: it pulsed with the urgency of Time and the potential for growth. The life of a tree is slow, measured in centuries, but the life of an arachnid is swift, desperate, and hungry. The spider's minute germ of thought sensed that it had found a place with room for expansion. It moved eagerly, following instinct, drawn toward the sapling of the Tree that had nurtured it. The house spiders might have tried to kill it, for it was still undersized, but most of them had gone with the ghosts, unsettled by corridors that felt suddenly too bare. When it reached the conservatory it ascended the tree trunk and crawled under a broken leaf, sucking the sap that bubbled from its veins. Soon, the leaf would no longer conceal it.

In his attic prison, Kal waited. Dawn came and went, a sunless affair that lightened the room only to show the dust. When he was sure Morgus would not return, he removed a package that had been tied up in his hair, a package looted from the cave beneath the Tree where the witches had dwelt for so long. He shook a little red powder out onto the floor, mixing it with spittle, using a wood splinter to pound it into paste. Presently, it began to steam; both the surrounding patch of floor and the splinter turned black. He took a scraping on the splinter's end and, bracing himself, applied it to his forehead. Only an indrawn hiss of breath, a fixed grimace betrayed his agony. He sat with his teeth locked against a scream while the sweat rolled down from under his hair and the pain ate into him. Eventually, he wiped the paste off with a rag of old curtain and daubed the wound with another rag soaked in saliva, which was the only moisture available. Then he repeated the whole process, slightly higher up on his brow. Not only would the rune of Agares find him for Morgus, but for anyone who knew the spell; it was more efficient than an electronic tag. With it, even beyond the prison, he would never be free.

In the evening, the hag came from the kitchen, bringing him a plate of food, the reward for his service. Switching on the single naked lightbulb, she did not seem to notice the acid mark on the floor. After she had gone, he peered at his reflection in the window, lifting the swatch of hair with which he concealed his brow. It was difficult to see clearly under the overhead light, but he was almost sure the fresh burns had begun to obliterate the brand.

Down in the basement, where Morgus kept her phials and philters, the head of Sysselore sat in a pickle jar, mouthing furiously.

"I will take you out when you are ready to be polite," Morgus said, smiling to herself as she moved from bottle to bottle, preparing another potion in a basin of stone. She had found little to please her since her aborted encounter with Fern and Gaynor, but now she smiled with genuine satisfaction.

She too had friends.

Fern felt she needed Sunday to herself, if only to think. But her thoughts went around and around like rats in a barrel, going nowhere, straying off at tangents concerning Luc or Kal and returning always to the place where she had started: the impossibility of destroying Morgus. She met Luc on Monday, this time at his own flat, situated in a mews over a two-Porsche garage. "Bankers measure their success in Porsches," he told Fern without visible humor. "I know someone with four. One for each suit."

"He only has four suits?" Fern said.

"Oh, yes. And one of them's Chinese red."

The interior of the flat was a surprise: its white-walled minimalism was negated by overcrowded bookshelves and unlikely paintings, including a huge grayish abstract resembling an enlargement of the cerebral cortex, a snowscape clearly influenced by Caspar David Friedrich, and some original architectural drawings of what seemed to be a chapel. The latest technology was slotted into designer units: widescreen TV, DVD player, and a music center with strategic speakers. There was a wafer-thin sofa with stick-insect arms, one armchair of the same design, two others from the Edwardian smoking-room era. A half-full ashtray and unwashed glasses evidently awaited the attention of a maid. Sleek glass lamps dispensed a slightly chilly light that made the apartment feel colder than it was. Luc switched on a fake fire with gas-powered flames that gave out no heat. "This place is a bit of a mess," he apologized. "I used to be tidy, but lately I haven't bothered."

"It isn't a mess," Fern said. "It's just—lived in. Not enough, perhaps."

"I prefer the hermit's cell," he explained. "Bare, uncluttered—but clutter always creeps in somehow. I grew up in nouveau riche luxury—my mother had no taste, my father no time—but Westminster and Oxford turned me from tough into toff, at least on the surface."

"How often have you used that line?" Fern inquired.

"Once or twice."

"It's quite good," she affirmed. "But the tough shows through. Sometimes."

He had removed his tie and poured her a G and T, himself a whiskey. "Like you," he said. "The witch shows through—sometimes. You said you were going to find things out."

"I saw your sister." The words were out before she had time to doubt their wisdom.

He turned his back on the liquor cabinet, giving her a long, still look. "You mean—*not* in the hospital?" The tone was muted, but she detected his reservations.

"Last seen wearing a long floating dress, many-layered, probably chiffon, and lots of hair, presumably false. The lost spirit tends to retain its latest physical appearance, clothes and all. I shouldn't think she understands what's happened to her. Even if she does, it's all dreamlike, unreal . . ."

"Where is she?"

"If I tell you," Fern said, "you must promise me not to rush into anything. One wrong move, and she might be lost forever. You have to believe me. I know what I'm doing." *I think.*

"You described her costume accurately," Luc said. "There's no way you could have known . . . unless you've spoken to one of the party guests."

"I might have done," Fern conceded. "Our social circles probably overlap. You can trust me—or not. It's up to you."

"I don't have a very trusting nature," he said, "but I believe you. Call it gut instinct." He passed her the gin, sat down in the modern chair. "Go on."

"She's at Wrokeby," Fern said. "She never left. Your father's tenant there is . . . a witch of a different color. A collector of souls. At a guess, she was at the party—I don't know why—and took offense at your sister's disguise."

"Took *offense*? I don't understand."

"She's Morgus—the real Morgus. She left the world a thousand or so years ago, but she didn't die, she was merely waiting—and now she's back. She wants power—control—revenge. She may be using your father in some way. She has a skill and a Gift far beyond mine. I'm just a beginner."

"Why should she want revenge on Dana?"

"She doesn't," Fern said. "Dana was an extra. Morgus is made of psychoses: she would steal a soul to torment, merely for an act of *lèse-majesté*. *I* am the object of her vengeance. When she took my spirit, I was to be her connection to the world of today. But I escaped, and betrayed her, and burned her in spellfire. She should have died, but her magic was too strong. She was reborn from the River of Death and returned without me, and now she cannot be killed by normal means, if at all."

"If this is true—" his face was cool, noncommittal, afraid of credulity, "—how could you know so much? How could you see Dana?"

"You came to me: remember? This is the truth you sought. As for *how*, I drew the magic circle: I wanted to call up certain spirits for questioning. I tried summoning your sister. The circle works in two ways: it can compel anyone in the vicinity to enter, and—if you have the power—it can open up a channel to another place. Dana appeared in the circle, but she was still imprisoned elsewhere. She has to be at Wrokeby."

"So we go there, and find her."

"No."

His mouth stiff, he sat back in the chair, turning and turning the whiskey tumbler in restless hands. "Explain to me why not. I am not afraid of witches."

"You should be. We're not talking old women in pointy hats. Morgus is mad—nearly all of the most Gifted go mad, sooner or later. She wants to rule Britain—she still thinks of it as Logrèz, Arthur's kingdom, which she tried to dominate through the son of their incest."

"Arthur never existed," Luc pointed out. "All the historians agree on that."

"They weren't there. *Someone* existed whom the legends call Arthur, whatever his original name. Myths grow from truth. Historians know only facts, and facts can lie."

"And you?" Luc asked. "Are you Gifted enough to go mad?"

"That's my second-worst nightmare," Fern said somberly.

"What's your worst?"

Unexpectedly, she managed a smile. "That I won't live long enough to find out."

Later, he took her to dinner in the darkest corner of a nearby restaurant, where discreet waiters served food, poured wine, and left them alone. She talked at greater length about Morgus, and the circle, though she said nothing about the goblins and gave few details on Moonspittle or where he lived. They progressed from steak to sorbet, from wine to brandy, and gradually the conversation relaxed into an exchange of life stories.

"My parents had to get married," Luc explained. "It was a shotgun wedding: Dad was eighteen when he got my mother pregnant. I don't ever remember him being very interested in his home life; it was all work. My mother must have been unhappy because of his neglect. She would be all over us one minute, and ignore us the next. A lot of that was the drink, of course. Dana—Dana was always very dependent on me. She didn't have anyone else."

"What happened to your mother?" Fern asked.

"Car crash when I was nineteen. She was drunk." His expression went rigid. "I never saw my father cry."

"Did *you* cry?"

"No. Maybe I was a stoic. Maybe I'm just coldhearted. Like my father."

"Careful. Your Oedipus complex is showing." He flicked her a grin. "My mother died when I was ten," Fern volunteered. "I cried when Daddy told me she was sick because I knew she would die, though he didn't say so. But I didn't cry after. I froze up inside. Sometimes your emotions do that. It's a form of self-preservation. If I had let go, I would have cried myself to death."

"Do you cry much?" he asked curiously, studying her face in the poor light, all smooth planes and clear-cut features. It was not a face made for tears.

"Sometimes," she said. He was clearly waiting for more, and the brandy had loosened her tongue, so she went on: "I cry in *La Traviata*, and *Gone With the Wind*, and whenever I hear Jacqueline du Pré playing Elgar. And I cried for first love, and the drowning of a city, and the loss of childhood."

"I dream of drowning," he remarked. "That's my worst nightmare. Didn't you say the dreams of the Gifted are significant? Assuming you and that nurse are both right, and I am Gifted. Perhaps I'm foreseeing my own death."

"Tell me your dreams," she said.

"I can't remember most of them in detail," he answered. "I

wake, and there's an impression of something—a bad taste in my mind—but that's all. You know the feeling. But after my mother died, I dreamed I had actually drowned—I was lying on the seabed, and crabs and crayfish were picking my bones, and a mermaid came to stare at me, not the Hans Christian Andersen kind but a creature with a corpse's pallor and eyes like a fish, no depth. She was in my dream the other night, too."

"Can you recall any of that one?" There was an odd note in Fern's voice, but he did not hear it.

"Too well. I was a sailor on an old-fashioned sailboat in a hurricane. I remember thinking how idiotic it was to be there—how we were all going to die—and then I realized somehow that I was the captain, it was my fault, I had chosen to set out. The mast was struck by lightning, and there was this hideous shriek, long drawn out, like a call, and then I was in the sea and *she* was there again. The mermaid. She put her arms around me and dragged me down, and I was breathing water and dying, slowly . . ." He shrugged, trying to disown the memory, or shake it off. "It was probably symbolic. A guilt trip—fear of the womb—woman—fish—sex. Whatever. Analyze if you like, but . . . Tread softly, for you tread upon my nightmares."

There was a pause that felt as if it might be endless. "No," said Fern at last. "I don't think it was symbolic. The dreams of the Gifted often involve memories, but not always your own. I believe . . . you dreamed your way into someone else's mind, someone long dead . . . but I don't know why." And she repeated, as if in anger or pain: "I don't know why!"

"Whose death did I dream?" he demanded. "Do you know that?"

But Fern did not answer.

They left the restaurant in silence, and in silence walked back to his flat. Belatedly, Fern realized where she was going. "I'll get a taxi—"

Luc pulled out his mobile. "My call. There's a cab company I always use. They'll put it on my account."

"I'd rather not—"

He ignored her protest. There was a sudden embarrassment between them, though Fern was rarely embarrassed and Luc never. When they reached the mews he said: "The cab'll be ten or fifteen minutes. Come inside and wait."

"I'll wait here."

He waited with her, close yet separate, not touching, barely speaking. His dreams, her doubts, the shadow of the otherworld came between them like an invisible wall. Only when the cab drew up at the entrance to the mews did he seize her shoulders and kiss her, swift and short, hard mouth on soft. Then he let her go without a word.

He said neither hello nor good-bye, she thought in the cab home, and she trembled, but not with desire.

It was after one when Fern reached Pimlico, and the ivy had gone from the door. In the drawing room, she switched on the light and looked around expectantly. The goblin was sitting on an armchair, having helped himself to an unidentifiable drink, possibly sherry. He evidently felt there was no further need for concealment: his feet were on the coffee table and he flourished his glass in her direction by way of greeting. His hat brim was tilted rakishly over one eye; the other gleamed purple-black in the lamplight. A multifingered hand waved her toward another chair.

"Make yourself at home," Fern said coolly, and noted with mild satisfaction a faltering of his impudence.

"We're friends now, aren't we?" Skuldunder asked anxiously. "Allies?"

"I hope so."

"I had to wait a long time," he offered in mitigation. "Anyway, I'm the ambassador of the queen. I should be made welcome."

"You're a burglar; I'm a witch," said Fern. "Drink uninvited at your peril. You never know what may be lurking in bottle and cupboard."

"I couldn't see anything." The goblin's confidence was ebbing rapidly.

"Of course not. Do you think I am an amateur?"

"It was labeled Toe Peep . . ."

"Tio Pepe," said Fern after a moment's reflection. "I might have known. I keep that for burglars: there's an attraction charm on it." The goblin set the glass down, eyeing it uncertainly. Fern relented. "Drink it with my blessing. It won't harm you—this time. I have news for your queen, though it is not good. The witch we spoke of is indeed dangerous, more dangerous even than we feared. I have learned her identity— through the power of the circle I saw her face-to-face. She is Morgus, who dwelt for years uncounted beneath the Eternal Tree, and has returned to the modern world with all her ancient grudges intact and her ambition sharpened to megalomania. I will defeat her, but I need the aid of your people."

"Megalo-what?" Skuldunder was frowning, his small face screwed into a caricature of bewilderment.

"Lust for power," Fern translated. "Tell the queen, it is time for witchkind and goblinkind to work together. Mabb knows how Morgus treated the denizens of Wrokeby, both ghost and goblin; she will destroy wantonly any creature that offends her, werefolk or menfolk, small or large. The threat is to us all. This young sapling that she nurses could well be a sprig of the Eternal Tree, perhaps planted now in the true soil of this world, its power subject to her. Who knows what fruit it may bear? We must act now. Tell the queen."

"A goblin cannot confront a witch!" Skuldunder protested, his voice squeaky with sudden panic.

"I am glad you realize that," Fern murmured without undue emphasis. "I would not ask it of her. But goblin powers are those of skulking and hiding, of sneaking and spying. I want certain people followed—contacts of Morgus, but ordinary humans. I want to know where they go, what they do, who they meet. This is goblin work. If I write down a list of names and addresses, can Mabb arrange this?" She knew the goblins would make unreliable, if unobtrusive, detectives, unlikely to adhere to the task in hand, but she had to use whatever troops were available. In addition, she wanted to cement her alliance with Mabb, if only because it was the one alliance she had.

"The queen will require more gifts," said Skuldunder, swallowing audibly.

"Of course. I will fetch them." She really must buy some more makeup, she thought to herself. Her supply was becoming depleted. "There will be some now, and more later. Wait here."

When she had fetched the gifts, Fern lingered over the list. Principally, she wanted Kaspar Walgrim followed, a discreet vigil maintained by Dana's bedside in the clinic, and a watch kept on Wrokeby, though she knew it would have to be from a safe distance. With some hesitation, she added the name of Lucas Walgrim and his mews address, telling herself it was for his own protection. Needing to trust him—somehow fearing that need—she reassured herself that he would never know. Skuldunder took the list, his finger tracing the words as he read it through.

"It is for the queen," Fern reminded him. "If she agrees, ask her to send me a sign."

"There will be a token beside your door by midnight tomorrow—"

"No. Other tenants use that door; it might be dislodged, or removed on purpose. Leave it in here, on the table." Skuldunder nodded and took a careless mouthful of sherry; then fixed it with a suspicious glare.

"You'll have to leave now," said Fern, glancing at the clock.

"I must get some sleep. Tell your queen I honor her, and my
goodwill goes with her and all her folk."

When he had gone she went to bed, but she slept fitfully,
torn between waking thought and intrusive dream. She pic-
tured Luc's rare smile, with the tooth missing in his lower jaw,
and tried to superimpose it on another face, half-forgotten,
blurred with the passage of too much time. That other smile
lacked a tooth—she remembered it now—but whether it was
the same, whether it was chance, whether it was important,
she didn't know. She strove to match feature to feature, present to past, but memory was rusty, and she told herself sternly
that as Luc was drawn to her, by necessity if nothing more, so
his Gift might show him her most intimate history. If you
truly love, Ragginbone had told her, you may meet again—
Someday. They say the spirit returns, life after life, until the
unknown pattern is completed, and it can finally move on.
But who are They, who say so much, and so often, and how do
They know? The mind is confined within one body, one life,
but might the spirit remember? And has Someday come at last?

Fool, cried her thought, despising the reasoning that went
beyond reason. Sentimental fool! You tried so hard to be ra-
tional and cool, but within its shell of ice your heart stayed
sixteen. What you call true love is only a wisp of a dream—a
romantic fancy—a shadow. You cannot even picture his face . . .

She had lapsed into slumber without realizing it, and now
she found herself in a high place, high as the Dark Tower,
though the panorama beneath was of folded hills and check-
ered fields and the jagged blue lumps of mountains wrapped
in the mist of distance. From the pinnacle where she sat even
the greatest of them looked no bigger than boulders. A road
or path came twisting toward her, climbing the impossible
scarp from the remoteness below. Some way down it she
made out a moving speck: the figure of a man. She leaned forward, narrowing her eyes, desperate to see him clearly; but a
voice at her back said: "I am here." And there was the dragon

charmer, Ruvindra Laiï, whom she had known only through magic and death. In that knowing she had loved him, as one may love the tiger for its stripes, the serpent for its hug: there had been a bond between them that had seemed, in that hour, deeper than romance. His eyes were ice-blue in a face of ebony—a face she thought she could never forget. But he changed and shrank, becoming an apple rotting on the Eternal Tree, and down among the roots she heard a scrabbling of hands, and she knew Morgus was buried there and must be digging her way out. She ran down into the Underworld, but the caves became the alleyways of Atlantis, and Rafarl Dev took her by the hand. They were running together, up winding stairs and over sun-scorched roofs. In a minute he would turn, and look at her, and then she would know. She would know the truth. And sure enough he turned, and smiled, and her heart gave a great leap—

She woke up. That instant of dazzling insight vanished with the dream. A second longer, and she might have been sure. But there was no surety, and the dream was gone beyond recall. When she slept again she was sitting with Luc in a wine bar, playing chess. The white queen was Morgus, wearing a dress that glittered when she moved. The black queen was herself, in a sheath that clung courtesy of Lycra, and a dark lipstick that drew her mouth into pointed curves. She was on the chessboard, with the squares stretching away forever, and Morgus was before her, and the next move was hers. The black knight protected her, and she knew he must be Luc, but once again there was a voice behind her, and turning she saw Luc was the king. "I was your knight before," he said, "and you threw me away to win the game. But now I am the king, and it is your turn to be sacrificed." She began to run away across the endless squares, and there was the Dark Tower, and the scarlet-clad guards, and the door was open. She struggled to resist, but her feet carried her forward; she screamed—*No! No!*—and woke again, and lay on her back in the pallor of morning twilight, until the alarm told her it was time to get up.

That night in Yorkshire, Mrs. Wicklow left around six. She had done a little cleaning and a lot of puttering, since Robin Capel, Fern's father, had spent the weekend there with his long-term partner, Abby. After they had gone Lougarry came padding into the kitchen, an expectant glint in her eye. Mrs. Wicklow was lavish with leftovers. Lougarry received a terse welcome and a plate of steak-and-kidney pie. "I'll leave t' back door on t' latch, shall I?" the housekeeper said. Long association with the Capels and their assorted friends had had its effect: when she talked to herself she guessed there was someone listening, and she trusted the she-wolf to mind the house in her absence. As it grew darker Lougarry went to the kitchen door and stood for some time staring out into the dusk. A barn owl, ghost faced and silent, swooped down from the moor and circled the building, apparently hunting field mice. But Lougarry knew there were no barn owls in the vicinity. The last time an owl had haunted Dale House was two years before: a raptor from the upper branches of the Eternal Tree, ageless and grown to gigantic size. But such birds were magical, cunning beyond nature, and able to adapt to any scale of normality. The visitor perched awhile on a gable, and cruised past the empty windows, before skimming the hillside and disappearing from view. The night closed in, and stars peered between the clouds. Far into the small hours Lougarry kept her vigil, the fur bristling on her nape, knowing with the instinct of her kind that she was watched in her turn.

A gaggle of magpies came the next day, picking at the grass for insects. When she looked at them sideways, the wolf thought they were overlarge and banded with blue, but when she gazed at them directly they seemed quite ordinary. She counted nine of them, the witch's number; they hung around all afternoon, chattering in the bird language that is all nonsense and noise. She wished she could inform Ragginbone, but although she could speak mind-to-mind with the few humans she was close to, she needed to be in their presence or near at hand; London was much too distant. One or two of the birds hopped near the open door, but Lougarry's unwinking stare deflected them, and the lift of a lip showed fangs that could tear them in half. They left late, streaming into the sunset, and the shadow of the hill grew long and dark, creeping over the house. Lougarry shut the door, slotting the latch into place with her nose. She hadn't eaten all day, but although the house was unoccupied she did not want to leave it to hunt for a meal. She settled down for the night by the stove, her chin on her paws.

But Dale House was never completely unoccupied. The house-goblin appeared in the kitchen later that evening, carrying the ancient spear he had brought with him from Scotland. He and Lougarry were linked only by their loyalty to the Capels: he still regarded her warily, and what she thought of him no one knew. To a wolf, a goblin was small-fry, little bigger than a rabbit and nowhere near as tasty. But Bradachin was stronger than most of his race, and bolder. He kept a careful eye on her while he lit a candle and rummaged in the cupboards for rags and various cleaning fluids. "I'm thinking we may be needing this," he offered presently. "I dinna ken what comes to us, but it isna guid. I saw the birds in the garden, nine of them, and their colors changing when the sun went in. Nine, aye—and nine is three times three. Some witch has been awalking in the fields aheid o' me. But nae doot ye ha' counted them yoursel."

Lougarry lifted her muzzle, twitching her ears to indicate that she was attending.

Bradachin set to work on the spear, sampling the different cleaners to find out which was the most effective. Rust spots and other stains that had been there for centuries were gradually scoured out of existence. "This is the Sleer Bronaw," the goblin said. "D'ye ken that, werebeastie? This is the Spear of Grief wi' which Cullen's Hound slew his best friend, and his ain son, sae he cursed the day it was forged, and the doom that lies on it. The auld laird, he used it but once, tae kill the mon who stole his wife, but she cast hersel atween them, and the spear took the baith of them. So he gave it to me, because I'm a boggan, and nae doom o' Men can fritten me. I wouldna give it tae ony man now—lessen it was a choice o' life or death."

The she-wolf watched him while he worked, evidently listening. Gradually, vigorous polishing began to impart a dull luster to the metal. The blade at the tip was heavy and blunt-looking, too thick in the haft. "There are spikes here," said Bradachin. "They'll open up in a man's belly, aye, and rip oot his guts." He rifled through the drawers for a knife sharpener, and for some time there was the grinding sound of iron on stone, until the blade had acquired an edge that glinted evilly in the candlelight.

Outside, a barn owl flew to the window ledge and thrust its spectral face close to the glass.

VII ⁓⁓⁓⁓

There was little progress for the next few weeks. A wilting flower on Fern's coffee table conveyed Mabb's agreement, and the goblins kept a casual watch on their designated targets. Skuldunder reported back, once in a while, with much detail and little substance: goblins can observe human society, but few have any understanding of how it works. Fern was certain Kaspar Walgrim was involved in some dubious activity on Morgus's behalf, probably financial, but she needed a computer hack, not a kobold, to investigate. She met his son several times, hospital visits and drinks extending to dinner, with her repeatedly having to dissuade him from storming Wrokeby. "As long as we do nothing, Morgus won't harm Dana any further. She's divided her soul from her body: there's little greater damage she could do, short of murder. But if we try a rescue mission and it fails, Dana will be the first victim. Morgus might send Dana through the Gate of Death, or worse still, into the abyss, as she did with the ghosts. When we make the attempt, we *must* be sure of success. Morgus has to have a weakness, if I can only find it . . ."

They discussed possibilities until the subject wore out, and moved inevitably on to more personal matters, to their likes and dislikes, their lives and loves, their tastes in food and music, literature and politics. Fern found herself giving him an edited version of her time in Atlantis—her journey into the

Forbidden Past when she was sixteen years old, her entanglement in the fall of the island empire, even a few details of her never-to-be-forgotten love. "He drowned?" Luc said at the end, his face darkening.

Fern nodded.

"How long ago?"

"About ten thousand years."

She saw him shiver.

"I watched him," she said. "I watched him die—in a spell, in a dream. His ship broke up, and a mermaid dragged him down beneath the waves."

"But . . ."

"The Gifted can sometimes tune in to another mind, another life. You have the Gift—I don't know how strongly—and circumstances have thrown us together. You seem to be picking up on my memories. He lay on the seabed till his bones were coral, like in the play. Those are pearls that were his eyes . . ."

Luc said sharply: "I had those dreams long before I met you."

"Don't!" said Fern.

"Don't?"

"Don't cheat me with fantasies!" In that moment, he saw her composure splinter, and there was naked pain in her face. "Don't let me cheat myself! The soul may return—we don't know—there may be unfinished business, a quest unfulfilled, some doom that might last a thousand lives, but we can't be sure. *We don't know.* Anyway, Rafarl Dev was not like you. He tried to be cynical, but he couldn't help believing in things; he tried to run away, but in the end he stayed. He was one of those who are born to fight, and lose. You are—a creature of another mettle. You have a harder edge, a colder eye."

"What you mean is, I wouldn't have waited for you when the city was falling about my ears."

"Would you?" she asked.

"No. I would have gone long before and made you come with me, against your will if necessary."

Fern smiled fleetingly, and then grew somber. "No one has ever *made* me do anything."

"Maybe it's time."

If we weren't in a restaurant, she thought, he would kiss me again. But they were, and the table with the remnants of their meal was between them, and a cruising waiter topped their glasses, and the moment passed into oblivion, never to return. Or so she fancied, wondering if that kiss might have lasted longer, and tasted sweeter, and whether, with his mouth on hers, she would have known the truth at last. She struggled to recall how it had felt to kiss Rafarl, but it was all too many ages past, and few kisses can stand the test of so much time.

"I don't believe in reincarnation," Luc resumed when the waiter had moved on. "I have never really believed in anything. Not God, or the soul, or true love. We are flesh and blood—water and clay—and when we are gone, that is all that remains."

"You said it," Fern pointed out. "*When we are gone.* If there is only flesh and blood, who is the 'we' that has to go with those elements? Besides, your sister's soul is in a jar in Morgus's spellchamber. You believe that."

"Just because it may be true," he said, "that doesn't mean I have to believe it." After a pause, he went on: "Your Rafarl, did he look like me?"

Fern sighed. "It's awful, but I can't visualize him, not clearly. His eyes were dark—yours are light. I think his bones were similar, but . . . more regular. He was beautiful, like a god. If he'd been alive today he'd have been advertising Calvin Klein. You're interesting-looking, attractive, but not beautiful." He grimaced at her, revealing the gap in his teeth. "How did you lose that tooth?"

"I pinched my father's car when I was eleven, drove it into a wall, smashed my face on the wheel."

"Why don't you have a false one?"

"Why should I?"

"Raf had a tooth missing," Fern said. "I think it was there."

"Coincidence," he said. "This is all nonsense. You and I couldn't have loved each other, or we would feel something now, and I'm not in love with you."

"Nor I with you," she responded. She felt no disappointment, or hurt. His light-gray eyes were fixed on her with a strange intensity.

"I recognized you, though," he said. "In the first dream. And the first time we met."

"Then you are more sensitive than me."

When they left the restaurant, he put her in a taxi and kissed her, but this time only on the cheek.

Gaynor, meanwhile, had summoned the tatters of her resolution and telephoned Hugh Fairbairn. He seemed less eager to see her than before, which is always the way; possibly he had found another sympathetic female to whom he could pour out his woes. Gaynor knew she ought to be relieved, but she wanted his attention, if only so she could demonstrate to Will her competence at research. "I need your help," she told Hugh. Not being an adept liar, she continued with a bowdlerized version of the facts. "I have a friend who's in trouble. I can't explain everything, but it's all to do with investment banking. I was hoping you could sort of fill me in."

"Depends what you want to know. Most of the stuff I deal with is very confidential."

"Of course, of course," Gaynor stammered. "But you're the most important banker I know . . ." This was true enough, she reflected, since he was the only banker she knew.

Hugh mellowed audibly. He was a man who mellowed easily, particularly in response to such stimulants as wine, women, and flattery—even if the flattery was offered in Gaynor's slightly hesitant manner. After explaining that he would be busy being important for the next week, he suggested lunch on the following Friday at the latest Japanese restaurant in Berkley Square. Gaynor accepted, despite private reservations about raw fish.

She arrived punctually, dressed in black—not clinging, sexy black but the kind worn by widows and orphans, guaranteed to discourage masculine advances. Gaynor favored black, though she suspected it did not suit her: it went with everything, did not show the dirt, and at night it blended effortlessly into the semidarkness of pub or party. One of her worst nightmares was entering a very large room full of people whispering, and realizing she was wearing scarlet. Hugh, however, was uncritical; possibly he could not differentiate between various degrees of black. He wore charcoal, with his hair brushed back from an ascending forehead and a city pallor that sat unnaturally on the face of a country squire. His genes should have made him jolly and easygoing, but the high-stress, dog-eat-man atmosphere of the City had rendered him aggressive, sometimes pompous, and chronically misunderstood. Gaynor found herself thinking that what he really needed was to retire early and live in the country with two or three Labradors who would not fail to understand him whatever he did.

Like most people who claim their work is very confidential, once he started to talk the sluices opened and Gaynor was inundated with information she did not need or want. Apparently, he was a merchant banker, which was something subtly different from an investment banker. It took several vain attempts before she was able to nudge him away from his own field—"I was doing business with Brazil only last week, an expanding timber company—timber is very big out there. Of course, we don't want to destroy the rainforests, but they have to earn their keep"—into the field next door. (*Earn their keep?* Gaynor wondered. They're forests, not inefficient employees.) Investment bankers, as far as she could tell from Hugh's rather rambling discourse, simply advised their clients on where to invest their money, sometimes, though not always, investing the bank's own funds as well. They were supposed to be cunning judges of which stocks would provide the biggest dividends, which were the most trendy, whether the market would go up or down, which companies would sink with the ship or swim with the tide. "They're clever buggers," Hugh conceded with only moderate enthusiasm. Naturally, he favored his own branch of the profession. "When they get it right, investors can make a mint. When they're wrong, you're down a few million. Or more. Look at—"

"What happens to the banker then?" Gaynor interrupted.

"Damages his reputation. Bad for business."

"But he doesn't have to pay compensation or anything?"

"Christ, no."

Realizing she was in danger of being sidetracked, what with the inefficiency of the rainforests and the nonaccountability of senior bankers, Gaynor launched abruptly into the reason for her inquiries. "Do you know someone called Kaspar Walgrim?"

"Lord, yes." Hugh seemed unable to affirm or deny without a religious qualification. "With Schindler Volpone. Known as Schindler's Ark ever since they went into the biotech industry. You know: fatter, juicier tomatoes and more of them, fatter, juicier cows, greener leeks, that kind of thing. Now it's mapping the genome. They do other stuff, but that's their specialty. Kaspar Walgrim is their biotech wizard: got the lowdown on every top scientist in every company and whether they're going to come up with a cure for cancer in ten years' time and designer babies in twenty. Or vice versa. Bit scary if you ask me, but that's where the money is—miracle medicines and producing a generation of six-foot supermodels with the brains of Einstein. Personally, I like my women a tad shorter and cuddlier." His grin hovered close to a leer. "What do you think of the black cod?"

"It's gorgeous." Gaynor had been agreeably surprised by the fish, some of which was cooked and all delicious.

"Good. Thought you'd like it. Nice to see you again. So how come you're interested in Wizard Walgrim?"

"Is that what they call him?" Gaynor asked, secretly entertained.

"Got a sixth sense, so they say. Uncanny. He'll pick out some little company with one laboratory and a couple of postgrads and a year later they'll be replicating your internal organs or growing a zucchini that eats its own weevils."

If Luc is Gifted as Fern says, Gaynor speculated, maybe his father is, too. Could you use the Gift for high finance? "What is he like?" she went on. "As a person, I mean."

"Only met him once. He's a sort of legend in the City, but not for his personality. Not the flamboyant type, you know. Gray sort of chap, doesn't show emotion, may not have any. Cast-iron integrity. Wife died a long time ago; no obvious replacement. Must have married very young—probably got the girl pregnant—for he's not yet fifty and there's a son of thirty-odd and a fucked-up daughter who spends all her time in rehab with the stars. Doesn't seem to bother Daddy much: he can afford the bills. Still, you never know. Where does your friend fit in?"

"My friend? Oh yes . . . well—" Gaynor succumbed to temptation "—I'm afraid it's frightfully confidential."

"Come on now. I gave you the goods. Not sporting for you to clam up on me now."

"Actually," Gaynor admitted, "my friend knows the son. Lucas . . . Luc . . ."

"Met him, too. Bright boy, so they say. Not like the sister. Supposed to be attractive—couldn't see it myself. One of those dark, bottled-up types. Hope your 'friend' isn't really you. Like in old whodunits: the lady never says she's being blackmailed or having an affair; it's always 'my friend.' "

"No," Gaynor assured him. "I really do have a friend. Well, lots."

"Not little Fernanda? Shouldn't have thought a City whiz kid was her cup of tea: she usually goes for mature men in the meedja."

"It's not her," Gaynor said hastily. "The thing is, according to Luc, his father's mixed up with a woman . . ."

"About time."

"She's not very desirable," Gaynor said, anxious to steer the conversation away from Fern. "At least, she *is* desirable, if you see what I mean, only not—not as a human being. We think she's a really bad lot—she could affect his cast-iron integrity."

"Sons always hate prospective stepmothers," Hugh said wisely. "Probably fancies her himself. Good for Dad, if you ask me. Van's seeing someone: did I tell you? Arty type, looks like a poof. Interior designer of some sort. I think she's trying to show me up. Says he's a New Man, changes diapers and that. Fine, I said. Let's start having sex again, have a couple of rug rats and *he* can do the dirty work. What's the point of a diaper-changing poof when she refuses to get pregnant?"

Gaynor lapsed into sympathetic mode and concentrated on her sushi.

In the lower branches of the Tree the spider spun its fragile webs, catching the few insects that invaded its airspace, drinking the sap from split stem and torn leaf. As it grew larger it ventured more often to the ground, exploring corners of the conservatory that the builders had not touched, behind stone jars and carved troughs where tropical plants flourished grimly, accustomed to the jungle gloom. There the spider spread its nets, no longer fragile, thickening the shadows. One day it caught a rat.

Morgus found it there on a night of the waning moon when she came to commune with the Tree. She stumbled into a sticky silken rope that tore her dress when she pulled it away, but she was not angered. Seeing the clustered eyes watching her, malevolent as Oedaphor's and intelligent as an aphid's, she laughed softly. "So my Tree has acquired a guardian! It is well. It is very well. What have you been eating?" She poked among the plant debris with her foot, dislodging a pile of little white bones. "Mice, perhaps? Too meager a feast for such a prodigy. I will bring you something more substantial." The next day, she ordered a car and was driven into the nearest town, where she asked to be taken to a pet shop. There she bought an entire litter of pedigreed puppies.

"I want the best," she told the assistant.

"These are purebred," the young woman assured her. "Look, aren't they adorable? Are they for your children?"

"For my—child," said Morgus.

"They're not like cats, you know. They have to be properly looked after."

"They will be taken care of," Morgus replied.

She paid with plastic, where once she would have had to pay with gold. She had concluded that money in the twenty-first century was at once vitally important and completely meaningless. Rulers mislaid or misspent unimaginable sums, running deficits that outran her comprehension. And even the lowest peasant seemed to borrow and juggle and gamble in ways mysterious to her. She left all such matters to Kaspar, her helper, her counselor—and her slave. His name was on the plastic, but no one queried it.

The puppies cost two hundred pounds apiece.

Later, the spider hunted something that yapped and squealed, until the venom took effect and it was paralyzed into silence.

"When you are hungry, there will be another," promised Morgus. "Eat well, and grow!"

In her basement spellchamber, she mixed a potion from the sap of the Tree and left a bowl out nightly for the spider to drink.

Upstairs in the kitchen, Grodda watched over the remaining puppies, stroking them and making inarticulate cooing noises, until one by one they were all gone.

Ragginbone stood outside a building site in King's Cross, reading the graffiti on the barrier walls. Among the usual scribblings of the lewd and crude there were signs that he recognized, or thought he recognized, though some were so ancient he was unsure of their meaning. All were freshly painted in various colors; he had a feeling each color, too, had a unique significance. He wondered who had done it. There were many strange creatures lost in the London crowds: werefolk, spirits in human or semihuman forms, a few of the Gifted who, like Moonspittle, had outlived their time and lingered on, furtive and ineffectual, telling fortunes, weaving petty spells, too old to die. But it did not really matter who was responsible. What mattered was that there could be something on that site which needed protection, or isolation, and there were those who had sensed it, or thought they had sensed it, and had taken the necessary measures. Ragginbone walked around the perimeter for some time before seeking admittance.

"I was hoping to talk to the archaeologists," he told the guard at the gate. "I am something of an expert myself."

The man took one look at his eccentric garb and believed him. Ragginbone followed him through the site to an area crisscrossed with trenches where about a dozen people, mostly of student age, bent or squatted over various inscrutable tasks. Both sexes wore jeans, T-shirts, long untidy hair, and, in a couple of cases, designer stubble. The guard called: "Mr. Hunter!" and one of them straightened up, glancing toward the intruders with a preoccupied air. "Visitor for you. Says he's an expert on this stuff."

The man murmured an "Okay," and the guard returned to his post, showing no further interest.

"I don't want to disturb you," Ragginbone said, "but I was intrigued when I read about your excavation. You seem to think you may have found traces of something very ancient, or so I gathered. The roots of London run deep."

"What's your interest?" asked the young man. He had a slight American accent, possibly Californian. "You're definitely not the press."

"I am also an archaeologist—of a kind. Purely amateur, I'm afraid. My name is Watchman."

"Pleasure to meet you," the young man said. "I'm Dane Hunter. I'm in charge here. Most of my fellow workers are student volunteers. Everyone approves of salvaging our heritage, but no one wants to pay for it. Still, we welcome informed enthusiasts."

"I was hoping," said Ragginbone, "that *you* would inform *me*."

The young man was actually not so young, he noticed. Perhaps thirty-five or so. The long off-blond hair, pulled back into a disheveled ponytail, and the jeans-and-T-shirt uniform gave him an air of superficial studenthood, but the planes of his face had hardened and there were faint lines around his eyes and barring his forehead. His mouth was slim and set, its seriousness belied by the more quizzical of the lines; his light tan and the muscles in his forearms indicated an outdoor lifestyle and regular physical exertion. But then, Ragginbone reflected, glancing around the site, much of archaeology did take place alfresco, involving digging with pickaxes or dental probes, exploring caves and graves, grubbing among stones and bones. Dane Hunter looked at once the man of action and the man of thought, though the action was undoubtedly careful and considered, his thought processes probably rather more rapid. Ragginbone noticed how the female volunteers glanced around at his approach and took their time before reverting to the work at hand.

Hunter talked easily about the indications of a building, possibly a temple from the layout, predating the Romans. "We've found some fragments of a skeleton or more than one, though they don't appear to be human. They could point to some kind of sacrifice. There are also a few artifacts: a stone knife, a broken cup or chalice, and some pieces that may have a religious significance. We don't yet know what religion. There were so many primitive gods around, and we have so few written records of any of them. We think this would have been the altar . . ."

He stopped beside a rather deeper depression, where stone showed beneath the earth. A youth in his late teens was sweeping a brush across a partially exposed surface.

Dane said: "We're hoping for an inscription. That would at least give us the language, which would be a starting point." He added, politely: "You said you were an expert. Have you any ideas?"

"Yes," said Ragginbone, "I have. But I think for the moment I shall keep them to myself. I trust you won't object if I return from time to time?"

"No," said Dane, clearly slightly nonplussed. "I don't object. But—"

"And if you find an inscription," said Ragginbone, "I should like to see it."

He did not go straight back to the shop that never opened but made his way instead to Fern's flat, walking south through the park, taking his time. London flowed past and over him, a river blended of many million lives, many million stories. His tale was just one droplet in the flood, a single strand in a vast embroidery, and somehow it comforted him to think of this, to catch in faces anxious or hopeful, vivid or closed, a glimpse of the wider spectrum of existence. In the country, it had often calmed him to watch the ever-changing sky and think of Keats: "Huge cloudy symbols of a high romance," but here Man, even more than nature, set him in his place in the world.

He reflected with the philosophical outlook that comes from great age that if they lost their particular battle, it might matter for a little space, a moment of eternity, but somewhere else, someone would win.

But he knew Fern would not see it that way.

She was home from work when he reached Pimlico. Whether his journey was long or short, fast or slow, he had acquired the knack of arriving at the right time. Maybe it had something to do with the Gift he had lost.

"I haven't seen you for a week," she said. "What have you been up to?"

"Walking. Thinking. I visited a building site today. I think you should come and have a look sometime."

"At a *building site*? Why?"

"Rescue archaeologists are at work there. They have made certain discoveries, not much yet, but there may be more. My heart tells me this is important."

"What have they found?"

"Something very ancient," said Ragginbone. "Maybe a temple. It smells of death. Old death, long gone. But the runes on the outer wall were new, scribbled among the graffiti. That in itself is an indicator. Someone thinks the place is in need of occult protection—or isolation. Death connects with death: it may once have held a link to the dark kingdom, the source of Morgus's invulnerability. There could be some clue—"

"I have been to the dark kingdom," said Fern. "Remember? It's empty now, a waste of vacant caverns, full of ghosts. There were no clues."

"Nonetheless," said Ragginbone, "it would be foolish not to check."

"I'll check," said Fern, with a hint of tartness.

Later, they sat down over a salad supper, discussing their researches. "Gaynor rang today," Fern said. "She got a colleague in Cardiff to e-mail her the photofiles of some manuscripts they have there. Very obscure mythology predating the Mabinogion. Unfortunately, they're in Welsh, and he forgot to e-mail the translation. She said she'd get back to him, but . . . I can't really believe we're going anywhere with all of this. I think . . ."

"Yes?" Ragginbone encouraged. "What do you think?"

"I have this feeling the real answer must be something very simple—something so obvious that we've overlooked it. That sounds like a whodunit, I know. Only this is a howdunit, and I'm the murderess, and the crime has yet to be committed."

"The crime is *being* committed," Ragginbone pointed out. "Dana's soul is imprisoned; her father may well be subject to some kind of mind control. What Morgus is doing at Wrokeby we can only speculate. You said she still dreams of ruling Britain. Her thoughts are limited by her past; she cannot look beyond old ambitions. But that does not limit her power. She could do great harm. Save your conscience for after the deed."

"I know," said Fern. "The native hue of resolution gets sicklied o'er by the pale cast of thought. And all that. I will try to stop thinking."

"How do your relations progress with Lucas Walgrim?"

"Relations? We don't have *relations*. Just dinner. Sometimes."

He saw the doubt in her face, the holding back. "What troubles you?"

It was a while before she answered. "I dream about him. He dreams about me. He dreamed long before—of things that touch my life. He dreamed of *drowning* . . ."

"You said he was Gifted. The Gift may reach out, mind to mind, binding two people together long before they meet."

"*You* said the soul returns. That if I truly loved, I might find Rafarl again—someday. I've always wondered: when is Someday?"

"Did you truly love? You were still only a child, after all."

"I don't know. That's just it. I don't *know* anything. I can't properly remember his face. Rafarl's, I mean. He had a tooth missing from his lower jaw: I remember *that*. So has Luc. Does that mean something?"

He thought she looked suddenly very young and unsophisticated, almost pleading with him, her expression naked.

He said: "We have no answers. Only questions. Maybe there are no answers to find. Some things you have to take on trust. But beware of sentimentality."

"Thanks," said Fern, relapsing into a smile. "You have, as usual, given me contradictory lines of advice. Both a warning and an endorsement. There are times when you behave *exactly* like the best wizards of fiction. It's a pity you don't have their power."

"The greatest fiction is always founded on truth, if not fact. I used to meet a man in a pub in Oxford, many years ago. He was an academic, a scholar of ancient languages. I remember he wanted to create a mythology for Britain. We talked a lot about this and that. He struck me as intelligent and imaginative, a Catholic as I once was. Perhaps that was why I gave him one of my Italian names: Gabbandolfo, Elvincape in English. I believe he was a genius, in his way. His stories have the true magic, the Gift that holds the reader. A story is only another kind of spell."

"In that case," said Fern, "you have not lost all your power. That is the best story I've heard from you yet. But is it gospel, or apocrypha?"

"It is as real as your tale," said Ragginbone. "But whether the man learned from me, or even remembered our conversation, that is another matter. He was probably too wise for that."

"False modesty," Fern said. "*Not* a wizardly quality. You haven't helped, you know—but you've given me something to smile about, in the night watches. Whether it's true or not."

Ragginbone's face—an old man's face, tough as oak and not always entirely human—scrunched into a thousand lines, brightening with unwizardly mischief. "Good," he said. "Then fact or fancy, it isn't wasted."

I visited the prisoner yesterday. Even without the nightmares, his condition had deteriorated. Being only semihuman he can go a long while without nourishment, but since his return I had instructed Grodda to bring him food each evening, and he was daubed in his own filth, his hair hanging over his face, clogged with a thick grease that seemed to be made from a mixture of dust and urine. It was as if his self-disgust required a physical manifestation, the need not merely to loathe his own being but to wallow in that loathing. What little dignity he once assumed was long abandoned. He stank. I mocked him from a distance, savoring his torment, but in truth he was almost too far gone for me to take further pleasure in my revenge. It was the man in him whose suffering I could appreciate, and now he was all beast. Vengeance is satisfying in its completeness, but I had hoped to delay that end a little longer, and play out my games with him, and watch the pain behind his eyes. Last night, I did not want to get that close.

"He has paid the price of betrayal," I told my friend. I had taken her head out of the jar and stood it in a shallow basin of the preserving fluid, which continued to seep upward from the neck and permeate the whole fruit. Regular periods of immersion were still necessary to stave off decay, but in the basin, she could talk to me.

I am not sure this is an advantage.

"What of *your* treachery?" she shrilled. "You hold me imprisoned in this state, fruit of the Eternal Tree, prolonging my torment, keeping me from both death and the chance of further life. Find me a body, a vessel to inhabit. You have the power, and such things have been done before. You know the long-lost words spoken from beyond the grave: *The damned are not forever lost*. That girl you have stolen must be young

and strong. Give me her physical being, and let her soul
wither, bodiless."

"I do not have her," I explained. "Her body lies in a hospital; only her spirit is mine. Still, the idea is interesting. I might
find you a body of another kind, say, that of some animal,
maybe a pig. That, too, has been done before."

"Do not taunt me!" she hissed. "Remember: we were as
sisters. We shared *everything*."

"I had a sister once," I said, "a blood-sister, Morgun, my
twin. We too shared everything. Our first pleasure was in
each other's arms, our spirits were interwoven, our minds had
a single bent. But she was wayward and seduced by her own
lusts. She gave up the way of witchkind and the pursuit of
power for the chimera of love and the forgiveness of men. She
turned against me—even me—in search of something she
called redemption, and she died in bitterness, and hung on
the Tree cursing my name. That is the nature of sisterhood."
The cat Nehemet purred as I spoke, a soft throbbing sound
not altogether pleasant to hear, and rubbed her naked flank
against my legs.

"I was a different kind of sister," insisted the head, fear-
pale. "I never failed you, or cheated you."

"Ah, but not for the lack of wishing!" I said, half teasing,
seeing in her fear that it was true. I stroked her cheek, still
young and full in the first ripeness of the fruit. "Do not trouble yourself, Sysselore my beloved; I will treat you only—
always—as you deserve." I knew she would have flinched
from me, if she could, but I would not harm her, not yet. Her
company is still sweet to me, for all the sourness of her
tongue.

In the kitchen, Grodda was nursing a baby. I had wanted a
human child, but these days such things are difficult to obtain.
There used to be many babies, wanted and unwanted—the
peasants bred like rabbits—but now they have pills to stave
off conception, and venomous creams, and sheaths to contain

the male secretions, and then women complain that they are barren and go to the doctors as once they went to witches, begging a spell or a philter to fulfill their dreams. The future is a strange place. There are more people but fewer babies, and the infants are so watched and cared for that even the maimed and sick grow to a gibbering adulthood, and are nursed and nannied into age. But Grodda had found a calf, I did not ask where; no doubt some farmer would miss it, even as the mother misses her child. It was twig legged and doe eyed, its soft ears lay back, and it suckled milk from a bottle. It would do, I said. I looped a cord about its neck and led it to the conservatory.

The guardian was waiting, its pale body, shadow mottled, lost among the eerie patterning of moonlight and leaves. The Tree stirred at my approach, rustling, or maybe it was the rustling of crooked limbs uncurling across the floor. I released the calf, and it stood there, emitting the mewling noises that small creatures make when calling for their mothers. Then moonspots and shadows seemed to gather together, bunching into a spring, and the calf was blotted out. It screamed once— a curiously human sound, touching me with pleasure—but the second scream was stifled into a whisper, and then it was silent. There were scrapings and scratchings as something was bundled up and dragged away to be consumed at leisure. Later, from a corner, I heard nibbling and crunching. When I went back in the morning there were only a few of the larger bones and a shell-like fragment of skull, picked clean. I could not even smell the blood.

He was lurking behind some giant pots, in an undergrowth of untended plants. After careful scrutiny I could make out a protrusion shaped like a claw, and a splinter of eye peering through the foliage. I wanted to coax him out, to see how big he had grown—in the dark, it had been impossible to tell— but I sensed the smallness of his mind brooding in the swollen body, a tiny insect mind focused on hunger and survival, and

I knew it would be better not to disturb him. I had no fear of him, but I did not wish to have to kill in order to protect myself.

The Tree, too, was growing: its trunk was as thick as my waist, and its spreading leaves darkened the daylight. I walked in its gloom, caressing quivering branches, listening to its whispering voice. And then I found what I had sought for so long, a small green thing like a misshapen crab apple, without flush or feature. Fruit. At that sight, my blood quickened to the Tree's quickening, my heart beat with its pulse. I touched the rind very gently, though it was firm and hard, willing it to swell and ripen, trying in vain to discern what form it might take. The heads of the dead grew on its Eternal progenitor, but the fruit of my Tree might take almost any shape. My imagination shivered at the possibilities. Already it seemed to me there were lumps on the little globe that could develop into nose and browbone, cheekbones and chin. I must have stood half the morning, watching it, as if I might actually see it grow. No sun penetrated this green cavern, but it came from a dimension without the sun, where day and dark sprang from the will of the Tree, and I knew it would ripen even by night. "Guard it well," I told the creature in the corner.

Later that day, I brought him a bowl of the potion mixed with tree sap to drink. He was large enough to eat a calf, and quickly, but I wanted him large enough to eat a man. Neither ape nor urchin, Adam nor Eve would steal my fruit from me.

"So what have we learned?" asked Fern. They were having a council of war at her flat in Pimlico. Although it was high summer, rain beat on the window, and she had switched on the artificial fire to ward off the chill. Gas-powered flames leaped and danced around a convincing array of coals; Gaynor, Will, and Ragginbone sat in a semicircle, warming themselves at its glow. Luc had not been invited.

"Nothing and nothing," Fern went on, answering her own question. "Morgus still looks invulnerable; Dana is still in a coma. We're going nowhere."

"Gaynor did well getting the lowdown on Walgrim senior," Will pointed out. "Anyone with that much integrity is always iffy, particularly a banker. Once you're above suspicion, you can get away with anything."

"Get away with anything?" Ragginbone inquired.

"Invent a company. Get people to invest in it. Pocket the money." Will's expression quirked into cynicism. "The easiest kind of fraud. And if Morgus has got her claws into him, he won't be worrying about the future. Magical influence makes your mind furry around the edges. Your sense of self-preservation goes. At least, that was how it felt all those years ago when Alimond summoned me. I should think this would be something similar."

Ragginbone gave a nod of acquiescence. Gaynor said: "What about the goblins? Have they come up with anything?"

"They don't investigate," Fern explained. "They simply watch. Dana is watched, Luc and Kaspar are watched—"

"Luc . . ." Ragginbone murmured, with a swift glance from under lowering eyebrows.

"Even Wrokeby is watched, from a safe distance. A couple of weeks ago, Morgus bought a litter of puppies. I know it seems unlikely, but Skuldunder was very positive. Any suggestions as to why?"

"Maybe she likes dogs," said Gaynor doubtfully.

"She's got a cat," said Fern. "Witches have cats. It's traditional. She isn't a doggy person. I could imagine her with a tank full of poisonous octopi, a pet cobra, a tarantula on a golden chain—but not puppies. She would kill anything that slobbered on her skirt."

"What kind were they?" Will asked.

"Don't know. Goblins don't like dogs of any description. Does it matter?"

Will shrugged. "We can't tell what matters. Maybe you should draw the circle again . . ."

"Too dangerous," said Ragginbone. "Have you forgotten? Potent magic attracts elementals. The many eyes of Oedaphor would be watching: Morgus has called him up, and he could betray Fern's whereabouts. We were too quick for him last time, but that would not happen again. We are not yet ready for the big confrontation."

"Does it have to happen?" Will said. "If Fern can't defeat her, maybe there's some other way . . ."

"She's looking for me," Fern said. "There were magpies around Dale House. Bradachin tackled the telephone—he thought it was important I should know. He says they were marked in blue, though it didn't show when you looked at them directly. They're birds from the Tree, spies for Morgus."

"Bradachin used the phone?" Ragginbone was distracted. "Goblins hate all technology: they see it as a kind of sinister contemporary magic. He *must* have thought it was important."

"He's exceptional," Will said shortly.

"I have to face her." Fern was following her own train of thought. "But not now."

"What about the Old Spirit?" Gaynor asked diffidently. "Is he involved in all this?"

"Gaynor has a point," said Ragginbone. "He is always involved. We would do well to keep that in mind. If any of you see or sense him, even in your dreams—especially in your dreams—" something in Fern's expression, in her silence, drew his attention; the other two followed his gaze "—share it with us."

"Haven't you told him about your dream?" said Will.

"Not yet." She didn't like talking about it, having to describe it again: the high office, and Azmordis, and the scritch-scratch of the quill as she signed the document she did not need to read. "It came again last night. It feels more real every time. I know it's the Dark Tower, like in stories, only it's modern, a black soaring skyscraper, all glass and steel. I think it's in a dimension of its own, like the Tree, but not separate: it connects to the City, maybe to all cities. I'm looking for it, so I find it, and I sign in blood, sealing the bargain. Selling my soul, my Gift. My Self."

"It can't be a prophecy," said Will. "It might be a warning."

"Maybe," said Ragginbone.

"I thought Azmodel was *his* place." Gaynor was frowning. "I don't understand about the Tower."

"He has many strongholds," Ragginbone explained. "Azmodel—the Beautiful Valley—is the most ancient. But the Dark Tower is old, nonetheless. Once it had dungeons and arrow slots, a spiral stair where now there is an elevator and an escalator, a stone chamber instead of a carpeted office. It has fallen and been rebuilt, adapting to history. *He* moves with Time, growing closer to Men, battening on their weaknesses. Long ago the Tower stood in a barren waste; now, as Fern says, it is in every city. He makes it easy for the great and the good to beat a path to his door."

"Not Fern," Will asserted positively. In a rare gesture, he reached for his sister's hand. "Don't worry. We know you would never do that."

"Worry," said Ragginbone. "Prophecy is a gray area, but the insights of the Gifted are not to be ignored. What are you thinking, when you sign?"

"I don't really want to," Fern said instantly. "It's as if I have no choice. There's someone in danger—someone I love."

"That old chestnut," said Will, and "One of us?" from Gaynor.

Fern shook her head. "I don't know."

"We can take care of ourselves," Will said.

"I remember."

"Don't be sarcastic. People can learn from their mistakes. You should learn, too, and not just from dreams."

"Meaning?" his sister queried.

"The Gifted are always alone. Not just Alimond and Morgus; think of Zohrâne. Even Ragginbone, in his wizardly days. Power isolates. Like Hitler, Stalin, Pol Pot. Maybe they had a Gift of a kind: who knows what drove them? The point is, they didn't have friends, only minions. Henchpersons to do their dirty deeds, courtiers to adore them and listen to their rantings. No one they truly cared for or who cared for them, no one to take them out of their little selves. Their lives were bounded in a walnut shell, and they tried to fit the whole world in there with them. Result: madness."

"I respect your arguments," Ragginbone murmured, "but I would like to point out that I at least am not mad."

"Debatable," said Will. "Anyway, you lost your power. More important, you gained Lougarry. She may well have saved your sanity."

"Are you saying," Fern interjected, "that without you lot I might end up like Zohrâne?"

"Yes," said Will. "That's exactly what I'm saying. You keep things from us, you distance yourself, you try to 'protect' us. That's incredibly dangerous—for you. I think that's the principal danger of the Gift. Power plus solitude equals disassociation from reality. Hence arrogance, paranoia, and so on. You told me if Zohrâne became attached to one of her body slaves, she would have him killed. Your friends and family aren't your weakness: we're your strength. You have to accept that."

"And the risk?" said Fern.

"All life is risky. For myself, I believe it's better for me to die than for you to become a megalomaniac witch queen."

"Me too," said Gaynor, before Fern had a chance to ask.

"Wisdom," Ragginbone remarked, "springs from unlikely sources. Your brother may indeed have pinpointed the true peril of Prospero's Children."

"Did they all turn to evil," Fern asked, "in the end?"

"Let us say that few turned to good."

"I lose either way, don't I?" said Fern. "My friends, or my head."

"The choice isn't yours to make," Will retorted. "We've chosen. Forget your dream for the moment, and the Old Spirit. We have to deal with Morgus first."

"If we can," said Fern. She turned to Gaynor. "Did you get hold of a translation of that Welsh stuff?"

"Mm."

"And?"

"It was all about Wales."

They kicked the subject around for a while longer, going nowhere, as Fern had said at the beginning. Yet afterward, she sensed a difference in herself, as if a shadow had been lifted from her mind, a barrier removed. She remembered how alone she had felt when, at sixteen, she first confronted the dark and became aware of her own power. But I am not alone, she thought. I never was. And for all her fears, relinquishing that burden of solitude and ultimate responsibility gave her a new lightness of heart, a different angle on their problems. I will find a way, she concluded. *We* will find a way.

That night, what dreams she had were beyond recollection, and she was at peace.

The conservatory at Wrokeby was a vast semicircular structure built toward the end of the Victorian age, when wealthy botanists headed into the Himalayas with mules and native porters, returning with the stolen flora of the mountains. Once, it had been the home of majestic gardeners, potted palms, wagging bustles, afternoon tea parties. But its north-facing situation, with the trees crowding close outside, meant that little light could pass through the towering glass walls, and any that did seek admittance was rapidly choked out of existence by the jungle inside. The builders had restored broken panes and replaced roof joists, but they had not tried to penetrate the thickets of plant life within. Now there were new shadows to strangle the intrusive light, woven webs whose weight bent the palms. The spider had grown too big for its surroundings, and the miniature rainforest could no longer contain it. There was no prey for it to snare, no food to sate its growing appetite, save at Morgus's whim. The tiny brain grappled with its overgrown body, filled with a nebulous rage at an existence that was against all instincts. Somehow, it sensed that there should have been webs to spin which did not snap their supports, juicy flies to eat, haphazard mating rituals. Instead, it was trapped in this shrunken world, hand-fed by a creature who was far from arachnoid in appearance. It stayed close to the Tree, finding it familiar, pining for a Tree that constituted its whole universe, and the safety of sheltering under a single leaf.

Morgus felt its bewilderment and its fury, and was glad.

She came day and night to look at the fruit. On one occasion the spider drew too close, lured by the scent of edible flesh, but a lightning flare scorched its foreleg, and it withdrew. Nehemet hissed at it, secure in the proximity of her mistress. Her fur would have bristled, but she had none, and only the goose bumps along her back betrayed her. "Do not threaten me, little monster," Morgus admonished. "Am I not the hand that feeds?" She did not give it a second look, turning back to the fruit, examining its colors in the murky daylight, the gradual development of its features. "It is a head," she told the goblin cat, and her sudden shortening of breath revealed her eagerness. "It is truly a human head. See the uncurling of its ears, the flattening brow, the hollows around the eyes. A head—but whose? Man or woman, living or dead? The skin is growing paler . . . there is the first tuft of raven hair. Whose head is ripening here for me? And *why* here, and not on its parent Tree? Ah, my kitten, we shall see. Soon, we shall see."

The head matured swiftly in the world of Time. Its complexion was almost white, the shadow of its brows very black.

Its hair grew thick and long, a tangle of dense curls that snagged on neighboring twigs and writhed downward like snakes. Dark lashes lay against its cheek. Morgus gazed at it as into a mirror. "It is my sister," she said at last. "My blood-sister, my twin. Morgun. But why should she come here to haunt me? I saw her on the Eternal Tree long ago. Her fruit withered, she passed the Gate—I know she passed the Gate—her soul cannot come again. Yet here she is: her eyes will open soon. I must understand. When the moon waxes I will draw the circle again, and question the seeresses and the Old Spirits—even the ghouls who gather in graveyards, looking for ghosts to eat. Someone will tell me the answer, if I have to interrogate the Powers themselves! The life of the Tree runs in my veins, and I flow in the sap of its sapling, so it responds to my thought and my need. But why Morgun? I have hardly thought of her in a thousand years. I had hoped it would give me the head of my erstwhile pupil, to show me the way to revenge. It is long overdue. But . . . Morgun? Why Morgun?"

The cat arched its spine; a flicker of static ran across its bare skin, visible as a leaping spark, but Morgus did not see it.

It was evening now, and together they stepped out into the sunset, watching the sky kindled to gold behind Farsee Hill, where the silhouette of blasted trees rose up like finger bones. The golden light reached even to the west lawn, long unshaven, stretching the shadow of a veteran oak across the grass. The witch and the cat swam in the light, gilded phantoms of the fading day, until the sun vanished, and the slow dusk crept out of the woods, and the house, purged of its past, stood like an unoccupied tomb, filled with an uneasy expectancy.

The owl followed close on the dark, cruising on motionless wings. Morgus extended her arm, and it alighted there, speaking in soft owl noises. "So she has not been there," Morgus said. "I dared not hope for it. But keep watch. She must come out from under her stone sooner or later. Meanwhile, Grodda will give you your reward."

The owl sped toward the kitchen windows, and Morgus went back into the house. The cat stayed outside for a while, until the moon rose and an owl-shaped shadow skimmed across its face, flying back to the north.

A couple of days later Ragginbone returned to the site in King's Cross with Fern in his swath. He was amused to note the altered manner of the guard on the gate, taking her, perhaps, for a student to Ragginbone's professor, elevating him from eccentric to academic. She had come straight from work and was dressed accordingly in soft pale gray trousers and collarless jacket, looking elegant and out-of-place as she picked her way across the excavations, followed by admiring glances from the guard and a lingering builder. Beside the bejeaned volunteers she seemed to be a different species, sophisticated and unnatural. Dane Hunter, climbing out of a ditch to greet Ragginbone, surveyed her without enthusiasm. "Your granddaughter?" he hazarded.

"My friend. Fern Capel. Fern, this is Dane Hunter." They shook hands formally, hers white and well-manicured, his rough and dry from grubbing in soil and brick dust, with dirt under the nails.

He said: "You don't look like an archaeologist."

"I'm not. I work in PR. Mr. Watchman—" she shot Ragginbone a malicious look "—thought you might need some."

"It's an idea," said Ragginbone, fielding the ball. "You could do with backers. I know Fernanda feels she spends too much time promoting products and not enough promoting causes."

Dane said: "I doubt if we could afford you."

"Her services would come gratis," Ragginbone assured him, ignoring Fern's steely glare. "Her gesture to posterity."

"Really." Dane looked skeptical, Fern irritated by them

both. Then her mood changed. They were bending over a
stone now fully exposed, his candidate for the altar. Fern, letting her witch senses take over, caught the long-lost scent of
blood, the shadow of ancient death—a shadow that could be
felt but not seen, lurking in the crevices and at the roots of
walls now all but razed. She laid a hand on the bare surface,
touching the deep pulse of the earth. Her eyes closed.

"You're a psychic?" Dane inquired, conscientiously polite.

Fern opened her eyes again. "Not exactly," she said, at her
most matter-of-fact. "I'm a witch."

"In PR?"

"Absolutely. I sell largely useless products to people who
don't need them. That takes witchcraft."

Dane, taken by surprise, relaxed into a smile. "Are you
really interested in archaeology?"

"Isn't everyone?" She glanced down at the stone again. "I
think it's the wrong way up. Fallen forward, maybe, or deliberately overturned. Christians vandalizing a pagan temple—a
rival sect—whatever. There is an inscription underneath."

"You know, do you?"

She nodded, ignoring sarcasm. "It's in a language you
won't recognize. It says . . ." she hesitated "—*Uval haadé.
Uval néan-charne.* I'll write it down for you if you like." He
did not seem to like, but she searched in her bag for pen and
paper. She wrote down the words in block capitals on the
back of a business card.

"And—er—what does it mean?" Dane asked. The smile
had gone and his courtesy was wearing thin.

"The Gate of Death. Well, not Gate . . . Portal is better.
Uval means that which opens. The Portal of Death, the Portal
to the Abyss. I know you don't believe me, but this isn't a
spiel. I'm not mad, either."

"You look sane, and rather decorative, but appearances can
be misleading."

"No doubt." She looked him up and down, as if criticizing

his soil-stained garb and student-length hair. "Dig. That's what you're good at, isn't it?" And, turning to Ragginbone: "There's nothing more here. We may as well go."

Hostile female eyes watched as she made her way back across the site to the exit. Dane Hunter turned the card over, scrutinizing it thoughtfully. His fingers left smudge marks on the white surface. Of course, she had been talking rubbish; that air of cool confidence was just a part of her professional artifice. He thrust the card into the back pocket of his jeans and returned to his work.

Fern summoned a further meeting at her flat on the following Tuesday. This time, she brought Luc. "This is Lucas Walgrim," she told the others. "He has to join us now. We need him. Luc, this is my brother, Will—Gaynor Mobberley—and a shady friend of ours whom we usually call Ragginbone. Mr. Watchman, if you want to be polite."

Luc nodded curtly and, after a moment's hesitation, shook Gaynor's extended hand. "I'm sorry about your sister," she said. "We've all been through it, with Fern. We know how awful it is."

"Have a drink," said Will, offering the contents of Fern's cabinet with vicarious generosity. "Just why do we need him, sis?"

"Don't call me sis." Absently, she poured herself a large G and T, but did not drink it. "I've got a plan."

"Is it a good plan?" asked Ragginbone, watching her expression.

"No," said Fern baldly. "But we can't go on waiting, doing nothing, and it's the best I can come up with."

"You've figured out a way to kill Morgus?" asked Will.

"Nope." Fern never said *nope*. "But we have to save Dana, and I want a look around Wrokeby. A chance to find out exactly what Morgus is up to. If I can't kill her, I need to get her out of the way. A diversion. Only it's going to be dangerous."

"You're always dabbling in danger," said Will. "There are times when I suspect you like it, in some deep-buried vein of your soul."

"It won't be dangerous for me," Fern said unhappily. "If we do this, *you're* going to have to stage the diversion. *You'll* be the ones in danger. You'll have to face Morgus—on your own."

For a minute, there was absolute silence. The screaming of a police siren somewhere nearby cut in sharply; inside the flat it seemed that nobody breathed.

"You wanted to be a team," said Fern. She looked very pale, even for her. "Welcome to the major league."

At last, they spoke. Will said: "Finally."

Gaynor murmured, "Shit," which was out of character.

Ragginbone contented himself with one of those glowing looks from beneath the overhang of his eyebrows.

Luc demanded: "Does that include me?"

"Not this time. You're coming with me—to Wrokeby. We need a fast car, and you're a banker. You've got a Porsche or two."

"Porsche and classic Jag," said Luc. "But I think I can do better than that. I've got a bike as well."

"A Harley?" Will was distracted.

"I'm scared of bikes," Fern said.

"Good," said Ragginbone. "That way we get to share the fear around. You'll need Lucas at Wrokeby: as her close kin, he could be the only one who can restore Dana to herself. Even if her spirit is released, without the Gift she may be unable to find her own way back."

"Can you tell me what to do?" asked Luc.

"Later. Tell us your plan, Fernanda."

She told them.

"You were right," said Ragginbone. "It isn't a good plan. But it will have to do. Were you thinking of drawing the circle here?"

"You know the room's not big enough, and the vibes are wrong. We'll have to use the basement again."

"Moonspittle won't like it," Ragginbone said. "Whatever you offer him won't be enough."

"You'll have to twist his arm. You've done it before. The point is, will it work?"

"Sorcery always attracts attention," the Watcher conceded. "The elementals are certain to be still around, and the eyes of Oedaphor miss little. Once she's found you, there's no doubt that Morgus will come. Whether we can divert her for long enough . . . well, that is a matter for us. But creeping around a witch's lair in her absence is hardly a safe option."

"I'll walk on tiptoe," Fern said. "And I'll put spells of protection around you, especially Gaynor. I'm sorry, but you're the weakest, and my friend; she's bound to target you. She already thinks you're a reincarnation of Guinevere."

"Maybe I could use that," Gaynor heard herself saying, surprised to find her voice unshaken. "I know all the legends."

"Legends only tell you what's legendary," Ragginbone said. "We don't know the truth, or what memories we might reawaken. That could be the most dangerous game of all."

"It's worth a try," Gaynor insisted valiantly.

"Definitely not," said Fern. "Just keep her talking for a while. When she gets angry, tell her where I've gone. That'll make her so mad she should forget about you immediately. Broomsticks are out this year: she'll have to get back to Wrokeby by car. With luck, we'll be away before then."

"You are relying too much on luck," said Ragginbone.

"You mean *we're* relying on it," said Will. "You'll be in the firing line, too. No more simply the observer."

Ragginbone made no answer, and his eyes were hooded.

"Are we agreed?" asked Fern.

The response came in nods and whispers.

"When do we do it?" Gaynor inquired tentatively.

"Friday," said Fern. "I won't wait for the moon; I don't

want to run the risk of the circles intersecting again. Morgus will have to get to London by some normal means of transport, probably a car. That's vital for the time factor." She did not add: I don't want to leave myself leisure to think. There was a darkness in her head that might have been mere dread or genuine premonition, but now that she had told the others of the plan—now that she had their agreement—she knew there was no going back. She glanced at Luc's face: the geometry of his bones, the straight bar of his brow, the clamped mouth. He would be with her. On some instinctive level, he believed in her—in her power, in her ability to help. Suddenly, it mattered to Fern very much that he did not see her fear or fail. Whoever he was.

"We'll be lucky," she said.

In her gut, she thought her luck had run out.

VIII ~~~~~

It was daylight in the backstreets and alleyways of Soho, but beneath the shop that never opened the basement was dark. The window slot was screened; lumpen candles guttered in a phantom draft but did not quite go out. Moonspittle quaked in a chair, his head retreating between rounded shoulders like a tortoise into its shell. On his lap, a restless Mogwit unraveled layers of cardigan with a kneading of claws. "I won't do it," Moonspittle muttered, over and over. "My place. My secret place. Intruders. Danger . . ." Ragginbone did what he could to soothe him. He was uncharacteristically gentle, but it had little effect. Fern, now that the initial arguments had ended, paid no further attention. She was walking the perimeter of the circle, spellpowder dribbling through her fingers, and chanting in a voice so soft that no individual words could be distinguished. The shadow of impending danger was not gone from her mind, but she had been able to thrust it aside, immersing herself in the present moment. For this little space she felt in control, sure of herself and her actions.

Will and Gaynor stood back from the circle. Luc remained near the door. Earlier that day, Gaynor had bought a style magazine and a quantity of makeup, darkening her eyes to smoky slits, hollowing her cheeks with blusher, painting her lips the color of black plums. Strands of her long hair were braided and twisted with glittering threads. "Gwennifer," she had told herself, gazing in the mirror; but the transformation

didn't work, she simply looked like a Gaynor whose face—
like so many of her clothes—didn't quite fit. "A change of image," she excused herself to the others. Will glared somberly
at her from time to time. In the flicker of the candlelight, forgetful of her appearance, she did indeed look different, as if
the memory of another face played over hers, someone more
beautiful and more alien, a stranger whose specter had returned courtesy of Chanel and Aveda to haunt her features.

Under the influence of magic, the room began its usual an-
tics, stretching and bending away from the circle. Luc, unprepared and unaccustomed, stared around him wildly, but
seeing his companions apparently indifferent, forced himself
to stay calm. Fern completed the perimeter, drew the runes of
protection outside. Then she commenced a new incantation, a
shielding spell to cover Will, Ragginbone, and Moonspittle,
and most of all Gaynor. She was not certain of the wording,
only that she must call on a power long gone, but as she spoke
her vocal cords were seized with paralysis and her lips moved
without feeling, and another voice vibrated through her, one
deeper than hers and wilder, startling even Moonspittle from
his fog of private terrors. Man or woman, spirit or witchkind,
Fern could not tell, but the voice filled her like wind in the
trees, like rain on the sea, and the spell rang out strong and
sure. For an instant they all saw it, glittering in the air around
them, and then it was set, and the vision vanished with the
words, and Fern was silent a long minute till her own voice
returned.

"What was *that*?" asked Will.

"You are meddling with powers that should not be disturbed," Ragginbone said predictably.

Fern did not deign to answer. She was carried along by the
momentum of the enchantment, not oblivious to distractions
but unaffected by them. *"Nyassé!"* she commanded. The candles flared upward. The circle became a ring of pale flame.
Luc saw the shadows fragmented, swirling around the room,

swarming like flies against a ceiling that seemed to arch away from the potency of the magic. He thought: She *is* a witch; and his heart shivered, but not with fear. She spoke words that he knew somehow were those of summoning, though he could not understand them. In the background, Moonspittle whimpered in protest. "Eriost Idunor!" Fern cried, and at the circle's hub a stunted column of smoke appeared, condensing swiftly into a fair, slight form. The Child. Luc tried in vain to discern its sex. It was leaf crowned, flaxen curled, and its eyes were old.

"You summon me again, Morcadis," it said. "You are profligate with your Gift, calling on ancient spirits so often and so carelessly. I thought you had mortal friends to bear you company."

"I am never careless," said Fern. "Tell me about the Tree."

"The Tree?"

"You know to what I refer. Morgus has brought a sapling of the Eternal One into this world and planted it. Even as I speak she watches it grow. Does it bear fruit?"

"I have no knowledge of such things," Eriost replied. "I am not a seer—or a gardener. Ask elsewhere."

"You are one of the first Spirits," Fern insisted. "You see far. Tell me what you see."

The Child tilted its head to one side and gazed mockingly at her.

> "Maerë, Maerë, witch of Faery
> How does your garden grow?
> With gallows tree and nooses three
> And pretty heads all in a row."

"Riddles and rhymes," said Fern. "A fit pastime for a child."

"I know another." Eriost laughed an infant's laugh tainted with mischief—or malevolence.

"Little Miss Capel sat at a table
Under the apple tree,
Along came a spider and sat down beside her
And ate up Miss Capel for tea."

The Child faded as it spoke, vanishing into a giggle and a puff of vapor.

Fern let it go. She could feel a change in the atmosphere, a thickening of the shadows that was not the onset of nightfall. It was midsummer: outside, beyond the city lights, the evening was still blue and clear. She felt a draft of bitter cold as *something* passed through the basement; eyes blinked from the darkest corners and were gone. "Oedaphor," she whispered.

"Boros," said Ragginbone. "They have found you."

"How long before they reach Morgus?"

"They will be with her now. The bait is taken. Last time, the circle held and blinded them. This time, they were outside the perimeter. They could see everything. They will lead her here."

"No!" shrieked Moonspittle. "Not *here*! My place—my secret place . . . Close the circle. Seal the door. If we hide down here in the quiet—dark and quiet—maybe she will not find us . . ."

"I am sorry," said Fern, trying to suppress her growing fears. "We must go." And to Ragginbone: "Take over. Keep the circle open as long as you can—as long as you dare. She *must* believe I'm here."

"I won't do it!" Moonspittle squeaked, but the Watcher's hands fell heavily on his shoulders, pressing him into the chair, and the stronger will took control of him, channeling his power. Mogwit hissed, fur bristling in ragged tufts, claws burrowing into his master's bony knees.

"Will he be all right?" Gaynor asked.

"I hope so." Fern was halfway to the door, Luc gripping her

arm. "Good luck. Take care—if you can—" They were gone before Gaynor or Will could respond in kind.

"Get after them," Ragginbone ordered Will. "Lock the outer door."

Will groped his way up the lightless stair. Above, Luc was wheeling the motorcycle from its parking place in the hallway out into the alley. It emerged into the dusk like some technomonster thrusting its foreweel from the shelter of a hidden cavern. Slivers of light ran over the chromework; a dim luster curved its way around the metallic black chassis. It was the war chariot of a modern Phaëthon, horseless, driven by its own power, moving lightly for all its heavy build. Fern struggled with the strap of her helmet; Luc turned to adjust it for her. From the rear, Will said: "What model is it?"

"A Harley-Davidson Fatboy; 1450 cc Evolution engine—"

"How fast does it go?" Fern interjected.

"How fast do you *want* to go?"

The engine jerked into life with a rattle like machine-gun fire: echoes ricocheted off the narrow walls of Selena Place. Heads turned, doors cracked open, and in the sewers below, rats pricked their ears. Fern mounted behind Luc, hastily zipping herself into the baggy depths of his second-best leather jacket. Will's valedictory "Good luck!" was drowned out as they roared down the alley and slid into the traffic stream, threading their way snakelike between lorries and cars, taking advantage of every widening gap. Fern closed her eyes and then opened them, deciding that if death was coming she wanted to see it. "This isn't a small bike!" she shouted. "We can't get through—"

"I thought you were in a hurry?"

After a while, she remembered to unclench her teeth.

They headed westward out of London, leaving the choked streets behind, scorching along the motorway at a hundred and twenty plus. There was little exhilaration at such speed, only the brutal buffeting of the wind as it filled the space under Fern's jacket, trying to tug her off the bike, and shook the overlarge helmet so the chin guard yanked at her jaw. She kept her head down, using Luc's body as a shield. "I won't be able to hear you at high speed," he had warned her. "Tap my leg if you want something"; but even when she thought the wind's pull might break her neck, she made no move to slow him down. She had staked her stake, rolled the dice: it was too late now to falter. She wondered if they would pass Morgus going the other way, but on the triple-laned motorway divided from the oncoming traffic, she knew they would not see each other. She had feared that Morgus might sense their passage. At the same time she wanted to be sure Morgus had really taken the bait. Fern's witch senses were strained to the limit, expecting nothing. When the touch came it caught her unawares—a cold blast on the edge of feeling, gone in less than a second. She turned, squinting through the visor, catching a flying glimpse of taillights, red streaks vanishing into the dark. The wind seized her helmet, wrenching at her neck. She ducked below Luc's shoulders, sheltering against his back, hoping Morgus was focused entirely on her goal and had no thought to spare for passing vehicles. Fern would have worried about her friends, but she dared not, lest her fears destroy her.

They left the motorway, following a minor road deep into the countryside. There were no lights, save for the clustered windows of the occasional village or hamlet. The moon was hidden. Shadowy hills reared on either hand, the fringes of hedgerows and coppices. The bike leaned steeply on every bend, and it took all Fern's courage to lean with it, trying to ignore the proximity of the pavement. They were going slower now, a mere ninety-odd. Peering around Luc's body she saw the single beam of the headlight slicing through the night, the dazzled eyes of some small animal blinking back at them. She heard him call out: "Not long now." The light stabbed between stone gateposts; gravel scrunched and spat beneath their wheels. Briefly, she glimpsed the house: ivied windows, crenellations, the stubby shape of a tower. Then at last they came to a halt. The engine cut off, and the light. Fern's first reaction was sheer relief, because she seemed to be still in one piece.

She dismounted awkwardly; her legs trembled with muscle strain and her bottom felt numb. Luc assisted her with her helmet. "Did you enjoy the ride?" he asked her.

"No."

There was no sound now but the murmurous quiet of a country night: seething wind, stirring leaves, whispering grass. Fern listened with more than her ears, but she could not catch even the distant beat of a bird's wing or the ultrasonic chitter of a bat. The undergrowth was untenanted; only insect life ventured near Wrokeby. She heard the slither of a passing adder, but it did not stay. She walked toward the house, her footsteps loud on the gravel. There were many windows, some rectangular, some arched, all blank and dark, eyeholes in an empty head. For the first time she understood the true meaning of what Dibbuck had told her: there were no ghosts here, no memories, no past, only walls and roof, and hollow spaces in between. But something had invaded the spaces, blowing in like the wind under her jacket, a hungry darkness pouring through wall chinks and splintered panels into every room. She could feel them there, tiny motes of spirit teaming like bacteria around a corpse, drawn not merely to Wrokeby's emptiness but to the sorcery that dwelt within. She wondered if Luc's senses prickled as hers did, and if he felt the same dread.

She said: "The door key?"

He produced it, stepping up to the main entrance, switching on a flashlight to find the lock. The oblong of light skimmed over black oak and curling iron hinges, steadied on the keyhole. Metal scraped on metal.

Fern unfastened her jacket, freeing her movements, looking around her with night-adapted vision. "Skuldunder?" she murmured. She had heard nothing, even she, but the werefolk were quieter than quiet. The goblin appeared a little way off, his hat brim pulled down to his nose, the hunch of his shoulders betraying his apprehension. "Where's Dibbuck?" Fern demanded. "I told you we would need him."

"He would not come, mistress," said the goblin. Fern noted that nervousness had made him excessively polite. "He curled up like a frightened hedgehog when we asked him, shivering and weeping. The queen herself could not insist. She ordered me to assist you myself, because—" he licked his lips, such as they were "—because I am the bravest of her subjects."

"You are?" said Fern, fascinated. Luc had unlocked the door and stood rooted to the spot, staring at the newcomer.

"Burglars have to be brave," Skuldunder declared. "Dibbuck described to me all the ways of this place. I will guide you."

"We can get lost together," said Fern. She turned to Luc, nudging him back into motion. "Come on. Let's hope you know your way around."

"A little. I hardly ever come here."

The door opened without a creak; presumably Morgus had had the hinges oiled. They went in, with Skuldunder trailing reluctantly in the rear, and it swung shut behind them with a soft final thud.

In Selena Place, Will locked the outer door and fastened the various bolts and chains that Moonspittle had installed over centuries of paranoia. Back in the basement, he gravitated automatically to Gaynor's side. Moonspittle was weeping in a mixture of panic and protest; Ragginbone had so far failed to calm him or assert his authority. The magic was getting out of hand. Glimmering rings rose like ripples from the circle and shrank inward, disappearing with a pop into the center. Power was building there, sucked into a nucleus too dim to distinguish clearly. "It isn't supposed to do that," said Gaynor. "Is it?"

"Control it!" Ragginbone commanded. "Or it may implode and destroy us all."

"Can't," Moonspittle mumbled. "Not my fault. Not me. Sitting here like rats in a hole, waiting for the rat catcher . . ."

"Control it!"

The ripples were rising faster now. In desperation, Gaynor stretched out her hand in a gesture she had seen Fern use—the other hand gripped Will's wrist—and stammered one of the few words of Atlantean that she could remember. *"Fiassé!"* Ragginbone had told her once before that she had a Gift of another kind; maybe, with the excess power already boiling over, it would suffice.

"Again," said Will.

"Fiassé!"

The ripples ceased. A crackle of flame ran around the perimeter, and at the hub the darkness condensed into a form. A bulging, familiar form, made of lip, dividing slowly into an immense toothless gape. Cthorn.

"Envarré!" said Will and Gaynor, as one.

"Envarré!" Ragginbone was shaking Moonspittle into submission, forcing words into his mouth with the brute strength of his will. The thing in the circle dissolved, melting back into a blackness of fume. "Gaynor!" Ragginbone gasped, breathless with effort. "Block it! Quickly!"

"How?"

"Conjure something."

"What? Who?"

"Anything. Anyone. Anyone useful. It is ill done—to waste spelltime . . ."

"But—" Gaynor stopped, trying not to founder, groping for inspiration in a vacuum of thought.

"A seeress?" Will suggested.

"I summon . . . someone from the past. Someone from Morgus's past. Friend or foe—kith or kin—it doesn't matter. I summon someone who *knows* Morgus!"

"Too general," said Ragginbone. "Anyhow, she had no friends and all her foes are dead. It was a long time ago. You'll have to—"

But someone was there. A woman. Gaynor, startled to the point of horror, saw with slight relief that she looked rather like a middle-aged water maiden who had spent too long in the shower. She was as thin as a pipe cleaner, her attitude languishing, almost drooping, with straight wet-look hair hanging to her waist, a dress that clung damply to her bony figure, and skinny arms with drooping, long-fingered hands. Her face was beautiful in a haggard way, fine-penciled with lines, heavily shadowed in the eye sockets. She gazed around her with an air of vague surprise, until her regard came to rest on Gaynor.

"Who are you, child? I think we have not met before."

"I'm Gaynor. Gwennifer. Aren't I supposed to ask the questions?"

"Don't you know?" said the woman. "Dear me. This is very confusing. I thought you summoned me."

Gaynor glanced wildly at Ragginbone, but he was studying the visitant with a frown and offered no advice.

"Go on," said Will.

"I summoned . . . someone," Gaynor explained. "Someone who knows Morgus. The witch. Do you—"

"Oh, yes. I know her. I've always believed she was dead. So much time gone by—so many centuries—I never kept count. Are you telling me she lives after all? That would be bad news for the world, or at least our corner of it. How could she manage to evade the Gate?"

"She hid," said Gaynor, "in a cave among the roots of the

Eternal Tree. Now she's back in this dimension, and we don't know how to deal with her."

"I can't help you there," said the woman. "No one could ever deal with Morgus. The gods themselves were afraid of her. Mind you, there were many gods around in those days, and some of them were small and nervous. I used to suspect it might be due to their digestion: too much red meat at the sacrifice, not enough herbs—"

"Who are you?" Gaynor interrupted, prompted by Will.

"I am Nimwë. I thought you knew. I was an enchantress— quite a good one, if I may say so; that's why I'm still around. I've slept through much of history: I didn't like the way it was going. I was waiting for something, though nowadays I don't always recall what. It will come back to me. When the time is right."

"But you knew Morgus once?" Gaynor persisted. "You knew her well?"

"Well enough. Did you say you were Gwennifer? Little Gwenny? You look like her—in a bad light. She died, of course, way back. In a nunnery. There was a fashion for such things. Repentance, you know, and a life of chastity. Locking the safe when the treasure has already been stolen. Poor Gwenny. They married her to a king, but she loved another and blamed herself when it all went wrong. A sad tale, but common enough. I hear they still make songs for her, even now. Something about a candle in the wind . . ."

"Wrong princess," said Gaynor.

"Same story," said Will, "more or less. Can't you get her to keep to the point?"

"I'm trying," Gaynor said indignantly. She turned to Nimwë. "Please tell us about Morgus."

"Ah . . . *please*. Always the magic word. I like courtesy in the young. They say it has gone out of style, but I'm glad to see they're wrong. Gwenny was a polite child, I recall—very important for royalty. She could be sharp with her equals, but she was always charming to the peasantry."

"Morgus . . . ?"

"She was never polite, not even to the gods. She cowed the weak with hard words and the strong with harsh deeds. Succor, valor, honor, that was the knightly code, but she twisted it and mocked it. She had no fear of any man, neither king nor wizard."

"Nor any woman?" Gaynor asked.

"Certainly not me, if that's what you mean." Nimwë fidgeted with her long hair, her eyes dreamy under drooping lids. "Of course, we wanted different things. She was concerned with dominion over others and earthly power; I wanted illusion, and enchantment, and love. She went mad; I didn't." Her gaze lifted, focusing on Gaynor. "I am quite sane, you know, even after all these years. *Quite* sane. Shall I show you something?"

Gaynor hesitated, unsure how to respond, and Nimwë shook her hair, scattering water drops on the circle. Segments of the fire ring were extinguished, damped into a smoking rim that leaked magic. The floor at Gaynor's feet sprouted grass that shriveled and died within seconds, like a high-speed nature film. The earth crumbled and heaved with white worms. Something that might have been a hand came groping upward, greenish with long decay. Moonspittle, frightened out of his panic, for once reacted quickly, jabbering a succession of Commands. The circle closed again, the hand sank, floorboards scabbed over the worm-ridden earth. Nimwë laughed sadly, a curious sound. "He isn't ready to wake yet," she said. "One day . . ."

"Morgus must have feared someone," Will said, "else why did she flee?"

"She feared winter," said Nimwë, when Gaynor passed on the question. "The Northmen came, bringing the ice in their hearts. Or maybe it was Time she feared, because hers had run out. Who knows? They say she feared her sister, but Morgun went away and did not wait for the future. They were identical twins, coequal in power but very different in character. Morgus was—and no doubt still is—a creature of cold passions, greedy, cruel, heartless. She feeds off others' pain, even as did the Spirits of old, but her weaknesses are human. The insecurities of a mortal ego. Morgun, too, was passionate, but her blood was hot. She was reckless, driven by love as well as hate. In the end, so they say, love conquered her, and she sought redemption. She and her maidens took the wounded king from the site of the last battle and carried him to the lost isle of Avalorn in search of healing. So they say. In some stories, I was there: did you know that?"

"Were you really there?" asked Gaynor.

"No. I stayed. I had other business. Someday, I may complete it. When *he* wakes." Her head dropped; her thin body sagged like a willow overburdened with leaves. Suddenly, she looked up again. Her strange eyes met Gaynor's: they were dark, with smoky lights moving in their depths. "Why did you call me?"

"I needed your help," Gaynor replied. "Against Morgus."

"None can defy her. Her sister dared to try, and ran for her life. They were lovers: did you know? Twin cherries on a single stem, as the bard says. A later bard, that; doubtless he stole from his predecessors. Anyway, they were wound together, Morgus and Morgun. Rumor said the demons themselves would go to spy on their lovemaking: they were so beautiful, and so perfectly matched. They would lie lip to nether lip, limb tangled with limb, their secret skin rose kissed, beaded with the moisture of love. The very gods of desire fainted with lust at the sight. But Morgun betrayed her sister for the love of men and left the world, and Morgus is gnawed ever by vengeance unfulfilled. Mention her sibling, if you wish to strike at her empty heart. She may not be injured, but she will be annoyed."

"Thank you," Gaynor said uncertainly.

"Are you done with me, child? I am very tired now. If we cannot wake the sleeper, then let us join him."

"Of course. I—I release you. Is that right?"

Nimwë faded slowly into what looked like a shower of silver rain. Her last whisper fell softly into the silence of the room. "We will meet again . . ."

"Now what?" asked Gaynor.

"Nothing," said Ragginbone. "We close the circle. It is dangerous to continue. I did not know Nimwë was still around: the Gifted can be a long time dying. She must have bound herself in an enchanted sleep, waking intermittently as the spell wore thin. I suspect she is only . . . *quite* sane."

Moonspittle finished the ritual, the fires died, the power drained, the circle was cold and dead. Only a faint tingle in the air indicated that the protection spells were still in place. Mogwit, no longer restrained, prowled around the room, pouncing on shadows.

Will said: "I need a drink."

"What do we do now?" Gaynor reiterated.

"We wait for Morgus," said Ragginbone.

The flashlight beam darted around the entrance hall, slicing the dark into segments of shadow that twitched and shifted around them. More shadows slid under doors, leaped up the stairs; eyes peered from a portrait. Luc said: "There's a light switch here somewhere."

"Leave it." Fern was curt, perhaps from nerves.

"We needn't fear discovery. With Morgus absent—"

"There may be other occupants. Besides, our burglar here would not like too much light. You're meant to be our guide, hobgoblin. Start guiding."

Luc swung the flashlight, but Skuldunder was gone; Fern picked him out as a black hump shrinking in the lee of the stair. "Point the light elsewhere," she told Luc. "Come on out, burglar. You do your queen no credit, running from a single ray of electricity. Where is the spellchamber Dibbuck spoke of?"

"Tell him to leave me alone," Skuldunder muttered. "Spellchamber . . . upstairs. Dibbuck said it used to be a sitting room. *He* should know." A crooked digit indicated Luc. "She uses the cellars as a storeroom. Below the kitchen. That's where Dibbuck saw the Tree."

"What about the servant?" said Fern. "The hag? We should deal with her."

"In the kitchen."

Luc said: "This way, I think . . ." He shone the flashlight ahead; Skuldunder followed behind Fern, well away from the prying light. Luc had visited the house only rarely, but eventually he found a descending stair with a yellow gleam beneath the door at its foot. Fern thrust it open and walked boldly in. The hag was backing away from her, lips working on some primitive charm or the voiceless mouthings of panic. Her narrow black orbs seemed to exude a mixture of malevolence and terror. The cowl had fallen back from her head and her gray hair, dense with tangles and small insect life, fanned out from her scalp as if animated with static. Fern seized a handful of her filthy robe—Grodda was light, scant flesh on gnarled bone—and thrust her effortlessly back, and back. Then Luc was there, lifting the lid on a chest freezer, and between them they bundled her in, slammed it shut, and placed a stack of ceramic casserole dishes on the top.

"Won't she die in there?" Luc asked without any particular concern.

"Doubt it," said Fern. "I don't know much about hags, but they're supposed to be incredibly tough. Like cockroaches."

"Where next?"

"The cellars. Morgus's storeroom."

They clattered down another stair in the wake of the flashlight beam. Luc kept a hand on the wall, but Fern seemed to see beyond the meager light. "There should be a cat," she muttered. "The goblin cat . . ."

"Maybe she took it with her," Skuldunder suggested hopefully.

"We'll see."

The cellar door was locked. Luc had the key, but when he tried to slot it in his fingers cramped and pins and needles ran up his arm. Fern produced a glove from her pocket and put it on: her hand became a lizard's paw, mottled patterns rippling over it, fading above her wrist. She turned the key without difficulty and they went in. Here, she switched on the main light. The illumination was poor but enough to show the shelves of bottles and jars, hanging bunches of herbs, saucers for burning oils and gums stained with toffeelike residue, white candles skewered on iron candlesticks, scribbled runes marking cupboard and drawer. The contents of some of the jars moved; at the tail of her vision, Fern glimpsed drifting eyeballs that appeared to watch her, following her progress around the room. Using her gloved hand, she opened drawers, finding knives, ladles, pincers, and took down bottles, peering closely at the labels. Some were in Atlantean, some in Latin, Greek, and what might have been Arabic. She didn't know what they all meant, but several bore the emblem of a tree. She uncorked one or two and sniffed cautiously, catching a familiar smell of dankness and greenness, growth and decay. Behind her, she heard Luc say: "What's this?" and turning, she saw the small table standing on its own, the empty jar with the crystal stopper, the sigils written in red.

"You don't want to touch that," said Skuldunder hastily, but Luc was already reaching out, and the air thickened around the jar, so his hand seemed to be pushing through glue, and shadows slid from the corners of the room toward them. As Fern drew closer she saw the jar no longer looked empty: a glitter of vapor coalesced inside and assumed a shape, too vague to specify, which beat like a trapped butterfly against the glass walls.

"It's her!" said Luc. "It's Dana."

"I think so. Wait—there's bad magic in here. I need to penetrate the shield."

She selected a bottle with more optimism than knowledge—one with a colorless liquid inside and red label bearing the Atlantean word for "burn"—and let a single drop fall on each of the sigils. They hissed and smoked, stinging her eyes; scorch marks blackened the table. *"Uvalé!"* Fern ordered, and the spell barrier, worn thin over the months and never renewed, crumpled at a touch. Fern picked up the jar in her gloved hand and passed it to Luc, who took it gingerly, as if it were very fragile, though the glass was thick and the base solid. "You know what to do," Fern said. "Imagine her body in the clinic; hold that picture in your mind. When you take out the stopper say the words Ragginbone taught you. Call her by name. Send her home."

Luc nodded, his dark face at once set and brittle. She saw his throat muscles flex as he swallowed. He seized the stopper, twisted it—for a moment the wax resisted, then it began to crack. A red flake peeled off, and another, and at last the crystal came free. He murmured in Atlantean the spell of unbinding, and a thin vapor streamed out, growing swiftly, spreading into an ill-defined form with trailing wisps of hair and clothing and wide frightened eyes whose whites gleamed as her gaze turned this way and that. "Dana," Luc said softly, and: "Dana!" a little louder. "Find yourself. Go to your fleshly home. You know where it is . . ." Fleetingly, her eyes met his. Then there was a sound like a rush of wind, and the vapor was blown away, and the vacant jar fell to the floor, cracking into pieces, and Luc started at the sound as if wakened from a trance. "Did I do it right?" he asked.

"I hope so."

"I must go. I must go to her."

"If you want. Freeing Dana was your task; the rest is mine."

He looked around the cellar, no longer searching, only skimming. "You need me. I'll wait, but hurry."

She walked along by the shelves, stopping beside the flask containing the eyeballs. They lined up against the glass, focused on her; she fancied there was a kind of pleading in that dreadful lidless stare. She picked up the container and unscrewed the cap, murmuring a charm similar to the one Luc had used. "Be free," she whispered. "Pass the Gate. *Vardé!*" The eyeballs bobbed in the preserving fluid and then went still, revolving slowly, no longer in alignment. A thin chill fled past her and was gone. "Rest in peace," Fern adjured, "whoever you were." A vision flickered through her brain of a golden island sea-ringed and a young man with a beautiful face whose bright brown eyes were narrowed against the sun. She turned and saw Luc was standing close by her, and she knew he had seen it, too.

"Come on. If you want to look over the rest of the house . . ."

"One moment."

There were few cupboards, but all were marked with runes of guard. She opened them with her lizard's paw, scanning the contents: spellbooks plastic-wrapped against possible damp, more flasks and phials, what appeared to be a winged fetus curled up in a greenish fluid. She took nothing, though she retained the bottle with which she had destroyed the magic symbols. The last cupboard was set deep in the wall, its double doors padlocked.

Luc asked: "Can you break the lock?"

"Not with magic. For a lock, there must be a key. What have you got?"

Luc's collection of house keys proved unhelpful, but Fern found the right one in an adjacent drawer. "Almost as if the padlock is for show," she remarked. "A gesture." She unfastened it, and the doors swung wide.

It was Luc who screamed, a cry of astonishment and horror abruptly cut off. There was a single big jar inside, and it contained a human head. Fern, more accustomed to such things, merely froze and stared. It was the head of a woman with her eyes closed as if in sleep and her long hair floating in the liquid around her. Her skin was almost translucent, showing the faint blue tinge of veins at her temples, though no blood beat there; her mouth was as exquisite as a half-opened rose, but very pale. Luc said: "What kind of a hellhole *is* this?" And: "Do you know her?"

"I think so," Fern answered slowly. "Don't worry: this isn't human. It is . . . fruit. Unalive and undead. We will not disturb her now." She closed the cupboard, replaced the padlock. She added with the edge of a smile: "Of course this is a hellhole. It's a witch's lair. What did you expect?"

"I don't know." Luc shrugged. "Black velvet curtains—black candles—an altar to worship the devil."

"Witches worship no one but themselves," said Fern. "You're thinking of Satanists. They have no true power, only the crumbs they can borrow from whatever Spirits they invoke."

"Can we go now?" The voice of Skuldunder piped from the corner where he had retreated as soon as they entered the cellar.

"Where next?" Luc demanded.

"The spellchamber. That might have black velvet curtains. I wonder what Morgus did with the Tree? She must have planted it somewhere." Fern checked the level in her stolen bottle: it was still three-quarters full. As they passed through the kitchen, ignoring the sounds of the hag hammering inside the chest freezer, Luc helped himself to the longest of the skewers and thrust a vicious-looking knife through his belt. "You look like a pirate," Fern commented. "Aren't you going to carry one in your teeth?"

Skuldunder muttered something and appropriated the

nearest implement, which turned out to be a carving fork.
Wielding it, he resembled a clumsy miniature Beelzebub,
rendered even more comic by the hat brim screening most of
his face. But nobody laughed. The emptiness of the house
would have sucked up laughter, like a vacuum swallowing air.

When they reached the ground floor again, Luc said: "If
you're looking for a tree, there's a conservatory. One of those
Victorian monstrosities big enough for a small jungle. As far
as I can remember, it's badly in need of repair."

"Dibbuck mentioned it," Skuldunder volunteered. "He
said there was a gypsy working there."

"We'll try it," said Fern.

Luc switched on the flashlight again and led them along a
dark corridor toward the back of the house. They saw the conservatory entrance across a sitting room full of slumbering
mounds of furniture: a many-paned glass door set under a
high arch that flashed the light back at them in broken glints.
Luc opened the door without any hindrance. "No hex this
time," he said. "There can't be anything here of importance."

"Then let's go," said Skuldunder. "I don't like it."

Fern peered ahead into a different kind of darkness—a
leafy darkness rustling without any wind. Fear emanated
from it, tangible as a smell. She said: "There's something here."

Luc had seen enough that night not to argue. As he stepped
over the threshold, Fern touched his arm. "Go carefully," she
said, "and very slowly."

"I'll wait," said Skuldunder.

"If you run away," Fern tossed over her shoulder, "I'll spit
you on your own fork."

They moved forward down a kind of aisle between unseen
thickets. The flashlight beam glanced over huge moth-eaten
sprays, the withered fronds of dead palms, a cracked urn
hatching a writhing nest of stems. The rustling had ceased:
every sprig, every blade was still. Their soft-shod footsteps
and the susurration of their breathing made the only sounds.

At one point Fern's toe nudged what she assumed was a piece of snapped branch, only it gleamed white in the gloom, like bone. And then the beam, probing ahead, found something she recognized. She did not speak, but her grip tightened on Luc's arm, and he stopped in his tracks. He had no alternative. In front of them, filling the end of the aisle, was a tree. The Tree. It had been planted in a stone trough, but the stone was already cracked; groping roots reached out across the floor and thrust down between the paving stones. Its trunk, twisting slightly so as to spread itself within the confines of the conservatory, was broader than Luc's waist. The light beam moved upward, taking in the oaklike foliage, blinking back from the convex panes of the roof beyond. "Back down," Fern whispered. (She didn't know why she chose to whisper.) "I saw something . . . *there*." The beam fixed on what might have been a misshapen apple hanging from a low branch, its rind very pale, a wisp of black down sprouting from the junction with the stem.

"What is it?" asked Luc. He, too, kept his voice low.

"Look further," said Fern. "There may be one more advanced."

The light roamed to and fro among the leaves. The beam was weak, but it traveled almost down to eye level now. It lit up another apple, smaller and greener, and then at last, within easy reach, it alighted on the object Fern sought—and dreaded to find. This time, Luc did not scream. Fern heard the hissing intake of his breath, saw the smudge of light tremble before it grew steady. The head hung there, life-size and complete in every detail, its milky skin glistening faintly as if with predawn dew. Jetty tangles of hair snaked down below the neck stump; eyes and mouth were closed. Luc held up the skewer like a sword, pointing at the monstrosity. "Explain."

"This is fruit," Fern said, "of a kind. The parent Tree is the one I spoke of: it grows in another dimension. The heads of the dead ripen there: it is said all who have done evil must hang a season on that Tree. Sometimes many seasons. This—it can't be a seedling: the Eternal Tree has no seeds—it must be a cutting, nurtured by magic. But I don't understand how it can bear fruit, here, in the real world—or what fruit this might be. It looks like Morgus herself, but she lives. It must be her twin sister, Morgun . . . Maybe this Tree is so imbued with her power that it will carry only those who are part of her history."

"Like that one in the cupboard?"

"I . . . doubt it. That's Sysselore—she looks much younger than when I knew her, but I'm sure. I believe she was taken from the original Tree and brought here. It's been done before."

"By whom?"

"Me."

"This one's alive." She felt him start. "I saw its eyelid twitch. She's *alive*—"

"Oh, yes," said Fern. "She's alive."

She had seen that moment before, when the eyes jerk open, and the whole face springs into animation. But she had never before seen such an expression on any of the heads. The eyes stretched until the iris was fully exposed, the mouth spread into a smile—a wide, happy smile devoid of laughter, eager, exultant. "At last!" it said.

At last? Fern was bewildered. The heads of those in purgatory were not usually elated or fulfilled.

"Take that light from our eyes," it continued peremptorily. "Let us see you."

Luc shifted the beam a little to the left. Under Fern's clasp his muscles felt rigid.

"The dark cannot hide you, Fern Capel," said the head. "Have we not possessed you, mind and body? Did we not steal your very soul?"

"Morgus couldn't keep it," Fern retorted. "Why do you say 'we'? I didn't know you identified so closely with your twin."

"My—twin?" The head scowled as if confused.

"You are Morgun? Aren't you?"

"Morgun! Do not insult us. That our own flesh and bone should turn into a milksop, mewling after the world's approval and men's love. She hung in bitterness on the Eternal Tree in a time outside Time. She wanted forgiveness, but not ours. Her mistake. We did not wait to see her wither; we had better things to do."

"Then—who are you?" But she knew the answer.

"We are Morgus."

"How—?"

"We are one with the Tree. Blood and sap, root and sinew, we are bound together. Long before, we plucked it from its progenitor with the most secret rituals, and it was brought to this world—first to Syrcé's island, then here. This fruit is the symbol of our union. Others will follow: we will be many. The power of the Eternal One is in us, and with it, we will engulf this kingdom of Britain. The network of our roots will burrow deep in its soil and our unseen branches will overspread the sky. Already, there are those who have drunk of our sap and serve our every need. One in particular, who was rich and powerful and called himself honest . . . his mind is in our keeping. He brings us Money, which in this latter-day world opens all doors. We have watched long in the spellfire and learned much: there is no more nonsense of succor, valor, honor. Now Money is men's credo and their grail. The gods have fled: their place has been taken by small men with big bank accounts. Your leaders are no longer warriors or greathearts but mere performers, posturing before the multitude. Once, they would not have sold their honor for gold; today, they sell it for a sliver of plastic, a scrap of paper inscribed with many zeros. We will buy our way into their inmost circle and dose them with our potions, and Logrèz will be ours forever. Oh yes, we have learned much, Fernanda. We did not need you after all."

"I am Morcadis, or have you forgotten? You named me; I cannot be unnamed."

"We do not forget. We will taste of revenge before all else. You may sneak in here when our earthly self is absent, but you cannot hide for long—"

"I am not hiding," Fern pointed out. "Can't she see through your eyes—or you hers?"

"Not yet. This fruit is still strange to us. We do not comprehend what our sorcery has engendered. When we meet, we will be whole, and all will be made clear."

Fern felt a sudden surge within her, beyond knowledge, beyond reason, as if all her instincts cried out with a single message. She said: "Then I will take you to her!" Turning to Luc, she added: "Give me that knife."

"The thing is insane," he said. "A disembodied head hanging on a tree, and it—she—wants to rule the world."

"All the Gifted are mad," said Fern. "I told you that."

"And you?"

"Getting there." She took the knife, approached the head.

"You cannot touch us," it said. "We are protected." There was such malevolent satisfaction in the face that Luc stepped back, suddenly wary, directing the flashlight in a swift circuit around them. Maybe it was a trick of the shadows, but to their left where the foliage was thickest a shudder seemed to run through the leaves. He gripped the skewer tight in his other hand.

"There is no spell here," Fern said, reaching up toward the stem. And even as she spoke, she knew there was something wrong. This fruit, of all things, would have been shielded. She hesitated, half turned—

She had a brief vision of the darkness itself rising up and springing upon her—she heard the head give a cry of evil triumph. Then her skull struck the ground, and she blacked out.

*   *   *

In the basement in Soho, they waited. Now that the circle was closed the room had shrunk back to its normal proportions. Ragginbone lit more candles, Moonspittle switched on the electric light. Gaynor found herself studying the prints on the wall, but when she saw them close up she wished she hadn't. Will unstoppered a glass retort containing a liquid the color of urine and sniffed, concluding hopefully that it was whiskey. "Can we drink this?" he asked. "I'll bring you another bottle tomorrow."

Moonspittle's boot-button gaze squinted beadily at him. "Tomorrow," he said, "we may be dead. Thanks to the witch."

"All the more reason to drink it now," said Will.

They drank out of chipped cups, sat down, stood up. Talked little. Mogwit continued to prowl, his patchy fur sticking out from his body as if he had received a violent electric shock. "If you had any sense," Will remarked, "you'd get out."

"He'll stay with me," Moonspittle said indignantly. "He's my familiar."

"No sense," said Ragginbone.

Gaynor suggested timidly: "Shouldn't we have weapons?"

"Against Morgus?" Ragginbone shrugged.

"I've got a knife," Will said. He drew out of his jacket something like a hunting knife but black, both haft and hilt. When it moved through the air Gaynor thought she could hear the faint sigh of molecules being sliced in half.

"What do you expect to accomplish with that?" said Ragginbone, at his most inscrutable.

"It will cut through both iron and magic," Will insisted.

Moonspittle eyed it apprehensively. "There is a darkness on it that is more than sorcery. Or less."

"Maybe," said Will, "but it's mine. I know: I stole it."

They fell into silence. The rumor of the city night sounded far away. Gaynor thought the books on the shelves seemed to squeeze together as if to make their spines less visible, and wished she could do the same. A cockroach scurried out of a crevice, thought better of it, and scurried back in again. Time passed. Gaynor almost began to hope that Morgus would not come.

They had left the basement door slightly ajar, and the first they heard of an arrival was the stifled rattle of a bell that no longer rang. There was a pause, then came a series of thuds on the front door, as if from a heavy fist. Gaynor imagined the whole building shook. She said quickly: "Surely she can't come in? If we don't invite her, she can't come in?"

"This is a shop," said Ragginbone, "even if it's always closed. The taboo doesn't apply. In any case, Morgus will have ordinary human henchmen to whom such laws mean nothing."

There was the sound of breaking glass, the squeal of bolts, the rasp of a chain. Someone was forcing their way through Moonspittle's multiple security devices, smashing what they could not undo. Moonspittle shrieked: "No! No!" and doubled into a crouch behind a chair, his head tucked down like a hedgehog in a ball, shaking all over.

Will indicated the basement door, but Ragginbone only frowned. "No point." And then came the footsteps striding through the shop, reaching the top of the stair. The tap-tapping footsteps of high-heeled shoes. They began to descend the stair, slowly—it was narrow and hazardous—but without faltering. Will drew his knife for a second, then changed his mind, sliding it back into the sheath inside his jacket. Gaynor's heart was beating so hard she felt physically sick. Under the weathering of centuries, Ragginbone's face was pale. Mogwit leaped clumsily onto the back of a chair, his claws raking great troughs in the upholstery. The heel taps ceased and they knew she was there, behind the door, beyond the light. Even the cat froze.

"Uvalé!"

The door slammed back against the wall. A gale screamed through the room, snuffing the candles; the electric light flickered and went out. Morgus stood in the doorway, outlined in wereglow, her Medusa locks crackling with live energy, her night-black stare scanning the shadows. She cried: "Morcadis!" and her extended fingers cast a lance of radiance that roamed across the faces of the occupants. Ragginbone. Will. The disappearing tail of Mogwit. The humped shoulder of Moonspittle. Last of all, it found Gaynor. "The friend," she said, and her tone softened, but it was not pleasant. "Little Gwennifer. Where is she? Where is Fernanda Morcadis?"

"Your sister has gone," Gaynor said, and was surprised to find her voice steady.

"My . . . sister?"

"She went with the boat," said Gaynor. Desperately, she drew on her knowledge of legend, on the words of Nimwë. "They took my king. Have you forgotten?" She had no idea how the others were reacting to her improvisation and she did not dare to look; her only hope was to divert Morgus. The witch queen was wearing the clothes she evidently considered suitable to her status: a twenty-first-century evening dress of some silky material, in the deep purple of vintage wine. Her high heels were probably Prada. To Gaynor, the costume appeared incongruous, and somehow this gave her courage.

"I will never forget," said Morgus. "What of it? Morgun died long ago. I seek Morcadis. She was here—they told me she was here—"

"She was here," Gaynor echoed. "She has grown in power, since her death."

"My twin *died*: that was final. Morcadis—"

"Death has many kingdoms, but only one portal," Gaynor said. She thought it was a line she must have read somewhere.

"Enough! You were never bright, Gwennifer, but dabbling in magic has made you witless—or are you trying to deceive me? That would indeed be folly. Speak! Or I will split your brain in two and pick out your thoughts with red-hot pincers. *Where is Morcadis?*"

"Why don't you ask me?" Will interjected. "She was never here. It is your spies you should punish—they were cheated by a ghost."

And Ragginbone, quick to follow: "The world of Time has blinded your thought, queen of Air and Darkness. Are you so sure your sister passed the Gate? Did you close it behind her?"

"Do you mock me?" she snarled. The tiny needle of doubt jabbed her into greater fury. She tossed the wereglow upward into a hovering ball of light, unleashing a whiplash of power from her hand that might have taken the Watcher's head clean off. But Fern's spell encased him, and the lash rebounded, flicking sparks from the barrier. Morgus screeched with rage, cursing in several ancient languages, striking again and again at Ragginbone, Will, Gaynor, even the little she could see of Moonspittle. But for the moment, Fern's magic held.

Gaynor tried not to flinch, struggling to keep what was left of her nerve. Nimwë was right, she thought. Mention her twin, and Morgus stops thinking clearly. Anything to distract her from Fern . . . "Morgun was here," she reiterated. "She came to the circle. She left you a message."

The witch strode forward until her face was within a yard of Gaynor's. "You're lying," she said. "I can read the lies in your mind. They run to and fro like mice in a cage, looking for a way of escape. Stupid, pointless lies. Morgun is a fruit hanging on my Tree. As for this barrier—Fernanda has called on an old power, and she does not know how to harness it. How much longer do you imagine it can resist me? An hour—or merely a few more minutes?" Her hands pressed against the spellfield, squeezing it tighter, tighter—Gaynor saw her mouth ruck into a grimace of pain, the red weals springing up on her palms. Yet there was nothing visible between them but a glittering on the air. Will seized Morgus's arm to pull her away—the protection spell did not impede its object—but she shook him off almost without effort.

"Try reading my mind!" he challenged her. "What do you see?"

"That you're a better liar," Morgus snapped. She was still focused on Gaynor, intoning a counterspell: *"Xormé abelon, zinéphar unulé—"*

Disregarded for the moment, Ragginbone drew on the surrounding magic, attempting a charm of banishment. He knew the risk—he was draining his own spellscreen—but Morgus caught the whisper of his chant even through her own, and she rounded on him again. The lash of her power did not break the barrier, but he was flung to the ground, the charm scattered. He knew they had very little time left.

Morgus clasped her hands once more around Gaynor's spellfield, compressing it closer and closer to her face. The witch's skin blistered and cracked where it touched the magic; sweat ran in great drops from under her hair. Will returned to the assault, but a vicious kick dented his shield, knocking him sideways. *"Xormé!"* Morgus cried. *"Néfia!"*—and all spells broke.

IX ❧❧❧❧

Luc saw very little of the attack. The leaf shudder became a
surge—a vast shadow sprang past him—there was a smell
like no other animal he had ever smelled. Fern went down
without a cry. The jerking flashlight beam showed him few
details: a grotesque forelimb, many jointed, barbed with stiff
white hairs; a pallid hide spiked with more hairs, thick as
spines. And then the light was fragmented into a thousand
pinpoints, gleaming back at him from twin globes, multi-
screened, lidless, and below he saw the venom bubble quivering on the tip of huge fangs inches from Fern's neck.
Somewhere behind the eyes he could sense a mind, ludicrously small, appetite driven, baffled by the glare. He lunged
forward with the skewer, jarring against the carapace. There
was a minute that seemed to last an hour with legs thrashing at him, spiny hairs scratching his cheek, claws hooked
into his motorcycle leathers. Beyond the hunger and magic-
induced madness the creature had a race memory of hunting
flies: you caught one, and the others flew away. They did not
band together and fight back. Even the puppies and the calf
had not done that. It lashed out in confusion, in rage, in fear.
Surely this man-fly was too puny to defeat it. Somewhere in
the background a voice screamed: "Kill! Kill!" But Luc was
taut muscled from the squash court and the gym, and his
kitchen weapon was very sharp. Even as the monster pulled
back he drove it home, stepping athwart Fern's body, forcing

the deadly fangs away from her. He heard the crunch as the skewer pierced the head armor and the point plunged deep into something soft. The leg thrashing became a spasm; froth scummed the jaws. The head of Morgus cried out in fury and chagrin. On the ground, Fern gave the subdued moan of returning consciousness.

Luc half dragged, half lifted her across the paving stones, clear of the corpse, which was still twitching horribly. "She's dead," said the head. "It bit her."

"Fuck off."

Fern was struggling to regain control of her senses. She murmured: "What . . . the hell . . . was *that*?"

"Whatever it was, I killed it," Luc replied. "Are you all right?"

"Mm." Her head ached, but her thought was clearing. "Stupid . . . stupid of me. I should have known. She would never leave the Tree unguarded." She tried to stand up, holding on to Luc for support, fighting vertigo. Her knees swam.

"Take it gently."

"I'll be fine." She drew on her Gift, sensing the slow trickle of strength stealing through vein and sinew. Luc felt her grip relax, saw the brightening of her gaze.

"Let's see." She took the flashlight from him, directing the beam toward the thing he had killed. The blur of light traveled over the death-curled limbs, the swollen, needle-haired body, the arachnoid face with its curved jaws and the blunt end of the skewer jutting between the eyes. The glimmer of the light in the empty facets gave it a hideous illusion of life. "It's a spider," Fern said, unnecessarily.

"I thought so," said Luc, "only I didn't believe it. What happened to make it so big?"

"God knows. Some sorcery of Morgus's weaving, I expect . . . Maybe we should ask her." She turned to the head.

"It was not our doing. It must have come here with the Tree, or perhaps when Sysselore was brought to us. In the other place everything is in stasis, but this world pulses with growth and Time. So the little crawler grew big. We merely encouraged it."

"You made it mad," Luc said unexpectedly. "I felt its mind. It was too small for the body, bewildered, afraid—"

"Hungry," said the head.

Fern dusted loose dirt from her shoulders. "Do you pity it?" she asked Luc.

"No. Maybe. It wasn't a self-made monster. We are the only ones who do that."

"Thought for the night." Fern bent down to retrieve the knife, which she had lost when she fell.

"You won't take us," said the head. "We must await our Self here."

Fern said only: "Shine the flashlight so I can see," handing it to Luc, reaching up once more to sever the stem. Suddenly the head twisted, sinking its teeth into her arm. Fern gave a short scream; Luc thrust the flashlight in a pocket, found the mouth by touch, and managed to force the jaws apart. But as soon as he loosed his hold they snapped shut again, almost taking off his fingers. When the two of them jumped back from the Tree they were both bloodied and angry. The head crowed gleefully, its lips and cheeks flecked with red. "You won't take us!" it repeated. "We have no stomach, but we can still gnaw. Come near, and we will suck the flesh off your bones like the harpies of old! We need no protector. We are Morgus!"

Luc said: "This is worse than the bloody spider."

"Cloth," said Fern. "Thick cloth. Let's go back into the other room. We may have to desecrate some ancestral curtains."

They returned with a quantity of velvet ripped into strips and approached the head more cautiously. It watched them with sly eyes. When they were within range it swung wildly, flailing them with its hair, snapping at their hands, teeth gnashing at every miss. Its strength was unhuman. The branch that sustained it lashed from side to side; leaves leaped and crackled. The coarse hairs cut like paper; the motion of the head was snake swift. In addition, it maintained a tirade of insult and derision that only ceased when they finally forced a gag between its jaws, knotting it tight at the back of the skull. Then Fern wound another band of cloth around it, blinding the eyes. When the head could neither see nor speak, bite nor butt, Fern cut the stem. It still twisted and writhed in her grasp, but bound in the thick velvet it could do nothing. Fern tried to hack some of the hair off with the knife. Although several clumps broke away there always seemed to be more of it. "We need to wrap it in more of the curtains," Fern said. "We may have to carry it a long way."

"Back to London?"

"I'm not sure."

"What about the others?" Luc, who was holding the light again, pointed it at the unripe fruit.

"I'll have to deal with them. Hold this."

He took the head, gripping the stem close to the scalp, feeling the jolt as it tried to yank itself free. Fern had produced the bottle abstracted from the storeroom and now, with a muttered injunction in Atlantean, she dripped the acid contents onto the bole of the Tree. A shiver ran through leaf and branch; the flashlight beam revealed the bark near the base turning black, peeling, crumbling, flaking into ash. The canker spread: roots withered as if in a sudden blight, leaves crisped into brittle skeletons that blew away as dust on the air. The leftover fruit bruised and darkened, thudding to the ground like windfall apples. Branches moldered and fell; the trunk was consumed from within. At last, all that remained was a mere husk of dead wood scabbed with char. Fern stood for a moment in silence, as though according it a formal farewell. Then she turned to Luc and, carrying their dubious prize, they left the conservatory.

*   *   *

All spells broke. Morgus's hands closed on Gaynor's throat; Will and Ragginbone rushed to help her but were hurled aside with a word of Command. "Now," cried the witch, "*now*, little Gwennifer, I will squeeze the truth out of you drop by drop, like juice from a plum, until you are dry and empty. I can see into your fears, into your vain hopes, into the shallowness of your soul and the cringing vessel of your heart. You have run out of lies. You are afraid for your friend, but you are more afraid for yourself. Wise child. There is nothing you can do for her now. Tell me where she is, and I *may* let you live. You can't speak, but I will hear you think. Think clearly, Gwennifer— think for your life."

In the wereglow, Gaynor's face was livid; she gasped like a fish. Will said: "Wrokeby, Morgus. Fern's at Wrokeby. Were you too stupid to figure that out?"

"Wrokeby?" Gaynor felt the choke hold slacken. Morgus had switched her attention to Will.

"Of course: what did you expect?" Inwardly, Will prayed to a God Whose existence he had always doubted that Fern had already left. "We used your spies to decoy you here so Fern could have a look around your country home. If you hurry, you might just be able to join her for breakfast."

"If Morcadis is at Wrokeby," Morgus was suddenly silken, "I will *eat* her for breakfast—cold. Do you really imagine I leave my house unguarded? Even now she must be the main course at dinner, all warm and sweet and tender. I will send you a morsel, if there is anything left—a knucklebone, or a finger—then you can bury it. But there may not be much to send; my pet is always starving.

"As for you—" to Gaynor "—you are almost too pathetic to kill. But not quite." Her grip tightened again, slowly. Her mouth smiled.

Gaynor thought: This is it. Her agonized gaze swiveled toward Will, because she had no voice to say good-bye.

And then somehow Morgus's grip failed, and Gaynor slid

to the ground, half fainting, coughing and gulping air. Will's arm was around her, and Ragginbone was lifting her head, but Morgus—Morgus was doubled over, heaving, greenish vomit spattering the floor. When the paroxysm had passed she tried to straighten up, supporting herself against the wall; but she could barely stand. As the ball of wereglow faded they saw her face was gray. "What has she done?" she croaked. "Morcadis . . . *what has she done to me?*"

No one offered any answer. Ragginbone found the light switch, clicking it up and down, and the electricity came on again. Will thought it was like that moment in a dream when you think you have woken up, and everything is normal again, and then you look around and all the trappings of nightmare are still with you. Morgus's very lips were ashen, but her vocal cords at least seemed to be regaining strength. She called out: "Nehemet! Bring Hodgekiss!" The cat came pouring down the stairs, noiseless as a ripple, her shadow-blotched skin and basilisk stare more monstrous than feline. The driver followed. He was burly of stature, heavy muscled, accustomed to chauffering the so-called Mrs. Mordaunt, asking no questions, being overpaid for extras. Possibly he had drunk of her potions. "Don't mind me," she told him. "Take the girl." He moved forward.

Will drew his knife. Light was absorbed into the blackness of the blade, returning no reflection. *"Try it."*

The goblin cat hissed menacingly, but neither animal nor man advanced any farther. Then Morgus groaned, and they turned to her, the man supporting his witch, the cat following, and they mounted the stairs to the shop. The listeners below heard what was left of the front door as it clanged shut.

Moonspittle poked his head out from behind the chair. "Has she g-gone?"

Will was hugging Gaynor. "Are you all right?"

She nodded. Her throat felt too bruised to talk.

"That was quite a performance," said Ragginbone. "Not so much brave as foolhardy."

"Insane," said Will. He hugged her harder. "I thought I'd lost you."

"What happened to Morgus?" Gaynor managed in a whisper. "Was it Fern?"

"We've no way of telling," said Ragginbone. "I only hope that when the witch gets back to Wrokeby, Fernanda is long gone. Whatever she's done."

At Wrokeby, Fern, Luc, and Skuldunder were standing in the spellchamber. The goblin had rejoined them when they left the conservatory, having witnessed the previous events from the comparative safety of the doorway. He had missed little: werefolk have good darksight. "Seems that gibbering house-goblin left a lot out," he brooded. "House is empty, he said. Even the spiders have gone, *he said*. Nothing about giant ones that try to eat people, oh no."

"It wasn't native to these parts," Fern said. "It probably arrived after he left."

"In a crate of bananas," murmured Luc. His façade of sangfroid was back in place; slaying an oversized arachnid with a kitchen skewer can do a lot to restore one's self-assurance. He was carrying the head in a Hermès shoulder bag they had found in Morgus's bedroom. From time to time it would vibrate as though with violent shivering, or thrash about, butting against his hip, until he slapped it back into immobility.

"Nothing about *that*, either," muttered Skuldunder.

The spellchamber was clearly empty but he entered it reluctantly, staying near the door and fading into the scenery.

"Don't disappear altogether," said Fern. "It's bad manners."

"What's wrong?" Luc asked him, looking for a nook where something unpleasant might be in hiding.

"It was here that she did it," Skuldunder said. "She opened the abyss. You can feel the pull of it . . ."

"He means, this is a place on the edge of reality," Fern elucidated. "If you open a portal between this world and another—between dimensions—between present and past—even though you may close it afterward, it changes things. There is a weakening in the fabric of existence. It happened once at our house in Yorkshire. It's never been quite the same since. Reality once broken can be mended, but if you are sensitive to atmosphere you will always be able to feel the crack."

"And open it again?"

"Maybe. If you have the power."

The emptiness of the room became oppressive, somehow more terrible than the menace of hidden presences that they had experienced in the conservatory. Fern conjured a ball of wereglow but it went out almost immediately, as if deprived of oxygen. By its fleeting light they saw the circle burned into the floor and the clustering shadows far above. Fern found herself standing within the perimeter, and she shivered. "This is where the ghosts were lost," she mused. "All the tiny phantoms from the history of the house—the living memories that gave it its identity—all wiped out in an instant. Others have come to take their place, but these have no past, no purpose. They are the bacteria of the spirit world, drawn to evil as to an infection. The air is choked with them: can't you sense it? They feed on the overspill from the void, and it fills them. This house will never be whole again."

Luc said only: "Black velvet curtains. Gratifying. I like to be right." The head became restless, pounding at his side, until he clamped it into stillness with a hand on the bag. They left, disquieted, almost wishing they had found another monster to fight.

"*Now* we go?" Skuldunder said hopefully. "My spine prickles. The witch is coming back."

"The witch is already here," Fern reminded him. "As for

Morgus, she has a long way to come. May she be stuck in traffic."

"Is that a spell?" Luc inquired.

"No. Wishful thinking." They were on a gallery, dark beyond the flashlight beam; below yawned the cavern of the ballroom. "Dibbuck said something about a prisoner in the attic. Which way?"

"He said it was a monster!" Skuldunder objected. "Huge— hideous. An ogre . . . Haven't we had enough of monsters?"

"I need another skewer," Luc remarked.

"Which way?"

Eventually, they found the attic stairs. Skuldunder had become increasingly jittery; Luc's manner hardened into tension. Fern's resolve acquired an edge of obsession: she spoke curtly or not at all, leading them up the stair, the flashlight clenched in her grasp. The beam stabbed the gloom ahead, unwavering, certain of its goal. Fern had stopped thinking now. She knew what she would find. She realized she had known all along, on some deep level of instinct, that *he* was here somewhere. He was imprisoned, suffering, and it was her fault, because she had vowed him friendship and had done nothing to keep her vow.

It did not matter that he was a monster.

As they entered the first of the attics they made out the gray square of a skylight, but there was no visible moon and indoors it was almost completely black. The whole house had that hollow silence of a place deserted by its genius loci: the floorboards did not trouble to creak, there were no scufflings behind the wainscoting, no soft murmurs of settling drapes or lisping drafts. But here, the quiet seemed muffled, as if the room was lined with blankets. "There is heavy magic here," whispered Skuldunder, and his small voice was deadened, despite the space. Fern made a werelight, only a cautious flicker of flame, but it burned green from the magical overflow. She switched off the flashlight and handed it to Luc.

He said: "I'll lead."

But she removed his restraining hand, crossing the second attic with the werelight trembling in front of her. At her side, Luc made a sound of disgust. "What a stink!"

"Drains," suggested Skuldunder. As a wild goblin, he had never figured out the mechanics of modern life.

"In the attic?"

Fern made no comment. By the next door, she halted. She could feel the spells ahead of her, a thick mesh clogging the air, impenetrable as jungle growth. She remembered the flexible screens she had woven around her friends, and realized with a sudden cold trickle down her spine how flimsy and inadequate they were. But it was too late now to do anything about it, and she tried to push her fear away, stepping forward into the last attic, ignoring the growing stench. The wereglow dimmed to a sickly corpse candle, giving little illumination. She could just distinguish a window square striped with what must be bars, and more bars, closer at hand, turning the end of the room into a jail cell. Beyond, in the corner, the darkness appeared to congeal into a shape that was humanoid but not human—a shape that might have had slumped shoulders broader than a man's, legs that terminated in the paws of a beast, twisted horns half-hidden in a matted pelt of hair. The stink of sweat and excrement was overwhelming. Fern fought down nausea.

Luc said: "I can't see anything."

"I can."

She approached the bars, touched the spellnet that reinforced them. It was so potent the jolt ran through her whole body, like an electric shock. The werelight could not pass the barrier, but it showed her the rusty gleam of chains snaking across the floor, a shackled foot, a tail tuft.

She said: "Kal."

He did not speak, but she heard the rasp of his escaping

breath and sensed that until then he had not known who his
visitor was.

"What is it?" Luc demanded in a hiss. "Do you *know*
this—"

"Quiet." And again: "Kal."

"Little witch." The voice grated, as if from lack of practice.
"Tell me you're real. She haunts me with nightmares. It
would be like her to plague me with a phantom of hope."

"I'm real." She thought he sounded near the breaking
point, or past it, and her heart shook. "I should have come
sooner."

"Simple Susan sewing samplers . . . You owe me. Don't
forget that. When I get out of here I'm going to call in the
debt."

"You'll get out." She roamed her hands over the barrier, an
inch or two away, testing for weaknesses.

"It is too strong for you," he said. "She made it to resist
both crude force and brute magic. Even if you found a chink
and thrust your finger through, the spellburn would eat your
flesh to the bone. What are you doing here, little witch? You
cannot fight *her*."

" 'Everything that lives must die,' " Fern quoted. "Or so I
have been told. Even Morgus."

"Her word or her death would unbind the spell," said Kal.
"Nothing else."

"We'll see." She stood back from the spellnet, raising her
hand in the gestures Morgus herself had taught her, focusing
all her power on what she hoped was a vulnerable spot.
Sparks flew; the backlash hit her like a physical blow. Luc
prevented her from falling, but she would not listen when he
tried to calm her; she flung charm after charm at the barricade, running through every Command she knew, exhausting
her strength and her Gift in a fruitless assault.

"Leave it," said Kal, and the words dragged. "Now I know
you are a phantom. The real Fernanda would have been more

sparing of her powers. She was never reckless. Her head was always cool, her heart quicker to feel pity than passion. Not that I want *pity*."

Fern said: "I offer you none."

The chains scraped along the floorboards as Kal shuffled slowly, awkwardly closer to the bars. For the first time the corpse light fell on his face: Fern saw it dirt smeared, shadow gaunt, the half-human eyes no longer ruby-dark but blood-shot red beneath the ledge of his browbone. Ragged twists of hair hung down over his forehead, obscuring the upper part of his visage, but she could make out the skin there raw and puckered as if from an acid burn. At some point not long before, sweat or tears had made runnels through the grime on his cheeks. "Kal," she murmured. "Oh, Kal," and Luc thought he had never heard her speak so gently.

"I said no pity!" His tone became a growl.

"What happened—there?" The direction of her gaze indicated his forehead.

"I did that," he said. "Don't imagine her torturing me. She marked me with the rune of Agares—the rune of Finding—and that was the only way to get rid of it. If you are just a stray specter, some *tannasgeal* she has harnessed, tell her I have no forehead left for her to mark. It might amuse her; you never know."

"I *must* get you out of here," Fern said.

"Air dreaming."

"Witch's dreams can have more substance than reality."

"Have you any substance, dream witch?"

"You know I—"

"Prove it. Let me touch you. A specter cannot be touched. There is a weakness in the spell wall, just *here*. Push your hand through—your left hand—and I will know you are in truth Fernanda."

Her left hand. He had seen her dip it in the Styx; he knew it would heal at once. Fern's look matched his, stare for stare.

"Very well," she said. She turned to Luc. "Stand back. And whatever happens, don't interfere. *Whatever* happens."

Reluctantly, Luc withdrew. Fern probed the magic from a short distance, checking the place Kal had pointed out. She knew it was best to allow herself no time for anticipation. Concentrating all her power on resisting the initial shock, she forced her hand through.

It was like thrusting it into a furnace at five hundred degrees. Her flesh fried instantly; her blood bubbled and steamed. She had intended to be stoic, to clench her teeth and bear it, telling herself it was only for a moment; but she screamed in agony. Luc ran to her, seizing her shoulders, pulling her away. She managed to articulate: "NO! NO-O-O—" And Kal, reaching through the bars, touched fingertip to burning fingertip in an instant's contact, old as creation—until she was dragged away, and fell to the floor, sobbing in the extremity of anguish. Without her thought to energize it the werelight failed, leaving them groping in the dark. Luc shouted to Skulldunder for water, dropped the flashlight, swore. Fern wrenched her injured arm free of Luc's grip and clamped her other hand around it, above the wrist, squeezing tighter than a tourniquet. Now she was rocking to and fro, her sobs diminishing to moans. Luc located the flashlight, flicked it on. But when the beam found her hand there was nothing but a red shadow on the skin that swiftly faded, and was gone. Her head drooped, perspiration dripped from her hair. Gradually, her breathing slowed to normal.

Luc said: "Your *hand* . . . ?"

"It's all right." She didn't explain.

Kal's voice spoke out of the darkness. "Fernanda." An affirmation.

She crawled toward him, until there were only a couple of feet between them. And the spell wall. And the bars. "I'll get you out," she reiterated. "I have an idea."

There was a jangle of chains as he pressed against the

grille; she thought she saw the red glint of his eyes. She whispered something to him that Luc could not hear.

"Are you sure?" Kal asked.

"My stomach is sure," said Fern, "but not my head. If it works, I will send someone to loose the shackles."

"These?" Kal's tone was contemptuous. "I could chew them off. It is the spells which hold me here. *Her* spells."

And, as Fern got up to go: "Good luck, little witch. You will need it."

Once they were outside, Fern addressed Skuldunder, adjusting with an effort to diplomatic mode. "Convey my thanks to your queen for the loan of your services. Tell her what transpired, if you think it will interest her; you never know with Mabb. I will send her suitable presents when I have leisure. And Skuldunder . . . tell her I think you are a worthy burglar, and a credit to her court."

The goblin's chest swelled; he raised the brim of his hat an inch or two. Then he made an unexpected bow and went off toward the driveway, vanishing into invisibility even before the darkness swallowed him.

"We should get back to London," said Luc. "And what are you going to do with this?" He tapped the head, which emitted a choked grunting noise, probably of rage.

Fern had extracted her mobile from one of the many inner pockets that always adorn men's—if not women's—jackets. She pressed out Will's number, waiting through a half minute of horrible suspense before he answered. "Are you all right?" she asked him, and Luc, hearing the note of desperation, realized that her coolness was purely external.

There was a rapid exchange while they swapped experiences. "She's coming for you," Will said. "Don't hang about. Get back to London. All together, we might stand a chance."

"N-no." Fern hesitated, struggling with her doubts. "I think it's better if I face her on my choice of territory."

"London."

"Yorkshire. That was where I first used my power. That's my place. The magic goes deep there, but it's mine, not hers. If I have to fight her, I want it to be on my home ground."

"Why would she look for you there?"

"Bradachin said she'd been watching the house: remember? She'll know I'm there. Anyway, I have the head. It is a part of her, though she isn't aware of that yet. It will draw her."

"I'll meet you there."

"No, Will. Don't come. Not this time." She felt a shiver like a surge of power.

"Take care, for God's sake."

"I always take care. For mine."

She cut the call and said to Luc: "I expect you want to be with Dana. If you could take me to a place where I can hire a car . . ."

"At this hour of night?" He shrugged. "Anyhow, I won't leave you. I'd like to see Dana, yes, but it can wait. You need me."

"I have to get to Yorkshire."

"I heard. Where, exactly?"

"A village called Yarrowdale. North York Moors, near the coast between Whitby and Scarborough."

"Direct me." He handed Fern her helmet. He couldn't see her face, but he sensed her hesitation, knew she was picking her words.

"I really appreciate this," she said at last, conscious of how inadequate it sounded. Help will be found, she had been told once, long long ago, in a dream of the past. And Rafarl Dev had never failed her, though her task was not his task. He had threatened—no, promised—to leave her, but he had always come back, always been there for her. She wanted to say something about that, something to acknowledge the link, to wake the sleeping magic between them; but she did not dare.

The bubble of potential illusion was too fragile; she feared it might burst at a touch. In the end, she added only: "Thank you. And, Luc—" as she mounted behind him "—avoid the London road. Morgus is looking for me now. We could not pass without her knowing."

The engine kicked into life and they roared off down the drive, churning gravel. Fern was trying to picture Raf handling the boat, sailing into a tempest, but the memory was small and faraway, like an image seen through the wrong end of a telescope, and in front of her Luc's leather-clad back felt solid and strong, a back of the modern world, square shouldered, gym muscled, designer wrapped, bearing no relation to the phantasms of memory and heartache. She thought: If he is Raf, if his soul has returned indeed, then he is older, and colder, and more ruthless, but . . . so am I. Oh, so am I. And she knew she was not sure, she would never be sure, because uncertainty is the essence of the human condition, and death is the one barrier beyond which we cannot see. There is no hope but faith, no knowledge but the acceptance of ignorance.

Yet still she hoped that one day she would know.

At a minor road junction, Luc scanned the sign in his headlight and turned north. Not long after, Morgus passed the same junction, urging her driver faster and faster toward Wrokeby.

"But what can *we* do?" Gaynor demanded as Will switched off the call.

"Personally, I could use a large whiskey. How about you?"

"Don't be flip. Mine's a G and T—I mean, it would be, if we didn't have more important things to think about."

"Actually, we haven't. Fern's got some sort of plan—I know her—but it evidently doesn't include us. We can take the rest of the evening off." While they talked they were standing at the entrance to the alleyway, where reception was better: Selena Place tended to inhibit mobile phones. Possibly it was the magical leakage from Moonspittle's basement.

Ragginbone said: "I trust you're right. At any rate, there's very little we can do until Fern requests help. I shall stay with Moonspittle. He has been deeply shaken by the events of this night. He is not comfortable dealing with friends, let alone enemies."

"*Are* we his friends?" Will inquired dryly.

"We used his home for various sorcerous activities before staging an extremely dangerous diversion there in which we—and he—could easily have been killed. After that, I think the least we can offer him is friendship, don't you?"

Will said: "When you put it like that . . ."

"Should we come back with you?" asked Gaynor.

"Not now. He finds too much company rather overwhelming. Leave it a little while—a century or two—and he may almost be pleased to see you."

Gaynor was not entirely convinced this was intended for a joke, but Will flicked him a quick grin. "A century or two will be just fine," he said, and, seizing her by the hand, he steered her up the road and turned off in the direction of a club that would be open into the small hours. Although he was not a member, a friend of his was located in the noisiest of the bars and signed both of them in as guests.

"Very smooth," said Gaynor, trying for disapproval. "Do people always succumb to your blarney?"

"I'm not Irish," Will pointed out. "It ain't blarney, it's charm."

"Funny how I missed that," said Gaynor.

"Yes, you did, didn't you?" She was disconcerted to see him looking suddenly serious. "Shame."

He got their drinks and led her through the relative quiet of a long sitting room with a piano (fortunately, no one was playing), down a couple of steps, and into a side room with two or three tables, assorted chairs, and a pair of actors, plainly oblivious to all else, who were deep in theatrical scandal. "Privacy," Will said. "Good. Now you can tell me exactly why you were so careful to miss my charm."

Gaynor fiddled with a strand of her hair. "I don't think we should be talking about that now," she said. "Not with every-thing so . . . unfinished. Fern's in awful danger, and we're—"

"Doing nothing? Fiddling while Rome burns—in your case with your hair? You did something earlier on and it nearly got you killed. You deserve a break. As for Fern—well, she trusted us, and now we have to trust her. It wasn't easy for her: she has the power, so she feels she should take the risk. But she trusted us, and somehow, through luck or fate, we didn't fail. You obviously have a Gift of some kind, though it's not like hers. Maybe it's a sort of supernatural understanding. After all, unhappy men always turn to you for a shoulder to cry on, don't they?"

"This isn't about me," Gaynor said hastily. "Look, it's not that I don't *trust* Fern, it's just—"

"You doubt her ability to win. Yes, you do. God help us, we both do. We love her, and fear for her, but . . . in the last few weeks, I've come to realize something. Her Gift—the con-flict with Morgus—all this stuff—this is more important to her than anything else in life. I'm an aspiring producer who dabbles on the dark side. You're a manuscript restorer dab-bling with the same. But Fern is a witch who dabbles in PR. The magic is in her blood and her bones. Morcadis is her true self. We can't deny her that. When I saw her drawing the circle—when I saw her confidence and her certainty—I knew in some ways she is more akin to Ragginbone, even to Alimond, than to me."

"Do you mind?" Gaynor asked. She did not question his conclusions.

"Not yet. If she hadn't trusted us—if her trust ever failed—*then* I would mind. If she ever came to look on us as less than her, merely human, in need of protection . . . That's the true danger of the Gift, I'm sure. People like Morgus, like Alimond, they see themselves as above ordinary mortals, isolated, *special*. So they lose touch with reality altogether and go insane."

"Like Stalin and Hitler," Gaynor recalled. "So you said."

"Just a theory," said Will. "Under the action-man exterior, I have the soul of a thinker."

"Hang on to it," Gaynor said. "Isn't Morgus meant to be the stealer of souls?"

"Morgus again. This conversation wasn't supposed to be about her. Somewhere back along the line, it was supposed to be about us."

"Is there an 'us'?" Gaynor asked, half in hope, half in doubt.

"I don't know," Will said. She tried to avoid his gaze, but somehow there was nowhere else to look. It struck her that these days he always seemed to have a suntan, summer streaks in his hair, the slight roughness of designer stubble on his jaw. He was nearly four years her junior, but he appeared to be catching up fast. He had always had more self-assurance, even when he was a larky sixteen and she a college girl visiting Fern's family; now, she suspected, he was rapidly acquiring more experience of life. He would sample everything the world had to offer, snatch an extra slice of the universal cake and then give it away to a friend in need, fly off into the sunset because it was quicker than sailing and come back two months later expecting a hero's welcome. He had no money, but he managed to patronize the latest bars and ignore the celebrity drinkers with the most successful of his peers. He apparently found the business of living exciting, effortless, a game, a gamble, a romp.

While Gaynor was a quiet girl, too sympathetic for her own good, who liked losing herself in the past and whose life consisted of stumbling from one minor disaster to the next. All we have in common, she thought, is Fern, and the adventures we've shared with her. And most of those weren't much fun.

"Is there an us?" Will repeated. "I'd say my balls are in your court—so to speak."

She accorded the pun a perfunctory smile. "I'm not your type. It wouldn't last. What's the point of a casual quickie? Isn't it better just to stay friends?"

"I don't want to be friends," Will said bluntly. "I want more. And I decide who's my type. As for casual . . ."

"You only want me because I'm the one that got away," Gaynor found herself saying, and instantly regretted it.

"If you think I'm as juvenile as that," Will snapped, "I'm not surprised at your reluctance."

"Not—not juvenile, exactly," Gaynor stammered. "Just a man."

"Sexist."

"I'm making such a mess of this . . ."

"All you have to tell me," Will said with deceptive gentleness, "is that, although you like me, you don't find me remotely attractive, and then I won't bother you anymore. Of course you could hedge, and say *I'm* not *your* type, but that's a plus because your type is usually some creep who complains his wife doesn't understand him, and you don't need another one of those."

"Has any woman ever told you she didn't find you attractive?" Gaynor inquired innocently.

"No, of course not. Your sex, unlike mine, is far too considerate."

"What happens if I say yes? I mean, yes, I find you attractive, not yes to anything else."

"Sooner or later, we go back to my flat. Tonight, or tomorrow night, or whenever. If it's tonight, we can just talk, open a bottle of wine. I'll sleep on the sofa. No hurry."

"You're lying," said Gaynor.

"Yes."

"I think I'd like another drink."

By the time they got back to Will's flat, the hour was so late it was beginning to be early. He was sharing with his business partner and friend Roger Hoyt, who had acquired what should have been a loft conversion in South London, only no one had troubled to convert it. The floorboards were unvarnished, the beams splintered. Large unframed canvases, some of them bearing Will's moniker, hung on the walls or were propped against them; blown-up photos peeled from the sloping ceiling. The bathroom and kitchen facilities were rudimentary. Opened bottles of both red and white wine stood on the table, and after a quick search Will found clean glasses. Gaynor, staring up through a naked skylight, saw a darkness bleared with the glow of the city, or possibly the advent of dawn. There were no visible stars.

"Why does it always happen this way?" Gaynor wondered, accepting a glass of red. "Here we are in the middle of trouble and danger, falling in—" she checked herself "—in lust. And when the danger is over . . ."

"I won't run away. Will you?"

"I'm scared," she admitted.

He tilted her face to the light, seeing the exotic eye makeup, now slightly smudged, and the vulnerability of the eyes underneath. "Ah." He didn't offer easy reassurance. "You're afraid of being hurt. So am I. Who ain't? If you care, you get hurt. But if you don't care, you get nothing. I can't promise not to lie to you, though I'll try. I can't promise anything, except that I care. Seeing you again, just lately, I've come to realize how much you matter to me, how much you've always mattered, only my poor punctured ego wouldn't let me face it. I don't know why: you just do. Chemistry. Fate."

Love, thought Gaynor. Oh, bugger.

She said: "I don't want this to go wrong."

"Relationships don't come with a guarantee." He grinned at her. "All I can say is, if it does fail, it won't be my fault."

"Yes, it will," Gaynor said indignantly.

"No, it won't." He took her glass and put it on the table, and then his arms were around her, and he was kissing her, and she was kissing him, and it wasn't difficult at all. Her hesitation crumbled, her doubts and fears retreated to the back of her mind. They wouldn't go away, not for a long time, but for the moment at least they no longer had a voice. She was young and healthy, and desire took over, a desire fueled by long waiting and vain suppression, sharpened by the horrors of the preceding evening. Eventually, they stumbled to his bed—a double mattress on the floor—and rolled on top of the duvet because it would slow them down to get under it, and sometime later the stealthy predawn twilight showed her sprawled limbs pale against his, her makeup kissed off, her dark hair puddled across the tumbled pillows. He stroked her shoulder, bird's-egg freckled from a brief stint in the sun, and the smoothness of her back, and the curve of her bottom, and when he thought she was asleep he tugged the duvet out from under her and covered her with it. She was awake, but she kept her eyes closed, faking slumber, because the attention was so dear to her. In the end it was Will who slept while Gaynor lay wakeful, unable to relax in the strange bed, and, like Elizabeth in *Pride and Prejudice*, knowing rather than feeling that she was happy. As a lover, he had been skilled though not yet blasé, which hadn't surprised her, but he had seemed startled when she responded in kind, gasping with pleasure and saying, only half-teasing: "My God, it's true! Older women really *are* best . . ." She worried for a minute that the age gap bothered him, though she knew she was being foolish, but the memory of his pleasure warmed her, right down between her legs, and presently she forgot to worry, and touched herself very gently, finishing the stimulus that he had begun, climaxing beside her sleeping lover, something she had never been able to do in bed with any man. She thought she would tell him when he woke, and the next time, or the next, it would happen with him. On that thought she slipped into a doze, and the daylight forced an entry around the pinned-down curtain on the bedroom window, only to find there was no one awake to object.

It was Roger Hoyt who roused them, banging on the wall because the door couldn't take it, reminding Will they were due for an informal drink with a contact from the BBC. "Get rid of Annabel—" Gaynor had left female apparel scattered across the main room "—and get moving."

"It isn't Annabel," Will said through teeth that were both gritted and gritty.

"Sophie—"

"Wrong again."

"Sinead—Lucia—Véronique . . ."

"I don't know a Véronique." To his relief, he saw Gaynor was giggling. He got up and opened the door, disposing of his friend with a few well-chosen words, mostly four-lettered. Then he reached for his jeans and offered tea or coffee. "There's probably no milk, but I'll get some. D'you want any breakfast? I could buy some croissants . . ."

He's making an effort, she realized, astonished and pleased; but she declined. "Just tea. I was wondering about Fern. Has she phoned?"

Will checked his messages, without result. Then he tried Dale House and her mobile. The former did not answer; the latter was switched off. "Or out of range," he said. "She could have crossed into a dimension beyond the ken of mobile phones. Maybe just Yorkshire." His lighthearted irritation with Roger had darkened; a frown cut double lines between his brows. "I don't like it."

"What do we do?" asked Gaynor. The intermission was forgotten or set aside: they were back where they had left off last night.

Will's mouth set; he looked at his unresponsive mobile as if it had committed a personal offense.

He didn't try to answer her.

∾∾∾∾∾∾ Part Three

Honor

X ⚬⚬⚬⚬⚬

I had forgotten what it was like to feel ill. For time outside Time I had dwelt beneath the Eternal Tree, out of reach of the diseases that afflict lesser mortals. In the spellfire, I saw people sicken and die, I saw plague and pox and cancer and AIDS, I saw microbes wriggling under a lens and doctors fighting to cure the incurable; but I could never recall being ill myself, save for the minor maladies of childhood. The nausea that came over me, the deadly faintness, was so terrible that I believed I was dying. My driver had to carry me to the car; Nehemet followed, mewing in sympathy. I lay back against the seats, but their softness galled me, and the smell of the leather turned my stomach, and I sat up and heaved— heaved like a drunken peasant or a pregnant whore—and the stuff that came out was greenish, and tasted of acid, and stank like rotting vegetation. I knew I could not be poisoned: the River had made me invulnerable to both weapon and venom. Yet I *felt* poisoned, though I had ingested nothing harmful. When the vomiting ceased my stomach drew, and I curled on the seat, trying not to moan, with my cheek on the cold bare flank of Nehemet (goblin cats are creatures of the Underworld: they are never warm), while Hodgekiss sped me home. He was a reliable servant; I had dosed his coffee, often and often, with the juice of the Tree. "Go swift," I told him, "and smooth." Above all, smooth. Whatever had happened to me, it must be some magic of Morcadis, some evil that she had encompassed when she had sneaked into Wrokeby in my absence. Fool that I was, to fall into such a trap! Yet I had not even the strength to summon the elementals, and send them to detain her. When the nausea was past my rage still sickened in me, and that did not go away.

Somewhere in the very core of me, in the sap of my heart, I knew what was wrong, but my brain refused to think and the knowledge lurked just out of bounds, over the borderland of the subconscious. I did not reach for it; I think I dared not, though I have dared much in my time. The spider has eaten her, I told myself. I will find nothing left but her bones. There are spells in the house that could fry her to ash . . . She was a mere novice, a stumbling pupil who has forgotten the little she ever learned. She has neither the skill nor the will to injure *me* . . .

When we reached Wrokeby, I knew she had gone. I could sense the wake of her departure like a violent eddy in the still hollowness of the entrance hall. I felt where she had been as if she had left a spoor. The conservatory.

I remember I ordered the driver to wait. I had forgotten his name, so dreadful was the tension of that moment, but it did not matter. I was stronger now, but it was a damaged strength, as if I had had a limb amputated, or a vital organ removed, and there was an aching vacancy in my being I did not try to comprehend. I walked through the house, Nehemet at my heels. The hag, I assumed, must have been slain. I switched on the lights as I went—the lights of the modern age, which need no flame and work from the same power that makes the lightning in the storm and the crackle on the hair of a cat. Normally I prefer the dark, but something else affected me, beyond weakness, beyond fury, something rare and strange and familiar, draining me more than any physical infirmity. It was a while before I remembered what it was. Fear.

There were no lights in the conservatory: I had never needed them. In the overspill from the house I saw crushed foliage, snapped stems; I heard the silence where once there would have been the soft leaf-murmur of recognition. And I saw the guardian, his great body scrunched like that of any common spider, swatted, stabbed through the head with a single thrust. It had not even taken sorcery: only a pin. My creature, my pet, whom I had nursed and nurtured, skewered through its tiny brain as if by an idle collector! There was contempt in that. I felt my fury grow, reviving my force, but the fear nudged it, and would not go away. When I reached the Tree, I thought I was prepared. It would be uprooted, its bark torn—leaves scattered—branches smashed. It might take me days, weeks, years to restore it to life.

But there was no Tree.

My darksight was returning, and I stared about me in bewilderment and horror, thinking I knew not what. There was the stone pot, cracked when the radix had forced its way through and penetrated deep into the soil beneath. But beside that there was nothing save a spill of blackened earth, a few leaf-shaped cinders, a long resinous smear on the paving stones. And ash powder, finer than dust, sifting through my scrabbling fingers. My nostrils caught the faint, acrid afterscent of something I recognized, a potion I had made myself, distilled from the stolen waters of Azmodel, deadlier than fire. My potion had destroyed my Tree! Now I began to understand both the seeds of my malady and the source of my fear. It was as if a part of my self had been torn away and brutally cauterized, leaving me limping, crippled from within. I may have cried out; I can't recall. My rage grew from a creeping surge to a great flood, overwhelming fear, restraint, pain. This was a loss that would be too long in the mending. I would have to go back to the parent Tree, take another cutting, trading power for power—and there are some places to which there should be no returning. I have never gone back, always forward, forward to a new conquest . . .

Morcadis had done this. The lost soul I had fostered, the

viper I had nested. In that moment, I swore that I would ea
her heart.

But what of the fruit—the fruit I had charged my guardian
to protect? The first fruit, trembling on the verge of ripeness
the thought of it gnawed my spirit. Surely there would be
some trace—a charred lump, a hunk of hair that had escaped
the burning. But I found no sign, and I knew now what I
feared most. *She* had taken it, the thief in the night, to learn its
secrets and use them against me. And then I felt it, reaching
out to me from somewhere far off, with a summons as insistent as a child's cry to its mother. It was the head, not *her*
whose trail I had sensed screaming through the house—the
clamor of a voice unheard, an echo of my own. I almost forgot
that Morgun had betrayed me, remembering only that she
was my twin. I had to take back what was mine, to exact revenge for this ultimate violation—

I went through the house like a gale, Nehemet hissing in
my swath. In the kitchen, she sprang onto the chest freezer
and there was a hammering from within. I swept off the pots
that weighed down the lid and Grodda clambered out, scattering peas like grapeshot, her garments crackling with frost
her face the color of bile. In the basement, I found flasks rifled, one bottle gone, my little menagerie liberated. The jar
that had held the whimpering spirit of the girl was already
smashed, but I crushed the remaining pieces and stamped on
the eyeballs of the blasphemer. But there in the cupboard was
the head of Sysselore, intact, eyes closed as if mocking me
with its slumber. I wrenched it out by the hair, pinched it into
wakefulness. "She was here!" I cried. "Here in *my* place—my
storeroom—breaking spells, stealing bottles, releasing *my*
phantoms into the ether. May that sniveling girl never find her
way home! Did you see her?"

"What girl?"

"Don't dare to taunt me. She was here—Morcadis—she

would have seen you, you must have seen her. Feign ignorance again, and I will squeeze you into pulp."

"I feign nothing," the head whined. "You confuse me, with your shes and hers, your this girl, which girl. Morcadis came, she saw me, but she wasn't interested. No doubt she had other objects in view."

"What did she say?"

"To me? Nothing. I was locked in a cupboard, in the dark, with preserving fluid filling my mouth; I was blind, deaf, dumb, as you ordered me."

"You are my coven sister, my—" I fumbled for the word "—my *friend*. You must have seen something, learned something."

"She was with a man."

"A *man*?" I was taken aback. I had thought better of her— even her. "What kind of a man?"

"Not handsome, as you or I would have it, but who is? What can I say? I saw him briefly, through my lashes. If he were a knight, his armor would be black. He would win in the joust because he could not endure to lose. If he had come to my island, I would have snared him with a will. I would have turned him into a black boar, but he would have kept the mind of a man, even to the moment when I set him on the spit for roasting. He had power, of a kind. The Gift, or something else."

"This is nonsense." She was rambling; she had often rambled. "Death has done nothing to sharpen your wits. Forget your brain-soft fantasies. As for his Gift, how could you know?"

"I did not know. I *felt*."

"Are you sure?"

"No. How could I be sure? I kept my eyes closed—"

"Venture further with your impudence," I whispered, "and I will lance your core with an auger, and watch the mold ooze out."

"I am dead. You cannot harm me."

"I can hurt you."

"Then hurt me. I will tell you this much: Morcadis has grown. Not in inches, but within. Her power, her spirit waxes to a new fullness. I saw her face, and it was as cold and implacable as the moon. She will find a way to defeat you: it is her fate, and yours."

"There is no way!" My grasp tightened on the severed stem and gossamer hair.

"There is always a way. Don't you remember the stories? The door that cannot be opened, the task that cannot be completed, the battle that cannot be won, and yet there is always a key, completion, victory. Your doom was in her face, Morgus: I saw it as if it were written. Do you believe in stories, my coven sister, my friend? Do you—"

"Go to hell," I screamed, "the quick way!" and I hurled the head against the wall with all my strength.

Maybe that was what she wanted. I have wondered.

Half her face was squashed into a red mess; the debris dropped to the floor; blood-bright juice ran down the wall. The remaining eye rolled, and was still. "That was swifter than your deserts," I said, but she was silent now, and I had no means to retrieve her voice. She had been my sole companion for endless ages under the Eternal Tree, but Morcadis had slain her, and now she was gone indeed. (Morcadis, always Morcadis. There was too much to add to the reckoning.) I did not miss her. There had been love between us once, when our exile was still fresh, but it had worn out long, long ago. I would not miss my Sysselore.

Nehemet waited, her tail twitching, her feline features impassive. What goes on behind her unchanging expression I will never know.

"I must find Morgun," I said. There were secrets to be whispered, tales to be told. Somehow, I sensed that with my twin I would learn the answer to the final question, the question I could not frame. I must have forgotten she, too, was only a fruit.

I went to the spellchamber, but it was undisturbed, though

they had been there. Who the man might be with Fernanda I
did not pause to speculate; some henchman presumably, a
servant or an admirer she had enspelled whose potential for
power Sysselore had undoubtedly overestimated. He was not
important; I had other concerns. The trail led to the attic, to
the prisoner whom I had not visited for weeks. The stench
made my senses reel. The spell barrier was undamaged as I
had been sure it would be; none other could unravel the com-
plexities of that pattern, nor would have the power to counter
my Commands. But she had been there, with Morgun: she
had stood by the door, staring into the barred gloom, seeing
the downfall of the creature she had used and discarded. She
might have considered him her ally, but I doubted it. She had
learned that much from me: accord no man respect that he
cannot compel, give no man gratitude that he cannot demand.
My prisoner had always been less than a man; now he was
less than a beast. He cowered in the corner, below the single
window casement. Outside, no moon sailed, no star peeped.
Within, the darkness was yet darker, but he still skulked behind dirt-clogged hair, arms wrapped around his torso, tail
hiding his feet. His eyes were mere slits between puffball lids.

"Morcadis was here," I said. "Your little witch. Was she
pleased to see you?" And, when he remained silent: "I asked
you a question. Answer it, or I will send the nightmares to
plague you again! Was—she—pleased—to—see—you?"

"She didn't say." The response came as if wrung from
his lips.

"What *did* she say?"

"Hail and farewell. What was there to say? She tried to let
me out."

"And she failed! She will always fail. Hope if you will: it
prolongs your suffering. Despair is the more terrible when it
succeeds a period of hope."

"I will remember that."

"Only my will can release you—"

"Or your death."

"My death! I snapped her charms like cobwebs, yet she could not penetrate mine. I am the greatest of witchkind, twice-born, once into life, once out of death; my body was anointed in Stygian magic and the sap of the Great Tree runs in my veins. I cannot be slain, nor conquered. There is no power in the world that could engender my death."

"Then why are you afraid?"

I would have boiled his meager brain inside his skull, but I had made the spell wall too strong, and it would take time to bypass it. He was right, of course. That was unforgivable.

"When I have leisure," I said, "I shall enjoy refining your punishment, since there is clearly still something left of you to punish."

"Not much . . . but something." He tried to grin, baring ragged teeth. I saw them, a yellow gleam in the darkness. Stained, chipped into bitter sharpness. Probably he had attempted to bite through his shackles or tear up the floorboards. It would avail him nothing. The magic held him.

"Good," I said, and turned to leave.

"She has—something—that belongs to you," he called after me.

"I know. Did you see it?"

"It was in a bag, I think . . . gagged. It may have tried to speak."

My eagerness redoubled, and my urgency. "Don't worry: I will get it back. She will regret her theft—but not for long."

Only later did I wonder why he should have told me that. Maybe it was the nearest he would come to wheedling, to begging a diminution of his punishment. But I would hear him beg, and see him rot, before I reduced it by as much as an ounce of suffering or a minute of time.

When I left him, I descended to my bedchamber. I was in too much haste to draw the circle, but there were questions I wanted to ask, though I doubted the answers would be very instructive. A seeress cannot lie, but she may be enigmatic with the truth. And although the sisterhood see farther than other beings, there are none left who can read the future, save in the indices of the present—and that is a trick anyone with a little wisdom can assay. I passed my hands across the oval mirror above my dressing table, murmuring the words of summons. In such a mirror, Snow White's stepmother fished for compliments; mirrors have many uses. They can be an all-seeing eye, a dimensional breach, a portal between reality and dream. This particular mirror was old and knowing: there were times when I had seen my face in it the way it used to be during my sojourn beneath the Eternal Tree, a bloated pallor, slug lipped, the nostrils like pits. But the eyes do not alter, whatever visage I choose to wear. As I spoke the glass clouded and my reflection was lost. Gradually, another face emerged, broad and ebon dark, veiled in scarlet. Léopana Pthaia, Léopana the Black. A hand removed the cloth and set the Eye in one empty socket.

"You are peremptory, Morgus, to call me with so little ceremony. A seeress should not be summoned as if she were a familiar imp, and to a looking glass, forsooth!"

"Yet you came." I had the power, and she knew it. It would have cost her dear to deny me.

"Question me, and be done with it."

"I planted a cutting from the Eternal Tree in this world, and it bore fruit. The fruit has ripened into the head of my sister Morgun—or so it appears. Is it indeed my twin?"

"That is beyond my Sight."

"Then tell me this at least: she was fruit on the parent Tree, but did she pass the Gate?"

Léopana's gaze grew misty as she peered backward in time. "She did not. She was strong in enchantment, and she found a way to put her spirit elsewhere."

"So it is her! But why? Why would she linger? And why is she ripening on *my* Tree?"

"I am a seeress," the Pthaia responded, and her Eye flashed. "I can tell you what is, and what was, and what may be, but it is not for me to reason or deduce. The magic is yours: search your own thought for understanding."

"If you know what is," I persisted, though her evasion vexed me, "then you know Morcadis has stolen my fruit. Is it unharmed?"

"It is."

"Am *I* in peril?"

"The waters of the Dead River rendered you invulnerable, and your power is greater than that of any other mortal, greater than many of immortal kind. Even I, the Black Sybil, must be at your beck and call. What could threaten you?"

Seeresses never refer to themselves: impersonality is a rule of their vocation. Her gaze appeared fixed, but her mouth was sly. "Do not answer a question with a question," I said sharply. "Can Morcadis injure me through the head?"

"Perhaps."

"I must regain it! Where has she taken it?" I could follow the trail, but it would help to know where it led.

"The house of her family in the north country, near a village called Yarrowdale. You should know the place: your spies have been watching it for some weeks."

"Of course I know it: that is where I first found her. I have seen it often in the spellfire. It is far from any major town, isolated and remote. She will have little protection there, save her own feeble magics. Is my power indeed greater than hers?" I had no need to ask, but I wanted to hear a straight yes—or no.

"Why pose a question to which you know the answer? Do you seek to test me?"

"Is my power—"

"Yes. I told you, you are the mightiest of Prospero's Children. Morcadis is still young; she has far to go. Gift for Gift, spell for spell, she cannot match you."

"It is well, but I think she will not go much farther." I
smiled at the thought, though I had not smiled all night.
"Have you any other word for me, ere I release you?"

There was a pause. A pythoness is never irresolute, yet it
seemed to me that she hesitated. "Only one," she said at last.
"Beware!"

My temper hardened. She was trying to frighten me, and I
knew it, yet still I was afraid. I had been too much afraid of
late, and I am not accustomed to fear. "You tried that one before," I said. "Beware of *what*? Be more specific."

"I cannot. It is between you and your fruit. Find the head,
and the truth will be revealed."

She was speaking in riddles, as seeresses so often do when
they wish to conceal ignorance. I dismissed her brusquely,
and watched the mirror clear. My own face reappeared, a
flawless structure sculpted in flesh, tinted with the hues of
youth renewed. But the eyes—the eyes were always old, black
as the Pit, luminous with secret power. I thrust the warning
aside, deeming it empty, shared another smile with my reflection, and hastened back downstairs to the car. Nehemet, as
ever, was at my heels. Hodgekiss had been sleeping, but he
woke on cue and we drove off, heading northward.

On the other side of morning my enemy was waiting, with
the stolen apple in her hand.

The summer dawn came early, but they did not stop. Despite
the discomfort of riding pillion, Fern found herself nodding off
and wondered if it was possible to sleep in that position, and
whether she would fall, but fortunately she never found out.
Luc had the head under his jacket: it had chewed through
most of the gag and was now trying to bite its way out of the
bag that imprisoned it, so far without success. He could feel
it pounding against him; he even imagined he could sense the
grinding of its teeth. He had occasional flashes of horror at

the nature of what he carried, but after all he had seen and endured that night his nervous system was numb and he thought nothing could shock him anymore. Around six they halted for breakfast: rubbery eggs and leathery bacon (or vice versa), and coffee that consisted of milky water on a basis of sediment. They didn't talk much. Luc's jacket heaved with the struggles of its captive. "Cat," he told the waitress, in case she was interested, but she wasn't. By the time they reached Yorkshire Fern's body was one huge ache, and she was chilled to the bone and could barely manage to stutter directions. She knew she must get some sleep before she could face Morgus, and it was with relief she saw the solid façade of Dale House. Dimly, she recollected that it was Saturday. Mrs. Wicklow wasn't there. Fern unlocked the door with shaking hands, stumbled into the hall. Lougarry slipped out of the kitchen on noiseless paws and thrust a cold nose into her outstretched palm.

Sometime later, when Will telephoned, Fern was asleep in one bedroom, Luc in another, while Bradachin kept watch from an upper window and the she-wolf from the moor above the road. Both mobiles were switched off. The house-goblin contemplated answering—he was conversant with the mechanics of telephones and often disconcerted sales callers with the incomprehensibility of his curious brogue—but he did not want to leave his post. Fern heard it ringing, somewhere in her dreams, and rolled over, and the sound was smothered by the pillow.

It was well into the afternoon before she got up and tottered sleepily downstairs to find Luc already awake and attempting to make coffee without a percolator. "Tea for me," Fern mumbled. "Please." And: "Any movement?"

"Not that I can see. Maybe we weren't the only ones who needed a rest."

"Maybe." Fern wasn't satisfied. "She's thinking," she concluded, "planning something. She won't just come storming in here."

"Perhaps she's learned to fear you." Luc produced a wry smile. "God knows I do."

Fern missed the aside. "That's not good," she said.

"Why not?"

"I prefer being underestimated. When Morgus starts to think, she's more dangerous than ever. I want her impetuous and arrogant. She should be off-balance, not careful and calculating. Oh well, there's nothing we can do about it now. We may have to play it her way for a while. I'd better ring Will." She had left her phone upstairs.

"Use mine." Having mastered the coffeepot, Luc began to look for tea bags. "I called the clinic."

"Is Dana—?"

"She's conscious. Doing fine."

"You should have been there," Fern said. "Not absconding to the wilds of Yorkshire with me."

"It's only because of you that Dana came around at all. I pay my debts."

Fern asked, without looking at him: "Is that why you're here?"

"No." He poured himself coffee, made her a cup of tea. "I found fresh milk in the fridge. Also sliced bread, butter, cheese. Do you always keep emergency rations here?"

"That's Mrs. Wicklow. She used to be our housekeeper, till she became part of the family. She likes to be prepared. If we don't come, she'll eat the stores herself. If we *tell* her we're coming, she'll cook enough food for a small invading army. Should we survive the encounter with Morgus you'll probably meet her. She's very dour, but don't let it fool you. That's just the Yorkshire *persona*."

"Soft as butter underneath?" Luc suggested.

Fern investigated the fridge, removing a slab of butter that was frozen hard. "Depends on the butter."

The day dragged. It had been a bad summer, but in Yorkshire it was worse. Great siege towers of cloud came rolling out of the west, ready to topple over the landscape; eastward, a defiant sun beat down on the chilly sea, turning it to burnished steel. A few flurries of rain formed a prelude to the approaching squall. Lougarry trotted in around five, communicating with Fern mind-to-mind, as she did with those who knew her well. "She's out there," Fern reported. "The car's parked about a quarter of a mile away. She's keeping her distance, waiting for her moment. Lougarry says she's standing up on the hillside, looking toward the house. One arm extended . . . first and fourth fingers pointing . . ."

"She'll get wet," said Luc.

"Not she. Raindrops would evaporate before they touched her." Unusually, Fern locked the back door. "I think we should all stay inside now."

The afternoon was growing swiftly darker. Too swiftly. Luc, watching through the kitchen windows, saw a cloud-shaped blackness gathering over the house; flying specks wheeled past and seemed to be sucked up into it. The gray daylight was cut off and there was a rustling, whirring noise like the beat of a thousand wings. But it was a minute or two before he realized what was out there. And then Bradachin came tumbling onto the table, materializing from midair with the carelessness of haste. "Birrds!" he exclaimed. "Muckle birds! No they piebald glitterpickers but great corbies wi' beaks as long as your hond! Ye maun be working on some powerful cantrips, hinny, for these will be coming in without ony inviting." As he spoke the first one hurled itself against the window: a carrion crow twice normal size, scissor-beak jabbing at the pane. Then another, and another. Each bird hit the glass in the same place, and on the third impact it cracked as if from a gunshot, splinter lines webbing outward. On the fourth, the glass disintegrated, and the birds were in the kitchen. Luc had snatched a broom and lashed out with the bundled twigs; Lougarry bared her fangs; Bradachin, spearless, grabbed both knife and rolling pin. Fern focused her power, and live energy crepitated from her fingers, searing anything it touched. There was a smell of burnt feathers, and two bodies fell to the floor. The rest took flight.

"They'll be back," said Luc. "This house has too many windows. We can only cover those in here."

"I'm thinking the corbies hae been told tae gang after the maidy," opined Bradachin. "Wi' luck—"

The crash of breaking glass came from Will's old studio. Luc slammed the kitchen door, jamming the latch with a fork. "We can't stop them invading the rest of the house," he said. He turned back to the shattered window—the breach in their defenses—kicking the corpses out of the way. "They're so *big*. Are they ravens or crows?"

"Baith," said Bradachin. "They wouldna normally flock thegither, but these maun come from the other place—"

"They're from the Tree," said Fern. "Morgus has called them."

"They won't get the head." Luc had regagged it, and stuffed it in a metal trash can, and weighed it down with a sack of potatoes.

"I'm wishing ye would stop bringing them things hame, lassie," Bradachin remarked. "I hae told ye afore, I dinna hold wi' necromauncy."

"It's important," Fern said tersely. She was listening to the sound of birds blundering down the hall, battering themselves against the kitchen door. "The house is going to be full of birdshit, apart from the breakages. Mrs. Wicklow won't like that at all."

"I'm no sae blythe mysel," said Bradachin darkly.

Another attack came on the windows, only this time there were more of the birds—giant ravens hacking at the remaining panes, gangster crows in an unending stream, even a couple of the blue-banded magpies swooping in to loot what they could. The dull afternoon was completely blotted out; charmlight strobed through the flock. Fern scattered a boxful of matches among them, crying one word: *"Inyé!,"* and every match flared. Many of the invaders concentrated on Luc, raking his arms with beak and claw, trying to home in on his face. Others swarmed around Bradachin and Lougarry. The metal can rocked as the head strove to leap out. And then, with a noise like the crack of Doom, the storm began.

It was a summer storm like no other, brief but violent. Rain rattled on what was left of the windows. Hailstones the size of golf balls bombarded the flock outside, fragmenting the spell-driven mob into panicked individuals. Some of those indoors turned and fled; some were isolated and killed. Eventually the battle of the kitchen was over; crockery was broken, sink and table fouled. Avine corpses strewed the floor. The assault on the closed door had ceased. Fern pressed the switch for the main light, but the cord was ripped; Nature's pyrotechnics provided the principal illumination. Lougarry had been protected by her coat, the goblin by his tenuous substance; Luc bled. Fern did her best to staunch the flow with a dishcloth. "This storm," he said, "was it you or Morgus?"

"Neither. Weather can be controlled, but it's very difficult to conjure. There are other powers in the world far stronger than mine—or hers. There's even supposed to be someone called Luck, though I'm told you shouldn't rely on him." The premature gloom lightened a little as the water-cannon rainfall slowed to a monsoon.

"Does Morgus really hope to defeat us with those birds?" Luc pursued, frowning. "Or is she just an obsessive Hitchcock fan?"

Fern accorded the remark a smile that was merely polite. "She may be aiming to exhaust my Gift," she said.

"If I have the Gift, too, can I use it?"

"I . . . I don't know. If you have, you haven't learned to discipline it—or channel it. And it won't work the way mine does: different people always have different talents. Stick with the broom: it's safer."

There was a quality in the somber, almost-handsome face that she could not read. Possibly it was withdrawal. She had forgotten to look for Rafarl in him: in these moments he was only Luc. "Presumably, when the birds run out, she'll come herself," he was saying.

"I hope so," said Fern.

The flock, dispersed by the storm, did not regroup in the same numbers: Most of the birds had fled back to the place from whence they came. In the shelter of the Eternal Tree there were no extremes of weather, and the birds dwelt there in relative safety, menaced only by each other. A few ravens remained behind, circling the house, perching briefly on gable and chimney, calling to their mistress in harsh voices. She waits for dark, thought Fern; but the evening was long and light. The cloud cover split, and an unexpected sunset overflowed the gap, spilling its yellow fires across the underbelly of cumulus, irradiating the landscape. Lean shadows stretched out behind hump and hummock, hill and tree. Fern and Luc relaxed their vigil enough to begin tidying up and cleaning off the droppings. In Will's old studio, they covered the broken pane with a black garbage bag, since all the plastic wrap had been used in the kitchen. Fern even leafed through the Yellow Pages and telephoned a repairman, booking him for the following Monday, hearing her own words spoken with a sense of dislocation in time. There was no Monday, she would not be there, the universe must turn around before Monday came again . . . She told herself sternly not to be a fool. There was always Monday: in a world of working weeks it was the one thing you could depend on.

"What's the matter?" Luc must have been watching her more closely than she realized.

"Nothing. Nerves."

She knew Will would be waiting for another call, but she did not phone, not yet. She felt less and less able to talk normally.

The sunset faded slowly, leaving a wide green pool of

empty sky beyond the departing cloud. Some kindly god switched on the evening star, its tiny, friendly glimmer winking at her down the light-years. Gradually, one photon at a time, the day died. Night fell like a black velvet curtain.

Morgus came.

She came to the front door, not the kitchen. They heard the heavy hand of the driver pounding the knocker, heard him call something that might have been: *We know you're there.* Then another voice, whisper soft but so resoundingly clear it seemed Morgus could have been in the room with them already: "Let me in, Morcadis. You know you cannot keep me out. Don't waste your strength. Let me in, and I may spare you, at the end."

As you spared Kal? thought Fern. Break the taboo. I dare you.

But she made no audible answer.

There came the thudding of an ax or machete hacking at the door, splitting the weathered oak. Then footsteps entering, pausing. Hodgekiss. "Come in, mistress." She thinks to cheat the Ultimate Laws, Fern realized. She instructs an ordinary mortal to break in and issue the invitation . . .

"Shouldn't we do something?" Luc hissed, scowling.

Fern shook her head slowly. They drew away from the kitchen door, positioning themselves by instinct, without any prearranged plan, Fern in front of the patched window and half leaning on the trash can, Luc to her left, Lougarry to her right, Bradachin lurking unobtrusively in the lee of the cupboard. Luc found he had picked up the broom automatically, and propped it in a corner, reaching instead for one of the larger carving knives. Morgus's voice sounded again, from the hallway just outside.

"Let me in, Morcadis."

The kitchen door shook. The fork-wedge was back in place, but it flew out with such force that it shot across the room and stuck, quivering, in the opposite wall. The latch lifted of its own volition. The door opened. Morgus entered, not on a gust of rage as she had done in Moonspittle's basement, but slowly, deliberately. Her gaze locked on to Fern's. Nehemet slid into the room behind her in a single fluid motion, like a worm through a crack. Her muzzle swayed, catching the scent of goblin; but the sight of Lougarry deterred her. Hodgekiss waited in the rear, faithful as an automaton.

Morgus said: "At last," but there was no exultation in her tone. She seemed taller than Fern remembered, perhaps because she was so slender. The serpentine tangles of her hair made an irregular black halo around her face; contemporary makeup emphasized the fixity of her expression, staining the set mouth, outlining the deadly eyes. The room appeared to rearrange itself around her, becoming mere background for her personality. Yet Luc, glancing at Fern, thought there was something forceful in Fern's face, too. For all its delicate angles and fine-drawn features, something indefinably, elusively similar was matching Morgus look for look, meeting power with challenge. A hint—a phantom—the shadow of a resemblance.

"You have stolen something that belongs to me," said Morgus. "You crept into my house by night and took the one ripe apple from my Tree. Like Eve, you will pay dear for your theft. Give it to me. Give it to me *now*."

"No," said Fern. The monosyllable seemed to escape her with difficulty. She was clenching her power. Braced. Armed. In the can behind her, the head hammered against the sides with a muffled *boom . . . boom . . .*

"So!" cried Morgus. "It is there!" The familiar lightning flashed from her hand. Fern made a quick gesture of defense, but she was just too late, and the jolt knocked her off balance. Luc and Lougarry leaped from either side, but Morgus's movements were thought-fast: she singed the she-wolf's fur and sent Luc reeling, burned even through his leather jacket. The lid flew off the can and the head sprang out in a volley of potatoes, bandage and blindfold unraveling. The lips were bitten raw from the savagery of its struggles; the eyes rolled. Morgus caught it by the hair, her Medusa stare meeting its true reflection. "Morgun?"

"Morgus," said the head.

And in that moment of comprehension, they were one.

"It's . . . *me*," Morgus shrieked at Fern. "You stole—*me*. You stuck my guardian like an insect on a collector's card—you slew my Tree with my own poison—and then you rob me of my *Self*, a *part* of me—!" A hissing stream of Atlantean issued from her mouth, and Fern's bare forearms bubbled into blisters that burst immediately, evacuating tiny maggotlike creatures that wriggled into her clothes. She fought to stay calm, muttering a counterspell, suppressing a scream when the maggots began to burrow under her skin. A frustrated Bradachin hurled his rolling pin, but Morgus batted it aside with barely an effort. The larvae were crisping into coiled cinders, dropping off Fern's body, but she was bleeding from a hundred minute wounds. She tried to shield, knowing she should have done it before, cursing herself for her stupidity. Morgus's incantation continued relentlessly. *"Sangué luava, duum luavé invar . . ."* The trickle of blood became a gush. Fern fell forward, seeing spots, too weak to fight back . . .

On the floor, straining to push herself up, she saw Nehemet squirm between her mistress's legs as if in affection—and nip her ankle. There was an unexpected touch of malice to the action. Morgus broke off her chant, crying out more in shock than pain, and stumbled backward over the cat, losing her grip on the fruit. The spell failed. The head, teeth bared, bounced toward Fern. But she was drawing on her Gift, reviving swiftly, using the respite to flood her limbs with pure power. She snatched at the hair, scrambling to her feet—"Luc! The knife!"—seizing the weapon when Luc kicked it over to her.

Morgus appeared briefly paralyzed, staring at the cat.

"You betrayed me," she said. *"You . . ."* She heard again the words of the seeress speaking of her sister: *She found a way to put her spirit elsewhere.* But not in the Tree, nor any of its later fruit . . .

"This is you," Fern said to her, holding the prize that writhed and snarled in her grasp. "Your Tree, your head. You've seen it, touched it, acknowledged it. The magic is complete. And it's never been dipped in the Styx."

The witch queen raised her hand, began to speak—but this time, it was she who was too slow. Fern plunged the knife into one eye; it felt soft, like butter, like all the clichés, and then there was denser matter, muscle or sinew, an instant of resistance before the point penetrated the brain. Two voices gave vent to a single scream, less a cry than a choke, cut off in seconds. Scarlet juice burst over Fern's breast and splattered the floor. Scarlet blood streamed down Morgus' cheek, clogging in her hair. But the wounds did not close. There was a splinter of time when she seemed to be still alive, when the scream still gurgled in her throat and a hand groped toward the hideous injury and her good eye gaped and stared in final malevolence. Then her body jerked and folded, slowly, slowly, and her face emptied of all but the terminal impress of pain. And there she was on the floor, a disorderly heap of flesh and bone, suddenly shrunken to mortal proportions, smaller with the smallness of death. Deprived of health and heartbeat, the power of the Tree could no longer sustain her or her fruit: the head rotted in Fern's grip, the juice stains fading to brown, while the corpse was already beginning to decay, a thousand years of aging compressed into less than a minute. The flesh greened and shriveled, wafting a foulness through the kitchen, withering to a tumble of white bones that brittled visibly and subsided into dust. Even her clothes were gone, caught in the magic, perishing with their wearer. The goblin-cat approached the little dust pile that had been her mistress, sniffed it, and then, inexplicably, slashed it with her paw. The last atoms of

Morgus were scattered across the stone flags, blown on a sudden draft and lost, not on a battlefield as she might have wished but in a scullery. Nehemet lifted her head, looking at Fern for a long moment in a way she did not understand; then she slunk out.

She was never seen again.

Luc got up, wincing from the burns on his chest. He came to Fern and put his arms around her, not speaking; her blood soaked into his shirt. Presently, he said: "Did you know that would happen?"

"No," she admitted shakily. "I just hoped."

"You're hurt."

"So are you."

Lougarry was licking her scorched fur, Bradachin ground his foot in the dust that had once been Morgus. "Guid riddance," he said. "Howsomedever, lassie, next time ye couldna be mair siccar? That wa' a wee bit close for my liking." He picked up the knife that Fern had let fall and put it on the table; the fruit had rotted away to an evil-smelling smear. Hodgekiss walked in, looking like a sleepwalker suddenly and rudely awakened.

"Mrs. Mordaunt . . ." he mumbled. "Where's Mrs. Mordaunt?"

"She's gone," said Luc, "and she won't be coming back. If I were you, I should take yourself home. Leaving now. It's a long drive." And, as an afterthought: "Tell your company to send the bill to Kaspar Walgrim."

"They always do."

"What we need," said Bradachin when the man had gone, "is usquebaugh. Usquebaugh tae fight the devil, usquebaugh tae heal the hert . . ."

"Robbie Burns?" said Fern.

"Boggan," said the goblin.

He fetched the whiskey. He knew where it was kept.

*   *   *

In the study of his Knightsbridge home, Kaspar Walgrim was sitting in front of his PC when he had the sudden impression that Time jarred. He found he had upset his sherry, and looked around the familiar room as if unsure where he was. His recollection of recent weeks—months—was inexplicably blurred. And then he blinked at the computer screen, and saw the details of the company he had invented, and the vast sums of the bank's and clients' money he had poured into it. In a frenzy he flicked through account after account, watching the money dodge here and there, acquiring a will of its own, ducking and diving, switching identities, bleeding away into the ether. He had never done anything criminal in his life, and now, seeing the evidence of his madness unfolding before him, his brain spiraled into panic. It was a dream, a nightmare—but no, the nightmare was over, and this was the awakening. He saw the name of Melissa Mordaunt and wondered fleetingly who she was. And then the memory returned of a woman with a bird's face, a spike-haired harpy who melted into a raven goddess caressing him with fingers of silk, transporting him into a dark Paradise . . .

At Wrokeby, the spell wall in the attic shimmered into view, a woven net of strange and sinister beauty—and vanished. Kal reached through the bars, probing the air, feeling nothing. He withdrew his hand, his expression undiscernible beneath the mask of grime, the lice-ridden hair. (He had eaten the lice when he was hungry.) He knew what it meant. Morgus had been his mother, had rejected and tormented him, punishing him for his birth, his being, for the monster she had made him. And now she was dead . . . There was something in his eyes that might have been pain, or perhaps simply a longing for the pain that was suddenly no longer there. Then he thought of Fern thrusting her hand through the barrier. He seized the chains that fettered him, the muscles in his arms stiffening into rigidity. He was part werefolk: captivity had not weakened him. The chains creaked, link grinding on link, straining at the ring that held them to the wall—then snapped like breadsticks. His legs were free; a few more minutes and his arms followed. The manacles still clasped wrist and ankle, loose ends of chain clattering as he moved, but he could deal with those later. He grasped the bars, trying to force them apart, wrenching, bending. It took a long time, but he had time. His strength was more than human though his soul was less, and gradually the gap widened, and the bars twisted, tearing up the floor where they were embedded, sending great cracks zigzagging across the ceiling. After nearly two hours, there was enough space for him to insinuate his body between them. On the other side he straightened up, stretching; the muscle web across shoulders and torso flexed, tensed, and relaxed into suppleness. Then he moved through the attics, chains rattling faintly, his stench following him like a darkness. In the ghostless house there were no eyes to watch him go.

Downstairs he met Grodda, who at Morgus's whim had brought him food: Nehemet's leavings, mice she had trapped, worms from the garden. On the rare occasions when she had arrived with a proper meal, she always spat in the dish. Seeing him, she turned to run, but she was not fast enough.

He broke her neck.

Then he went out, leaving the door ajar, letting the country night flow in to fill the emptiness.

In Dale House, Fern and Luc were patching up their injuries. A search of the bathroom cabinet had yielded a selection of antiseptic creams, one or two suitable for minor burns, and such antiquated remedies as iodine and hydrogen peroxide. There were also Band-Aids of assorted sizes, lengths of bandages, pads of gauze. Luc had stripped off his damaged jacket and unstuck the bloodstained shirt from his burns;

Fern spread cream gingerly on the blistered area and insisted
that he wash every spider scratch even though, as he pointed
out, those lacerations were old and dry. "I'll deal with them
later," he said. "Your turn. Take your top off. And your bra.
And your jeans."

"I'd rather—"

"And don't fuss."

She complied. The maggot bites on her upper torso were
tiny, but there were very many of them, and Morgus's magic
had seen to it that she bled freely. Her top was already stiffening from the drying blood, and she squirmed out of it with
difficulty; underneath, her white bra was blotched crimson.
Bradachin dematerialized tactfully, muttering something about
a robe, while she peeled off her jeans. Her body was very
slender, twiglet boned, curving slightly outward at the stomach, like a child's. When she removed her bra Luc saw her
breasts were small and conical, tapering to nipples like hard
pink shoots. She did not work out, and her thighs were slim
and soft, her thin arms lacking the reinforcement of visible
biceps. Her fragility and the number of her wounds roused
him to an unfamiliar gentleness: he wiped away the blood with
cotton balls dipped in a bowl of boiled water and peroxide,
feeling her every wince, every instance of teeth-clenching
pain deep in his own loins. "How come these don't self-heal
like your hand?" he asked her.

She explained, trying not to react to the proximity of his
naked chest, the hurts that made him vulnerable, her own
nakedness and vulnerability. Despite the stinging of the peroxide, the touch of the cotton ball was cool and pleasant.

"They're not deep," he was saying. "I could bandage half
your body like an Egyptian mummy—"

"Don't bother. Let them breathe. But you ought to cover
those burns."

"Perhaps we should let them breathe as well." The cotton

ball moved along the crease beneath her breast, daubed her nipple. She felt suddenly warm inside, very warm, though her customary pallor did not alter. And then Bradachin reappeared with a bathrobe, and she put it on, fumbling clumsily with the tie, and turned away to see to Lougarry, and Luc resorted to the whiskey bottle.

Later, unexpectedly ravenous, they raided the fridge and opened cans of soup from the larder. Fern telephoned Will, telling him at length what had happened, absentmindedly sipping her way through a large glass of scotch on the side before she hung up. Lougarry lay in her preferred spot by the stove; Bradachin, seeing the two humans did not need him, faded unobtrusively from the scene.

"Do you still wonder if I am your first love reborn?" Luc demanded abruptly, cutting the thread of conversation. "Are you afraid to believe it?"

"Not afraid, no. It just doesn't matter anymore." Her eyes, green with latent magic, looked straight into his. "Rafarl was part of the Past—even when I met him, he was part of the Past—and it's wrong to look back. I've learned that much. If you're always looking back, you can't move forward. You're you, whoever you are. You stood by me, you killed the spider, you defied Morgus. I don't want you to be anyone but yourself."

This time, she knew he would kiss her, and he did, pulling her to her feet, holding her carefully, carefully, the only roughness in the pressure of his lips, the invasion of his tongue.

"Mind your injuries," she said, in a moment of respite.

"Mind yours."

And somehow, somewhen, they were in bed. She thought she was falling into darkness, a blindness all touch and sensation, a slow, inexorable intimacy like serpents twining in a living rope, like two rivers running together into a drowning sea. After a while, she no longer knew where her body ended and his began, whether the pleasure she experienced was his or hers. Luc's initial caution grew into certainty, and they forgot their wounds, and the soreness, aches, tiny jabs of anguish only intensified the dark sweetness of their lovemaking. If it *was* love they were making. To Fern love seemed such a little word for something that was so fundamental, so primal, a plunging into the roots of being, an exploration not simply of the physical self but of the spirit. She had never felt so defenseless, so totally exposed, even to her very core, and she luxuriated in it. And at last she understood that what they were making was not just love but magic, and the Gift in him woke to hers, and the power flowed through them both, so all their nerve endings were alight, and their senses were magnified. They fed off each other like succubi, and drank each other like vampires, and gave themselves as willing victims, until hunger was sated and thirst slaked, and their souls were drained to the dregs. Fern saw Luc open himself to her, saw the layers of dissemblance that hid his heart peeled away one by one, until in the moment of ecstasy he appeared as a deity of the night, demigod or superhuman, his body arched backward in a terrible splendor, the darkness spreading out from him like wings, his face racked with ultimate agony, ultimate bliss. When the magic finally ebbed it felt like dying, if dying is a terminal relaxation, a drifting away of self and thought. Fern slid voluptuously into the blackness of sleep, and dreamed.

The same dream. The surreal city, the Dark Tower, the office with its window on the world. And the shadow who showed her the file bound in red, and the document with its strange calligraphy: the document she signed in blood. She saw the knife nick her arm, and the blood run down, staining the quill, saw the unreadable signature begin to trace itself across the page . . .

She woke up. The moon had put in a belated appearance, nearly full now, shining low through the windowpane. Its long rays reached across the bed, silvering Luc's uncovered chest, his left arm extended toward her. She saw the V-shaped scar of the knife wound, clear in the moonlight. The dream filled her.

Now she knew what it meant.

XI ✐✐✐✐✐

Luc woke to find himself bathed in moonlight; Fern lay in the darkness beyond. He reached for her, but she was as motionless and unresponsive as stone. He could not distinguish her expression; only the glitter in her eyes told him she was awake and aware. "Come to me," he said, and his voice was soft and sure.

"No." She said it the way she had said it to Morgus, a grudging monosyllable wrung from her lips.

"What's wrong?"

"You ask me that." She did not even turn her head.

"Yes. I'm asking."

She lay unspeaking, letting the silence do its work.

"What is it?" he persisted, but he did not touch her again.

She felt so cold. At last she said: "Why? Why did you do it?" but she knew.

"Do what?" His tone had flattened; he could not maintain his air of bewilderment.

She sat up brusquely, thrusting her face into his. The moon spotlighted her, showing the tumult in her eyes; he drew back from that look. "I have the Gift," she said. "Don't you know what that means? I can dream my way into your head. The face can hide your feelings, but in the soul, nothing hides. I have been inside your soul. Only it isn't yours anymore, is it? You made the ancient bargain, you gave him your Self. For Dana? Was that the excuse?"

"It was the reason," Luc said. "But not the only one."

She lay back again, disappearing beyond the light. "Honesty. At last."

"The nurse at the hospital—the one I told you about—sent me to the place. I had seen it before, in other cities, always from a distance—a few streets away, between buildings, a tower among other towers. I felt it was my destiny."

"You were afraid," she said.

"Yes. And desperate."

"But he showed you all the nations of the world and promised to spread them like a carpet beneath your feet. He promised you wealth, power, and an eternity of—what? Servitude? And Dana. He promised to restore Dana. But you and I did that, without his help."

Luc said: "He showed me the way to you."

"And I thought it was chance, or fate. He told you about Rafarl, didn't he? He told you what to say. He plucked the tooth out of your lower jaw." Still she lay in the dark, on her back, unmoving.

"The tooth . . . yes. But my dreams were my own. My soul knew you long before we met, with or without Azmordis. Maybe I am your lost love, maybe not, but I loved you tonight. You know that's the truth. With your Gift, you know it."

She was silent so long he might have thought she slept, but for her body's tension. "If you are my lost love," she said eventually, "I would you had never been found. As for tonight . . . that was not love. That was Judas's kiss. With my Gift, I know it."

"If that is what you wish to believe."

"Believe . . ." She picked up the word as if to sample it, to taste its poison. "You told me once you believed in nothing. No pattern, just chaos. But you believe in *him*, don't you? *His* pattern? *His* chaos?"

"He gave me something to believe in. Someone. Neither evil nor good. The power at the heart of things, the pulse along the wires. The one who makes skyscrapers grow and sparrows fall. He said he would teach me how to use my Gift, would mesh my power with his. He named me Lukastor, Fellangel, Lord of the Serafain, and gave me wings to ride among the stars. Do *you* believe in a kindly God with a white beard who leans down from a cloud once in a while to pat you on the head? Do you believe in harps, and cherubs, and pearly gates? He is the real thing, the only thing. He has my belief."

"There is a Gate," she said, "but it isn't made of pearl. I have seen it."

And, after a while: "Lord of the Serafain. He gave you a *title*. A little thing, at so high a price. Lukastor, Son of Morning, how thou art fallen. Farther than any sparrow."

He said: "You're talking nonsense. Without him, I would not have found you, or saved Dana."

"How do you know? There was always chance, or fate."

"You make your own fate."

"Not anymore." She almost sighed. "*He* will shape your fate for you."

She was thinking: You might indeed be Rafarl. There is weakness as well as strength in us all. Light and dark. Fear and courage. We are the choices we make. I loved you tonight, I loved even the dark in you. But not the choice you made, not the you who chose . . .

She said: "So what was the price—the whole price? What service did he require, to prove your loyalty?"

She had guessed the answer.

Luc said: "I am to take you to him."

"And?"

"He will offer you what he offered me. He says your Gift is great, and you can be great among his people. Morgus was a test: he was certain you would find a way to kill her. He wanted you to kill; he said it was necessary. Come with me— come to him—and we will be together always, sharing our power and his. So many live their lives without meaning, dying from a night's cold, a whiff of disease, and we can do nothing for them. But we can do this for ourselves. We can live *our* lives with a purpose, we can make our mark on eternity. Fern . . ."

"I like eternity unmarked. I am content to live my life in doubt, with no questions answered."

"Fern—"

"He lied to you, of course." She was tranquil now, if emptiness is tranquillity. "Would you have taken me to him openly, or by subterfuge?"

"He said I mustn't tell you. Not immediately, not till—"

"Not till it was too late for me to run away. Not till we crossed the threshold of his office. And then he might have made his offer, and he might not. Or he could have chosen slow torment for me instead. Petty tyrants have so little imagination; they always favor slow torment. Not that it matters. I won't be going."

"You must."

The moon had moved now, leaving them both in shadow. She was still lying on her back, motionless; he leaned over her, loomed over her, like a lover or a murderer.

"Must?"

"You don't understand. It was part of the bargain. I hadn't met you then; I swore—"

"Well, *I* didn't."

"You must come," he reiterated. "He won't harm you: I know that. I don't want to force you, but—"

"Then don't. I knew someone who broke his bargain with Azmordis." She used the name, in defiance or indifference, but no demon stirred. "He wasn't a good man—in fact, he did much evil—but he was brave. The morlochs set on him—have you seen the morlochs? The goblins call them pugwidgies. They have no feelings, no *minds*, only hunger. Oh, yes, Ruvindra was brave. They ate him alive. How brave are you?"

"Fairy tales don't frighten me."

"You are *in* a fairy tale, in case you've forgotten. Only no one lives happily ever after. Magic . . . magic is just another way of playing without the rules." He thought she smiled, but it was only a trick of the dark. "I play by witch's rules, didn't you know? Witch's honor."

"Fern." He bent down to her, and his voice was softened again. "Stop hiding in your own nightmares. Listen to me. We could do so much, be so much. The other week I saw a girl dying in a doorway—drugs of some sort—and I knew I was helpless. And there are so many like her. Don't die that way, don't live that way. I love you too much." He kissed her parted lips, a long, long kiss. She did not resist, did not respond.

When he was done she said in a flat voice: "I would rather die in a doorway than walk another yard with you."

He swung his legs off the bed and began to dress, finding his clothing without the light. Witchsight, she thought. Then he turned. There was an object in his hand that gleamed a thin reflected gleam. The knife. The knife that had lain on the desk in the tower office.

"You have no choice," he said. "I chose for you."

Silence. Shadows and silence. And in the silence, in the shadows, the glitter of her eyes.

"I am a witch." Her voice was very quiet. "I killed tonight. Do you think you can compel me?" And to the knife: *"Rrassé!"* But the blade had its own power: it trembled, but did not break.

"Do you think you can fight me?" said Luc.

She rose out of the bed, naked, all pale slenderness. He said: "Dress."

"Why?" She seemed indifferent to her nakedness, like a wild nymph or fey child.

"You will be cold."

She dressed, carefully, still in the dark. Always in the dark.

She whispered a charm, but it did not reach him; Azmordis must have shielded him from her sorcery.

She said: "Naked or clothed, I won't go with you."

The gleam of the knife blade stirred in his hand. They stared at each other for perhaps twenty seconds, then in the same moment, the same motion, he sprang, she dodged. There was no magic between them now, only strength, his and hers. He flung her on the bed, pinioning her arms almost without effort. The knife was at her throat. "Don't call the dog," he said. "You're fond of her. I should hate to have to harm her."

"You might find that difficult." She strained, but could not break his hold. "I won't call for any assistance. We are one to one: that is fair enough. Except you have a weapon, I don't."

"We are witchkind. As I understand it, we don't play fair."

"You learn fast." But not fast enough. I am on my home territory. I don't need to call: there is already someone there.

"Give me your word you will come with me in the morning, and I will release you."

"My word?" She was playing for time.

"What was that phrase you used? Witch's honor."

Witches have no honor. But that was something he had yet to assimilate.

She said: "Witch's honor."

He drew back, the knife gleam still bright in his grasp. She sat up. Stood up. "When I have a weapon," she said, "*then* this will be a straight fight."

He made out the shape crouching in the dark beyond her— the shape he had not seen before. He heard the whispered admonition: "Ferrn! Carlin! I hae the weapon for ye—"

Her hand closed on the haft. She felt the weight of the spear pulling her into the thrust, guiding her. The Sleer Bronaw, the Spear of Grief. Grip, pull, thrust. It was a single movement, smooth and inevitable. The death strike of the cobra, the warrior's lunge, the swordsman's *coup de grâce*.

The knife gleam leaped toward her.

(But was there a hesitation, a fatal instant of doubt?)

The blade dropped harmlessly from his hand. He made a noise: not a scream, a sort of choking grunt. He fell heavily. She said: "Luc," and she was on her knees beside him, trying to pull out the spear, but the barbs had opened in his belly, and she could see the blood, lots of blood, black in the moonlight. She called for cloths or bandages but not light, not electric light, no light to see what she had done, to make it real. She was holding a wad of cloth against his stomach, watching it turn black with the blood. Her hands were black. "Luc," she said, "Luc," but he did not answer. At some point she tried to find a pulse in his wrist, in his throat, but she wasn't sure how. Her face was wet, though she was not aware of crying.

Bradachin said: "He's deid," and "There wa' nae help for it."

Much later, nudged by Lougarry, she rose and went to wash her hands. The blood swirled around the basin in the stream of water, ran down the drain. She thought: This is what murderers do. They have to wash the blood off their hands.

None of it was real.

Back in the bedroom, she switched on the light. She didn't want to, but she knew it was necessary. *(He wanted you to kill: he said it was necessary.)* The body lay there, its face waxen from the blood loss. Not Luc, the body. A dead thing, solid and real, filling the room, filling the house. Taking over. It did not crumble into instant decay like Morgus: it stayed there. Unmoving. Immovable. She saw it in the light as if for the first time.

In London, Will's phone rang.

"I've killed Luc." His sister's voice was almost unrecognizable, close to hysteria. "Come now. You've got to come. The body's here and it won't go away. I don't know what to do with it. Please . . ."

Will said to Gaynor: "We'd better go."

* * *

Driving through the small hours, much too fast, they reached Yarrowdale before eight. The remnants of the front door had been jammed into place with a chest of drawers; it took Fern several minutes to shift it. "You said you'd killed Luc," Will said, once they were inside.

The explanation came out in a stammering rush, close to incoherence. "He had a knife—the little dagger from the tower office. Like a paper knife. I tried to break it, but the spell failed. All my spells failed. He said I must go with him. We s-struggled, and Bradachin gave it me. Sleer Bronaw. The spear." Her mouth shook; her gaze seemed to be fixed on something they could not see. "It went in so quickly—so quickly. There wasn't time to . . . to pull back. He hesitated. I'm sure he . . . He had the knife, but he was slow, and I was fast, and it went in, and I couldn't get it out. I couldn't . . ."

Will put his arms around her, and she began to shudder violently, dry sobs racking her like an asthmatic fighting for breath. "It's okay," he said with what he hoped was authority, though he knew it wasn't. He had never seen her like this, frantic, falling apart; it shocked him as much as what she had done. "Why did he pull a knife on you?"

"Sold himself—to Azmordis." For a moment, she looked up at him, and her eyes were wild. "It was my dream: do you see? Him, not me. Luc—Lucas—Lukastor, Son of Morning . . . I saw the scar. He said—I must join him. My third chance. Third time lucky."

Gaynor said: "Dear God."

Will: "I see."

"We made love. He l-let me think—he made me believe— he was Rafarl, Rafarl reborn . . . True love—Someday . . . Maybe he was. That's the worst. Maybe he was, and he betrayed me." The tears were coming now, leaking from her eyes, scribbling rain trails down her face. "We slept—and I dreamed—and when I woke up . . ."

"All right," Will said. "Gaynor, make her some tea. Strong

and very sweet. Or coffee; whichever you find first. As long as it's sweet."

"I don't take sugar."

"You do now. You're in shock." With Fern still curled within his arm, he followed Gaynor into the kitchen, refraining from comment on the broken windows. Lougarry emerged from the shadows to accompany them; Bradachin was already there.

"I tried to help her," he said. "But she waur just sitting there, on the floor, trembling like a wee pippit. The dog was licking her, like she wa' herrt, but she didna say aught. It wa' nae blame to her, the laddie was a baddun. He would hae killt her."

Fern shook her head numbly. Her voice had dropped to a whisper. "He hesitated. I didn't. *I didn't.*" The tears came faster now, healing, or so Will hoped.

He addressed Bradachin: "Where is he?"

The goblin jerked his thumb, pointing upward. "Her bedchamber."

They went upstairs. The body lay where it had fallen, cold and pale in the morning light. Will surveyed the face for a minute, thankful that the eyes were closed. It was the color of tallow, or the color he imagined tallow ought to be, the black hair, flattened by the crash helmet and deprived of gel, falling in limp spikes over the forehead. He didn't look at the wound, or remove the pad of reddened towels that concealed it. There was blood on the carpet, stiff and dry now. The spear had gone; Bradachin must have extracted it somehow. "Ye maun bury him deep," the goblin said. "I'm thinking there's those that wouldna understand what the maidy had tae do."

"I know." He would have to dispose of the body. He thought about it coldly, matter-of-factly, because that was the only way to think right now. "Can you help me?"

"Yon's tae pondersome for me."

He would have to ask Gaynor. He didn't want to, but there was no one else. "I won't bury him: digging takes too long, and new-turned earth is always obvious. There's a lake about an hour's drive from here. Far enough."

"And the motorcarridge," said Bradachin. "Ye maun get rid o' that, too. Folks will be noticing it muckle soon."

"Pity." Will was concentrating on detachment. Fern, who never panicked, had panicked—Fern who had faced dragon and witch queen, who had stolen a fruit from the Eternal Tree, walked the paths of the ancient Underworld, ridden out the tempest at the Fall of Atlantis. Now everything was down to him. "I didn't like Luc, for the little I knew him," he remarked with studied flippancy, "but it's a shame about the bike."

"Aye," said Bradachin. "I dinna approve o' carridges without horses, but yon's a bonny machine. I would ha' liked to gie it a try."

Back in the kitchen, Will said to Gaynor: "I'm really sorry, but I'm going to need your help, if you can bear it. It'll take two of us to carry the body."

"Body," said Fern. "Luc. The body . . . Like s-something on TV." The tea mug rattled in her hands.

Gaynor said: "Yes. All right."

"Hell of a way to start a relationship," said Will, giving her shoulders a quick squeeze before they entered the bedroom.

Gaynor made a wry, unhappy face. "Hell of a way to finish one."

Mrs. Wicklow arrived around lunchtime, but Will had anticipated this, and he and Gaynor had already moved Luc, wrapped in a sheet, to a room on the third floor, and put Fern to bed, claiming she was ill. The motorcycle had been wheeled into Will's studio and covered with another sheet, though they trusted the housekeeper would have no reason to go in there. She expostulated over the breakages and traces of droppings, attributing them correctly to some sinister cause, and cooked a sustaining meal that neither Will nor Gaynor could eat. Fern, exhausted and heavily dosed with aspirin, had finally fallen asleep and was left in peace. Fortunately for the other two, Mrs. Wicklow ascribed their lack of appetite to what was clearly a blossoming romance, and her superficial dourness led her to ask few questions. She went home at last around four and Will and Gaynor, with a bizarre sense of relief, lapsed back into tension.

"When do we go?" asked Gaynor, stroking the she-wolf's head for reassurance.

"Not till ten. We need full dark. Dark for dark deeds. It's Sunday night: there shouldn't be many people about. Let's hope to God anyone who *is* out is unobservant."

"Fern shouldn't be left."

"It can't be helped. Bradachin will take care of her. Lougarry will go in the car with you; I'll lead on the bike. Strange: I've always wanted to ride a Harley, but now—" He shrugged.

"Mrs. Wicklow's made steak-and-kidney pudding," Gaynor remarked, pale. "Her steak-and-kidney's awfully good."

"Afraid we'll have to freeze it," Will sighed.

The lake lay cupped in hills, reflecting the moon. It was an authorized beauty spot, a tourist destination of the kind that forbade picnickers and where angling was allowed only with a license. Will had gone there in his college days, to lie in the sun smoking dope—that didn't count as a picnic—and attempt the seduction of a girl he had been pursuing. Now he couldn't even remember if he had succeeded. There were legends attached to the lake, one concerning a drowned village, or maybe just a church, a priest who sold his soul to the devil, a local beauty who killed herself, and the bells that could be heard tolling sometimes, far beneath the water. Older stories spoke of kelpies, and a green-haired nix, and a lake god bearded with weed who lurked in the deepest places. More recently another local beauty had been pulled out, or part of her, after a ten-year absence, on the end of a fishing line. The prime suspect was her husband, who had collared her money, changed his name, and gone to live in the Balearics. Extradition proceedings were still under way. The lake had a bad name, for all its picturesque qualities; perhaps that was why Will had thought of it so quickly. Almost as if some dark intuition had invaded him, prompting his subconscious. Somehow, he felt it was the only choice.

They arrived just before midnight, driving along an unsurfaced lane to an empty parking area. Gaynor pulled over under trees, switching off her lights. Will told her to wait and, joined by Lougarry, cast around for a footpath to the water. The one they selected was stony and would show few tracks; Will took the motorcycle and followed the path up to a low bluff, wishing he could extinguish his headlight but afraid to negotiate the rough ground without it. At the top, he dismounted, shutting off the engine, and wheeled it across the grass to the edge. Above, a pale blur of moon shone through thin cloud, silvering the wind-scudded water farther out, but immediately below he could see only blackness. "Is it deep enough?" he whispered.

Lougarry turned her head.

Yes.

He inched the Harley forward until the front wheel dipped over the brink. One last shove and it plunged down, swallowed up in a huge splash that sounded very loud in the dead midnight. Spray rose toward them and fell back; the disturbed water seethed and bubbled for what seemed like an age but was really less than a minute. Walking carefully in the dark, Will trailed Lougarry back to the car.

"Now for the nasty part," he said to Gaynor.

She turned to him a face whose expression he could imagine, though he couldn't see it. "I've been thinking—are you sure we can't tell the police? After all, it *was* self-defense. His prints must be on that knife. She could say he went mad or something . . ."

"And she just happened to have a spear on hand?"

"Sorry . . ."

"Look, if you want to back out, it's not too late. I could drive you somewhere, Lougarry and I will finish this, and I'll pick you up later. Disposing of dead bodies wasn't in the job description when you opted to become my girlfriend."

"No," she said. "I'm with you. All the way."

She got out of the car. He took her hand for a second, clasping it tight and hard.

"I'm okay," she averred.

Lougarry led them to another path, shorter and muddier, skirting the lakeshore in the opposite direction. Will produced a flashlight—Luc's flashlight—and shone it along the bank. The moon had vanished altogether, and they moved in a world of dim shapes, groped by the occasional outstretched arms of bush or stunted tree, feeling rather than seeing the expanse of water beside them. Lougarry, trotting ahead, came to a halt at a point where the flashlight showed them the bank sloping steeply down and a thin breeze chilling the water into gooseflesh.

"Here?" asked Will.

Yes. I can smell the depth. He will roll down and the weed will bind him. It will be many years and an ill chance ere anyone draws him out.

"Right," said Will. "Let's go and get it."

Back at the car, they opened the trunk. The light panned over the contents, the terrible guilty thing muffled in sheeting, folded into lumps and mounds. Will said: "You take the legs." With no hands free they had to switch off the flashlight, groping for purchase on their load, dependent on Lougarry's guidance to take them back along the lakeside. The body was awkward and very heavy, with the additional weight of the leather jacket and pockets stuffed with stones. Gaynor found herself wondering about rigor mortis and whether the mild warmth of Dale House could have delayed it; the limbs still felt supple enough. But she had little space for thought: physical effort took all her concentration. More than once, she had to rest, setting the legs down while Will supported the torso. The second time the sheet fell back, and she saw the head lolling against him, a pallor of skin, a darkness of hair.

She said: "I can't believe I'm doing this. I could believe in the other stuff—dragons and goblins and magic circles—but not . . . *this*."

Will said: "Nearly there."

It seemed to take a long time, staggering sideways, or forward, or backward, encumbered by a bundle that felt heavier with each step. A soft drizzle began, powdering everything with damp; Gaynor felt her hair adhere clammily to forehead and neck. Her sneakers slithered frequently on the muddy path. "It'll blur our footprints," Will said. "Not that anyone'll come looking."

We hope, Gaynor thought, and shivered with the rising terror of discovery, the idea that someone, somewhere might be watching—a nocturnal dogwalker, lovers at a rendezvous—that police might come, the next day, or the next, searching for the impression of distinctive shoes, fishing in the black water . . . She mustn't think like that, or she would never sleep again. The task itself was enough to burden her conscience.

She stumbled on.

And eventually Lougarry halted and turned—Gaynor saw the yellow blink of her eyes—and Will said: "This is it."

They hefted the body over the edge, half dropping, half rolling it down into the lake. They could see almost nothing: rain blotted out their surroundings, darkness filled them. The splash this time was muted, but they heard the water slurping against the bank like the licking of giant lips. Will said: "Has it gone?"

Yes.

"Better get rid of this, then." He threw something out into the lake; Gaynor realized it was the flashlight. Then his arm came around her, guided more by instinct than sight, and he hugged her close, and suddenly she knew that she loved him, that he loved her, not for a month or a year but for always. He had done this for his sister, this terrible secret thing, and he had taken her with him, trusted her, and she knew in her gut— in her soul—that he would have trusted no one else. It seemed strange and wonderful to her that at such a moment she should experience this revelation. So they clung to each other, staring across the water, into the rain. The darkness looked thicker out there, drawing into itself, condensing into a core of blackness deeper than the engulfing night. It was difficult to be sure, but Gaynor thought she could distinguish it as a billowing mass, hovering above the lake, drifting shoreward.

"He sold himself to a demon," said Will. "Maybe the demon is coming to collect."

He pulled her back from the bank and hurried her along the path, though she needed no urging. Lougarry was already there, visible as a gray movement flickering ahead of them. They were almost running now, despite slithers and stumbles. They didn't look back.

As they turned away from the lake toward the parking lot, Will thought he caught a faint echo of sound somewhere behind them, like a bell tolling far away, or deep under water.

A fortnight went by. Fern had returned to London and work immediately but struggled to cope with the simplest tasks and was instructed to take a week's leave to recover, though nobody knew from what. ("Lovesick," opined an associate. "It turned out badly. He doesn't call anymore.") Gaynor stayed a few days with her and Will visited constantly, usually bringing therapeutic videos since she didn't seem to want to talk things out. Ragginbone, who was not much of one for videos, went back to Yorkshire. In the *FT* and the *Economist*, they read the breaking news of an investment banker with a hitherto unblemished reputation who was implicated in a vast fraud involving both clients and colleagues. By the time the story reached the tabloids, a mystery woman was included who had since disappeared, the protagonist's son was said to have absconded, also—according to rumor—with large sums of ill-gotten money, and the whole business had acquired a flavor of Greek tragedy or TV saga. Kaspar Walgrim was shown in photographs and on television, between arresting officers, turning away from the cameras. ("Poor man," said Gaynor. "It wasn't his fault.") Lucas Walgrim had been sighted at the gambling tables in Monaco, on the top of the Empire State Building, in the souk in Marrakesh. Dana was reported to be in rehab, then was said to be recovering from a "long illness" in a private clinic somewhere.

"I ought to go and see her," Fern said out of the blue. "I owe it to—to Luc. Or to her."

"You don't owe *him* anything," said Will.

"I'll go if you like," Gaynor offered. "As your representative. It isn't as if she knows you."

"Would you?" Fern sounded truly grateful. "It must be terrible for her. In a coma for months, and then coming around to all this. And not—not understanding any of it."

"Should I explain?" Gaynor asked uncertainly.

"I don't know . . ."

"Use your own judgment," said Will. "I'll go with you."

But she declined, feeling that two of them might be too much for someone in Dana's presumed condition. The next day, she took the afternoon off and arrived in Queen Square behind a large bunch of flowers, only to find Dana had been moved and staff were reluctant to reveal her present whereabouts. "You might be a journalist," said a senior nurse, bluntly. "She needs privacy right now."

"I'm not," said Gaynor. "Honestly I'm not. I restore manuscripts. You can check." She gave her work number. "I know Luc—Dana's brother. He came here a couple of times with another friend—Fern Capel—who'd been in a coma too and was trying to help them. Support stuff. She's not awfully well now, so I'm here instead of her. We just want to know Dana's okay."

"I'll get back to you," the nurse conceded.

Gaynor took the flowers to Fern, and they returned to their perusal of the papers, who were getting nowhere in their search for the mystery woman. Melissa Mordaunt was clearly a fictitious identity, but since the person behind it had no records of any kind—no birth certificate, National Insurance number, passport, or driver's license—they were unlikely to track her farther than Wrokeby. Luc's defection continued to baffle, but no one suggested he had been murdered, and the issue was clouded still further when someone in his office managed to shift responsibility for some dubious financial transactions onto him. Meanwhile, Kaspar Walgrim's lawyer expressed remorse on his client's behalf and called in psychiatrists to explain that he had acted while the balance of his mind was disturbed. Pictures appeared of Dana at various society events over the past several years, but the newspapers were beginning to abandon the carcass of the story for lack of meat when the clinic finally contacted Gaynor.

The following day, armed with more flowers, she drove down to an exquisite Georgian country house where those who could afford it retired to convalesce, generally from drug addiction, alcoholism, or nervous breakdown. Knowing a little of Dana's history, Gaynor wondered if she had been there before. During the journey she had dwelt unhappily on the fact that this was Luc's sister she was going to see, and although she had done her utmost to put that night at the lake out of her mind, she could not help feeling steeped in guilt. Dana's opening remarks nearly sent her bolting straight back to London. "I don't know who you are," she said, "but I'm told you're a friend of my brother. Have you any idea what's happened to him?"

She didn't resemble Luc, Gaynor thought, striving desperately for a natural reaction. She was a little thin and pale, which suited her, and had the type of good looks that result more from grooming than nature: well-cut, high-gloss hair, clear skin, manicured hands. There was none of Luc's suppressed intensity or Modigliani bone structure. Unable to find a suitable answer to her question, Gaynor handed her the bouquet and hovered undecidedly by a visitor's chair.

"Actually," she said, "I'm only an acquaintance, really. I didn't mean to deceive you, but it was too difficult to explain properly at the clinic. The thing is, Luc got in touch with Fern Capel—she's my best friend—because he'd heard from a doctor that she'd gone into a coma in circumstances very like yours. Luc thought maybe she could help him. I know she went to see you a couple of times when you were unconscious and she wanted to visit you now, but she isn't very well at the moment, so she asked me. I'm sorry: does any of this make sense?"

"Nobody makes much sense right now." Dana looked bleak. "Look—sit down. I could ask for some tea. They don't allow alcohol here."

"Tea would be lovely," said Gaynor.

Dana pressed a bell and ordered the tea, and Gaynor, in a painful attempt to adhere to the truth, said: "I'm afraid I—I haven't seen your brother in a while. I don't think anyone has."

"They're saying he's gone off with money from the firm," Dana persisted, "but he wouldn't do that. He's unscrupulous sometimes, but not a thief. He's not that stupid. He had a great life—plenty of dough—why quit for a few extra bucks?"

Gaynor mumbled: "I don't know."

"Some people came from the Serious Fraud Office," Dana went on. It occurred to Gaynor that she was short of a real confidante and desperate to talk to almost anyone. "About Luc and—and Daddy. They said Luc might have debunked because he'd found out about Daddy, or been involved with his business affairs, but that's nonsense. I told them, he would never just *leave*. Not without a word. We hadn't seen much of each other lately, but when we were kids he always looked after me. He would never, *ever* run out on me. They didn't believe me. They didn't say so, but I could see it. They looked awfully cynical, and tired, and *sorry* for me . . ." She began to cry helplessly, trying to sniff back the tears. Gaynor groped in a flowered box for a wad of tissues and decided this was quite the worst afternoon of her life.

"I'm so sorry," she said, feeling like a criminal. Technically she supposed she was one.

"No . . . no. *I'm* sorry . . . I keep crying at people. They say it's okay—therapeutic . . ."

"Of course it's okay."

"The psychiatrist's very kind—she's quite young, you know, and not patronizing like some I've had—but it's so nice to talk to a *real* person."

"What about your friends?" Gaynor asked unguardedly.

"Oh, a couple of them came down. They were excited about all the stuff in the papers and kept sort of looking at me sideways, to see if I knew something I wasn't telling, but I don't. And Georgie's always fancied Luc, but he didn't reciprocate, so she was mouthing off about him. My best friend's in Australia, having a baby. She's phoned several times, but she's nearly eight months gone and she doesn't want to fly. I might go over there after the baby's born." She mopped her face with the tissues and glanced up blearily as the tea arrived. She didn't say thank you, so Gaynor said it for her. "Tell me about your friend—Fern what's-her-name. You said she'd been in a coma like me."

"It was two years ago," Gaynor said. "She was supposed to be getting married, and we went out for her hen night, and she drank too much and passed out and didn't come around for a week."

"A *week*?" Dana sounded mildly scornful. "I was out for months."

"The thing is, there was nothing wrong with her. Like you. It was as if—" Gaynor trod carefully "—her body was in suspension, and her spirit had gone . . . somewhere else."

Dana's expression froze into sudden stillness. "That's how it felt," she said. "I had such awful dreams. I was shut in a jar, in this huge laboratory. I kept banging on the sides and shouting, but no one came to let me out. I felt like an insect trapped under a glass. I was terrified they were going to perform some horrible experiment on me."

Gaynor said: "They?"

"There was this woman who would come and peer at me sometimes. She was huge, or maybe I was very small, and she had this big red smile full of teeth, and black eyes—really wicked eyes, like looking into a dark cave when you know there's something dreadful lurking down there. She always seemed to be wearing evening dress; all wrong for a laboratory. And there were these other faces, nightmare faces, distorted and leering, like an illustration for 'Rumpelstiltskin' in a book I had as a child. That picture always scared me so much I was afraid to go to sleep, but now it was as if I had, and the picture had turned into reality, and I couldn't wake up. I couldn't wake up."

"Fern had bad dreams, too," Gaynor offered. "About a pair of witches, and a gigantic Tree that filled her whole world."

"Sounds more fun than mine," said Dana. "Lindsay—the psychiatrist—says it's frightfully interesting and Kafkaesque." A note of gratification flickered in her voice. "But at the time, it was so . . . not exactly real, but horrible, because I was stuck in the dream or whatever it was, and I couldn't get out. Lindsay says it was symbolic, but it didn't *feel* symbolic. Apparently it all has to do with my mother dying when I was young and my relationship with Daddy."

"I'm sorry about your father," Gaynor said.

"I can't believe he would do anything against the law. He's always been so aloof, and stuffy, and high-minded about things. It can't all have been hypocrisy . . ."

She sounded hopelessly bewildered, and Gaynor found herself thinking: She doesn't love him very much, but she must have relied on him. He laid the rails that she had to go off.

She couldn't think of anything to say in the way of comfort.

"How did you get out of the jar?" she asked eventually.

"It's funny, isn't it?" said Dana. "That's what Lindsay asked me. She said dreams of this kind have their own logic. I don't know: I never had logical dreams before."

"But you do recall getting out?"

"Not very clearly. All I know is, Luc was there. And some-one else, I think, but I only remember Luc. His face was huge too, all bendy through the glass, and then it shrank back to normal size, and went far away, and I suppose after that I must have woken up. And now he's gone . . ."

"I'm sorry," Gaynor said for the umpteenth time. "So sorry . . . I'm sure he would have done anything for you. Any-thing at all."

That evening, she gave Fern an edited version of the inter-view, and Will, later, a rather more detailed one.

"She seems pretty self-absorbed," Gaynor told Fern. "She didn't appear very interested in what might have happened to you. As far as I could make out, her psychiatrist thinks she had some sort of dream sequence symbolizing her relation-ship with her father."

Fern attempted a rather shaky laugh. "If the Eternal Tree was a hallucination," she said, "what the hell does that say about my family background?"

"The point is," said Will, "there's nothing you can do for her. She may be confused and upset, but she's well off, well looked after, and in a month or so she'll be winging her way to Bondi Beach to forget. You don't need to agonize over her."

"No," said Fern. "After all, I killed her brother. There isn't a lot I can do to make up for that."

"You had no choice," said Will.

How often had she heard that phrase? Her face twisted. "There's always a choice," she said.

She had been back at work for a while now, struggling to concentrate although the world of PR appeared completely surreal. The launch party for *Woof!* magazine was due in a few days, with a full complement of celebrities and their pets, most of which seemed to have even more rarefied tastes and eccentric habits than their owners. Fern felt so detached from the action, she found it curiously easy to retain what was left of her sanity. But the nights were difficult. She would lie staring vacantly into the darkness, trying not to relive that final moment, blanking out the terrible wonder of their lovemaking, thinking about nothing till her head ached from the strain of it. Every evening she drank a glass of wine too much in the hope that it might soothe her, or warm her, or chill out the pain. If it *was* pain. Mostly, it seemed to her that her life had ended when she ended Luc's, and the rest of her days would be filled with emptiness and the taste of dust. Gaynor dosed her with Mogadon, and Rescue Remedy, and kava kava bark, all of which Fern took meekly, and then she would laugh a little, or cry a little, or sleep a little, but the emptiness inside her devoured both laughter and tears, and sleep would not drive it away.

"I'm really glad about you and Will," she said once, with something approaching true feeling. The two of them were alone together; Will was out charming a commissioning editor.

"I didn't know you'd noticed," Gaynor said candidly.

"Of course. I suppose . . . I'm afraid to say too much. Everything I touch turns to ashes these days."

Later that evening, Skuldunder arrived. Fern didn't notice

him before he materialized, perhaps because she didn't want to look.

"The queen is coming to see you," he announced from under his hat brim, his one visible eye straying toward the chardonnay on the table. Evidently he had acquired a taste for it.

Gaynor glanced at Fern, who said nothing, and spoke for her. "We will be honored."

Mabb duly appeared, garlanded with dying flowers and carrying a particularly vicious thistle stem by way of a scepter. Her eyelids were painted purple with iridescent spots that spread over her temples, and her customary rank odor was mingled with overtones of what might be Diorissimo. Gaynor saw Fern flinch slightly as the smell hit her. ("The perfume was a mistake," she admitted afterward.)

"Greetings, your highness," she said, adding bravely: "You are most welcome."

"I show you great favor," Mabb declared, perching herself on an armchair. "My loyal subject here, the Most Royal Burglar Skuldunder, has told me how you commended him for his courage in the witch's house."

There was a note of doubt in the assertion, so Fern responded: "Yes."

"I have also heard how your companion slew the giant spider, aided by my burglar, and how, with Skuldunder's help, you stole the demonic head from a sapling of the Eternal Tree."

"Absolutely," Fern said faintly.

"And now the witch is dead." It was not a question. News of the events at Dale House, or some of them, had obviously reached Mabb. "It was a great feat," the queen continued. "She was mighty among witchkind, but you proved mightier."

"Not really," said Fern. "Everyone has their weak spot. I found hers. I am not—" she shivered "—in the least bit mighty."

"You don't look mighty," Mabb agreed. "You have not my regal presence, or the mien of one of the great. But by your deeds you are known. You will be the most powerful and most dreaded of Prospero's Children—you will be as Merlin, as Zarathustra, as Arianrhod of the Silver Wheel. None will be able to stand against you. Therefore I salute you, and cement our allegiance." She made an imperious gesture, and Skuldunder disappeared, reappearing an instant later holding a curled shard of tree bark piled with herbs, a few wildflowers, and a small green apple.

"Thank you," Fern said. "I'm afraid I haven't anything for you right now."

"It doesn't matter," Mabb declared magnanimously. "You were unprepared. You may send your gifts later, with my subject here. This apple is from my special tree," she added. "No other in the world has the same sweetness."

"Thank you," Fern said again.

Gaynor felt it was time to rush into the breach. "How is the house-goblin—Dibbuck?" she asked. "Will he be able to go back to Wrokeby now?"

Mabb's face seemed to darken. "None of goblinkind will go there for an age and more," she said. "When all the spirits are driven out of a place by some great evil, it brings the abyss very close. Sometimes, it is an act of sorcery; sometimes, a mortal deed. Mortals talk loudly of honor and chivalry and the code of war, but they surpass werefolk in evil, when they wish. Are not the witchkind mortal, at birth?"

"We are always mortal," Fern said bleakly. "We just forget."

"About Wrokeby," Gaynor said hastily.

"Even the birds will not go back there for a long while," said Mabb, "or the little nibblers and scrappickers who live in old houses. Only malignant elementals will roost in its rafters, the kind who are drawn by the nearness of the void and the black humors that gather in such places. If the house-goblin returned, they would send him mad."

"Will he be all right with your people?" Gaynor inquired.

The queen shrugged, twitching her wings. "Maybe; maybe not. He is not strong like us wild goblins. He pines for his lost wardship. He may pine away until he loses his hold on existence and sinks into Limbo. Or he may live, and brood, and wither slowly in a long, long autumn. Who can say?"

"I wish him well," said Fern. "Tell him that."

Unexpectedly, Mabb inclined her head in acknowledgment. "The wish of so great a sorceress is a potent thing," she said. "I will tell him."

Gaynor saw Fern suppress a wince.

The queen declined a glass of wine, to Skuldunder's disappointment, and departed, leaving behind the barkload of gifts and the lingering reek of Dior and dead fox. Studying Fern's face, Gaynor replaced the chardonnay with gin.

"Mighty," said Fern, almost musingly. "Such a horrible word. It sounds *heavy*, like a mailed fist. Mighty is righty. I don't *look* mighty, I don't *feel* mighty, but I am a great sorceress. I destroy my enemies even when they think they are invulnerable and I slay my lovers lest I grow too fond of them. That is what I have become, or what I will be. It is written."

"Written where?" said Gaynor.

"In the annals of Time—in a prophecy of stone—in the rushing wind and the running water."

"In other words, nowhere," said Gaynor, determined to be pragmatic. "Nothing is written till we write it ourselves."

"Who said that?"

"I think I did."

"It's a good one," said Fern. "I like it. But I already wrote *my* fate. In blood."

At work the following day, a prolonged session with the creators of *Woof!* magazine did much to take the edge off her mightiness. Hitches sprang up like toadstools: Gothic rock star Alice Cooper, invited to the launch because he was rumored to sleep with a couple of pythons, admitted to a snake phobia, and writer Carla Lane had gone into print to boycott the party since so many of the superstar pets were endangered species. A joke memo circulated the office saying that Richard Gere would be bringing his collection of gerbils, Freddie Starr a born-again hamster, and Tara Palmer-Tomkinson her new coat. (The last item turned out to be true.) Fern did not smile. She was about to quit her desk for an unavoidable stint in the Met of socializing with clients when the phone rang. Her hand hovered, hesitated, lifted the receiver. She wasn't looking forward to the bar.

"Can I speak to Fern Capel?"

"Speaking."

"Dane Hunter." Of course: the American accent. A little to her surprise, she remembered him at once. "I'm the archaeologist you met at the site in King's Cross. You were right about that inscription. We won't be working there much longer—the developers never give us enough time—but I thought you might like to come and have a look before they build over it."

"Yes," she found herself saying. "Yes, I would."

XII ⸎⸎⸎

Fern went to King's Cross the next day, stretching her lunch hour. It was raining in a thin, drizzly, disheartened manner, but despite rat's-tail hair, dripping noses, and crumpled windbreakers the volunteers were still working with enthusiasm. Dane came to meet her in a damp sweatshirt and straggling ponytail, his tan faded to sere in the gray of a British summer, his smile switched on a little too late, as if something about the sight of her disconcerted him. He was thinking she had lost weight and looked indefinably more fragile, less perfectly composed than before. He said: "Those shoes won't do." She wore high-heeled mules that seemed to hang loose on her feet; even her ankles appeared brittle.

"Damn," said Fern. "They'll have to. I forgot to bring any others."

He took her arm to assist her over the rough ground.

"How did you get my number?"

"You wrote out the inscription on the back of your business card," he reminded her. "I hope you didn't mind my calling."

"No, of course not."

"I tried you two or three weeks ago," he went on, "but they said you were on holiday. Since then, things have been a bit busy. I've been attempting to convince the developers this site is important enough to be preserved, but we can't get any backing from English Heritage—they say it's 'interesting' but there isn't enough here. What they mean is, there's nothing to pull the tourists. And no one but you has been able to decipher the language on the stone. Take a look."

The trench was much deeper now, the fallen stone raised so that the engraved lettering was visible on the side. Dane sprang lightly down and, without asking, lifted Fern after him. She leaned closer to read the words she had already seen in her mind. The script was Roman, not the far older Atlantean alphabet that is similar but more complex, including a separate sign for *th* and several different vowels for variations on *e*. *"Uval haadé. Uval néan-charne."* A tremor ran through her as she recalled what Mabb had said about Wrokeby. "I think . . . something happened here a very long time ago, maybe thousands of years. It's left its mark. It isn't a place for the curious to stand and stare."

"My team don't seem to mind," Dane said. "At least . . . one of the girls was diagnosed with depression, but she probably had it anyway. Someone fell in a trench and sprained his ankle, we had the usual cuts and bruises, and one guy's eczema came back. Is that enough to justify a curse?"

"Not a curse," said Fern. "Just . . . leftover evil. The aftertaste of emptiness."

He didn't mock. "I guess I know what you mean. I always need a drink when I quit the site. But that's pretty standard, too." He scrambled back up out of the hole and reached down to swing her up after him. "I could use a beer now. How about you? There's a pub around the corner."

"I have a meeting at three-fifteen."

"That gives us at least an hour."

The pub was small and poky inside, yellowed with cigarette smoke, patronized by a handful of barflies who looked as if they had been there since the Stone Age, or so Dane said in a murmured aside. "So has the beer," he added.

"I don't drink beer," said Fern. She asked for a mineral water.

"No alcohol at lunchtime?"

"Not really. Oh all right, a G and T. Thanks."

The barflies stared at Fern, but were evidently accustomed to Dane. He paid for the drinks and led her to a corner table. "If you're hungry they do sandwiches, but they're not very good."

"I'm not hungry."

"Excuse me if I'm being too personal, but have you been ill lately? You look kinda thin."

"Stress," said Fern. "Lots of stress."

"I thought witches could just wave their wands and magic their problems away."

"I left my wand on the tube," Fern said with the flicker of a smile.

"Must be real easy to do. Like umbrellas. When I first came to England I always carried one, but I kept leaving them everywhere."

"You go through a lot of wands in my business," Fern affirmed. "I don't see you as an umbrella person, somehow. More a getting-wet person. Like now."

Dane grinned, pushing back a damp forelock. "Maybe I exaggerated a bit. But when you come from California, and you've heard so much about English rain . . . well, I did have a couple of umbrellas to begin with. Till I lost them."

"It's been a lousy summer."

"So everyone keeps telling me."

"Have you been over here long?"

An hour later, she glanced guiltily at the clock. "I must get back. We've got the dog-biscuit people coming—they're sponsoring the magazine and paying for the party, so we have to keep them sweet." She had told him about *Woof!* "I— I've enjoyed this." She sounded slightly nonplussed by her own response. "I—thanks. I wish you luck with the site and everything."

He stood up with her.

"No chance your telepathic skills could find me a human skeleton lying around there? That always gets things moving."

"Sorry." Her smile flickered again. "I don't do bones. You need a dog."

"Well, thanks for your help, however you did it. I'll always believe in witches now."

Outside, they shook hands by way of good-bye, and he held hers a moment too long. Just a moment.

"How about dinner sometime?"

She went out with him on Saturday, starting with drinks in a pub and moving on to a Vietnamese meal in a restaurant of his choice. It was far less sophisticated, and less expensive, than her evenings with Luc, but she didn't care. At the liqueur and coffee stage, Dane asked her: "Are you going to tell me what caused all this stress you've been having recently—or am I being too nosy?"

"I was seeing someone," Fern said. "It didn't work out." She concluded, after a pause: "All fairly commonplace."

He heard the quiver in her voice. "Was he playing around?"

"Playing? No—nothing like that. It just . . . wasn't working."

"Rich guy?"

"How did you know?"

"You look like the kind of girl who pulls rich guys. I don't mean—hell, that came out all wrong. You look—high maintenance. And you must meet plenty of rich people through your job."

"I don't usually check," said Fern. "And for the record, I maintain myself. Anyway, what about you? Some archaeologists are rich. Heinrich Schliemann and co."

"He's dead," Dane pointed out. "For men like that, archaeology is a hobby, not a career. I get by. I lecture in term-time, dig in the vacation, sometimes both."

"Like Indiana Jones?"

"You got it. Picture me with a whip and a leather hat, stealing the green eye of the little yellow god from a gang of crooks. Beautiful girl on one arm—"

"Dead rat on the other?"

They both laughed.

"Whoever your guy was," Dane resumed presently, "he must have hurt you pretty bad. You look like you haven't laughed much in a while. Was he a fool or a knave?"

"Knave," said Fern, "I suppose. We—we had a disagreement . . . an argument. You could say it was a question of ethics."

"So it was you who ended it?" said Dane.

"Yes," said Fern. She produced a pale smile. "I ended it."

Back at the flat, feeling comfortably wined and dined despite the conversational hurdles, she drifted easily into slumber for the first time in weeks.

It was dark when she awoke, and a glance at the bedside clock showed the time was twenty past two. She lay for a few minutes feeling restful, even though sleep was ebbing from her brain. Gradually, she became aware of a presence nearby, or the imminence of one, an elusive pressure on the atmosphere that did not quite take shape and solidity. She detected a muted heartbeat, a sense of menace, yet she was not afraid. "It's all right," she said. "You're invited." He developed slowly, a thing of air and darkness hardening into flesh. He was clean now, his coarse mane softened into an aureole from recent washing, his hot, animal smell more unobtrusive than usual. Her witchsight could just make out the terrible pitting on his brow, but beneath the ridge of bone his eyes were almost calm, their red gleam deep and soft as burgundy. "It is good to see you," she said, and meant it. "If you go and wait in the living room—that way—I'll put something on and we can have a drink together."

"Is that what friends do these days?" Kal asked.

"Yes," she said. "That's what friends do."

They did what friends do. She opened a bottle of Corton that she had bought to share with Luc, and they drank their way through it. He looked bizarre sitting in an ordinary armchair, dressed in oddments of fur and hide, one leg outstretched, the other crooked, his lion's tail looped over the armrest. The man-made light shone on his giant muscles, his disfigured face, the twisted coil of his horns. He glanced around from time to time, when he thought she wouldn't notice, half-nervous, half-wondering, as if he had difficulty believing he was really there. Fern found herself filled with a deep warmth toward this mongrel creature with whom she had once traded friendship as part of a bargain, an offer made in cold blood to save her own life, and who had since become a friend indeed. It seemed to her that, more than anyone, he was the person she could talk to about everything that had happened, the one who would truly understand. She told him about the final battle with Morgus, and the courage Luc had shown, and that hiatus after when they came together at last. And the dream, and the wakening, and what followed. "I killed him," she said. "He hesitated—I know he did—but I didn't. *I killed him.*"

"It's natural," he said. "I have killed often and often. To feed—to win—in vengeance—in hate. I have killed the howling dog that disturbed my sleep and the fox that slunk from my path and the beggar who would not share a crust. Your little killing is nothing, Fernanda. It is your conscience that magnifies it, born of your soul. I have no conscience, no soul. I cannot comprehend such feelings."

"Then why did you never kill your mother?" said Fern. "Why did you love her, in spite of all she did to you? Oh, yes, you did—you loved her and loathed her, and when her death released you, in a corner of your heart you mourned, because now there was no chance she would ever turn to you."

"You are seeing phantoms," said Kal. "I never loved my mother, nor mourned for her."

"Liar," said Fern. "I can sense your emotions, even the ones you deny. They are prisoners as you were, trapped in your subconscious. Let them free."

"Give me the wine, and let my emotions be. We were talking of yours, little witch. Your lover betrayed you, and threatened you, and you killed him to save yourself. That is the right of any living thing."

"Is it?" said Fern. "Or did I kill for the sake of killing, because I could? Because he made love to me, and without killing him I knew I would never be rid of the taint?"

"You are not a killer by nature, I know that. Hence these torments."

"I am not tormented," Fern responded. "I am . . . diminished. I have always believed that your soul grows when you do something that is good and brave, a right thing, a true thing, and when you do evil—no matter what the motive— your soul is eroded. Well, my soul is less. I feel an emptiness inside. As if there was a little bright flame in the nucleus of my being, and now it has gone out, or withered to an ember. I don't . . . I don't quite know how to go on living."

"Yet you manage," Kal said. "That emptiness is familiar to me. I have always had it."

"You have a soul," Fern asserted. "At least, a soul *in potentia*. I can see it."

"My father was an immortal who had no seed. My spirit was plucked from the ether and forced to inhabit a fetus botched together by magic from an unholy union. My heredity does not include a soul."

"We are more than our heredity," Fern declared. "Someone said to me recently, nothing is written till we write it ourselves. I owe you, Kal: you are always reminding me of it. So I will give you something. I will give you a soul."

Kal's eyes gleamed red as flame. "You have a spare?"

"Wait." She left the room, returning some ten minutes later with Mabb's apple wrapped in tissue paper. "Take this. It is a goblin apple; the fruit is not good but at its core is a soulseed. Plant it, nurture it, and as it grows, so will your soul." She had put a spell on it to encourage rapid growth. "One day it will become a tree, and when the tree blossoms, your soul, too, will flower. But remember, magic is not enough. You must nourish it with deeds, you must try to—"

"To do the right thing, the true thing?" He cupped the apple in one swarthy hand. His tone was suspicious. "Goblins have little magic, only petty charms, slumbersongs, will-o'-the-wisp lanterns. I have never heard of a soulseed."

But Fern was ready for that one. "Mabb is a picker-up of discarded enchantments," she improvised, "a hoarder of secrets who will forget in a moment what they are or where she has hidden them. She gave me this, no doubt, because she did not know or could not recall what it really was."

"Why should the light-fingered queen of a race of malmorffs be sending you gifts?"

Fern explained about their allegiance, telling him of Skuldunder—Kal had barely noticed him at Wrokeby—and Mabb's recent visit.

"Truly you have mighty allies," he commented, with amused sarcasm.

"I hate that word," she said, suddenly cold. "Mighty. Mabb called me mighty. But I don't want to be."

"I think you need this apple more than I."

"It wouldn't work for me," she said. "I'm supposed to have a soul already. If it is damaged, no magic will make it grow."

"Then take your own advice. Nourish it with deeds. Live again, love again, whatever love may be—" his manner was mainly flippant, but not all "—and your soul will revive."

"Love again?" Fern shrugged. "I met someone lately, someone I could have—might have . . . but it's no good. If I loved him, I couldn't lie to him—I couldn't tell him the truth—it will always be there, the thing I did, like a great red wound that no one else can see. I won't be able to forget it, or ignore it, or set it aside. It will always be part of me—a part I can't share. I fear I am damaged for good."

"It is not for good," said Kal. He picked up the bottle and drained the last of the wine. "Thank you for my gift. I will grow myself a soul. Now I owe you, little witch—for many things."

"There are no debts between friends," she said.

"For that also I owe you. I will find a means to repay . . ."

She was growing tired now and she thought he had begun to fade, blurring from her sight. Then, as in a dream, there were strong arms lifting her, carrying her to her bed, and even as sleep supervened she felt the pillow beneath her head, and someone drawing the quilt up to her chin.

About three weeks later, she returned home from work to find a phial on her dressing table that had not been there before. Beside it was a note written in an ill-formed hand on a scrap of her own paper. *You know what this is. A single draft, and your Gift, and all you have accomplished with it, good or bad, will be forgotten. You can start again, no longer my little witch, just Fernanda. Good luck to you, however you choose.*

The phial was very small, the size of a perfume bottle, and seemed to be made of rock crystal. As far as she could tell, it contained about a mouthful of clear water. When she held it up it took the light and broke it into rainbow drops that danced and flickered around the walls.

She sat for a while, remembering the caverns of the Underworld where Kal had been her guide, and the silver notes of a fountain now little more than a trickle, all that remained of a spring that had once fed a great river. Its name lived on in legend, though the healing water had all but gone. The well of Lethe.

She closed her hand tight around the phial, but did not touch the stopper.

*   *   *

Summer declined into autumn with little appreciable change in the weather, except that it got wetter. Will's production company won its first significant commission, involving about six weeks' filming in the more inaccessible parts of India, as a result of which he decided he needed to cement his relationship with Gaynor by moving into her flat. "With such an unstable job," he announced, "I need a stable home life. Besides, when some unhappily married creep comes around trying to sob his way into your sympathy, I want him to see my socks in the bathroom. And I want photos of us all over the place. Soppy ones."

"Next you'll be saying you want me to get pregnant," said Gaynor.

"We'll see about that in due course."

They gave a party to celebrate and Fern brought Dane, who, perhaps under her influence, had cut his hair short and wore something that might have been a suit if the jacket and trousers had matched. "He's lovely," Gaynor told her friend in an aside, hoping desperately that with someone like that Fern might learn to forgive herself, and let go of a past she could not forget.

"Isn't he?" said Fern, and her expression went cold. "I don't really know what to do about it. I don't deserve him."

As Will was going to be away until the second week in December, they made long-term plans for Christmas. "Family, friends, all together," said Will, offhandedly including Dane. Fern said nothing either to confirm or deny.

"We could go to Yorkshire," suggested Abby, Robin Capel's permanent girlfriend. "The house is big enough."

"Not Yorkshire," said Fern, so flatly that no one attempted to disagree with her.

Ragginbone paid Will a visit, a few days later, on one of his occasional trips to London. Hearing about Dane Hunter, he remarked: "I knew something about that excavation was important to Fern. I didn't pretend to know what."

"Will she ever be able to put all that business with Lucas Walgrim behind her?" Will inquired.

"Who knows? She is who she is. That is something that cannot change."

"As long as Dane doesn't turn out to be the reincarnation of some psychotic Viking or a mad Celtic druid."

"He may well be," said Ragginbone. "So may you. Since you can't remember, what does it matter?"

In late October, Fern and Dane took a weekend break in the Peak District. He had asked her to come to America to meet his family, but she refused, insisting it would be inappropriate as theirs was only a casual affair. The peaks were mostly obscured by rain, but he dragged her out on bracing walks and warmed her up afterward by the log fire in their hotel, and she wished she had more to give him than just the outer layer of her self. She was driving down the motorway on the way home when it happened. That sudden jolting of reality—an image from the spellfire flashing into her mind—a blinding glimpse into the moment ahead. She was in the fast lane, doing perhaps sixty-five, the wipers swishing the rain this way and that across the windshield. On the other side of the central divide there was a lorry coming toward her—huge, dirty, anonymous—she saw it in great detail. And behind the sweep of a single wiper the driver's face shrank into a skull, and his teeth jutted in a grin of triumph . . .

Glancing around, hand on the horn, she swerved abruptly across the traffic flow, skidding to a halt on the hard shoulder. Dane cried: "What the *hell*—" but his words were cut off by the scream of tires, a horrific thud, the crunch of metal on metal. Even as Fern moved to evade it the lorry had mounted the crash barrier, bucking like a giant bronco, carried forward by its own weight and slamming straight into the car that had been behind her, mashing it into the road. The two interlocked vehicles slid across the wet asphalt, adding other victims to a pileup that finally stopped about thirty yards back.

Dane took one look and reached for his mobile, dialing emergency services with his left hand while his right arm held Fern very tight. She was still clutching the wheel, her teeth starting to chatter from shock. "How did you know?" he said. "How did you know to swing over like that?"

"I'm a w-witch," she said when she could speak. "I knew."

It had not been an accident—she realized that only too clearly. The death's-head was no hallucination; she didn't need to listen to the news the next day to learn that the driver of the lorry had mysteriously disappeared from the scene of the pileup in which two people in the car behind her had been killed and three others seriously injured. (My fault, whispered a still, small voice in the back of her mind.) She was at the top of Azmordis's hit list: she always would be.

Until they got her.

That night, for the first time in a long while, she dreamed of Atlantis. She was back in the Past, living it, at one with it, and she was sixteen again, and the burden of her years was so light, so light, and the Fern she was now dwelt in the mind of Fernani, the girl of those far-off days, and danced for joy in the cleanness of her spirit, the freshness of her heart. And there were the lion-colored colonnades, and the slaves sweeping horse dung, and the smell of perfume and spices and dust, and the great disc of the sun beating down on the dome of the temple, and the sound of the drums throbbing like heat on stone, like blood in the brain. In her dream she experienced all the sweetest moments again, jumbled together in a moving mosaic, a wonderful kaleidoscope of images and feelings, taste, touch, scent. She was in the dungeon with Rafarl, and escaping over the rooftops, and supping in his mother's villa in the sapphire-blue evening, and making love on a beach at sunset where the sand was made of gold and the sea of bronze, and the great arc of the sky hung over all. Rafarl's face was clear in her vision, and the beauty that came to him when he stood in a fountain shaking the water drops from his hair, or rose from the waves like a sea god, and they walked in the deserted orchard of Tamiszandre plucking the peaches that grew there, silver and golden, and the Fern of today thought her heart would break with happiness to be revisiting her city, her love, her self.

But the throb of the drums grew louder, until the mosaic shattered like glass, and she was in the temple with the priests chanting and Zohrâne opening the Door, and the shadow of the tsunami swept over them, blocking out the sun. The dome broke like an eggshell, and the columns cracked, and the *nympheline* Uuinarde was hurled into the maelstrom, and Fern fled with Rafarl down the tunnel to the harbor with Ixavo the High Priest in pursuit, clutching the wound in his head to stop his brains from oozing out. And they took ship, though it was too late, but at the last she threw herself overboard to delay Ixavo, and saw Rafarl sailing, sailing into the tempest, and thought he was saved. But the hurricane tore the ship apart, the mermaid took Rafarl, and the earthquake swallowed the golden city and everyone in it. The Ultimate Powers buried it deep and forbade even the vision of it to witch and sybil alike. But they cannot forbid my dreams, thought Fern, even as she slept, and in her dream she woke, and wept, wept a pool of tears, like Alice, then a lake, then her tears turned to starlight and she was sitting on the silver shores at the Margin of the World, waiting for the unicorn who would never come again. But because it was a dream he came, and bore her away, bounding through the star spray.

Where are we going? she asked, and he said: *Home,* and she was glad, though she knew *home* was neither Yorkshire nor London, nor even Atlantis. They rode on, and on, and the constellations were beaten to dust beneath his hooves, and the galaxies unraveled around them and streamed in ribbons through the flying universe.

When will we get there? she asked, and she knew it was the wrong question, because he answered: *Someday,* and with that word the stars vanished, and the world turned black, and she moved on to another awakening.

She was in the Cave of Roots beneath the Eternal Tree, gazing into the spellfire. She saw the graveyard of dragons in a mountain range beyond the reach of man or beast, the huge bones of one long-dead behemoth soaring upward like the skeleton of a cathedral, the dark-faced man who had come to steal the last dragon's egg walking under the arched ribs. She met his eyes in the smoke, in the instant before his death, and they were blue as wereflame and seared her like an ice burn. And she cut his head from the Eternal Tree, and brought it back to the real world, to finish what he had begun. He told her he was helpless in that form, without limbs to carry him or heart to care, but *I will be your limbs*, she promised him. *I will be your heart.* But he burned in dragonfire, and passed the Gate, and she knew him no more.

Fern turned over in bed, reaching for the head on the pillow where she had laid it, and started back, because it was not the dragon charmer, it was Luc. He was as pale as his own corpse, and there was blood on his lips, but his eyes lived. "Blood washes out," he said, "but not the sap of this Tree. My sap is on your pillow, on your hands. Look—" and he vomited a gush of red, and smiled, and the smile became Rafarl's, and the head was rolling over and over down the beach, bouncing on juts of rock, spattering her with sap. The tide had gone out, exposing the seabed, and tiny fishes flapped helplessly to and fro, dying in the air. The head of Rafarl lay among the fishes, half sunk in the ooze, watching her sideways. She struggled to get out of the dream, but she was floundering in a quicksand, and the darkness closed over her.

With an effort that felt like lifting gigantic weights she opened her eyes. But the dream went on relentlessly; she was trapped in its maze and it would not release her until she

was dreamed out. She was making her way through the city—
the unreal city of rain-soaked lights and people with animal
faces, beaked and furred and fanged. She reached the Dark
Tower, and the elevator whisked her skyward, and she stood
in the topmost office with the dripping quill in her hand, and
Luc said: *Sign.* And she must have signed, because he was
smiling, and his face was changed, becoming both more beautiful and more terrible, and his wings unfurled like angel's
wings, only black. The huge window vanished, and he drew
her after him on wings of her own, soaring through the cloud
wrack, and the city lights spread out far below, numerous as
grains of sand. Ahead they saw the storm clouds piled into
top-heavy cliffs, but they flew over them, and beneath them
the lightning stabbed earthward, and whole areas of the city
were darkened, but Fern knew it did not matter, because Luc
said so. *I am Lukastor, Lord of the Serafain. I will show you
your destiny.* But now it was all dark below them, blacker
than a black hole, and the last grains of light were sucked in,
and the storm clouds, and she knew it was the abyss. She too
was being sucked downward, and she snatched Luc's hand,
but her fingers slipped through his. *You are too heavy,* he said.
It is your soul that drags you down . . .

She was floating in a lightless vacuum of utter cold. Every
so often a face drifted past, billowing like a jellyfish. Some
she recognized, Morgus, Sysselore, Alimond; others were
merely familiar. One was just a pair of eyeballs trailing a few
thin filaments of nerve. She did not like this part of the dream
at all, but it seemed to go on a long time, the floating and the
emptiness and the cold that ate into her heart. Eventually
there were no more faces. She grew very afraid, and cried out,
calling on God, though she was not sure she believed in Him,
not the God of conventional religion with His constant de-
mands for worship and repentance. But there He was, drawing her out of the darkness, and she was sitting on a green

bank beside Him, having a chat. He looked rather like Ragginbone, only kinder, white-haired and bearded, wearing a sky blue cape.

"How do I stop the dream?" she asked.

"You know how," he said.

And of course she knew.

She awoke in the pale gray of early morning feeling like a traveler returned from a long, weary voyage. For a while she lay thinking and thinking, conscious of what she must do yet dreading that final irrevocable step. She would have to make the necessary preparations, close every loophole; a single mistake could cost her more than her life. And maybe she should say farewell, to Ragginbone, Lougarry, Bradachin— but no, it would be too hard, she would do what had to be done and leave the explanations to Will. (Will and Gaynor: she must talk to them.) At least now that she had made her decision there was no more need to agonize: she had only to plan, and to act. She had killed—whatever the motive, whatever the circumstances—and there was a price to pay. The price for Luc's life, and for hers. Now she knew how it must be paid.

December was passing. In the center of London there were Christmas trees on every promontory, shop windows festooned with tinsel and fairy lights and aglitter with snow scenes, elaborate montages with cribs, angels, shepherds, kings—goose girls, pixies, ogres, dragons. Children besieged the toy shops, demanding dinosaurs and video games, cuddly monsters and svelte princesses. The streets were infested with carol singers and people dressed as Santa Claus. It had rained recently, and in the premature dusk every glint of neon, every streetlamp, every fairy light was reflected back from puddled pavement and gleaming road, and the splashback from a passing car sparkled like fireflies. Fern was making her way through the City, past the bulging bosoms of turkeys hanging in a row, and pheasants in all their feathered glory, and old-fashioned puddings in linen bags, and chestnuts roasting on a brazier that smoked and spat in the wet. The faces around her were mortal, flushed with seasonal good cheer, happy faces calling greetings even to those they did not know. The demons had turned into latex masks, masks and games and toys, and this was the reality she wanted, this safe, human world. Safe if only she could make it so, if her gamble worked, if she dared to lose all, to gain all—or all that was left. She passed the entrance to a tube station, and saw the crowds boiling in the depths, and bumped into a man who did not smile but simply sidled away, muttering. And then she found the passage, just as she had known she would, because it was always there for those who looked. She paused for a moment—the last moment, when there was still time to draw back. Then she walked under the arch.

The lights behind her were cut off; it was very dark. She emerged into the square where the lamps were scant and wan, and the people, few or many, stood in little groups, always far away. At the center was the Tower. The city had receded into the distance, and the Tower stood alone, so tall it made her dizzy to gaze upward, plated with black glass, strengthened with black steel, outsoaring all other skyscrapers. Yet it is only a tower such as men build, she thought. Azmordis has no ideas, no imagination of his own, only what he has stolen from us, down the endless ages of dominion and envy and hate. She held on tight to that thought, hoping it might give her courage, or the semblance of it. The wide steps were before her, spreading out like waves on either hand, and the scarlet-cloaked guards with their metal faces, blinking once as she walked between them, and the great doors that parted automatically and swallowed her without a sound. She went up to the reception desk, hearing the tap of her booted feet on the marble floor echoing around the lobby. "I have come," she said.

"Do you have an appointment?"

"He is expecting me." He had been expecting her for more than fourteen years.

She crossed the narrow bridge to the elevator without looking down. Then as in her dream—in every dream—they rose upward, slowly at first, then faster and faster, leaving her stomach behind and making her ears pop and crushing her skull with the pressure of their ascent. At the top she stood reeling, pulling herself together. Then she stepped out. It is the same bridge, she told herself; only the drop is different. And somehow she walked across, with no noticeable hesitation, and mounted the escalator that traveled in a spiral around the outer wall of the Tower to the office. *His* office. The doors slid open with a soft swishing noise, and she went in.

The red lamp shone across the desk, but not on him. He was just a darkness in a suit. The carpet lapped the walls, and the curtains poured down from above, and the windows were huge and black with unrelieved night. She walked straight up to him, facing him across the ebony desktop. The walk seemed to take a long time.

He said: "So you have come to me at last." His voice was soft and deep as a purr, but colder, and it penetrated to the very recesses of her spirit. "The document is ready. I had it drawn up long ago." He pushed the red leather folder across the desk. Her name was embossed on the cover: Fernanda Elizabeth Capel, called Morcadis. She wondered how he knew about the Elizabeth. But he would always know.

"I sent you Lukastor, Lord of the Fellangels, to help in your fight against the witch queen Morgus," he went on.

"That was generous of you," she said. Politely.

"He was both brave and true," the demon said. "And he loved you. Yet you returned him to me with a spear in his belly. I valued him highly: his Gift was undeveloped, but under my tutelage he would have learned to use it, and he might have achieved much. You owe me for this, Fernanda, and for many other things. The debt must be paid. Therefore my terms are not so liberal as they might have been."

"I owe you nothing and you value no one," Fern said with all the scorn she could muster. "I have not come to accept your terms, liberal or otherwise. I have come to offer you mine."

There was a long, long pause—a pause such as that office had never felt before. The muted hum of something resembling air conditioning ceased. The whole force of his being shifted, focusing on her with a new and terrible intensity.

"Yours?"

"My soul is not for sale," she said. "But I will make you a deal for yours, such as it is, if you will hazard it."

"I—have—no—soul." The words grated, stone on stone.

"Then I will take what you have," said Fern. "Your unsoul—your spirit—your immortality."

"*You* will take—*you* will offer—! What deal would you dare to offer *me*, least of witches? What makes you think you will leave this place alive? A word from me will melt your bones where you stand."

"I have protection," Fern said.

"What protection could you find that would avail you *here*?"

"I invoke the Mother," she said.

Another pause, another jolt in his concentration. All his far-flung, casual power seemed to contract into the shadow before her; she could feel the glance of his unseen eyes like a ray of darkness probing her mind.

"She will not hear you," he sneered, yet there was doubt behind the derision. "She Who Sleeps will never rouse at *your* whimpering."

"She hears me," Fern said, and as when she had made the spell shield around her friends, another voice spoke through hers. In Moonspittle's basement, she had touched the ancient power by accident, not knowing what she did. This time, she knew. "She was stronger than you once, Ysis-Astolantë, Pan-gaea Allmother, but the priests bound her in slumber, and the world was ruled by men. You found them more apt to your hand than women, did you not? But the world changes, and maybe she sleeps but lightly now."

"So you are *her* handmaiden?"

"No. Not yet. I am no one's vassal; I told you that before. I have come to buy you, if you will sell. *She* is my surety."

He stood up, growing taller and darker behind the light. He no longer appeared to be wearing a suit. She was aware of clouds forming beyond the windows, pressing close to the glass with clammy hands. Stars shone through them, in pairs.

She kept her attention on Azmordis.

"What can *you* offer me?"

She took the phial out of her bag, holding it up. Even in that place its contents shone pure and clear. "This is a single draft of the Well of Lethe. If I drink it, I will forget the very name of Morcadis, and all that I have done as a witch—as the least of witches—all that I learned, all that I was and all that I might become will be lost. I will no longer trouble you, nor threaten your schemes. I will live out my life as an ordinary mortal, and grow old, and pass the Gate, and none will remember me. That is my offer."

"And what must I do in return?"

"Forgo your vengeance on me and anyone connected with me, distant or dear. You must pledge your unsoul, for you and all who serve you or seek your favor. The document is ready." She drew a file out of her bag, set it down on the desk. It was red. "I had it drawn up according to the correct procedures. There are no loopholes. It wants only your signature."

A wind came howling around the Tower; the cloud shapes were whirled away in a writhing torrent, all groping limbs and gaping mouths. But within the office it was utterly still.

"If I should give my pledge, and break it?"

"The effects of Lethe would be negated, and your immortality would be forfeit." The shadow was enormous now, filling the room, and all the winds of the world shrieked outside, and in the blackness there was only the dull red glow of the desk lamp, like the smolder of a dying fire, and the glimmer of the phial in her hand. But her tone strengthened, and the power of her will and the steel in her soul mastered her fear. "Break your pledge and I swear, if it takes a thousand centuries, if I have to waken the Allmother and every other Spirit who ever slept, I will destroy you. Morgus opened the abyss to banish a handful of ghosts, but I will open it for you, and cast you into the void. I swear it."

"And if I tear up your document and send you squeaking from my presence clutching your leftover life in your feeble hands?"

"The same. I can do it; you know I can. Among the million possible fates that lie ahead of me that is one. For all your might, for all the height of your Tower and the depth of your hate, you fear me." Her heart trembled as she said it, but not her voice. "Sign, and you will be secure from me, if not from others. For men are many, and have resources beyond the Gift, and despite your servants and your slaves, your countless faces and names, you are only one."

There was a rumble in his throat that might have passed for laughter, though it sounded like thunder far off. "Whenever men have tried to reject me, whether through some shining new creed or gentler religion, intolerance and pride have always turned them to my service in the end. Men are my creatures; they eat from my hand. The abyss itself will be filled ere they defy me."

Fern stood there, silent. Defiant. The chorus of winds screamed in mockery.

"You want me to ransom my very self to a mere mortal? I, Azmordis, ruler of both this world and the other! Who would you find to witness such a pact?"

"The Ultimate Powers," said Fern.

The tumult outside was suddenly quiet. The cloud thinned to a mist; the pairs of stars winked out. There was only darkness within and darkness beyond. The ember of the lamp was smothered and for the first time that night she saw *his* eyes, filled with a glow the other side of light. His voice seemed to come from everywhere and nowhere.

"They do not exist. Or if they do, they trouble themselves little with mortal and immortal affairs."

She spoke into the darkness, into the eyes. "Then sign, and break your pledge, and fear nothing."

She felt his enmity and his rage pressing against her. The blood beat in her ears; breathing became an effort. But the rage was controlled, though barely, and beneath the enmity she sensed his wavering and the seed of fear that she had dared to name.

"If I agree," he said at last, and in that "if" she knew she had won, "then you will drink your draft, here, tonight?"

The darkness was shrinking, becoming once more a shadow in a suit, and she stood in his office, and the light of the desk lamp shone red on the red file. "If you agree," she said, "then you will sign, and I will give the paper to someone I trust, and at the appointed time I will drink, and our pact will be sealed."

"When is the appointed time?"

She had thought carefully about that one. "Midnight on Christmas Eve."

There was a silence while he appeared to reflect, but she felt he had done with reflection. And at last he said it, the thing she had waited to hear, and the tension began to ebb from her muscles, leaving them weak and shaking. "Very well. I accept your offer. You have harassed me enough, Morcadis, and this way I can dispose of you without further trouble. I will make a deal with you for my unsoul, in exchange for all that you were, and all that you are, and all that you might have been."

She opened the file and took out a single sheet of paper, thick creamy paper, crisp and expensive, covered with spiky calligraphy. Her signature was already there, written clearly and carefully across the bottom; below it, a space remained for his. He picked up the quill, snapped his fingers to conjure an ink bottle. "That is not valid," she said. "It must be signed in blood, or whatever ichor flows in your immortal veins."

"There is no blade here that will draw blood from me."

She took out the knife—the knife with which Luc had threatened her—and thrust it quivering into the desktop. She did not have the force to thrust hard, but the point bit deep. He stared at it for a second or two before pulling it out. She saw him extend a shadowy arm, roll up the sleeve—if there was a sleeve—draw the blade across it. Some dark fluid welled out and dripped onto the ebony, smoking slightly. He dipped the nib in it and signed—Azmordis, for that was the name in which the document was drawn up, the name by which Fern had always known him—and the *scritch*, *scritch* of his pen was the only sound in the whole world. She waited for the clap of thunder, the lightning flash, but there was just that terrible silence. The paper wrinkled around his signature.

"It is done," he said, pushing the document toward her as if in contempt, but she wasn't deceived. "Take care of it. No other mortal has ever made such a bargain with me, and I may yet change my mind, ere midnight strikes on Christmas Eve. Then look to yourself, and all you hold dear."

She picked up the paper, replaced it in the red file. "Do not think to cheat me. The bargain may not be sealed, but it is signed, and the Ultimate Powers have borne witness. You know the cost of betrayal."

"Get out: I am done with you. Now you are self-ordained a nobody. Get out!"

She moved to the door, and it slid open in front of her—a part of her had believed she would never see it open again—and she was standing on the escalator, crawling like a snail

around the Tower walls. Her escort waited by the elevator.
She crossed the bridge as if it were broad and railed, and sped
earthward, and her heart beat fast as she went toward the exit,
and passed between the guards, and crossed the square. She
thought the knots of people turned to stare, but she paid them
no heed. She was running now, running and running, through
the passageway, under the arch, and she was back in the City,
the real City, teeming with people and lights and noise, and it
was Christmas, and she was crying, tears of sadness and loss
and relief and joy, blurring her view of the happy crowds, crying softly all the way home.

Epilogue

Exit Third Witch

It was Christmas Eve. Fern had been to a party with Dane Hunter, and joined Will and Gaynor for dinner, and had one digestif too many and sung carols out of tune and returned to her flat almost happy, almost sad. She and Dane would spend Christmas Day together, but she had told him that tonight she needed to be alone. She didn't say why, and he wasn't satisfied, but he left her with a smile and a kiss, not a quarrel, because he had always sensed that certain fragility about her, the burden of secrets she would not tell. She had entrusted the red file to Gaynor—after all, manuscripts were her area of expertise—explaining to her and Will what she intended to do. Now she sat in the drawing room with a single candle and a glass of cognac, playing a compilation of seasonal songs by the likes of Frank Sinatra and Nat King Cole and waiting for the hour to strike. It was barely eleven: she had time yet. Time to think, to regret, to relive all those bittersweet moments just once more. But instead her mind planed on nothingness, vacant if not at ease. Beside her, a folded newspaper told her Kaspar Walgrim's case would come up for trial next year. He had an expensive lawyer and high-level contacts; she doubted he would get a long sentence. Dana Walgrim had gone to Australia and engaged herself to a beach bum. No one had ever found any trace of Luc.

Soon it will be over, she thought, and the ghoulies and ghosties will go back in the shadows, and I will live out my life in the light, even if it is an artificial light. She remembered God in His blue cape, sitting on the grass to chat, and hoped He at least would not be lost to her. He had seemed a kindly God, a comfortable God; she would like to know more of Him. And maybe, when her time came to pass the Gate, He would open the locked door in her soul, and she would have Atlantis again, and the unicorn would be there, waiting to take her home. She could not know—you could never know—but she must hold on to her faith, because soon faith would be all that remained. All the memories—the passion—the darkness and the magic—everything would be gone.

She found she had drained her glass, and replenished it, just a little way. 'Twas the night before Christmas, she quoted to herself, and all through the house, Not a creature was stirring . . . But beside the curtain, something stirred. A burglar. A goblin burglar in a crooked hat, with a sprig of holly stuck through the brim. And because he was werefolk—the last she would ever know—because it was Christmas, because of the holly in his hat, Fern was more than pleased to see him. "Her highness sends you greeting," he said, "and wishes you a merry Yuletide."

"Thank you," said Fern. "Have a drink."

He choked on the cognac, but persisted.

"I didn't know goblins celebrated Christmas," Fern went on. "It seems a little inappropriate."

"We celebrate Yule," Skuldunder explained when he had recovered. "That is a far, far older festival than Christmas. This is the moment when the year turns. Under the deep cold, in the warmth of earth, the first shoots waken. The snow may lie thick, but after Yule, we know that spring will come again."

"There isn't any snow," Fern pointed out.

"Mabb has moved to the woods and mountains of the far north," Skuldunder said on a faintly admonitory note. "There, the snow lies thick."

Fern took a moment to picture the goblin queen careering

down a mountainside on a makeshift toboggan, or throwing snowballs at her hapless courtiers and allowing them to throw snowballs back, provided they did not hit their mark. She had no idea if it was a true picture, but it made her smile. "Tell the queen I too send her greeting," she said with something like a sigh, "but our alliance is at an end. Not because I doubt her, or have other allies in view, but because from midnight I will cease to be a witch, and become an ordinary mortal."

"Why?" asked Skuldunder, clearly baffled.

"The story is too long for now, and the ending too sad. It is enough to say I wish it."

"But—how can you cease to be what you are?" the goblin demanded.

"An ancient magic," said Fern, "and my last. Let's not talk of it. Merry Christmas! I mean, Yule." She raised her glass. "Go back to the north where the snow lies thick, and tell Mabb—tell her farewell. This is my final gift." She detached a tiny model of a violin from her Christmas tree. "It doesn't play, but it's pretty. Still, she has some magic. Maybe she will be able to wring a tune from it." She blanched slightly at the thought.

"It's a beautiful thing," said Skuldunder solemnly. "I never stole anything like it."

"Now go," Fern said. "Midnight is coming. After that, I will no longer be able to see you, nor any of your kind. But I'm glad you came tonight."

He faded, slowly and sorrowfully, or at least in bewilderment, and she was left alone with her vigil. She fetched the phial, and stood it beside her glass, and knew that soon it would be no more to her than a curiosity, an unusual perfume bottle that she had acquired she couldn't recall where. She would have liked to say good-bye to Kal, but she sensed it was unnecessary. He had given her the phial; he would know she had used it. And *now* the memories began, jostling for place in her head, memories of golden city and giant tree, of

starfoam and dragonfire, of Rafarl and Ruvindra, enemies
and friends, of riding the wind and feeling the heartbeat of
the earth . . . She needed leisure to savor every second, to live
it all one more time, before it slipped over the boundary into
the realm of dream and fantasy, never to return again. But the
clock ticked inexorably onward, hand closing on hand, and
her Time was running out. Three minutes left. With a little
difficulty, she unstoppered the phial. Her grip was unsteady.
It seemed to her that the memories had spilled out of her mind
and thronged the room, reaching out, calling to her: Fernani—
nevelindë—Simple Susan sewing samplers—Morcadis—
witch maiden—sorceress—lover . . . On the clock face, the
hands touched. The chimes of midnight began. She raised the
phial to her lips and drank.

And then there was only the music playing in the empty
room.

Glossary

Boros (Boor-ross) Possibly derived from Boreas, the Greek
    name for the North Wind.

Bradachin (Brad-da-chin) From the Scots Gaelic meaning
    "little thief." The ch is pronounced as in loch.

Cerne (Sern) The antlered god also known as Herne, Lord of
    the Hunt. This name, one of many, comes from Cernus,
    a Celtic deity about whom little is known.

Cthorn (K-thorn) An obscure name that may have some con-
    nection with the Greek *chthonos*, earth. Gods of the under-
    world are often referred to as chthonic.

Dibbuck (Dib-buk) Presumably from the Hebrew *dybbuk*, an
    evil spirit that possesses a living body, though why a
    house-goblin should acquire such a name is not clear.
    Perhaps he was considered to "possess" the house.

Eriost (Eri-osst) This may be a corruption of Eros, or from
    the Greek *eris*, strife. The other names mentioned for
    this spirit seem to come from a variety of sources. Val-
    lorn is from "valiant"; Idunor from Iduna, the Norse god-
    dess of youth; Sifril may also be Norse (Thor's wife was
    Sif of the Golden Hair); Teagan is a Welsh name mean-
    ing "beautiful"; Maharac sounds like a spirit name, pos-
    sibly of Indian origin; Varli may connect with Vali the
    Slayer.

Léopana Pthaia (Lay-oh-pa-na P-thai-a) Léopana is from the

Latin meaning "leopardess" or "lioness"; Pthaia is possibly from the Greek pythoness, or the Atlantean that predates it: *pythé,* seer.

Mallebolg (Mal-leh-bolg)

Morgus (Moor-guss) Also called Morgause or Morgawse, the half sister of Arthur. Her sibling Morgun (Morgana, Morgan Le Fay) is better known to common legend.

Nehemet (Neh-heh-met) The name sounds Egyptian, a land in which cats were revered and (it is thought) first domesticated. Bastet was the cat goddess.

Nimwë (Nim-way) Also spelt Nimuë, an enchantress who was in love with Merlin.

Oedaphor (Ee-da-foor) Probably from Greek, this could relate to *oidema,* swelling.

Pangaea (Pan-gae-a) Gaia was the Greek earth goddess; *pan* is a prefix meaning "everything."

Skaetha (Skay-tha) There may be a connection with Skuld the Vola in the Edda, the seeress who foretold the battle of Ragnarok.

Skuldunder (Skul-dun-da) This sounds like an uncomplimentary nickname of human origin, similar to "dunderhead," meaning "stupid."

Sleer Bronaw (Slee-a Broh-noor) A corruption of the Scots Gaelic *sleagh,* spear, and *bron,* grief.

Sysselore (Siss-se-loor) See *The Dragon Charmer.*

Ysis-Astolantë (Ey-siss Ass-toh-lan-tay) Isis was the Egyptian moon goddess; Astolantë is probably derived from the Assyrian Ishtar, or Ashtoreth.

Don't miss the first two books in the enchanting
series by the author of *The Witch Queen*

Jan Siegel's

PROSPERO'S CHILDREN

**"A lyrical, captivating first novel of
mermaids, magic, lost worlds, and found
souls that deserves the large and
enthusiastic audience it is sure to find. . .
This book will not be forgotten."**
—Terry Brooks

Ages past in fabled Atlantis, a mad queen forged a
key to a door never meant to be opened by mortal man—its inception would hasten her own
death and the extinction of her vainglorious race.
For millennia the key lay forgotten beneath the
waves, amid the ruins of what had been the most
beautiful city on Earth. But however jealously the
sea hoards its secrets, sooner or later it yields
them up. Now, in present-day Yorkshire, that time
has come. And for young Fernanda Capel, life will
never be the same again . . .

Published by Del Rey
Available wherever books are sold

Jan Siegel's

THE DRAGON CHARMER

"Highly imaginative and darkly charming."
—*Publishers Weekly*

After surviving a harrowing summer twelve years ago, Fern Capel renounces her mystical power and decides to marry. Her fiancé insists they wed at the Capels' summer house, a place swelling with magic. When Fern returns there, ancient, sinister forces reawaken.

Forced to confront the evil again, Fern realizes she can no longer run from her fate. She reclaims her gifts and is swept into another land, removed from Time. It will take all her skill to fight her way back to the present and save the people she loves from the growing danger that threatens them. To her utmost surprise, the key to survival is a dragon with the capacity to rule the world. . . .

Published by Del Rey Books
Available wherever books are sold

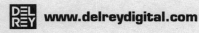